SHADOWLESS

ALISON ROBINSON

Published by Village Editorial Birmingham, Alabama
www.villageeditorial.com

First edition.

Hardback ISBN: 979-8-9910056-3-0
Paperback ISBN: 979-8-9910056-4-7
EBook ISBN: 979-8-9910056-5-4

Printed in the United States of America

Author: Alison Robinson
Editor: Anna Hartzog
Illustrator: Racheal Smithson
Cover Design: J. Caleb Clark

For Adam, always the best man in the room.

CHAPTER ONE

ARCHIBALD CUTTER HAD NO idea what was hidden next door. He believed what everyone else believed, that Haaris Faye lived alone. But there was something odd about Haaris's stone cottage—something he couldn't quite say. Despite Archibald's meticulous garden facing Haaris's shrub-shrouded one, and despite having just seen something inhuman in the attic window, Archibald drew his attention elsewhere. After all, if the ghosts of the widower's dead wife and baby lived next door, it was none of Archibald's business.

He rapped his knuckles against a bright orange gourd, frowning. Like the rest of Greymere, Archibald was in the final preparations for the Festival of Shadows. It was his garden which provided the pumpkins each year. And with only a few days left, Archibald was in a panic. Last year, his magic had produced a pumpkin the size of a toolshed. But the largest he'd managed so far was no bigger than a barrel, which was unacceptable.

A scrawny ferret with enormous round ears scurried up the pumpkin's vine and perched atop the stem. *If I press it much further, it'll burst,* the Shadow thought.

Archibald's lips crinkled. "Do it anyway."

His Shadow hummed with magic, and the pumpkin vibrated under his tiny paws. Archibald felt the sensation as if his own feet were perched atop the gourd.

Something flashed in his periphery. The attic window again. Despite himself, Archibald shivered, but then a sickening *crack* rent the air. The giant pumpkin burst, spilling the ferret atop a sticky mess. The Shadow and man cursed at their failed magic.

"Let's try another one," said Archibald.

The ferret shook seeds from his paws before scurrying atop the next pumpkin. His magic reached like invisible fingertips into the thick, orange rind, expanding it like a balloon. Archibald checked the round window at the top of Haaris's house. It was vacant as it ought to be.

Meanwhile, inside the attic, a girl shooed her Shadow away from the little round window. "You know the rules," she scolded her Shadow. Windows were to be skirted at every point.

Rowena Faye—fifteen years old and very much alive despite the people of Greymere believing her to be dead—stood before a mirror wedged under the steep ceiling, attempting to tame her curls. She managed to tie them back with a leather cord, but her fringe sprang loose. Something about that non-compliant hair bouncing atop her forehead roused a smile. She donned the sense of rebellion like a coat.

Through the old, weathered floorboards, she heard muffled noises. Footsteps. A cabinet was opened and then shut. Some shuffling, mutters, more shuffling. Her father was awake.

Rowena grabbed her bag from a peg on the wall, ignoring her trembling fingers when she slung it overhead. Her father would notice it, but that was the point. Perhaps he was feeling uncommonly generous that morning, and she wouldn't need her Plan after all.

That's how she imagined The Plan, with capital letters. It had started as a daydream nearly a decade ago. She had been only five years old when her father left her home alone. Despite the rules, she'd watched him leave from the front window downstairs, peering through the curtains. She would never forget the feeling. The cottage walls, which at that age had seemed so tall to her, felt as if they suddenly jumped inward, claustrophobic and choking. The silence had been the worst part; the absence of sound in the empty house had been deafening. That was the day the daydream came—like a ward. It happened every year after. "It's just one day," Haaris reasoned, but that was enough for Rowena. Left alone in the empty cottage, the suffocating loneliness worsened each year, hardening her daydream into an obsession until it eventually calcified into a fully formed Plan.

After a final check in the mirror, only to see her curls already escaping the cord, she grabbed the trapdoor rope and heaved it up out of the floor. Then she slid down the ladder on the inner soles of her shoes and, with a tidy jump, landed in the kitchen. Her father had already made tea, and she poured herself a cup. "G'morning, Papa," she greeted, but he didn't hear.

His lean frame reached atop the mantel, rummaging among an odd assortment of things. While the outside of the cottage showed no sign of anyone else living there but him, the inside barely contained the burgeoning evidence of Rowena's life. Her confinement overwhelmed the place, with books spilling from cases lining the walls, sketches tacked like wallpaper as high as she could reach, and contraptions made of scrap wood and iron (in various stages of completion) strewn about.

Haaris knocked a stack of papers from a chair, and Rowena lunged for them as if they were priceless, spilling her tea. She blotted the smudged pencil sketches with her shirtsleeve, but that only smeared the drawings further. It was her own design of a device involving mirrors and a pipe through which she might spy on her neighbors. She dropped the soggy pages back onto the chair. There was no time for them now.

"Where is the clock?" Haaris asked. His voice sounded distracted and distant like he was in another room.

"I needed a spring for my catapult and—"

"—and, naturally, you raided the clock." A twitch in his jaw belied his sarcasm. Without another word, Haaris left out the back door, tucking in his shirt and muttering about being late. His Shadow was a tawny spaniel with flopping ears and sad eyes. The spaniel followed at Haaris's heels, and Rowena followed the spaniel.

Behind the cottage stretched a stone walkway to Haaris's workshop. When Rowena was a baby, he had planted a laurel hedge to shield the path from view. Aided by magic, the evergreens had grown tall and thick just in time for her first steps. This past summer, however, a host of miscreant caterpillars had moved in, and no matter how many times Haaris's magic filled in the holes, new ones appeared each week. That's how Archibald Cutter saw Haaris all the way from his pumpkin patch, followed by a girl and something unnamable in her wake.

As soon as the workshop door closed, Haaris spun on her. *"Bazileus, help me; he saw you!"*

When Haaris looked at her, he had the habit of looking directly at her, his eyes never wavering from the center of her face, his periphery narrowed. The effect was more intense than he intended, and Rowena knew this. Still, she buckled under his look. "I thought your Shadow fixed the gap!" she cried.

He didn't answer, but at least his eyes unfocused. It would take his and his Shadow's combined attention to reach their magic through the wall, over the hedge, past the gate, and across the lawn all the way to Archibald's yard. Rowena touched the spaniel's head. His skull buzzed. It wouldn't be a full persuasion, not from this distance. But still, his magic managed to tickle the neighbor's mind enough for him to forget.

Rowena felt suddenly hollow. This was not the first time her father persuaded their neighbor to forget seeing her. But each time he did, it felt like a part of the magic worked upon her as well, erasing bit by bit. He'd done it hundreds of times and undoubtedly would do it a hundred more. But surely, someday, his magic would finish the job, and she'd be snuffed out entirely.

The spaniel nudged her kindly as if he could hear her thoughts just like Haaris's. She buried her fingertips into his fur, his body soft and warm. Tangible. Real. He licked her fingers, reminding her that she, too, was real, and no amount of magic would ever change that. The vibrations changed in resonance, and she knew what her father magicked next. Cracking the door, she could see young leaves unfurling in the gap in the hedge. A chubby caterpillar opened its mouth as if in praise.

Rowena closed the door, swallowing a lump of jealousy. Witnessing her father's magic always felt this way, the teeter between admiration and envy. But she knew such feelings were pointless. To prove to herself she wasn't bothered, she kissed the spaniel between his ears, knowing her father would feel it, too.

Sure enough, Haaris flashed her a bashful smile but then dropped it at once. "You're not coming today," he said.

"I didn't ask if I could," she said.

"You didn't?" He jutted his chin at the bag on her hip. He had noticed, and apparently, he wasn't feeling generous after all.

"I had to try," she said. He laughed, the sound more like a bark, rough at the edge.

A wooden cart, with wheels almost as tall as Rowena, stood waiting at the mouth of the workshop, full of materials bulging under a tarp. Haaris checked that everything was secured properly. His Shadow jumped onto the bench at the front.

"Here, let me help," Rowena said, shifting her bag around to her back. She checked the ties on the side of the cart nearest her.

Rowena only knew what he told her, but apparently, there was a king-dom-wide festival this time every year, and Haaris was hired to provide con-struction for a portion of it. Something involving a stage where people per-formed—honestly, she had no frame of reference for any of it, and Haaris wasn't really the explaining type, which meant his disappearance each year was mostly a mystery. Hence, her Plan.

The moment he looked the other way, Rowena grabbed a contraption she'd set aside the night before and shoved it under the tarp. This part of The Plan she had debated for months. It was risky. After all, he might see it. But she knew venturing out without any form of protection was stupid. She needed something, even if it were just a homemade catapult. If someone saw her, perhaps a well-aimed blow between the eyes would distract them enough for her to run away. It was weak, but it was all she had.

Haaris was too busy checking a wheel to notice. *Step one complete*, she thought.

He spoke as if answering a question she hadn't asked. "It's just, there's gonna' be people everywhere setting things up."

"I know," she said.

There was guilt in his furrowed brow, and she was glad for it. He ought to feel guilty, leaving her like this. It was as if he heard her thoughts because he pleaded, "It's hard enough convincing the neighbor. The amount of magic it would take—the number of laws I'd have to break—just so you could come."

For obvious moral reasons, persuasive magic against an unprotected mind was illegal in the Kingdom of Wyre. Civil society would be impossible if people kept magicking each other's minds to think whatever they wanted them to think. And yet, Haaris broke this law most days—for her. Still, his Shadow had limits.

She knew his excuses by heart, but she couldn't help but argue, "You take me with you every other time you leave."

He threw another strap over the tarp, gesturing for her to tie her side. She hated this tarp, but since it was the only way she was allowed out of the house, she had submitted to hiding under it countless times.

"This isn't an errand or a quick delivery," he said.

"I don't mind waiting so long."

"I won't be near to protect you." He tugged the twine harder than necessary, and it broke.

Rowena stared at the saw-dusted floor, chiding herself. The Plan had been for him to just leave. There was no point in arguing. But she couldn't let it alone. "When are you going to trust me?" Her voice cracked with more emotion than she meant to show.

Distracted by his hurry, something must have cracked inside Haaris, too, because he snapped, "When your Shadow becomes a *real* Shadow."

He hadn't raised his voice, but still, his words were like a slap. Rowena stung from it, the shame blackening like a bruise. Tears threatened to breach her eyelashes, but she held them in check. Haaris continued to secure the tarp alone. She watched him, her expression closed like so many curtains, shrouding her hurt from view.

Breaking his habit, Harris's gaze flicked to the thing at Rowena's side, then quickly flicked away.

There, like smoke from an extinguished candle, hovered a wispy creature no larger than a teapot. Where arms might be, there were only flippers and no legs, her torso ending in a curl of smoke. The Shadow's expression seemed interested but clueless as to what had been said. And maybe she was clueless. No one would ever know, least of all Rowena. For, while everyone shared a mind with their Shadow, Rowena had never heard one thought or word from hers. Her Shadow's lack of mind-link and corporeal form was enough to make her an aberration, but she was also the only Shadow in the entire Kingdom of Wyre with no magic whatsoever. In every conceivable way, Rowena's Shadow was empty.

So tiny with enormous almond eyes, the thing might have been considered cute—if one could look beyond her inherent sacrilege. Which, of course, no Wyrian ever would. By kingdom standards, Rowena's Shadow was, at best, an oddity. At worst, evil.

Like a cat, the Shadow batted specks of sawdust dancing in sunbeams. She seemed to be enjoying herself, although it was hard to tell. Without a mouth, she could neither smile nor frown.

"Ghost, stop it," Rowena muttered. She grabbed the misty Shadow by her curly tail and tucked her in the crook of her arm like a child with a doll. The Shadow submitted happily to Rowena's embrace—or at least she seemed happy. Rowena could never tell.

Haaris opened his mouth, but no words came. He and Rowena both knew he meant what he'd said. So long as Ghost was, well, ghost-like, Rowena must remain hidden. The kingdom's superstitions would never tolerate such an abomination.

Without a word, Haaris climbed onto the cart next to his own Shadow.

It wasn't until his back was turned that Rowena allowed a tear to escape. Ghost reached up to poke the salty ball of sadness. Her touch felt how Rowena imagined a cloud would feel: cottony and cold. The Shadow smeared the tear onto her own misty cheek as if wondering how crying felt. It was a pitiful gesture, but Rowena knew what Ghost meant by it. She kissed her bulbous head, and Ghost nuzzled back like a sleepy kitten.

Rowena turned on her heel and slammed the door behind her, but instead of going back into the cottage where she normally would have gone, she slid along the outer wall of the workshop. At the corner of the building stood a rain barrel. She crouched behind it for only a second, just enough to ensure her father and his Shadow faced away. Then she ran, muffling her steps on the balls of her feet and ducking as she went. Soundlessly, she hoisted herself over the back of the cart, slipped under the tarp, and, hunched awkwardly, wedged herself between a toolbox and some lumber. Just in time, the cart lurched forward, and she nearly congratulated herself, except it was then that she realized she was alone. In all of her planning, she'd forgotten to explain The Plan to Ghost.

Rowena lifted the lip of the tarp to find Ghost hovering by the hedge. She held a fuzzy caterpillar, rubbing it with her smoke-like cheek. She had a weakness for anything soft, especially things that were alive. The caterpillar, for its part, didn't seem to mind being snuggled by a specter, too busy munching new leaves.

Ghost, get in here! Rowena screamed in her head, but of course, Ghost couldn't hear. The cart lumbered down the driveway and Rowena wavered. She knew she should jump out, but then she wouldn't be able to get back in, and she'd be stuck at home. Alone.

But if she stayed…

The cart rounded the front of the cottage, and something sharp stabbed her chest. She shoved a fist against her lips. Every person in Wyre understood this pain, having tested the link with their Shadow at one point or another. It was why parents told scary stories to their children about people who died when their Shadow got too far. Soul's halves must never be parted.

Thanks to her father's Shadow, the cart gathered speed, and Rowena cursed magic altogether. It felt as if a knife were scooping out the inside of her ribcage. She had no choice but to abandon The Plan.

The pebble driveway was like rushing water below, soon replaced by cobbled bricks. Rowena's hand pressed against her chest, but the pain wasn't as bad as it had been just a second ago. Impossible. She should be in agony this far from her Shadow. But the pain only eased. She looked up, and sure enough, several yards back Ghost zoomed like a cannonball, flippers outstretched. Rowena would have reached out for her but for the blur of homes whizzing past. She hoped with all her might that their neighbors didn't notice the phantom chasing Haaris Faye's cart.

When Ghost caught up, she crashed into Rowena so hard she knocked the breath out of her. Rowena hugged her Shadow as if trying to bury her under her skin. "Oh, you little pest," she whispered but felt nothing but relief and a flicker of wonder at the hard-won proof she'd just acquired. Though Ghost lacked everything a Shadow should have, including any discernable good sense, the Shadow still contained some portion of Rowena's soul. Otherwise, they would have felt nothing from the separation. Ghost burrowed against her chest as if realizing the same thing.

The cart jerked, and the toolbox slammed against Rowena's side, cutting her wonder short. She had managed her escape, but The Plan wasn't nearly complete. Soon, they'd arrive at the festival arena, and she'd have to exit the cart before her father—or anyone else for that matter—saw her.

CHAPTER TWO

Autumn painted the surrounding forest in swaths of yellow and red, the air perfumed with crisping leaves and deadwood. But Rowena didn't notice, jostling in the back of the cart as it banged over cobblestones. A bruise formed on her hip where the toolbox knocked her at each turn.

No one in Greymere had a cart like her father's because few could handle the magic it required. It was a tricky animation that synchronized with the spinning wheels. Divots in the road, a turn around a bend, going uphill or down, all varied the wheel's movement, requiring Haaris's magic to counter like a dance. While some magics were static (like manipulating a worn pair of shoes to shine like new), animation was a roving, slippery endeavor. Yet, so long as there was movement, his magic could work indefinitely. Or, at least, that's how Haaris had explained it to Rowena. Having no magic herself, she had no idea what it was like.

Rowena pressed her face to a tear in the fabric, blinking against the cold. The city rolled past, a complex maze of stonework cut in the northernmost region of the Torborough Forest. Steepled buildings dotted endless lanes like spikes in a fence.

This wasn't Rowena's first time in the city. Anytime her father delivered orders to customers, he took her along, always stowed under the tarp. But she had never seen Greymere like this before. It seemed everyone was out today—in preparation for the Festival of Shadows, no doubt. Shop bells chimed like laughter as people poured in and out laden with packages. Animal-shaped Shadows followed underfoot or winged overhead. The smallest sat atop shoulders or rode in a pocket to avoid being trampled.

A whiff of something delicious made its way under the tarp, and Rowena poked her nose out, inhaling deeply. She realized then that she'd forgotten to eat breakfast. The air was spiced with cedar and honey, smoke from the butcher rivaling the haze of powdered sugar across the street. Rowena longed to swipe her finger along the dusted white windowsills where Greymere's baker had sprinkled nearly everything in cinnamon and sugar.

They rounded another corner, and Rowena nearly ripped the tarp to see better. "The castle!" she gasped. No matter how often she saw it, she would never get used to the impregnable fortress of limestone and steel. Colorful stained glass glittered like treasure just out of reach. Ghost jockeyed for a look, but Rowena's eyes were fixed, searching until she found the front doors where students entered laden with bookbags, their Shadows prominent in their wake. Her whole body strained against her tight enclosure, aching to walk among them. Ghost poked her in the ear, and Rowena jerked aside, allowing Ghost to witness the variegated menagerie of magical creatures parading past: all feathers, fur, wings, and scales.

Years ago, Haaris had explained that the castle housed a school where children of all ages learned to harness their Shadow magic. It wasn't long before Rowena had plastered their cottage with drawings of the castle. Every pen stroke was an act of love, her obsession evident in intricate details.

She had begged her father to allow her to attend the school, and to her amazement, he had consented with only two requirements: "Your Shadow must look normal, and she must have magic." While Haaris knew the impossibility of his conditions, Rowena hadn't then and so set to work.

For the first requirement, she captured animals found in the yard which she presented to Ghost as models. But when her Shadow failed to appear as anything but a bit of smoke, they were left with half-tamed rabbits, hedgehogs, a toad, some squirrels, and a rather cranky tortoise burrowing in the furniture and cupboards until finally, Haaris had to ban animals entirely.

Meeting her father's second condition had gone no better.

Every parent in Wyre anticipates their child's first magic with hope (that their magic might be strong) and apprehension (at what sort of havoc their infantile power might wreak). But Rowena's father never needed to worry. Her Shadow never set fire to the couch in a fit of temper like some children did. Nor did she shoot her supper across the table to smack her father in the face or turn her bedroom a violent shade of pink. As she grew up, she tried and begged and hoped and wished, but eventually, the truth sank in for Rowena.

The cart turned, and Rowena lost sight of the castle. A straggling student ran past them, close enough for her to make out the shiny salamander camouflaged against the student's green cape. It was then she recalled her father's words from earlier: "*When your Shadow becomes a* real *Shadow.*" The words stuck in her mind like a sweater caught on a splinter, unraveling her enthusiasm like yarn. She leaned back, allowing Ghost full view. Suddenly, Greymere seemed quite greyer than before.

It took almost an hour to pass through the city, but eventually, the cobbled stones gave way to a smooth dirt path. Buildings were replaced with the white-barked trees of Torborough Forest. Rowena knew when they arrived merely by the noise. Saws and hammers mingled with the hum of magic from a hundred Shadows. And the voices—so many voices!

Her eyes found the slit again. They'd come to a large meadow, much larger than she had expected. Indeed, the whole castle could have fit atop the swath of grass. Market stalls lined in winding rows, transforming the meadow into a miniature version of Greymere.

Her Plan had been to jump out of the cart and slink off into the forest. From there, she could watch the festival being constructed from a safe vantage. The Plan had seemed so simple when she was in her house with its safe hedges and walls. Even in the city, things felt close, buildings blotting out much of the sky. But here, the sky gaped like a giant mouth ready to swallow her. The market booths were made of canvas, open at the sides, and spaced apart so thousands of people could traverse the grassy lanes. She had no idea the world could be so big.

Regret zapped her veins like lightning. "Ghost, this was a mistake!" she whispered. Her Shadow dove for cover behind her ear.

The cart eventually stopped at the meadow's far end, where a deep arena sloped down like a ravine. Through the slit, Rowena saw a man the size of a bear jogging directly toward her. She recoiled against the toolbox.

"Haaris Faye!" the man's voice seemed to shake the whole earth. "Good to see you!"

"Sorry I'm late, Roderick," Haaris's voice greeted mildly. There was a slap of hands shaking. "Clock broke."

"Not to worry," the man named Roderick growled. "Fern sends her love."

Haaris chuckled in a way Rowena had never heard before. "I'm surprised your wife's not here herself, looking me over and demanding I eat something."

Roderick's laugh was like a mountain cracking in two. "Ha! She's around here somewhere; you'll hear it soon enough. So, how's the hermit life treating you, my friend?"

Panicked and penned though she was, Rowena's whole world seemed to lurch. She gripped the toolbox like a raft in a storm. The giant had called Haaris "*friend.*" The only person she had ever known was her father. But for him, it was not the same. He had a friend!

The giant whistled, and Rowena flinched, the tarp flimsy protection from such a man. She could hear a group of more men approaching loudly. Overlapped greetings jumbled in a confused mash. Rowena had no experience picking out individual voices from a group, but they all welcomed her father by name. She might have been bothered by his evident popularity if not for her mounting terror. Any moment, one of them would lift her pathetic cover, and she'd be caught.

She cocked her ear. It sounded like the men were at the front of the cart, meaning the back of the cart was free. A quick look confirmed this. Just a few yards ahead, a canvas booth displayed artfully labeled bottles. And beyond that—too far beyond for comfort—stretched the forest: her target. If she could get there, she'd be safe.

Men's voices garbled, and there was some coarse laughter. Straining her ears, she could just make out her father's voice.

Shifting her weight, she realized then that her legs had fallen asleep during the cramped ride. Pinpricks cascaded from her heels to her thighs. She grimaced against the pain and forced herself to move. With her catapult in tow, she emerged from the cart like an ungainly birth. Thankfully, thick grass softened her fall, but her torso landed on the catapult, adding to her bruise count. She groaned, regretting bringing the thing. But there was nothing for it. If she left it behind, her father might suspect.

She rolled under the cart, trying to muster the courage to run. Something tugged her hair, and she yelped. But it was just Ghost still buried in her curls. A smoky flipper pointed behind them where half a dozen legs congregated and, most serious of all, a few Shadows. Her father's Shadow must have remained in the cart because the spaniel wasn't among them. One of the Shadows was too massive to see below the cart, but the others could. A sleek hare flicked his ear toward her but otherwise showed no interest. Perhaps teenage girls were known for hiding in strange places.

"Ghost, stay," Rowena whispered, reaching up to check her Shadow was hidden in her mane of hair. Ghost squeezed the nape of her neck in answer.

Rowena shimmied out from under the cart, then clamored to her feet. The gaping sky made her dizzy, but she threw herself forward anyway. She rounded a booth and then another when her shoulder rammed into someone. A person. She'd touched an actual person. The sensation lingered on her skin like a burn. They, however, didn't seem as mystified by the touch. "Hey!" But Rowena didn't stop. Her focus narrowed on the trees ahead, everything else a blur. She pumped her legs and one arm, the other holding her catapult. She dodged two more people and their winged Shadows before escaping the market. With all her might, she hoped that she appeared like any ordinary girl, though maybe one in a hurry.

At last, she entered the forest, vaulted over a fallen log, then squatted behind its mossy bulk. It was hard to hear over her ragged breath, but it didn't seem anyone was coming for her. The din of the meadow went on unchanged.

She pressed her head against the log. The forest felt fresh and new despite autumn tucking the trees in for winter. Dead leaves crunched under her legs and bottom. Chilly air flushed her cheeks pink, awakening something inside, something alive and growling. It rose in her chest, and at first, she thought she might cry, but the bubble of emotion lifted into her throat and laughter burst out like a jailbreak. All the morning's anxiety vented in shocked hilarity until her sides ached. Her lungs gulped air like cold water.

Ghost sat on Rowena's knee with her head cocked, not understanding the joke. Eventually, Rowena mellowed to a hiccupping glow. With her head against the log, she closed her eyes, soaking in the busy noise from the meadow like an aficionado might a symphony.

But she had one last step of The Plan to complete. She spun on her knees and set the catapult on the log, mashed down the spring, loaded a stone, and then pointed it toward the meadow like a weapon. Only then, with protection in place, did she comfortably settle to people-watch for the remainder of the day.

Her curiosity feasted upon the scene, taking in every detail with hungry relish. Despite the exhilaration of beholding real people—and magic, too—she breathed deeper and steadier than she ever had at home. She was free, if only for the day.

While all of Greymere raced to be ready in time for the Festival of Shadows, none of them noticed the girl and her ghost watching them like a haunt.

CHAPTER THREE

Tʜᴇ ᴄᴀʀʀɪᴀɢᴇ ʀᴏᴄᴋᴇᴅ ʟɪᴋᴇ a boat inside the belly of Torborough Forest. Penalynn felt nervous among the papery trees etched with black knots that looked too much like eyes.

"Dirty backwater roads," she muttered. She needed a distraction, so she flipped open a novel, one that read like dessert: all sugar and no sustenance. But sunlight struggled to reach her through the dense canopy outside, and straining her eyes would only leave her with a headache, so she tossed the book to the floor with a frustrated huff.

You know you'll have to pick that up, her Shadow thought. *There's no servant here to do it for you.*

"Shut up," Penalynn snapped at the fox curled by her side. The Shadow's orange fur clashed brazenly with the carriage's red upholstery. Penalynn turned back to the window, preferring the creepy trees over her own Shadow with her veiled reminder.

It had been weeks since she'd been cast from her lifelong home in Riven. She knew she must not return. The king allowed one guard for her travels, but once she arrived in Greymere, she was on her own. Any attendant she might require, she must find in her new home where she knew not a soul.

Penalynn rocked in the carriage, alone, save her Shadow. Until this trip, she had never stepped foot outside the capital. Now, she would reside in the kingdom's farthest-flung city, deep in the forest. Greymere, she was told, served as a mini capital of sorts in the northernmost region of the Kingdom of Wyre. It also boasted the largest school of magic outside of Riven. Yet despite Greymere's importance to the Sceadwe's rule, hardly anyone from Riven ever traveled there.

The High Consul had called it a relocation, but Penalynn knew better. She still could not believe she hadn't seen this coming. *Inevitable* is what her Shadow had said. It had been naïve to think she could make her life in Riven work. She had been made a Scholastic only days before it happened. Her blue Scholastic cloak still chafed from newness when she was told.

Granted, the Sceadwe had not wanted to make her a Scholastic in the first place. It was the king, not the High Consul, who had appointed her to the role. In fact, it had been the king's first order after his coronation. The whole ordeal had been debated with animosity, the High Consulars venting their vexation in the marble halls of the palace. While Wyre's new king felt no repercussions for appointing so young a Scholastic, Penalynn had received unparalleled institutional resentment.

Like her appointment to Scholastic, her banishment had also not been the Sceadwe's doing. That had been the king's second order as Wyre's brand-new sovereign. The brand-new Scholastic would relocate to Greymere—indefinitely.

Anger and embarrassment swirled until Penalynn's thoughts were all a muddle. But who could blame her for not foreseeing this turn? Scholastics resided in Riven only. They worked in the Sceadwe castle, some even living there. All other regions had their own Hall of Sceadwe, with local Sages, Myth Keepers, and Lord Overseers to do the Sceadwe's bidding. Scholastics simply were not needed elsewhere. But Greymere would soon have the honor of hosting the first-ever resident Scholastic.

She fidgeted with her pendant. "Ugh, this thing is ridiculous. They can't expect me to keep it on." The Scholastic pendant thumped against her chest, the silver and blue image of a face—half human, half dragon—barely discernable in the twilight. "No. I refuse." She jerked the chain over her head. The sudden lightness flamed her defiance, and she unclasped her Scholastic cloak as well, wrenching it with a tug. She had difficulty extricating the fabric from her ample bottom, so she stood. The carriage jostled, and she fell headfirst onto the puffed bench opposite, her dimpled legs upended awkwardly. She yelped, a crumpled pile of flesh and velvet.

There was a *thump-thump* against the carriage roof, followed by a man's voice. "Everything alright in there?"

"I'm fine!" Penalynn panted loudly. She pushed herself up and hurled the wadded cloak as if it were a vile, offending thing. Then she scooped up the pendant and tossed it as well, hissing like an injured cat for good measure.

The fox sat perfectly still, watching Penalynn with regal disapproval. *You'll just have to put that back on when we stop.*

"Says who?" she snapped, mutinous even towards her own Shadow.

Says the Sceadwe.

"Well, the joke's on them. By sending me to Greymere, I am the highest-ranking official for days in every direction. *I* am the Sceadwe out here."

The fox made a snorting noise that sounded almost like laughter.

Night soon fell, and they passed a sign designating the bit of road sandwiched by buildings on either side as "The Town of Keatston." They rolled to a stop before a cozy-looking inn. Penalynn's black-clad guard jumped from his post and wrenched open the door, holding out a gloved hand. An orange lizard clung to his forearm. Penalynn took the guard's hand and hopped from the carriage, swaying after a long day's ride. Her Shadow followed primly behind.

"Are you forgetting something?" the guard asked.

"No." She glowered. Her head barely reached his shoulders as she brushed past.

The guard stifled a grin.

Inside, they stopped at the front desk, where a mustached man greeted them. His hairy Shadow lounged on the ledger.

"I would like a few rooms, please," Penalynn said politely. "One for me and however many you have for my company."

"How big's your comp'ny?"

"Besides myself, there are five men." He leveled her with a quizzical stare, so she explained, "Four drivers and my guard here."

The innkeeper glanced out the window where the first wagon hauled a tower of boxes, some furniture, and even a porcelain tub. "Lot of stuff for one lass. And are those *horses* pulling those wagons?" His mouth fell agape.

It was fair. Usually, people of means could afford a driver whose Shadow was powerful enough to propel a wagon by magic. Anyone who couldn't afford such a driver most likely couldn't afford a team of horses, let alone four sets. A horse-drawn carriage was not entirely unheard of, but it was definitely odd.

"My rooms, please," Penalynn pressed.

"No doin'." The innkeeper shrugged. "All booked up, I'm afraid."

Penalynn blinked. "You can't be serious."

"S'the festival in Greymere." Another shrug.

A new traveler entered the inn, wearing a green cloak signifying him as a Sage of the Sceadwe—an educator in Shadow magic. He queued behind Penalynn while the innkeeper continued. "Suppose I could set you up in the barn out back. The hay's fresh."

Penalynn's jaw dropped. "You expect me to sleep in a *barn?*"

He shrugged. She considered slapping him if his shoulders flopped like that again.

"Are you really so unprofessional as to offer *the barn* to a potential customer?" Her mind spun at the concept of sleeping in such a place. On hay, no less! Didn't animals *eat* hay? Preposterous.

"It's what I got, lady."

"I will take my business elsewhere."

"Good luck on that. Anywhere you go, it'll be the same. Like I said, it's the festival."

Penalynn moved aside, and the green-cloaked Sage stepped forward.

"Bran, what are we supposed to do?" she asked her guard, terror rising. She had never ventured so far from home and was hopelessly unaccustomed to the discomfort of traveling.

You just had *to insist on magicless travel,* her Shadow admonished, fox fur bristling. *Well, now we're going to sleep with those horses! HORSES!"*

Penalynn felt so angry she could spit.

"Of course, sir," she heard the innkeeper say, his voice noticeably brighter. "I got a key right here for nobility such as yourself."

Penalynn whipped around so fast she stepped on her Shadow, who scratched her ankle in protest. "Did this man have a reservation?" she demanded loudly. The innkeeper blinked dully, reservations a novel concept for such an establishment.

The Sage answered for him. "No, I arrived just now."

"You *do* have rooms!" she crowed.

"I always keep a spare for nobility and the like," the innkeeper said, daring to shrug his shoulders once more. Penalynn contemplated setting his desk on fire.

"You offered me the barn when you had a room."

Her guard murmured in her ear, "I suggest we go outside."

But her focus narrowed on the innkeeper. "I'm a paying customer. I demand you give me your spare rooms this instant, including that man's right there." She pointed at the Sage, who slid to the side, grimacing uncomfortably.

A black glove tapped her arm. "Outside."

"No doin', miss," the innkeeper said.

Penalynn planted her feet, but her guard spun her to face him, heading off the coming explosion. "Go put your cloak on," he said.

"No."

His breath was hot against her ear. "Pen, so help me. I will carry you outside myself." His stormy eyes told her this was not an empty threat. So, she stomped out the front door into the moody glow of lanternlight. When she reached the carriage, she wheeled around.

"Bran, you can't talk to me like—"

"I'll talk to you like the spoiled baby you are," he said, pointing at the carriage door. "Put your cloak on."

"No." She crossed her arms. He crossed his, too, his muscles bulging much more menacingly than her doughy arms. She dropped them. "*I* should be given those rooms. I arrived before that Sage, and I will pay good money. That is the only reason I should be given rooms."

"Well, those aren't the only reasons rooms are given, *Madame Scholastic.*" Her title sounded sarcastic when he used it. "Put your cloak on!"

She stood her ground. Bran's biceps looked near to bursting, and his Shadow's orange scales shone like a band of fire around his forearm. Penalynn felt the contrast of their statures; her soft roundness squared off against his broadness. But no matter how soft her body might be, her resolve was not.

"No. It's the principle of the thing!"

"Ah yes, your principles. And how much have your principles helped you lately, Pen?"

She picked at a wayward cuticle, melting a bit. "You sound like my Shadow."

He snorted. "You are the only person I know who fights with their Shadow. You know that's not normal, right?" He pointed at the fox. "She's *you.* I don't even know how you're mentally capable of it."

I've been saying this for years, the fox thought wryly, though only Penalynn could hear.

"Oh, shut up," Penalynn said. "Both of you." Bran laughed, and Penalynn allowed a small smile. "I could just perform a persuasion. That'd make him give us rooms."

"Yes!" Bran nodded emphatically. "Please. Yes. Do that. I'm sure your Shadow is aching to use her magic. How long's it been, exactly? You still counting in months or years now?"

The fox sprang to all fours, licking her lips. *Yes, magic. Let's do magic.*

"I was joking," Penalynn said, "Of course, I'm not going to do magic just for a couple of rooms."

"Fine, I'll do it."

"You're a royal guard."

"So?"

"So, persuasions like that are illegal!"

"Everyone does it."

Penalynn smacked him, barely missing the lizard who jerked out of the way.

"Ugh. Pen, please! Put on your cloak and get us some rooms. I didn't get to ride in a comfy carriage like you. I want a bed. With pillows."

Though she glowered, Penalynn obliged, reaching inside the carriage. Despite having been wadded up, the velvet unfurled like dark water. She draped the cloak over her shoulders, clicking the clasp across her collarbone. Bran swung the pendant in front of her, and she snatched it, dropping the heavy chain over her head.

"Do I look important enough to deserve a room now?"

He looked her up and down, and she blushed. She knew her stature alone would never invoke intimidation or even respect in some circles. But that didn't matter. The cloak would be enough. Scholastics were the closest thing to royalty a citizen outside of Riven would ever see. She blanched at the thought.

Bran noticed. "You okay?"

She nodded, then reentered the inn, though now as a Scholastic of the Scead-we. Immediately, the innkeeper took in the glistening blue cloak, the pendant glinting in the firelight. His jaw dropped. Penalynn didn't know whether to be furious or pleased with the response.

She approached the desk and said with forced sweetness, "I would like rooms, please."

"Ma-Madame Sc-Scholastic! Why, I had no idea you were..."

"Yes, that was obvious. Now, about my rooms."

"But that Sage got my last one."

Penalynn's smile froze.

The innkeeper jumped, and his Shadow rolled off the desk. "But I'll fix it! Nothin' to worry 'bout! You will have the very most—the very best rooms in no time!" He disappeared up the stairs, his Shadow scurrying after him.

"You better be careful," Bran warned her, "Your nose will get stuck if you keep pointing it up like that."

"Shut up. I do not act any different with this cloak on than I do otherwise."

"You're right. You're always pretentious."

"Please remember who you're talking to."

"Bah," he dismissed with a wave. "You like that about me. It's why you brought me."

"I was allowed a guard and figured it was my last chance to see a familiar face."

"And it helps that it's such a handsome face."

She snorted. "You know, for a man in your position, you ought to be more serious."

"How about this for serious." He leaned against the desk. "Like it or not, you've got to wear that cloak."

"I *am* wearing it."

"You know what I mean. Resent it all you want, but things are different for you now. But, despite what you think, being a Scholastic is a big honor. Except for the High Consul and the king himself, no one outranks you. Most people would kill for that kind of power."

Her voice was suddenly small. "I'm banished, Bran."

"More like relocated."

"Exiled."

"You have three wagons of luxuries, and you'll live in a castle. You will out-rank every person within a month's ride from you. This is not a prison sentence you've received. That cloak and all it signifies will give you a life out here. Don't resent it."

"I don't mind resenting it."

"Well, it makes you insufferable. More than you already are. You'll make no friends."

Friends? She heard disgust in her Shadow's voice.

Penalynn wasn't sure she agreed with her Shadow. After all, Bran was her friend, that same grinning, annoying boy from childhood. He may have been the son of a nobody, but he had been one of the few constants in a life that bent and forked like a river. Yes, though everything about them was opposite, from her preening tutors and his soldier's training, her lavish luxuries and his scant provisions. Fat next to muscle, her ideals against his pragmatism. Unlikely as it was, Bran was her friend.

"I'll wear the cloak," she promised.

The innkeeper gave Penalynn the Sage's suite. The Sage moved to a smaller room down the hall, so Bran could have the room across from hers. When she entered her quarters, a servant lingered in the washroom. It had been weeks since she'd seen a proper tub, so she'd requested a bath. The woman's Shadow hummed magic over a copper basin until the water steamed. When she left, Penalynn sank into the scalding water. Her muscles screamed after weeks on the road. She forced herself not to think about how many bodies had used the tub before her, inhaling the scent of peppermint—a thoughtful manipulation by the servant's Shadow.

Her fox perched beside the tub, thinking of Bran. *He's starting to forget. Another goodbye is coming.*

Penalynn couldn't tell if the regret she felt was hers alone or shared between them.

"You're glad to be leaving," she said.

Of course, I am. The fox's teeth showed, and Penalynn thought how animal-like she looked. A wave of offense pricked her heart, but she wouldn't claim it. The fox sighed. *Bran is right. We have everything we need to build a life out here.*

"I know."

But you won't leave it alone. A question embedded in the accusation. Dread. But not Penalynn's.

"I have submitted to everything without a fight, including this move."

But you won't leave it alone.

Penalynn didn't answer. She didn't need to.

When they climbed into bed, they slept back to back; the fox curled at the farthest edge, tail wrapped tightly to cover her face. Still, any dreams that came, they dreamed together.

CHAPTER FOUR

IT WASN'T LONG INTO her spying that Rowena observed how much people relied on their Shadows. Everything was done by magic, even things easily accomplished without. For instance, a woman erecting a booth. After assembling the poles and canvas, she needed to secure it in the ground. For this, she used a minuscule hammer small enough to be clockwork. She tapped it atop an iron stake as if cracking an egg. Rowena would have scoffed, except the stake shot into the ground as if smashed with a sledgehammer. The duck at the woman's feet waddled to the next stake, readying to magic another.

Everywhere, it was the same, Shadows magicking whatever they could find. At one point, competition broke out when a vendor manipulated his bland canvas into a garish shade of yellow—no doubt to stand out. Thinking this was a good idea, his neighbor magicked his own booth, a bright purple Rowena quite liked. Not to be outdone, the rest joined in until the whole meadow flashed like an undulating rainbow, turning Rowen's stomach. Eventually, the Lord Overseer himself had to intervene—the giant man from before, whom Rowena could now see properly. After that, they all chose a color and stuck to it.

By midday, Rowena fidgeted. Her hands weren't used to being still so long. She fiddled with her catapult, noticing a gear had loosened, no doubt from the morning's journey. She pulled from her bag a dog-eared book with cracked binding. It fell open to a much-used page where cramped scrawl framed the diagram of a catapult. Most of the book's inventions were beyond Rowena, but after several failed attempts, she managed this one, however smaller. After checking the page, her slender fingers moved expertly. She pulled tools from her bag when necessary. When she was happy with the result, she twirled a wrench on her thumb.

A noise caught her attention. She looked to her right where a group of kids congregated in an open patch of meadow. She tucked her contraption under her arm and snuck from tree to tree to find a better vantage.

Her pulse skipped with pleasure when she saw they were all around her age. The school must have let out, she thought, because some of them still wore the green capes she'd noticed kids wearing to the castle. They ran about, calling loudly to one another, and it took her a moment to understand they were playing a game. It involved magicking a rock in the air.

A boy with a raccoon for a Shadow caught her attention. He seemed uninterested in the game itself, preferring to pelt kids with the rock. Rowena found this behavior odd, but his peers all laughed—except a boy who'd just been smacked between the eyes. When it was his turn with the rock, he must have still been angry because his Shadow shot the rock so hard it landed in the forest. It came to a rolling stop just a foot from where Rowena hid. She dove behind a tree, expecting them to come looking for it. But someone found a new rock in the grass, and the game proceeded.

Rowena continued to watch but felt different somehow. It started as a vague longing, the same jealous tightness she felt when she witnessed her father's magic. But the feeling intensified until she snatched the rock that had fallen nearby. With no magic interfering anymore, it lay lifeless against her pale skin. Ghost prodded it, suspicious, but Rowena scowled at the thing as if it had insulted her. It felt like a challenge somehow, beckoning—no—demanding she play.

She could. There was nothing stopping her. Sure, Ghost might not have magic like the rest of them, but Rowena was not helpless, no matter what her father thought. She knelt, looked down at the catapult, back at the rock, and then at the meadow.

Her hand was perfectly steady when she set the rock onto the catapult's seat. With a fingertip, she tightened a gear until the spring was set, then checked that every student was facing away. She pulled the lever. The contraption convulsed exactly as designed. With a satisfied grin, she watched the rock arch across the field, just like the other kids had done. Magic or not, she could do what they did. She felt suddenly light, as if her body lifted up and out just like that rock. She smiled wide and toothy, pretending the cheers on the field were for her.

With a sudden jerk, her daydream dropped. A Shadow had noticed. The same boy who had sent the rock into the woods now snapped his head around.

Rowena snarled at herself. "Stupid!"

The boy scooped up the rock. He squinted, seeming directly at her.

Rowena ducked. "No, no, no," she muttered. Oh, what she would give to have magic so she could persuade his mind to look elsewhere! But Ghost floated dumbly as usual.

The boy walked towards her with a curious look. His teammates hollered for him, but the boy with the raccoon cried, "Oh, let him go!" and the game resumed.

Rowena dove behind a mossy boulder just as he entered the woods. It was then she noticed Ghost hadn't followed her. She heard a gasp and hazarded a look. It felt like a dream, Ghost hovering face-to-face with the boy. A nightmare, really.

"It's a spook!" he said as if it really was a nightmare.

He stepped back, but his owl-shaped Shadow winged forward and landed on the boulder. Rowena covered her head with her arms, a feeble gesture. Two enormous owl eyes blinked at her.

"I can see you," the boy called. Not knowing what to do, Rowena gave the owl a measly wave. The boy asked, "Want to come out?"

Hiding was pointless now. Besides, she needed to get Ghost. She stood and faced the boy, her weight on her toes, ready to run. He was tall, with broad shoulders, but gangly. She deduced he was close to her age—fifteen, maybe sixteen years old.

"I'm Titus," he said. He mussed his hair like a nervous tic, but somehow, the messy effect brought out the lines of his jaw and cheekbones. Rowena wavered, unfamiliar with introductions and considering which direction to start sprinting. He asked, "Where's your Shadow?"

Her eyes darted to Ghost and back to him. Her breath was shallow, like cornered prey.

"Your Shadow is the spook?"

In answer, she bit her lip.

The boy's face lit up. He leaned toward Ghost, her milky form like a minuscule cloud. "That's got to be the coolest Shadow I've ever seen!"

This was not the response Rowena expected. Despite her terror, her lips twitched. The owl winged in a tight loop, examining Ghost from every angle. Ghost spun to keep the owl in her sight.

Titus noticed the gadget by his feet. "Is this thing yours?"

Rowena found her voice then. "I made it."

"Oh yeah? What is it?"

"It throws things."

"Yeah? Show me."

She should run. She knew she should. But somehow, despite good sense like a warning voice in her head, her feet compelled her forward. Her father would be furious if he found her talking to anyone, but what could she do about it now? The boy had already seen her. Her whole life, he'd promised her that anyone who saw Ghost would be terrified. But this boy didn't seem scared at all. Besides, something in his inquiring look—matching her own aching curiosity—drew her in.

She knelt before the catapult and swung it away from the meadow. Keeping the boy in her periphery, she moved by rote, pulling levers, pressing springs, and winding gears. "I need something to throw," she said.

Titus offered the rock he still held, the one she'd foolishly let fly. His fingertips felt like static against her palm, a lingering shock. She placed the rock atop the seat. The catapult convulsed like a trap, shooting the rock to crash against a tree several yards away. A startled squirrel chirruped in protest.

Titus's lips parted. "Woah! You *made* this?"

Rowena tucked a wayward curl behind her ear. She felt bubbly inside. This boy with the disarming owl was impressed by her. The realization made her proud and lightheaded at the same time. "Yes," she answered.

"Do you animate the rock or the throw-y thing to aim?"

"Uh. It aims without magic."

"Show me." His cheek dimpled like a challenge but in a friendly sort of way.

Something like courage unfurled in Rowena's chest, tentative but real. "Alright," she said, then pointed to an empty bird's nest several trees away. She adjusted gears with careful precision. Titus produced another rock, and this time, she grinned at his quick touch. The rock knocked the nest, sending crumpled pieces to the ground.

"This is really amazing!" Titus dropped to his knees. Rowena flinched at his sudden proximity. Her heartbeat pulsed in her ears, heady but not unpleasant. "Teach me how to do it," he said.

Titus proved a quick learner, choosing increasingly tricky targets. While they took turns hurling anything they could find, Ghost inspected Titus's Shadow, which sat atop his shoulder. The owl didn't seem to mind. Soon, both Shadows took to the air, dodging trees in a game of chase. Rowena paid them no mind and so didn't notice when their latest shot hit Ghost square in the chest, knocking the little wisp to the ground.

"Woah!" Titus touched Rowena's arm, "Are you okay? That looks like it hurt."

She gaped at his hand as if he staunched a wound. "What?!"

"You just took out your Shadow." Her confusion was evident, and he slowly realized, "Wait, did you not feel that?"

Ghost emerged from a pile of leaves, dazed but unharmed. She zoomed back to Rowena. Titus' eyes narrowed back and forth between them, and Rowena felt the urge to run again. He reached across, and to her utter shock, he poked Ghost in her smokey belly. "Can you feel that?" he asked.

Rowena could hardly think, let alone speak. The boy had touched her Shadow—something even her father avoided. She shook her head.

Titus poked Ghost again, this time a bit harder. "How about that?"

"No," she whispered. The moment felt intimate, his face close and touching her Shadow. Her breath was shallow, but the urge to flee was gone, replaced with a different sort of urge she didn't understand. Titus should have been horrified, disgusted even, to touch such an unnatural thing. But he was all wonderment and awe, completely unaware of the kindness he bestowed. His finger tapped Ghost once more, and something fluttered in Rowena's chest, warm and tender.

"That?" he asked.

She smiled and shook her head.

Before he could do it again, Ghost reared back and smacked his hand with a sharp *thwack*. Her translucent face puckered with indignation.

"Ouch! Yeah, I deserve that." He chuckled, shaking his hand. "She's stronger than she looks."

Ghost turned to the owl and poked his wing, thinking the gesture was social convention. Or perhaps in retribution.

Titus laughed again. "You're tougher than you look."

When Ghost made to jab the owl again, Rowena caught her flipper, her cheeks hot with embarrassment. "Ghost, stop that!"

"Ghost?" Titus asked, "It's a real ghost, then?"

Color drained from Rowena's face. "NO!" she cried louder than she meant. "I mean, no, that's just what I call her."

"You really are spooky, aren't you?"

Unsure how to respond and feeling self-conscious, Rowena fidgeted with the catapult.

"You know what I think we need?" Titus said, mercifully changing the subject. "A moving target." He swung the catapult toward the meadow where the game was still happening.

Rowena's stomach lurched. "What are you going to hit?"

Taking aim, he muttered, "My brother."

"Which one is he?"

"The jerk with the raccoon."

On the field, half of the group hung their heads low, having just lost the game. The boy with the raccoon slung across his shoulder was stockier than Titus but seemed older in the face. Apparently, his team had won because he did a taunting dance, thrusting his hips.

Titus took aim but fell a yard shy of his target. He swore under his breath. Despite herself, Rowena twisted the gears helpfully. Titus shot again, and the acorn smacked his brother square in the back of the head. The raccoon toppled to the ground in a heap.

"*Ooh!* I hope that bruises!" His brother rubbed the back of his head, jaw agape in confusion. Titus cackled. "Look at his stupid face! He has no idea!" His laughter stopped short when he seemed to realize something. "Hey, I bet with our magic along with this thing, we could get a rock all the way to the cider tent over there." He pointed to the farthest end of the meadow.

In a way, their short time together had been like a dream, but the reminder of the world beyond the trees doused Rowena like cold water. "Umm, no—" she snatched the catapult and shoved it into her bag. "Actually, I've got to go."

"Oh," said Titus, disappointed. "Hey, what's your name?"

"Umm..."

He looked at her directly, open, unflinching, and chasing all thoughts from her head.

"Rowena."

"Rowena," he repeated as if securing the name in his memory. "Rowena, do you like dancing?"

"Yes." She had never danced in her life.

"Let's dance together at the festival. I'll look for you." He grabbed her hand and pulled her to standing. Rowena gaped at their interlocked hands, like cream and caramel swirled together. She jerked hers away, and he pocketed his own. His lips widened into the most confident grin Rowena had ever seen. "See you later, Spook."

"See you later," she mimicked. The lie lingered on her lips, bitter and cruel as she retraced her steps. It was time to go home.

CHAPTER FIVE

WHEN ROWENA RETURNED TO her earlier spot in the woods, Haaris was still at the bottom of the arena, building something on the stage. She scanned the meadow for Shadows, looking for instances where one wasn't visible. Most were too large to conceal, but a smattering of Shadows peered from a pocket or pouch, which was encouraging. Someone was going to notice her; there was no way around it. If they did, hopefully, they would assume her Shadow was a hamster or ladybug or something. And so, after ensuring Ghost was hidden under her hair, she stepped into the clearing with all the casualness she could muster. Her heart pounded so loudly in her ears that, for one panicked moment, she wondered if anyone else could hear it, too.

She walked quickly but not abnormally so. And to her relief, nobody noticed. She paused by a pile of empty boxes and discarded canvas—the throw-aways from the market construction. Her mind spun. With a glance around, she snatched a scrap of canvas. When she reached her father's cart, she crawled underneath. Laying in the grass, she arranged the canvas over her to look like a discarded scrap, then covered her head and waited.

It took a while for her father to return, but Rowena hardly noticed the passage of time, even when Ghost fidgeted. Her imagination was too busy replaying her time with Titus, mulling over every word, gesture, and look. She rubbed her hand where they had touched as if she might press the memory into her skin.

Haaris eventually returned and loaded his toolbox and some leftover materials into the back. Once he and his Shadow climbed onto the front bench, Rowena rolled out and slipped onto the bed of the cart unnoticed.

On the way home, Haaris stopped at a storefront. Rowena peeked at the sign above the door, which read *Patterfold Potions.* She frowned with a small twinge of worry. Night fell fast this time of year, so it was dark when he emerged from the shop carrying a small paper sack.

She knew they'd arrived home when banging cobblestones were swapped for crunchy gravel. Not waiting for the cart to stop, Rowena slipped out near the front of the cottage. Darkness hid her well. She entered through the front door (left unlocked as part of The Plan) and went to the kitchen straight away. Next year, she'd plan on taking food with her because she was famished. Ghost released pent-up energy by zooming several loops around the ceiling.

Rowena's previous worry was confirmed when Haaris awkwardly opened the back door with his opposite hand. His other arm was in a sling. "What happened?!" she said through a mouthful of bread and cheddar.

Haaris rolled his eyes at his own foolishness. "Fractured my wrist." His Shadow whined, sharing the pain.

"Are you going to be alright?"

"'Course I am. Stopped at the apothecary on my way home. He wrapped me up and gave me a potion."

Rowena took the paper bag from his good hand and fished out a brown bottle with a rubber dropper. She read the label. "'Mending Potion.' What does that mean?"

"It'll help the injury heal quicker."

Her fingernails tapped the glass like a question. "A potion can do that?"

With a tired groan, Haaris eased himself into his favorite chair. "They can do all sorts of things."

Rowena turned the bottle over. She opened it, sniffed the contents, filled the dropper, then squeezed oily amber drops back inside. Haaris cleared his throat and held out his hand. She handed the bottle over, but reluctantly. Sure, she'd seen a potion before, mostly when one of them had a cough or fever. Still, she eyed the bottle curiously.

Haaris dribbled some of the amber liquid onto his tongue, then swallowed with a shudder. "Would it kill him to manipulate the taste?" he muttered, screwing the lid.

Rowena knelt before the fireplace and struck a match, then held it to a log. Haaris's Shadow was sprawled on the rug close by, almost like a real dog. "Help me, will you?" she said to the spaniel. He didn't even lift his head in response. Still, she heard the hum of magic an instant before fire blanketed the log. She backed away from the heat and settled on the floor by her father's Shadow. Being more affectionate than Haaris, the spaniel rested his chin on her knee, smiling when she scratched his head. Haaris removed his boots with a gratified sigh, then leaned back, his expression softened by exhaustion. He faced Rowena openly, and she met his look with a twinge. Could he tell by looking at her where she'd been all day? Her hand flew to her hair, checking for leaves or twigs that might have come along.

But Haaris and said casually, "So, the Lord Overseer has asked me to do the lights for the ceremony at the festival."

"'Do the lights.' What does that mean?"

"Well, it, uh, it's hard to explain. There's a platform at the top of the arena, behind the audience. That's where I'll have to sit to do it. Pretty tucked away from everyone. But it's a great spot to see the ceremony."

Rowena's ribs collapsed in a hunch. So much for avoiding a day alone. "You're going to the festival too?"

Haaris looked down at his wrapped hand. "The platform's high, and the only way to get there is by ladder. Now that I've gone and busted myself, I'm not sure I can manage the ladder alone. So, I was thinking, if we got there before everyone else, you could help me up."

She hardly dared to breathe.

"If you kept low on the platform, I don't think anybody would notice you...that is...if you stayed."

Her eyes shone in the firelight like two polished coins.

Harris leaned forward with his good elbow on his knee. "I know I didn't show it, but I heard what you said you this morning. You're right. I need to trust you. You can come to the festival with me if you want."

The spaniel pressed his wet nose against her skin, and Rowena's face broke into a smile so big her eyes crinkled.

Haaris held up a finger in caution. "Now, you can't go walking around or anything. You'll stay on the platform and keep out of sight. It's not going to be comfortable up there. But if you promise to—"

"I promise!"

He looked at his Shadow before nodding. "Okay, then that settles it. We're going to the festi—"

"AHHH!!!" Rowena launched from the rug to throw herself upon him. She wrapped her arms around his neck, and he gasped with pain. "Oops, sorry!" She shifted off his injured arm and sat on his knee like when she was little. "Thank you, Papa! Thank you, thank you!"

She kissed his cheek again and again. Ghost zoomed in more loops around the room. Rowena giggled against her father's neck, and he smiled grimly as if his cheeks were sore from lack of practice. "I hope to Bazileus this isn't a bad idea," he muttered.

CHAPTER SIX

THE DAY BEFORE THE Festival of Shadows, Greymere's excitement bubbled like sparkling wine, nearly exploding when a carriage and three wagons rolled down the main promenade—pulled by horses, of all things. People leaned from windows and lined the streets to watch the caravan like a parade, though they clutched their Shadows as if the presence of real animals was bad luck.

Inside the carriage, Penalynn looked in a mirror and fussed with her hair, silently cursing the king who was responsible for her present predicament. She had never realized how much her personal attendants did to achieve her preferred style. Her hair lay limp and wholly uncooperative. The more she messed with it, the limper it got until Penalynn's skin blotched with rage.

Stop touching it, her Shadow thought. *You're only making it worse.*

The fox was right. Penalynn snapped the mirror shut so hard the glass cracked, a just punishment for showing such a meager version of herself. She hoped the king's new crown gave him a rash for humbling her so. "I can't be seen like this," she said.

Just then, the castle appeared outside the window. *It seems we won't have a choice,* observed the fox.

A sizeable crowd waited before the castle doors. Penalynn counted a dozen Sages in green cloaks. At the center stood a tall man in a Myth Keeper's cape and a small army of servants flanking behind.

Someone wants to make a good impression. That must be every resident of the castle.

Penalynn considered asking Bran to find a back entrance. Sensing this, the fox encouraged, *All anyone will see is a Scholastic. Which is enough.*

Her Shadow was right. The lustrous cloak and pendant would compensate for any lack Penalynn felt.

When the carriage stopped, she scooped up the fox, her russet fur coarse against her skin. The door swung open, and she accepted Bran's offered hand. The lizard around his wrist gave her a friendly lick, and she felt suddenly braver. That was until the smiles waiting to greet her froze. All down the line, brows furrowed, heads cocked, and most humiliating of all, The Myth Keeper himself hung his jaw agape.

Penalynn set her teeth. She approached the Myth Keeper directly, her heels clicking hard on the stone. The Myth Keeper recovered enough to step forward, thumbing his bushy brows uncertainly. "Ah! *Madame* Scholastic!" he greeted.

The fox shifted in Penalynn's arms. *He wasn't expecting a woman.*

The man folded in a bow, and the Sages and servants followed.

"Mr. Keeper," was all Penalynn said in greeting. She noticed him look her up and down, his frown deepening. Fire ignited her skin. She disliked him at once.

Ignorant of this, the Myth Keeper turned to the line of Sages and made introductions. Penalynn greeted them all politely, tucking their names in her memory. At the end of the line, she said to the Myth Keeper, "I trust you received my letters explaining my requirements?"

He seemed thrown off-center. The canary atop his shoulder hopped from foot to tiny foot. "Hm, yes. I hope you'll be pleased with our arrangements. But I, ah, might have made an unfortunate assumption—quite unfortunate, in fact—in selecting a personal attendant." Penalynn noticed a young man standing nearby looking oddly forlorn. The Myth Keeper winced with embarrassment. "Young Roger here was chosen because you see, I—that is, you signed your initials only—and I, ah..."

Penalynn was tempted to leave the man dangling in his mistake but forced herself to mercy. "My apologies, Mr. Keeper, it's entirely my fault. My name is *Penalynn* Graft."

"Yes, madame. I will find a female attendant before the day's end. Might I show you to your quarters to ensure we have not failed in that regard as well?"

Penalynn followed him into the castle. Bran poked her in the back to remind her to be nice. She flashed him an exaggerated smile, and he rolled his eyes.

Greymere's castle was similar to the one in Riven, though less opulent but tastefully so. The Myth Keeper led her past a grassy courtyard rimmed by outdoor walkways. They entered the eastmost turret to ascend a circular staircase all the way to the top, then emerged at a wide corridor.

"Our newly renovated Scholastic wing," the Myth Keeper declared with a sweep of his arm. His Shadow proudly winged ahead. Your living quarters are at the end of the hall. Your office and personal library are over there. And here—I believe you called it a laboratory? I'm afraid some of the materials only arrived this week, so we are still unpacking." He opened the door, and it was like upturning an anthill, servants scurrying about inside.

Before Penalynn could enter, her Shadow jumped from her arms and planted herself beside the door. Penalynn refused to give her Shadow the satisfaction of an argument and so entered the laboratory alone. The Myth Keeper and nearby servants all noticed but averted their eyes as if they hadn't.

It was a large room, well-lit from many windows, with arched beams spanning the ceiling. Glass cabinets lined the longest wall—made exactly to Penalynn's specifications, she was happy to note.

A stone counter stretched down the middle, like an altar that had been stretched to accommodate an especially large sacrifice. It was covered in metal contraptions freshly unboxed. The machines were foreign-looking, even to Penalynn, ominous in their complexity. She'd had them specially made in Riven and delivered directly. It would take some time for her to learn how to operate them all.

"Quite impressive...uh...things," the Myth Keeper said. Any disapproval he harbored toward the machinery, he hid well. "All of us are very interested to see what sort of work you intend. Hosting the first Scholastic in Greymere! Why, it is all very exciting."

Penalynn walked about the room and servants moved to give her a deferential berth. At the far end, a few women unboxed glass vials. Packing straw littered the stone floor. Penalynn had sent instructions for the bottles to be sterilized, so the woman unpacking them handed each vial to the next woman who dipped the glass into a basin of water and alcohol. Her Shadow hummed with magic, animating the solution to boil. After a few seconds, the Shadow cooled the liquid, and the servant removed the jar then handed it, dripping, to the next woman whose Shadow magicked it dry. The vial was then set on a high shelf along with the rest. Already, hundreds of vials stood empty, waiting to be filled with discovery. Still, the boxes held hundreds more.

The fox watched from the hall, half expecting the door to close and trap her like a sterile jail. Penalynn said, "Very nice," to the women, who all quaked under her approval.

"Are you polishing that with a *rag*?" the Myth Keeper suddenly barked, and everyone in the room jumped.

A servant paused her vigorous wiping of a boxy metal device.

Penalynn looked over and asked, "Is something the matter?"

The housekeeper overseeing the work hurried over, wringing her hands. "I beg your pardon, Mr. Keeper. We needed all the help we could get, so I called Freya up from the kitchens." She scowled at the woman holding the rag. The housekeeper's Shadow jumped onto the counter to magic the box the woman had been polishing. Within a moment, the surface reflected like a mirror; no rag needed. The housekeeper pushed the woman toward the door. "Freya, go...dust something, why don't you!"

"Stop," Penalynn said, and the entire room went still. "You dismiss her because she didn't use magic to clean?"

"Certainly, madame," the housekeeper said.

The Myth Keeper cleared his throat. "We apologize for the disgrace."

"I don't understand," said Penalynn.

"Her magic is weak." The housekeeper lowered her voice as if she spoke of something shameful. "The poor thing can barely heat a kettle."

Penalynn felt a maternal growl, but her Shadow stamped it down. *Don't be stupid.*

Penalynn ignored the fox. "Freya, is it?" The woman blanched at hearing her name on Scholastic lips. Stooped in submission, she stepped forward as if expecting a beating. Instead, Penalynn asked, "Who did your braid like that?"

Freya's face lifted, though she didn't dare look at the Scholastic directly. "Madame?"

Penalynn admired the meticulous braid artfully piled atop her head; it was not quite her style, but impressive nonetheless. "It's pretty. Who did it?"

"I did, madame."

"With magic?"

The girl dropped her chin. "No. Mrs. Finkle is right. My Shadow is weak." The pocket of her apron quivered where her Shadow hid, no doubt ashamed.

Penalynn looked across the room at Bran. He shook his head, barely perceptible. But Penalynn knew his thoughts as if he were her Shadow. After all, they so often agreed, him and the fox. But this was her laboratory, a new thing she was making, never seen in Greymere nor hardly even in Riven. The king might have the power to make her a Scholastic and even to drop her way out here. But being so far from Riven's reach, she was free to remake the role to her liking. Besides, Bran was leaving. He would forget her, no doubt, and she should try to forget him. So, despite his opposing look, she turned to the servant. "Freya, I need a new attendant. May I ask you some questions?"

"Madame, no!" Mrs. Finkle interrupted. Penalynn's eyes flashed. "Pardon me, but madame would not be happy with Freya."

"Because of her Shadow?"

"Yes, just that, indeed."

Penalynn continued as if the housekeeper hadn't spoken. "Freya, if you were my attendant, could I trust you to obey exactly as you are told?"

Freya nodded.

"Could I trust you to be discreet?"

The Myth Keeper's eyes narrowed at the word discreet. Freya, however, looked at her knowingly and said, "Your business is no one's but your own, madame."

Penalynn was satisfied. "What do you think of my hair? Can you make something of it?"

At this, Freya smiled outright. "Yes, madame."

"Good. Please go to the wagons and oversee the transfer of my belongings to my quarters. You will find a tapestry wrapped around a large frame. Make sure the item remains covered and put in my office."

Freya dropped a quick curtsy, professing her gratitude in fervent thanks, then dashed from the room. Penalynn said to Mrs. Finkle, "Freya is a Scholastic attendant now. She will need proper attire. No aprons. No gloves. No boots."

Mrs. Finkle looked thoroughly disturbed. "Madame, really, the woman has no magic!"

"No one has *no* magic," Penalynn corrected.

"Yes, but she's got about as little as a Shadow can manage."

"Enough!" Penalynn silenced, and the woman's mouth shut with an audible snap.

The Myth Keeper stood speechless. A gentle knock at the door startled him, and he cried. "Ah!" but then he recovered himself. "Oh, yes, lunch! Madame, I thought you might want to stretch your legs and see your new home, so I've prepared a castle tour. I figured we could eat while we walk."

Outside the laboratory stood two young men carrying trays of finger foods and crystal cups full of spiced juice.

The fox's ears perked. *He might not be as bad as he seems.*

Penalynn wasn't yet convinced, still sore from the Myth Keeper's blunder assuming she'd be a man. However, she said, "Thank you, Mr. Keeper. After thirty-two days in a carriage, a walk and lunch sound lovely."

CHAPTER SEVEN

Throughout the castle tour, Penalynn felt a mix of relief and contrition at her previous prejudice. In honesty, she had expected something much more primitive. But Greymere and its castle were impressive both in size and form, yet with a cozy quality she couldn't quite name—informal without being undignified. Traversing under carved ceilings like inverted tortoise shells, with stained glass windows cutting swaths of color across every path, it dawned on her she might actually enjoy Greymere. Her Shadow, knowing her thoughts, rubbed against her ankle in an *I told you so* fashion.

She listened politely as the Myth Keeper narrated the history of various castle elements. All the while, a vigilant servant kept a platter at her elbow. She munched along, quite enjoying herself and sharing her favorite samplings with Bran.

"The east wing comprises the school of Shadow magic, of which I am the headmaster," the Myth Keeper said in a steady monotone. "Our Sages use the classrooms on these three floors, relocating to the courtyard for livelier magic lessons. Now, let us make our way to the west wing. My little realm."

Through large glass doors, they entered an open, circular space with a towering domed ceiling embellished in mosaic detail. More stained glass glittered cheerfully. Bookshelves rimmed concave walls, with story upon story stacked overhead. A staircase spiraled along the outer wall to reach each balcony above. The Myth Keeper strode past aisles of bookcases arranged in concentric circles until he and Penalynn reached a round court. At the library's center lived an elegant, jeweled statue taller than a man. A dragon perched atop a mountain, hewn from deep blue stone in intricate detail down to each individual scale.

Penalynn's happiness emptied like a torn sack. She froze mid-step.

"If you notice the stained glass," the Myth Keeper pointed overhead, revolving on his heel. "Each pane tells the story of the Great Myth. My favorite window is just there, on the second balcony. A beautiful scene of the Bazileus and first king. Though this rendering of the Bazileus is much more impressive up close." He indicated the statue.

Penalynn's gaze never left the dragon. Its jeweled eyes were the same color as the cloak wrapped around her shoulders, and she felt an overwhelming urge to rip it off and fling it away. Her Shadow burrowed under her skirts, pressing her body against Penalynn as if trying to hold her up. She forced her breathing to slow, embarrassed at her heart's frantic skips.

The Myth Keeper droned on, "From the library, we have a beautiful view of the Torborough River, which wraps around the backside of the castle. Legend has it, it took ten Sages to manipulate the river to scoot over to make room for the castle's foundation."

Penalynn barely heard him, too busy controlling her breath, her skin clammy. The dragon smiled as if amused by her discomfort. She felt like a scolded child, ashamed and foolish.

Noticing what he assumed was rapture for the image of the Bazileus, the Myth Keeper said, "If you like that, I think you will appreciate what's next."

He walked toward another set of massive doors. Penalynn felt Bran pull her elbow, a question in his touch. But she jerked away, not daring to look at him lest her cool exterior shatter like ice.

They entered a vast theatre filled with cushioned benches. At the far end of the cavernous space spanned a dais with a podium off to the side. The Myth Keeper swept out his arms for effect. His black cape looked like a bell stopping at his elbows. "This is our Hall of Sceadwe. Used for ceremonies, school assemblies, what have you. But I'll draw your attention to the wall behind the stage." He led her down the center aisle toward the dais.

"Yes, I'm familiar with silver glass," said Penalynn, glad to hear her voice was steady. A wide expanse of pure silver hung on the wall, double the height of Penalynn and nearly as wide.

"No, that is not it," he said, then gestured to the wall surrounding the silver glass, which, Penalynn now noticed, was covered floor to ceiling in row upon row of statues. Each statue resided in its own individual alcove. Penalynn wavered, not understanding what she saw.

"It's the royal lineage!" the Myth Keeper explained. "Every king and queen who has been united to the Bazileus is represented here in order of succession. As we know from the Great Myth, the royal line stretches to the very beginning of man and Shadow, so the earliest ones are missing. But, we have the ones history has recorded. The lineage continues along the opposite wall, with the most recent royals. In fact, come with me."

He practically skipped down the aisle towards the back wall. Penalynn reluctantly followed. "I give you, most recently united to the Bazileus himself, King Callum!" With a flourish, he indicated the last statue. It was clearly new. "I went to painstaking care to have sketches sent from Riven, choosing only the best artists. Madame, surely you have met the king. Is it an accurate likeness?"

Penalynn beheld King Callum's carved form, noticing how blank his stone eyes looked. She was surprised at herself. A still calm overcame her, no trace of a quiver. She stood in the stillness as if in a pool of water, submerging herself in the feeling—or rather, the lack of feeling—blank as the carved expression of Wyre's new king.

"Yes," she said, "It looks just like him."

The Myth Keeper clapped his hands, thoroughly pleased. One of the servants, still holding the lunch tray, stepped forward to speak in the Myth Keeper's ear.

"Yes, thank you, Albert. Excuse me, madam, but I am due at the silver glass. Greymere's monthly meeting with Riven. Perfect timing, actually, if you want to join. Unfortunately, the Lord Overseer will miss it. He's leading the construction for tomorrow's festival and all."

Penalynn looked past the Myth Keeper as, all the way across the hall, the silver glass swirled like water within a limestone frame. Her peace was suddenly gone, and she realized then it had not been peace after all but merely the eye of a storm. Her heart sounded like a war drum in her chest, urging her to retreat. She sputtered, spit flinging—something about not feeling well and needing to lie down. Then, without waiting for the Myth Keeper's response, she dashed out the nearest door just as the swirling silver stilled to reveal the image of a man.

The door slammed behind her, and she realized she had no idea where to go.

Something touched her arm, and she yelped, but it was only Bran. "This way," he said, then led her directly toward her rooms.

The more distance they gained from the Hall of Sceadwe, the more freely Penalynn breathed until, at last, she burst into her quarters. Without even a glance at the rest of the rooms, she crawled into bed. It was midday when she fell asleep. She awoke only when knocking sounded in the dark. It took her a moment to gain her bearings. Moonlight stretched through high windows, and a fire danced in the hearth—no doubt her new attendant's doing.

"Pen?" a familiar voice called. "Are you alright?" The knocking sounded louder.

She fumbled to the door, bumping into furniture, then opened the door to find Bran ready to burst in. Upon seeing her, he relaxed.

She blinked in the light of the hallway. "What time's it?"

"Were you in bed this whole time?"

She yawned. "Took a nap."

"Oh. I just wanted…" he hesitated. "You seemed upset earlier, and I wanted to see if you're feeling better."

The day's events returned to her, and she winced, remembering how she had fled that horrible hall of statues to cry herself to sleep in an alien room that suddenly belonged to her.

"It was a long day," she croaked. Her mouth was dry.

Bran frowned at her swollen red eyes. "Listen, I know I said I'd leave tomorrow. My job is technically done. You've been delivered." Penalynn grimaced at the choice of words. "But I thought maybe I might stay for a couple of days until you get settled. I could leave after the festival."

Her eyes welled. Bran pretended not to notice. "That will be fine," she said.

He left. But before he reached the stairwell, Penalynn called, faint but clear, "Thank you, Bran."

He nodded, then descended out of sight.

CHAPTER EIGHT

IT HAD BEEN AN hour since Taiosech awoke, but he still hadn't left the comfort of his pallet. Under the weight of several wool blankets, he stared at the canvas and beams that made up the ceiling of his tent. Through fabric walls, he could hear the bustle of camp life: footsteps and rustles, children laughing or crying, their parents admonishing or consoling, and Shadows humming from every corner. The Wandering had arrived at the outskirts of Greymere only yesterday, but already their camp was complete. One of the few benefits of being nomads: The Wandering knew how to erect a city of tents in a single day.

From the beam overhead, a white bat hung upside down, his filmy eyes trained on Taiosech. They shared a comingled hesitation, a longing to remain in bed. But both man and Shadow knew that if he didn't rise soon, they would come for him.

Sure enough, the flap parted, and an auburn-haired woman with so many freckles that she looked like she'd been sprinkled with cinnamon entered the tent. Morning air entered with her. The cold forced Taiosech further awake.

"Are you well, my love?" his wife asked in the lilting tongue of The Wandering. She sat on the edge of their pallet near his head.

Taiosech took her hand and gently pulled, beckoning. "Come back to bed, and let's sleep the day away." This roused a smile so lovely Taiosech's heart ached, but she shook her head with infuriating prudence.

"The chief mustn't sleep when the rest cannot."

Her answer irritated him, and he wanted nothing more than to roll over and turn his back on her like a sulking child. But she was right. A chief was not allowed emotional indulgences. He was no mere man and could never be regarded as such, not by his wife nor even himself. He was the role, and the role was him. Duty outweighed his heart every time.

He emerged from the comfort of his blankets and rose at last, planting his feet atop the woven mat, his joints popping and muscles aching. He'd slept on the ground his entire life, but the older he got, the more his body screamed for a proper bed.

When he'd dressed, his Shadow dropped from the beam above and landed on him, hooking claws into the straps sewn onto the shoulders of his tunic. From there, the bat hung comfortably across his back. Taiosech emerged from his tent and breathed through his nose, the earthy scents of the forest made rich with dew and seasoned with campfire smoke. Snow usually dusted the ground by this time, but winter seemed reluctant to come this year. He sympathized.

Just then, his daughter sprinted past, chasing a couple of her young cousins who squealed with delight, their Shadows white blurs among them. He watched his wife's lithe frame as she stooped to prepare his breakfast and heard the quiet murmur among those seated on cushions surrounding the fire.

Taiosech's tent was one of ten side-by-side in a loop called the "elder circle." The Wandering camp housed dozens of such circles—small groupings of families and neighbors. Already, the nine elders sat around the fire at the center of the elder circle, sipping tea. Each Wandering Shadow was a shock of white contrasted starkly against the black forest floor. Taiosech admired how their Shadows matched the elegance of the forest; white trees staggered everywhere with blackened knots, like eyes. His entire life was spent around these campfires—sleeping in these tents. Their days were spent roaming, erecting camp only to take it down again. A meandering life for the people accurately named The Wandering. His people.

The story of how The Wandering came to wander was a centuries-long oral tradition. The details had been muddied from generations of telling, but even so, the core of the story remained intact. Ages past, the king of Wyre had sat on his throne when a great creature entered the throne room. Some claimed the creature was a horse or perhaps a large cat, like a lion. Some renditions said it was a dog. Whatever it was, it entered the king's court on a day when many people were gathered. At first, it was thought to be a Shadow, except no human accompanied the creature. And it was certainly no mere beast because when it approached the throne, it opened its mouth to speak—a prophecy—the Shadowless was coming.

When it had finished speaking, the creature was at once driven from the courtroom. Some say the king killed it right then and there for its treacherous words. The Sceadwe acted fast, squelching news of the prophecy at every telling until the story was forgotten entirely. But one man did not forget: a Myth Keeper who had been there that day and witnessed the creature prophesy the king's death. It had been a promise as sure as fate. The Myth Keeper kept what he heard secret, telling only his wife and his closest friend, or perhaps his brother, or his entire family (the tale changed with every telling) until word eventually reached the king of the Myth Keeper's treachery. But by then, a large band of believers in the prophecy had joined him. They were too numerous to imprison or kill, and so the king banished them, stripping them of all rights as citizens of Wyre—including the right to a home—thus cursing the group to a vagabond existence. They could make camp for no more than three weeks at a time. Beyond that, the Sceadwe would denounce them as squatters and land thieves, punishable by death. Thus, The Wandering race was born of exiles.

Countless generations later, breaking off into tribes as they grew, the Wandering still roamed.

From the bloodline of that ancient Myth Keeper, Taiosech was made a chief of The Wandering after his father. Like all chiefs before him, he was given a primary noble task. A task that would preserve the life of his people forever, one day freeing them from this nomadic existence of endless roaming, tents, and dirt floors: Find the Shadowless.

A voice lured him from the mouth of his tent towards the campfire. "So?"

"Good morning, Karah," Taiosech greeted, taking the open seat next to his most ardent devotee. He nodded to the rest of the elders, who talked among themselves around the fire. His wife handed him his breakfast: Flatbread, stone fruit preserves, and roasted mushrooms, floppy from being reheated by magic. Everyone else had already finished their meal an hour ago.

Karah leaned close like a conspirator. "So? Did you dream?"

"I did," Taiosech murmured, taking a bite.

"Was it the same vision as before?"

Taiosech nodded as he chewed. His head felt oddly heavy.

But Karah's countenance brightened. "It is confirmed then!" he slapped his hands, catching the attention of the other elders.

"Yes," Taiosech agreed. In his younger days, he would have found the news inspiring, liberating even. But today, it was merely a burden he would rather someone else bear.

"This is an honorable task you have been given, my chief. Why do you frown?"

Taiosech swallowed some mushrooms, made palatable by a generous glob of preserves, then said, "I am only tired. Three months of dreams does not lend for rest."

Every night of their long journey to Greymere, the same dream had visited him. In this dream, a giant creature that was neither Shadow nor animal delivered to him a proclamation. A new prophecy. Someday—in Taiosech's lifetime—The Wandering would wander no more. They would settle for good, with land of their own and houses of stone and wood and masonry. It was more than a prophecy. It was a promise. Every night, the dream came, and belief in this promise settled in his bones like marrow.

"It is confirmed," said a wheezy voice. Taiosech looked directly across the fire, where a grizzled old woman sat with a bowl of water at her side. Inside the bowl, a milky white fish swam lazy circles.

"But what does the dream mean?" another elder asked the group.

"It means exactly what the creature in the dream told him," the youngest and most optimistic of the elders answered. "Chief Taiosech will be the one to find the Shadowless. Our people will see deliverance in *this* generation!" His eyes shone, but Taiosech scanned around the fire. Most of them looked doubtful. He didn't blame them. He'd look the same if the dream had come to someone else and not him.

"The Wandering have been searching for centuries, from the first moment of our exile. Did this creature in the vision tell you *where* the Shadowless will be found?"

"No," Taiosech answered, taking a bite of bread.

He let the elders debate amongst themselves, staring into the fire as he chewed. Eventually, one by one, the elders left the fire, and his wife stood as well. She kissed Taiosech on the lips, and once again, he yearned to return to bed just the two of them—leave dreams and prophesies for tomorrow. As if knowing his thoughts, she touched her forehead to his, her long hair falling down his shoulder like a scarf. Her Shadow hummed, and he felt her magic touch his thoughts like fingertips, brushing away his worries with gentle encouragement. She left him by the fire, but her peace lingered. He never thought he could ever love her more, but then she did things like that, giving him exactly what he needed, and his love swelled all the more. He watched her walk away with a smile on his lips. Eventually, when everyone had gone, he turned to the only remaining elder across the dying fire.

The fish stopped its swimming to stare directly at him, magnified through the glass bowl. "You don't know what to do," the old woman wheezed, accusing.

Taiosech reached to pour himself a cup of tea from a pot hanging above the embers.

"You are chief. You must act."

He took a sip. It scalded the roof of his mouth, but he didn't wince—wouldn't give the woman satisfaction.

"What will you do?" It was more a demand than a question.

"What I have always done: watch and wait," Taiosech answered. His hot breath looked like smoke in the chilly air.

"You expect your Shadowless will just wander into our camp and expose himself, do you?"

"It is not *my* Shadowless, but all of ours," Taiosech snapped. "And I suspect nothing. This task was given to me, not you."

"Then do it!"

Taiosech took another scalding sip.

The woman rolled her eyes as if dealing with a petulant child. Her wrinkled hands balled into fists in her lap. "Karah!" she wheezed loudly, rousing a rattling cough from her lungs, which left her hacking into a handkerchief for half a minute. The elder, Karah, was about to leave the circle of tents, but he approached at the woman's call. Finally, she quit her hacking and asked the waiting elder, "Have the fireworks been delivered to Greymere yet?"

"No, they are checking them now to make sure none were damaged in the transport," he said, "They will be delivered at dusk."

"Good. The chief will deliver them."

Karah looked uncertainly between his chief and the eldest elder. Taiosech's serenity slipped, as well as his tea. It sloshed, staining his tunic and burning his skin. "Woman, I am your chief!"

"And I am your mother!" she growled, although she seemed pleased to have stoked something like fire in Taiosech's eyes. "In fact, Karah, go with him into town. Make sure my son is the one who lights the fireworks." She wagged her finger at Taiosech as if he were still a young boy. "You've grown indolent in your chiefly duties. It is your way. As a baby, I had to prod you in the ribs to get you to nurse. All you wanted to do was sleep."

Taiosech looked at the cup in his hands, his reflection hateful in the remnants of his tea. "I will not disgrace myself with those dragon-lovers."

"But you'll expose your people to them when they sell our wares? You are a coward."

He flinched and wanted nothing less than to hurl his cup at her. But like usual, the fire of emotion flared hot for only a second, then quelled. Something had occurred to him. He met her gaze, his forehead creased with puzzlement. "You think the Shadowless is Wyrian?"

After a long moment, she allowed a quizzical grin, the lines of her entire face crinkling like paper. "What does it matter if the Shadowless is Wandering or Wyrian? So long as he does what must be done. So far, our search has been orthodox, but where has orthodoxy gotten us?"

"Orthodoxy," Taiosech repeated. He downed the rest of his tea in one enormous gulp and, once again, wished he could go back to bed.

CHAPTER NINE

ON THE DAY OF the festival, Haaris and Rowena Faye were among the first to enter the meadow. They avoided the main entrance—where a hundred pumpkins squeezed together to form a bulbous archway—and instead trekked through a dense part of the woods to enter the opposite end. At the top of the arena, a wooden platform perched atop hefty pillars. Harris's magic flared steadily, his Shadow ready to persuade any eye that might wander their way. But no one noticed the father and daughter climbing the ladder to the platform. Haaris managed the ladder with his uninjured hand, but Rowena had to carry his Shadow. Ghost remained hidden under her hair, though she peered excitedly between curls. The platform was so high that if Rowena lay flat, no one could see she was up there.

She sprawled on her belly, waiting for something to happen. The hours seemed to drag until, finally, the sun sank out of sight, and stars blinked awake. A massive bonfire roared to life, spicing the air with the smell of burnt applewood and autumn leaves. Lines of firebulbs drooped like streamers overtop the many lanes of booths, casting the entire scene in a moody amber glow. It took a dozen men and women posted along the perimeter to keep them alight, their Shadows animating the fire inside the bulbs all night. Beside a spacious dance floor, the band sprang to life. A steady drumbeat summoned the people of Greymere like magic itself.

Rowena watched in wonder as the crowd poured under the entranceway to fill the meadow like water. Every person in attendance paid homage to their Shadow by wearing a costume. Even Haaris wore a coat of the same tawny hue as his Shadow. He had constructed a band for his head with two floppy ears framing his face. Rowena had even convinced him to line his eyes with coal to resemble his Shadow's baleful eyes. Even so, his frock was minor compared to the extravagance parading about that night.

Rowena lay with her chin propped on her hands, watching the scene below. People milled about eating and drinking and shopping among the merchant stalls. Here and there, performers were stationed in entertaining vignettes: singers, dancers, and even the odd acrobat or two—each using Shadow magic to enhance their acts beyond natural ability. Stationed closest to Rowena's perch, a bubble artist manipulated soapy spheres into fantastical shapes and colors. A portly man with a mustache lingered to watch. The artist manipulated a bubble into the form of a walrus in an uncanny likeness of the man. Those gathered nearby erupted with laughter, even more so when the mustachioed man went purple in the face. He swatted at the bubble when it tauntingly clapped its flippers.

Rowena chuckled with the crowd, her senses like greedy hands grasping for more. Her ears filled with chatter, applause, cheers, and gossip as if it were all a symphony. Costumes swished like a thousand whispers. Shadows hummed their magic. Near the dance floor, the music pulsed with an unrelenting drumbeat. Ghost bobbed in time to the music, though she remained hidden, so it seemed Rowena's hair moved independently.

Haaris sat beside her, upright, with his legs dangling over the edge. Rowena knew his Shadow's magic was alert should anyone look their way. But the festival pageantry proved too dazzling for anyone to bother with a boring old platform. After an uneventful hour, his defensive posture softened enough for him to ask, "You hungry?"

Rowena's face was already sore from smiling so much, but her lips widened further, and she said, "Yeah!"

"How 'bout I go grab us some dinner."

She could hardly believe her luck. "Seriously? From down there?"

He winked, then motioned for her to grab his Shadow. His magic surged, and the spaniel vibrated in her arms. She followed Haaris down the ladder just long enough to set his Shadow on the ground, then scurried back onto the platform to hide. The magic worked. No one saw her. Her eyes followed Haaris as he traced his way through the crowd. But her gaze diverted from him when he passed a tall young man wearing a feathered cape and headpiece.

The boy named Titus matched his owl handsomely, the brown feathers of his cape blending with his dark hair and tan skin. He strolled alongside his brother who looked as mischievous as a person could look, wearing a black mask to match the grinning raccoon atop his shoulder. The brothers meandered, stopping to chat with friends as they went. When they reached the dancefloor, they parted ways. The elder brother grabbed a giggling girl and spun her in time to the music. Titus hesitated at the periphery, looking as if he were searching for someone. Rowena's stomach clenched with something like hope or yearning or perhaps even regret. He was looking for her. She knew it. The girl from the woods with the ghost for a Shadow—forbidden to claim her promised dance.

Eventually, Titus gave up his search, settling for a dance partner with jeweled cat ears perched atop cascading blonde hair. Rowena's mood dampened. She scanned the crowd to find her father returning with food balanced in his one good hand. His coat pockets bulged with bottles of drink.

Just before he could reach the ladder, a man and woman intercepted him. "Haaris! Look at you, participating in the festival!" the man cheered, ruffling his costumed ears.

Rowena's nose poked over the platform ledge. She recognized the man. It was hard not to notice the Overseer's hulking size, made even more formidable by his costume. The shaggy grey wolf at his side was nearly as big as the man himself. On Roderick's other side stood a willowy woman with soft brown hair. Her face was painted with exaggerated eyelashes, a brown nose, and dappled white freckles. Beside her stood a fawn. The Shadow's eyes trailed upward, and Rowena recoiled, sure the woman had seen her, but the Overseer's wife conversed with Haaris as if she hadn't. So she peeked again to see the fawn had averted its gaze.

Rowena could barely hear their conversation over the festival racket. Every few seconds, people interrupted to greet the couple. It was clear the Overseer was beloved in Greymere, and from her safe vantage, Rowena could see why. Though his size was frightful, Roderick spoke animatedly, all smiles and hand gestures, his gargantuan demeanor somehow whimsical and boyish despite being a head taller than everyone else. But his charm seemed ineffectual with Haaris, who responded coolly, almost rudely. That was until a small group approached. Then he turned white as a sheet.

A slender man dressed like a canary walked up with a squat, round woman in a blue cape. They were followed by a foreboding-looking man who appeared impervious to the cold. He wore a black vest, leaving his muscular arms bare of anything but the orange lizard hugging his bicep.

Haaris looked close to vomiting at the sight of the newcomers. His Shadow looked directly up at Rowena; the spaniel's eyes sharp, like a warning.

Just behind Penalynn's eyebrow, a headache throbbed in rhythm to the drumbeat. Orange fox ears perched atop her headband—her only adornment for the occasion. She had never been one for crowds. However, Greymere's festival was nowhere near as immense as the one in Riven.

The Myth Keeper led the way. Even in the crush of the crowd, Penalynn wouldn't lose sight of him. His costume was a garish shade of yellow, looking less like a canary than a somber daffodil sprung to life. He took the festival as an opportunity to educate Penalynn on all things Greymere, rambling on in the same fashion as their castle tour.

When they came upon a popular stall under a banner that read "Corrie Cunningham's Confections," Penalynn lingered. After a quick survey, her eyes landed on a pile of iced tarts. Each masterpiece was topped with a glistening sugared cherry. Despite the traffic flow, Penalynn remained rooted, forcing people to squeeze around her until a man dressed like a goat stepped on her Shadow's tail. She yelped, sharing the fox's pain. Instantly, a black glove reached for her.

"I'm fine, Bran," she reassured her guard, although her trampled Shadow sulked within the folds of her skirt.

Behind the counter, an aproned woman stacked cookies. She was covered from head to toe in powdered sugar—a happy side effect of her job, no doubt. When she noticed Penalynn's blue cloak, she dropped the platter of cookies with a startled squeak before bending into an awkward curtsey. "A Scholastic here in Greymere!" she cried. "What a treat! Oh, please take whatever you want! On the house! No, I insist!" She grabbed a pink-striped box and tossed delicacies inside, ignoring Penalynn's half-hearted protests.

Bran muttered, "Get her to throw in a cinnamon bun, will you?" But the powdered woman had already added a few to the box. The top barely closed when she handed it to Penalynn. Then she dashed out of the booth without accepting even a "thank you." Corrie Cunningham was not only Greymere's premier baker but also the queen of all gossips. An encounter with a real-life Scholastic was too tasty a story to keep to herself. After that, news spread swiftly. A Scholastic of the Sceadwe was here.

Penalynn shook the swollen box at the Myth Keeper. "Here, have a pastry."

"Thank you, madam," he said, selecting a ball of caramel corn.

"Please call me Penalynn. The title is rather new, and I'm still getting used to it." Bran grabbed his sticky bun, and Penalynn selected a honeycombed something-or-other that stuck to her teeth.

They continued their walk, and the Myth Keeper said, "Yes, not to be rude, of course, but I noticed you seem much younger than any Scholastic I have met before. Being a Myth Keeper, my university training in Riven allowed me to cross paths with most of your colleagues."

It wasn't a question, but nevertheless, Penalynn answered honestly. "'The youngest in history' is how they described me when I was appointed a few months ago."

"Only a few months?" The Myth Keeper did a poor job of hiding his surprise. "And then transferred to an outer borough?" Penalynn chaffed at the question but couldn't explain, so she merely nodded. The Myth Keeper observed, "In such a quick relocation, it seems you have not had time to select an apprentice."

"You are correct. The move across the kingdom was a little distracting."

"Well, I offer my services for this purpose. I'm quite familiar with the local members of the Sceadwe. As headmaster of the school, I have worked closely with every Sage in the region and can offer my advice. Perhaps help you sift through candidates."

Penalynn didn't respond because they had just reached the dancefloor. A cascade of costumed couples swirled before them like a churning sea. Dutifully, the Myth Keeper held out his hand. "Would you care to dance, madame?"

"No, thank you," she replied with equal politeness. Her companion's evident relief did not slip her notice. To hide her embarrassment, she diverted the conversation. "How many teachers do you employ at the school, Mr. Keeper?"

"Sixteen Sages," he answered. "Four for each of the four branches of magic—Persuasion, Intuition, Manipulation, and Animation. Then there is our physic professor, though he isn't a member of the Sceadwe, of course."

"Only one instructor for physic?" she asked.

"One is more than enough. It is a school of magic, after all."

Quite right, Penalynn heard her Shadow agree. The fox, of course, shared the same prejudice against physic as the rest of Wyre.

Penalynn frowned. "Without a thorough knowledge of the physical world, how can students understand enough to perform the various magics?"

The Myth Keeper's eyebrow twitched. "Well, they do just fine, as I'm sure you'll see during the graduate trials tonight."

The fox nipped at Penalynn's ankle. *You're at a festival, for goodness's sake. If you're going to be so dull, at the very least, smile!*

Penalynn sighed. *Why is my socially agreeable half the part that doesn't talk?*

I wonder that every day, her Shadow thought sourly.

They turned down another lane, and Penalynn nearly tripped over the fox, who was startled to a stop. *Did you feel that?!*

What?

Persuasive magic.

The overstimulation of her surroundings left Penalynn feeling stupid. *But you're not using intuition—are you?!*

Of course not, the fox snapped. *There! That was a tug.*

Penalynn felt it, too, but still, she argued. *Maybe it's the music, or something else caught our attention? There's so much going on, I'm sure—*

No, it was magical, I'm sure of it. Someone's persuading us. But without magic, there's no knowing for sure. Penalynn looked all around, testing her Shadow's hypothesis.

A black glove squeezed her shoulder, and Bran spoke in her ear, "Pen, you need to use intuition. I'm picking up a persuasion." The lizard wrapped around his arm hummed with magic, though the din drowned out the sound.

"I know," said Penalynn.

"As your guard, I can protect you physically, but I can't protect your mind."

"What's the persuasion about?" She spoke in his ear so only he could hear.

"No idea." He scowled, clearly frustrated. "And with this many people, I can't tell who it's coming from."

"Is the persuasion nefarious?"

He gave her a withering look. "If that fancy word means *bad*, then no, I don't think so. But it doesn't matter. Please, just this once, tell your Shadow to—"

"No," Penalynn said flatly, ignoring her Shadow's internal argument. "If there's no apparent harm then—"

"Curse you, Penalynn! This is no time for one of your high and mighty principles."

The Myth Keeper had stopped to speak with someone and so missed their conversation. He turned to Penalynn to make introductions. Bran melted into place behind her, though he kept one hand on the dagger at his hip, his intuition magic flaring. Penalynn felt another tug. Something nudged her attention with a gentle touch, barely noticeable. She met Bran's eyes, and he nodded. He'd felt it, too.

Ignorant of Penalynn's tension or the presence of illegal magic at work, The Myth Keeper spoke with a pious lilt in his voice. "Madame Scholastic, might I introduce Greymere's Lord Overseer, Roderick Ashworth, and his wife, Fern."

CHAPTER TEN

RODERICK AND HIS WIFE welcomed the Scholastic to Greymere. The Myth Keeper, being tall himself, could easily look the Overseer in the eye. But Penalynn, as short as she was, had to arch her head back. Her neck strained as if her head were too heavy for the task. The couple chatted with the Myth Keeper while Penalynn struggled to force her gaze upward. Even without intuition, she knew magic was at work.

Whoever is doing the persuasion is talented, the fox thought, impressed despite her disapproval.

The persuasion intensified. The tug became a firm push against Penalynn's mind, and she felt an overwhelming urge to give in and let her gaze drift. Why did she want to look up there anyway, she wondered vaguely. After all, there was nothing of interest to see.

A gentle hand touched her elbow. She looked to see the Overseer's wife smiling warmly. Her voice was like satin. "Tell me, Madame Scholastic, have you ever witnessed the fireworks of The Wandering?" The question snapped Penalynn's focus like a twig, and the persuasion won. She shook her head, blinking rapidly.

It was then she noticed a man had joined them. His Shadow was unmistakably albino akin only to The Wandering. He spoke quietly to the Lord Overseer, then left.

Roderick smiled apologetically at the Myth Keeper and Penalynn. "Excuse me, I'm due backstage." He kissed his wife on the cheek, then jogged down the arena steps to catch up to The Wandering man.

The Myth Keeper's goatee twitched with disapproval. He explained to Penalynn, "The *Wandrels* provide our celebration with fireworks each year."

"It's Greymere tradition," Fern added diplomatically.

"A blasphemous tradition."

Penalynn mused, "I doubt it's The Wandering's *fireworks* the Sceadwe deems blasphemous."

The Myth Keeper sniffed. "Any association with that lot dishonors the Bazileus himself."

"Spoken like a true Myth Keeper."

"Do you disagree, madame?"

"If the Bazileus is offended, let him rise from his mountain and handle the matter himself. It's been, what, a thousand years since the dragon's been seen? I imagine the exercise would do him good." She had spoken without thinking, her mind still muddled from the fight with the persuasion.

The Myth Keeper looked like she'd smacked him across the jaw. Behind her, Bran cleared his throat, and her Shadow bit her ankle. Penalynn winced at her own carelessness. But before she could apologize, the firebulbs flashed overhead, signaling the start of the ceremony. The crowd instantly shifted as thousands scrambled into the arena, vying for the best seats.

Penalynn looked up at the flashing lights, mildly aware she was suddenly able to do so unimpeded. For only a second, her gaze traveled heavenward, but it was long enough. Peering from a platform she hadn't noticed before was a heart-shaped face. A pair of bright eyes locked with hers—a girl. Then, in a blink, she was gone. The platform was empty save a man and his canine Shadow.

*Is that what the persuasion...*Penalynn thought listlessly, her mind suddenly sluggish.

The fox yawned. *Just a kid.*

Bran asked, "Everything alright?"

Penalynn shook her head as if to clear it, then followed the Myth Keeper down the arena steps.

At the bottom of the arena was a stage rimmed in a thick curtain. Backstage it was dark. The only source of light came from a single torch which cast the area in a somber glow. It had taken several members of the tribe to deliver the fireworks, but as soon as they had, they returned to camp. All but two. Beside the wall of crates stood a man like a statue, still and watchful. The chief of The Wandering waited for Karah to return, bringing Greymere's leader with him.

Roderick's thundering voice broke the silence. "Tay-oh-sack! What brings you here, chief?" He grabbed the chief's hand, shaking it vigorously.

Taiosech's grim features soured to find his hand in the clutch of an enemy. Roderick's charm, though renowned in Torborough, had no effect on The Wandering chief. After all, the man's king deprived his people of a home, forcing them to migrate as punishment for their beliefs. A servant to such a king would only ever be an enemy. Still, The Wandering couldn't survive without Greymere's business. And so, the tribe fulfilled their order for fireworks every autumn.

"I've been practicing," Roderick bragged, impervious to the chief's scowl. "*Tay-oh-sack.* I sound just like a member of The Wandering myself. TAY-oh-sack!" He pronounced the name with an affected flourish, mimicking The Wandering accent.

Taiosech's lips pressed into a charitable sort of grimace. "Very good, Lord Overseer." As a young boy, he had learned the common language of Wyre but still preferred to speak in The Wandering tongue. To Roderick's ears, it was just a jumble of syllables, but in his mind, Roderick heard the chief's voice speaking the Wyrian language. It was the only agreeable quality a Wyrian could have, thought Taiosech, permitting such magic. Despite the Wyrian taboo against it, Roderick didn't seem to mind the magical interpretation.

"It's great to see you, chief," Roderick said, "But what are you doing here?"

"There is no task below a good leader," said Taiosech, proud but oblique.

Roderick nodded wisely as if he understood. Taiosech was tempted to roll his eyes at the buffoon. With a clap of his hands, Roderick said, "Well then, let me get this thing started, and when it's time, I'll signal you to light 'em up."

The Overseer entered the arena through the heavy curtain, leaving Taiosech and Karah alone in the dark backstage.

Karah whispered, "What now, my chief?"

Taiosech could feel his Shadow flex his wings against his back.

"What we always do, Karah. We watch and wait."

CHAPTER ELEVEN

WHEN THE AUDIENCE HAD settled into their seats, the arena fell into sudden and complete darkness. Not only did the firebulbs and bonfire in the meadow snuff out, but the very moon and stars went black. Rowena had still been lying on her stomach but sprang bolt upright in the pitch dark.

"It's all right," she heard her father say, his calloused hands squeezing her shoulder reassuringly, "It's mean to do that." Sure enough, she could hear his Shadow humming with magic. She marveled. So, this was what "doing the lights" meant. Her father's magic could manipulate even the light from the heavens.

Unlike Rowena, the sudden dark sent the crowd into a frenzy, their anticipation evident in cheers and whistles. But then the music began, and they fell silent, *shh-shing* their neighbors so as not to miss a single note. The orchestra's many Shadows magically amplified the music so even the latecomers in the back could hear. As the song swelled, so did the light. Stars blinked into life once more, faintly illuminating an artistic backdrop at the top of the stage, painted to evoke a snowcapped mountain range with a towering summit at the center crowned in sunshine. Rowena recognized the stage's design from her father's renderings at home.

In the faint starlight, a woman walked onstage. When she stopped, a spotlight erupted in a blazing circle with her at the center. Rowena felt something pull her sleeve, and reluctantly, she turned to see her father pointing up at the sky. She followed his finger to see the moon shining once more. But the glow was odd.

Haaris smirked in a satisfied way, and she realized with dawning wonder that his magic manipulated the moon, or at the very least, its glow. His Shadow gathered the light like a swath of fabric, bunching it to fall in a single beam.

Rowena turned back to the stage, where the full force of moonlight cast the woman in a dazzling cool glow. She was decked in feathers in homage to her Shadow: a strawberry-red cardinal which perched atop her outstretched wrist. With the help of her Shadow to reach inhuman notes, the woman sang a ballad about Shadows and magic, the king, and his dragon. Rowena had never heard the song before, but each time the chorus circled back around, the audience joined with hearty enthusiasm until, by the third stanza, everyone was swaying and singing with the affection of a cherished tradition.

When the woman finished, she bowed deeply and exited the stage. Rowena sat on her hands to keep from clapping with the rest of the crowd. She doubted anyone would look her way, but still, she didn't dare do anything to draw attention.

The Lord Overseer came next, so huge he filled every inch of the spotlight, too big for his Shadow to fit. The great hulking wolf looked even more intimidating from the dark. Roderick greeted the crowd heartily, bouncing on his toes as he talked. After some welcoming remarks, Roderick unrolled an important-looking scroll that, he said, held a message from the king of Wyre.

Rowena leaned forward, intrigued. She had a vague knowledge of Wyre's king—namely that he existed and lived in the capital city of Riven, which was so far away as to be like a fairyland—but beyond that, she knew nothing.

Roderick read in a kingly voice, "My citizens of Wyre, it is I, King Callum, newly melded with the Bazileus. It was with great sadness that we all grieve the loss of our late king, my dearest uncle, Irascus..." And so the message went on in mellifluous monologue. Rowena understood very little of it. In fact, she had no idea that the former king had died nor that another one had been crowned. And at the mention of the Bazileus—a meaningless word to her yet somehow steeped in consequence—her skin prickled. Instinctively, she reached for Ghost, pulling her Shadow to sit comfortably in her lap. Ghost happily submitted to the rare show of affection and seemed even more happy to be free from the confines of Rowena's hair.

The king's message was short, and soon, more singers replaced Roderick onstage, leading the crowd through several upbeat songs. Every tradition enacted by the crowd revealed in Rowena a chasm of ignorance. After another song where everyone in attendance knew the words (even her father!), she crossed her arms and hunched with ill humor, feeling stupid and embarrassed and thoroughly left out. Ghost, however, seemed to enjoy it all. She bobbed in time to the music.

After the last song, the crowd's levity deflated in an instant when a sober-looking man wearing bright yellow feathers took the stage. He plopped an ancient book onto the podium, where his canary Shadow perched.

"The Great Myth, a translation from the original text," the Myth Keeper read.

The audience sagged, the Myth Keeper's voice like a monotonous lullaby. Heads drooped; mouths yawned. Rowena, however, sat at attention, finding the Myth Keeper's part to be the most interesting element so far. She soaked in every word like a student who might be tested on the material.

The Myth Keeper read from the dusty book:

In the time before Shadows, three creatures inhabited the Kingdom of Wyre.
The lowest creatures were brute animals, finite in every way.
The highest creature was a dragon by the name Bazileus;
Filled with magic and eternal like a god.
Between them lived humans:
No power theirs, and prone to die,
But filled with the precious treasure of a soul.

The Myth Keeper paused with expectation, and the crowd roused themselves enough to drone in one combined voice, "We are vessels." Rowena's mind spun, trying to make sense of the ancient myth. The Myth Keeper continued to read:

Mankind was not content like his animal neighbor,
And so, he set his sights above, to where the dragon lived.
The courageous and foolish alike traveled up the hallowed mount
Where dwelt the Bazileus, in hopes of capturing his magic.
Some used weapons. Others used cunning.
But all failed to steal the magic,
Aspiration and avarice met in a firesome end.
Until one day, an honest man ascended to the dragon's lair.

The crowd responded as one, "Oh king, live forever!"

No sword in hand, with open palms, he spoke:
"Great Bazileus, I come not to conspire but to bargain.
Dragon, I would buy your magic.
I have a prize all creatures might desire."
The Bazileus was intrigued.
What could a mortal man possess that a god did lack?
Suspecting the dragon's thoughts, the man spoke again.
"Bazileus, look below your mountain there,
Outside your hollow cave.
See my palace, nestled within a great city and beyond,
Stretching as far as the eye can see, my kingdom.
These: my throne, my crown, my land, I trade you.

Your magic I will fairly buy."
"Oh, king of Wyre, live forever!" the crowd called out.
The Bazileus scoffed. "A petty sum you bring me.
Am I a beggar to be won with a chair, hat, and dirt?
Am I a fool to barter command of the wind, of the earth,
Of rain, and animals, and even the thoughts of men?
"Mighty Bazileus, full of power!"
"There is nothing I lack—but one.
Inside your heart, there dwells a soul.
I would have it.
If you desire my magic, then impart your soul to me.
A trade fairly made."
"We are vessels!"
At once, the king cast his soul aside to drink the dragon's power,
Like a cup, dregs, and all.
Immediately, power inhumane consumed the king,
Rending and tearing until madness overtook him.
The Bazileus fared no better.
The man's soul soured in the dragon's breast.
"We are vessels!"
With destruction near, they clung to one another.
And as they touched, scale and skin, with magic swapped for soul,
An ancient magic did work upon them, binding and tying.
A kinship deeper than blood and surer than the grave
Wove the man and dragon like thread until they were one.
Soul and magic fastened unbreaking.
"Oh, king and Bazileus, live forever!"
From their bond, a new humanity was born:
A humanity of soul and magic.
"We are vessels—soul, and magic!"
Shadows descend from Bazileus,
In the likeness of brute animals so as to remember
Our lowly place beneath the eternal dragon.
"Oh, Bazileus, live forever!"
But imbued with the power of a god
Over wind, and earth, and all that exists,
Even the minds of men.
"We are vessels!"
We all descend from that first king.
His courage is the price for our reward.

"Oh, king and Bazileus, live forever!"

The Myth Keeper shut the book with a loud *thud*. The audience was silent.

Rowena shivered. Something seemed to creep up her spine, a reluctant understanding of what she had heard. Instinctively, she reached for her Shadow, but her hands clasped each other. She looked down at her empty lap, then spun to cast about the platform, but only her father and his Shadow were with her. They were both wholly consumed in magical effort upon the night sky and so didn't notice her frantic searching. It took less than a moment to realize Ghost was gone, and it felt to Rowena like she'd been plunged into ice.

Something caught her eye, and she looked beyond the platform to see a wisp floating over the back row of the audience. Rowena nearly cried out but clapped a hand over her mouth. She looked at her father, but he was staring intently at the stage, sweat beading his forehead. His Shadow stared at the moon, unblinking.

Rowena slid herself off the platform to stand on the ladder. Her legs trembled so badly that she feared the ladder would wobble. Thankfully, it was nailed into posts. Holding the top rung, she leaned out, reaching. Ghost hovered in the air, misty eyes wide as if she were hypnotized. Rowena snatched her from the air, and the trance seemed to break. Ghost startled, but Rowena's hands were strong. She squeezed her Shadow in a fist and ascended back onto the platform.

Her skin prickling with panic, she retook her seat. She looked guiltily at her father, but he was oblivious. Rowena's knuckles were white as she clutched Ghost, squeezing perhaps too hard. The Shadow didn't seem to mind, transfixed on something far in the distance. Rowena's mind raced, trying to make sense of her Shadow's behavior. But there was never making any sense of Ghost. Any other time, Rowena would have made herself sick with overthinking, but the ceremony continued as if nothing had happened, and soon she was distracted. Any worry she felt was merely a vague itch at the back of her mind.

Onstage, the Myth Keeper and his podium were gone, replaced by a woman wearing the customary green cloak of a Sage. With a formal, academic air, she explained to the audience the next portion of the ceremony: "The Shadow trials prove advanced magical ability warranting graduation from the school of Shadow magic. This trial serves as the final examination for every graduating student. They will present their magic to the public with the intention of using their Shadow's magic to contribute to and honor their community. We are very proud of this year's class."

Several students in matching green capes walked on stage to applause.

The first student stepped forward to introduce his trial: a work of manipulation. He pushed a large wheelbarrow overflowing with flowers and recited a rehearsed speech detailing how his Shadow had manipulated each plant to grow either larger, quicker, or more visually appealing. The audience applauded politely.

The next student stepped forward. She asked for volunteers, and a dozen eager men and women took to the stage. They were each handed a drink manipulated to evoke certain emotions. One at a time, they downed their cups. The first volunteer giggled as if his cup had told a hilarious joke. The second drink was meant to mimic the feeling of falling in love, and indeed, it seemed to work because the woman sighed wistfully, batting her eyes and pawing at the wary volunteer on her right. She had to be escorted offstage when she attempted to pin the poor man with a kiss. Soon, all of the volunteers had to be escorted away. One burst into a torrent of tears. One became so inflamed with anger that he threatened to fight the entire front row to the death. Meanwhile, the last volunteer fell asleep right on the spot. The student being tried seemed equal parts pleased with her results and embarrassed at the scene her magical drinks unwittingly caused. She left the stage to chuckling applause.

One by one, students stepped forward. Some trials were as mild as manipulating the temperature of a block of wood until it erupted into flames, while Rowena's favorite was a student who attempted to take flight wearing a backpack with wings. His Shadow animated the wind to pull him aloft. But when a gust shifted unexpectedly, the student's limbs flailed like a panicked windmill, and he careened into the orchestra, landing head-first into an upright drum. The audience gasped and guffawed alike, eventually applauding when the student limped offstage, unharmed but with a dazed sort of smile.

Mesmerized, Rowena see-sawed between wonder and jealousy at the student's magical feats. Ghost shifted restlessly here and there, and each time, Rowena tightened her grip. But when a familiar figure stepped onstage, she nearly let go. It was Titus's brother. His rascal-looking raccoon waddled by his feet.

"Bruce Ashworth!" the Sage introduced the boy, "Performing for his trial, both animation and manipulation."

Bruce dragged a long hose across the stage. He explained to the crowd that the far end of the hose had been submerged in the Torborough river, a quarter of a mile away. His Shadow animated the water's course to pull up through the hose and spray out over the crowd. At first, the audience screamed, about to be sprayed with water in near-winter. But the raccoon was not done. His magic manipulated the droplets midair, freezing them. The effect was a harmless dusting of snow. They audience *ooh*-ed and *ahh*-ed with delight.

Rowena felt a sort of fondness for the brother of the only boy she'd ever talked to. She would have clapped with the rest of the crowd, sure no one would look her way with such exciting things happening onstage, except now Ghost wriggled like a violent fish in her hands. Tiny flippers struck her wrists with surprising force.

"Ouch! Ghost, that hurts!" she hissed, keeping her voice low. Her Shadow

answered with a furious *thwack-thwack!*

Rowena held her tightly, and eventually, Ghost wore herself out. The Shadow drooped her tiny head, woeful and beaten. If it weren't for the ongoing trials, Rowena would have questioned Ghost's odd behavior, but another student stepped forward, and she couldn't help diverting her attention again.

The student addressed the crowd. "I ask for permission to perform a persuasion upon all of you gathered here tonight. Do I have your permission?"

The audience answered as one, "We give our permission."

The girl held out her hand, which closed around something that seemed to glow. She opened her palm, and a firefly the size of a robin sprang into the air, glittering like stardust. It danced over the heads of the crowd, and soon, a bird made of diamonds joined in, followed by an eagle of emeralds. Lastly, a sparkling ruby dragon joined the complicated aerial choreography. Every pair of eyes was fixated upon the sky; their minds convinced that what they saw was real. In truth, the air was empty, the dream-like scene only a figment magically enacted upon their imaginations. Still, everyone gasped as one—everyone, that is, except Rowena.

She never saw what everyone else saw. Because Ghost had resumed her fight, this time so aggressively, she soon burst free. Ghost shot as if from Rowena's catapult, zooming down the nearest aisle and heading straight for the stage below. With her Shadow already halfway down the stairs, a sharp pain jabbed Rowena's chest, but Ghost didn't stop. She slipped through the black curtain that made up the proscenium and disappeared backstage.

Rowena could hardly believe what just happened. She gaped, helpless and terribly alone. The pain behind her ribcage intensified, proof of Rowena's soul link with Ghost slicing her chest like a knife. She groaned, wrapping her arms around herself.

A quick look confirmed her father was absorbed, either by his task or by the trial's persuasion. Rowena slid off the platform, down the ladder, and onto the top step of the arena. She paused on the grass, hardly believing she was about to do this. But she had no choice. She had to find Ghost—before someone else did. She crouched in the way one does when trying not to be conspicuous among a seated crowd, and ran like a hunchback, taking the stairs two at a time until she reached the stage. Miraculously, not a single person noticed her; all of them were too engrossed in the persuasion. And so, Rowena slipped through the curtain leading backstage just as her Shadow had done.

Chapter Twelve

Backstage, the light from a single torch was feeble. Even so, Rowena could tell at once that no one was there. The Overseer and Myth Keeper must have been in the opposite wing, and with the trials nearly over, Sages and graduating students had found seats among family or friends.

She couldn't see Ghost, but Rowena knew she had to be near because the pain in her chest eased with every step, barely a dull ache now. She searched within the folds of the curtain, under a table, and along the edge of the stage but didn't find her Shadow. She passed the torch, which stood before a tower of crates labeled "fireworks." Rowena stopped. Just beyond the crates hovered Ghost, facing the black forest which abutted the back of the stage.

"Ghost," Rowena whispered, "get back here—"

A man stepped from behind the tower of crates, and Rowena's voice dropped along with her heart. From the man's arm hung a huge white bat. A second man was just behind him, speaking low in a lilting language Rowena didn't understand. At the sight of the two men—and, more horribly, at *their* sight of *her*—terror-fueled adrenaline zapped her limbs. She dashed past them, past the tower of crates, toward the edge of the forest, reaching desperately for her Shadow. From the dark beyond, a pair of eyes reflected the light. Rowena stopped short. Ghost stretched her two misty flippers toward the eyes, beckoning in a way, but before she could touch whatever that thing was, Rowena snatched Ghost from the air.

At once, her Shadow revolted, grasping, straining, reaching for—well, Rowena couldn't make it out. There appeared to be a snout. Maybe some ears. Or were those horns? A mouth? Whatever the creature was, Rowena was uninterested in finding out. Anything that would cause her Shadow to abandon all reason and act so recklessly could be nothing good.

Rowena squeezed Ghost in both her hands, but somehow, impossibly, Ghost proved far stronger than her wispy stature implied. To keep from slipping, Rowena had to plant both her feet, using her body weight to counter. They grappled together, Rowena and her Shadow, a literal tug of war of conflicting wills. Rowena felt desperate; her own Shadow, her only companion, her very soul betraying her. And for a demon in the dark! Her father and the rest of the world had been right. Ghost was a monster, after all. Hot tears trailed down Rowena's cheek, her grip slipping, all hope nearly lost.

Behind her, the two men of The Wandering watched, their albino Shadows appearing like ghosts themselves in the dim light. But Rowena had no thought for them because, just then, the hidden creature stepped into the light, just enough for Rowena to make out the form of a giant hound—although it was closer in size to a pony than a dog. A disquieting intelligence met Rowena's gaze, and her grip upon Ghost broke at last.

Ghost slammed into the dog's neck, and Rowena fell back. There was a muttered "oof" and a flash of white as she toppled atop one of the men. His stately figure hit the stone floor while his bat flapped offended wings, knocking over the nearby torch. It crashed into the stack of crates.

At first, neither the chief nor Rowena noticed the fire, both transfixed by her ghostly Shadow nuzzling a giant dog. But a quick series of *pop-pop's* caught their attention.

Rowena convulsed, clamping her hands over her ears. She peered under her arm to witness flames spreading like water over the mound of crates. Straw packing ignited like tinder. Explosions burst from their boxed containment, shattering wood in every direction. Splinters caught in her hair, and she curled in on herself like a turtle in a hailstorm.

One of the men hoisted the other to his feet. Then, the two sprinted for cover, leaving Rowena laid out on the ground. Rockets whistled past to crash onstage in a shower of gold, blue, and acid green, dazzling glitter illuminating the scenery. A red-hot rocket shot directly for her, screaming like a warning. There was no time to move, so she merely covered her face from the oncoming blast.

A force like a battering ram slammed into her side. At first, she thought it was the rocket, except it came from the wrong direction. Whatever it was, it pushed her out of the rocket's path just in time, splaying her like a star on the floor. The world exploded somewhere beyond her feet. Rowena lay flat on her back and, with detached curiosity, noticed the moon just behind a sizzling shimmer of sparks.

It took her a moment to realize she was no longer backstage. With dim comprehension, she rolled her head to the side and beheld a sea of faces frozen in horror. An unrelenting succession of explosions shook the audience from their stupor as the cache of fireworks was set ablaze. Raw terror suppressed Rowena's instinct to flee. She merely lay there while *whistles, bangs,* and *pops* sang in a symphony of catastrophe. The glittering display might have been beautiful if not for its deadly proximity.

Soon, smoke flooded the air, and thousands of people coughed. Rowena's own breath was suddenly cut off with a wrenching gag. Something dragged her by the throat. She managed to rock her head back to see the collar of her dress in the mouth of the giant demon dog. Ghost glided at its side as if they were friends, her flipper clutching dappled fur. Rowena would have cried out at the cruel betrayal, except her vocal cords were constricted by the dog's toothy maw. But then it dropped her, and she gulped air in sucking gasps.

Rowena was at the front of the stage now, away from the worst of the explosions. The dog planted four paws the size of grapefruits on each of her sides. It angled its body like a shield so close its ribcage pressed her head. The fireworks unleashed a fury of colorful thunder. Ghost, as if suddenly noticing the danger, dashed for cover in Rowena's arms. Flames engulfed the curtain and backdrop scene. Her father's painted masterpiece blazed like melting glory.

A final, earth-shattering explosion erupted, and Rowena wrapped her body around Ghost. Something heavy pressed against her back. The dog lay on top of her, sheltering her from the flying wreckage. The last of the cache exploded in an epic finale of sparks and cinder.

All the while, the audience attempted to flee the horror show, but only a lucky few managed to make it out of the arena. The rest were blinded by the smoke, sandwiched among a frightened throng.

Members of the Sceadwe descended upon the scene. Soon, their Shadows snuffed the flames, but this only resulted in more smoke, caging the crowd in near-suffocation.

It was the Lord Overseer's Shadow who stretched his magic like mighty arms. The wolf seized hold of the wind. Like enormous bellows, magic animated the air, and the smoke wafted out and over the forest in a wave. The vanished smoke revealed a bedraggled audience, a horribly charred mess onstage, and the girl who lay among the wreckage. Over her stood an enormous hound with mottled black and white fur like spilled ink on parchment. The dog sniffed her head as if confirming her safety, then bounded upstage with great loping strides to disappear into the forest beyond.

Several Sages, the Lord Overseer, and even the Myth Keeper all stood in a semi-circle around Rowena, having battled the fire with their magic. The air was clear now; all smoke dissipated.

All smoke, that was, except the little wisp floating at Rowena's side.

As fast as things had erupted into chaos, a harried silence descended in the aftermath. At first, people weren't sure what they saw, their attention disordered, with several nursing injuries from their attempted escape. But one by one, their eyes locked on the wisp.

Rowena sat up and brushed ash from her eyes, only to behold a wall of faces noticing her for the first time. A thousand mouths opened, some in surprise, more in confusion. They murmured. The sound was faint through the ringing in her ears. But then she saw a finger raised. Pointing. Without looking, Rowena knew it was her Shadow they beheld in such horror—as if a real ghost had entered their midst.

Chapter Thirteen

WHILE ROWENA SAT THERE, her clothes and skin charred, staring at the people staring back at her, a body collided with her. Familiar arms enveloped her like a cocoon.

Her father's lips pressed against her ear. "Are you hurt?" he demanded. His Shadow sniffed her all over. She felt callused hands force her face upward; all care for his injured wrist forgotten. Haaris's face was a study of parental terror. "*Are you hurt?!*" Her head throbbed, but she shook it nonetheless. He clamped her to his chest, stroking ash from her hair.

Roderick knelt beside them. By this point, Rowena was too numb to be bothered by the man and wolf's sudden proximity. His voice was gruff as if he'd inhaled much of the smoke. "She alright?"

Haaris nodded.

The crowd churned. Several people called out, wondering why—how—*what in Bazileus' name*—had happened?!

"Get her out of here," Roderick muttered. He stood to face the crowd.

Haaris pulled Rowena to standing, and she felt vaguely glad that all her limbs seemed to be working. A quick look on all sides confirmed every exit was blocked. During the explosions, the crowd had filled the aisles. With their safety secured, they seemed uninterested in leaving. They wanted an explanation, they hollered.

"Ladies and gentlemen!" Roderick raised his hands for quiet. His Shadow amplified his voice, and Rowena winced, her ears ringing sharply. "I will ask that you exit the arena in an orderly fashion while we tend to the damages."

"What *was* that?" someone cried defiantly.

"This was an accident," Roderick answered, his arms still raised.

"That kid! She did it!" someone shouted. The crowd seemed to agree, and their voices overlapped.

"She did it!" more chimed in. Rowena was too shaken to make out what anyone said, but a few made themselves heard, and the rest quieted the listen. "She did it!"

"Who is that with her?"

"It's Haaris—Haaris Faye!"

"*Who?*"

"The widower."

"The hermit, more like."

"Didn't his child die?"

"Then who is that?"

"It can't be."

"*What* is that?!"

"Just smoke is all."

"That's not smoke."

"It's a ghost!"

"*She's* a ghost. Look at her, just like her mother—remember her?"

"It's Hazel Faye's dead child!"

"A ghost!!"

Understanding caught like fire. Roderick attempted to gain control but to no avail. The crowd whipped into a frenzy as they screamed about ghosts and hauntings and the supposed-to-be-dead child in Haaris's arms. Roderick's wolf raised his hackles seeming to double in size.

"ENOUGH!!" Roderick boomed. The arena fell silent. Many people stumbled back. The trees lining the arena trembled; brittle limbs crashed to the ground. "THIS WAS AN ACCIDENT. HEAR ME? YOU WILL EXIT IN AN ORDERLY FASHION. *NOW!!*"

The crowd shifted, reluctant but obedient.

One person, however, sat quietly in her seat. The fox in her lap flicked a bushy orange tail. Penalynn watched the man onstage with interest, the one with the sad-looking dog for a Shadow. His arm wrapped around the shoulders of the teenage girl in question, looking as if he expected someone to steal her away. It wasn't until the audience exited the arena and the man and girl turned to leave that Penalynn acted. "Bran," she said to her guard, pointing. She didn't need to say more.

Bran leaped onto the stage, catching up with the man and girl before they could enter the woods. The guard placed a gloved hand atop the man's shoulder. "Madame Scholastic wants to speak with you and the girl."

Father and daughter both turned toward the Scholastic, looking as if they faced their own deaths. Penalynn had approached the foot of the stage but didn't bother ascending the steps. She stood in the front row. Her face was blank, bored almost. She cradled her fox in her arms.

The Myth Keeper stood among those onstage. He spoke first. "Madame, I advise this man and child be detained and interrogated. It is clear the girl is to blame—"

Roderick interjected, "You have no proof of that, Julian!"

"Look at her! Her Shadow alone is evidence that she—"

"Mr. Keeper, that will be all," Penalynn said, satisfied with the way his mouth snapped shut. She looked at the man and the girl. "Sir, what is your name?"

"Haaris Faye, Madame Scholastic."

"And is this your daughter, Mr. Faye?"

Haaris nodded, swallowing thickly.

"She's supposed to be *dead!*" the Myth Keeper hollered. "I performed her funeral on this very stage, along with her mother's!"

Haaris winced. The girl in question merely gaped, the white of her eyes perfect circles around dark black irises. She pressed her hands over her ears as if they were all shouting.

"Mr. Keeper, that is enough," Penalynn said. "I recommend you and the

Lord Overseer do what is minimally necessary to settle things here tonight. I expect you both in my office tomorrow morning."

"The people of Greymere deserve an explanation!" the Myth Keeper demanded.

"And they will have one. After we have sorted out what happened exactly."

He opened his mouth to object, but she lifted a finger to silence him.

"Mr. Faye," said Penalynn, "You and your daughter will come to my office in the morning as well. You may go home now."

Haaris did not need to be told twice. Quickly, he moved, squeezing his daughter tighter when they passed the two Wandering men. Penalynn noticed the chief's gaze.

"Chief Taiosech?" He seemed reluctant to tear his eyes from the girl, and Penalynn had to snap her fingers to get his attention. "Did you have a hand in what happened here tonight?" she asked, then added, "You will speak to me in the common tongue—out loud."

Standing on the stage, surrounded by members of the Sceadwe, Taiosech distinctly felt the proximity of enemies on every side. But he wasn't afraid, only irritated at his own disheveled state among them. Even so, he kept his head erect as he looked down his nose to the squat, fledgling woman standing below. He was double her age and head of his own race. And yet she commanded him as if she were the queen of Wyre herself.

Taiosech grimaced but didn't dare break the dragon-lover's law against persuasive magic. He spoke aloud. The language tasted foul in his mouth. "I and my elder waited in darkness for fireworks at the end of night. This girl fell on me. My scead," he indicated the bat hanging from his arm, "Grew feared. He hit torch. Torch light fireworks." He seethed, furious to be forcibly exposed by his clumsy command of the Wyrian language.

Everyone onstage turned their attention back to the Scholastic, expecting her to make a judgment on the matter. She stood eye level with their feet and yet somehow loomed over them all. New as she was, she outranked everyone. For the first time since donning the title of Scholastic, Penalynn felt the weight of her role. Even the Lord Overseer waited for her word, his wolf at attention. Her legs itched, tempted to shift her weight from side to side. But, outwardly, she remained steadfast, allowing only her toes to wiggle, feeling the squishy grass through her shoes.

"Thank you," she said to the Wandering chief. "You are free to go." He moved to leave, but she added as if remembering something. "One more thing. You will remain in your camp for the remainder of your stay. If one of your people is found within the city limits, they will be arrested. My friend Bran here will escort you back."

Bran held out his hand, his Shadow wrapped around his forearm. "After you, chief," he said.

The bat flexed its wings, and a muscle in the chief's jaw twitched. Penalynn met his stare and knew she'd perceived him correctly. He had intended something with that girl. She felt her feet settle into place. The Wandering chief left without a word, escorted by Bran.

Penalynn turned to Roderick, who had watched this all with bushy eyebrows raised. "Get some rest, Lord Overseer," she said. "You and I have much to sort through in the morning."

CHAPTER FOURTEEN

FOG BLANKETED GREYMERE THE morning after the festival. The city slept late to make up for the late night before. The Fayes, however, were wide awake, though their cottage was so quiet as to seem empty. In the upper bedroom, Ghost sat on the windowsill, her translucent shoulders stooped, head propped against the pane in a picture of misery. A creeping vine tapped the glass in a half-hearted breeze. Rowena was still in bed, though. Like Ghost, she hadn't managed to sleep much. Their minds were linked in that way, at least: they both slept and woke in unison.

From under the covers came the sound of sniffing. Ghost looked over to see a new wave of tears leaking onto Rowena's already damp pillow.

Eventually, Rowena managed to stop crying enough to emerge from bed, looking like a mess. She went to the washroom first. Her father's Shadow had heated a tub of water for her. It took two thorough washings to get all the soot off her face and hands, but the smell of smoke seemed locked in her hair, no matter how much soap she used. With clean clothes and dripping hair, she entered the kitchen.

Haaris sat at the table. His fractured wrist was freshly bandaged, having splintered further in the chaos the night before. His good hand wrapped around a teacup long grown cold. Before him on the table lay a note in hasty scrawl:

Don't run. Trust me.
Meet me at the castle.

—Rod

Haaris had been halfway through packing when the note arrived in the dead of night. Rowena had sat in stunned disbelief, watching him. She didn't cry. Didn't move. She was speechless. She had burned down a sacred ceremony in front of everyone, and now her father told her they would leave their home and disappear into the woods. Her mind couldn't take it all in. Her change of fate felt like a living death, incomprehensible. But then Roderick's note came, and Haaris stopped packing. Now, staring into his tea, he looked like he regretted his decision. Things were still grim, but Rowena was at least grateful not to be waking up in the middle of the forest somewhere.

"It's time," Haaris said. The clock hadn't been fixed, so Rowena had no idea how he could tell.

They left the cottage in silence. For the first time in her life, Rowena rode in the cart next to her father, hunched against the cold. Morning light burned the fog away as lines of houses eventually gave way to shops. Ghost hovered near Rowena's shoulder, out in the open for anyone to see. The spaniel performed no magic to conceal her. There was no point to it now, although it didn't matter. Hardly anyone was out yet.

When they reached the city's heart, the cart stopped before the castle entrance. For the first time in her life, the sight of those great oak doors aroused no wonder, no joy. Her time had finally come to enter the castle, and she felt as wooden as those doors. The irony of the moment felt like a tragedy, the sweetness of securing her lifelong wish ruined by the condemnation that surely awaited.

Despite her misery, upon reaching the threshold, she gasped. The doors were towers in themselves, much taller than she expected. So close now she could see that it was not woodgrain that gave them their busy hue, but carvings—impossibly intricate and interwoven pictures stretched corner to corner. Rowena ached for time, for hours to examine them, sure that half the day wouldn't be enough to see all their variegated detail. She'd brought her bookbag. The heavy strap was a small comfort across her shoulder. Her fingers instinctively reached for the notebook inside, unable to rest until they sketched the doors. But Haaris cleared his throat, and she reluctantly peeled herself away.

Across the castle threshold was an empty passageway leading to a grassy courtyard. Their footsteps echoed in the quiet.

Roderick Ashworth waited for them in the vestibule, his Shadow was seated yet still almost as tall as Rowena. She kept her father's Shadow between her and the wolf.

"Thanks for coming," said Roderick.

"I almost didn't," said Haaris with a hint of regret.

"I know."

"So, what are we about to walk into here?"

Roderick spoke to Haaris, but his eyes darted to Rowena several times. "I'm not sure, exactly. I just met this new Scholastic last night. She's young. And from what I've gathered, spirited. But I've got a good feeling about her."

"I don't want Rowena in there for this," said Haaris.

Roderick flashed a sorrowful smile. "Rowena," he whispered. The quiver of his chin belied hurt somehow, although Rowena couldn't imagine how her name might upset him. Then again, she had hardly any experience talking to people beyond her father, and even he was an inscrutable mystery most days. She didn't know what to make of Roderick's intense look—so much unspoken emotion just under the surface. So she merely decided to look down at her shoes.

"Why did you never tell me?" Roderick asked Haaris. Haaris shook his head, seeming unable—or perhaps unwilling—to answer. "Fern is going to want to meet her. It took everything I had to keep her from coming here this morning."

Rowena had no idea what this meant, but Haaris replied, "The reunion will have to wait."

Roderick nodded, then led the way past the courtyard and up several flights of stairs.

Inside her new office, Penalynn sat behind a large cherrywood desk. Her weight shifted in the oversized leather chair—so high her toes hovered a few inches from the floor. She would need a different chair immediately. She had to reach to grab a pen, and as she moved, the leather squelched embarrassingly. She scribbled a note for her new attendant and underlined "not leather" twice for emphasis. The fabric made a burping sound under her legs as if in protest.

Stop fidgeting, her Shadow admonished, poised atop the desk like a statue, the perfect model of decorum.

Penalynn ignored the fox. She was about to have her first official meeting as a Scholastic, and her office was in shambles. Unopened boxes were stacked like towers while the bookcases lay bare. Her humongous desk was empty save a scrap of paper, a pen, and her judgmental Shadow. She felt untethered—far away from

Riven and not yet at home here. The door opened, and her stomach flipped. "Oh. Bran." She exhaled.

Bran pretended not to notice her nervousness. "They're here."

Her face fell. "Ah. Yes."

The Myth Keeper entered first, followed by the Lord Overseer, who ushered in the father and daughter. Bran stood sentinel beside the closed door.

"Gentlemen, good morning," Penalynn greeted. She caught herself and added to the girl, "Hello again to you too."

The Lord Overseer spoke first. "Madame Scholastic, may I more properly introduce my good friend Haaris Faye—Greymere's premier artist and craftsman—and his daughter, Rowena."

Haaris inclined his forehead, and the girl leaned against him. Her face was delicate, contrasted starkly by wide, round eyes. It took less than a second for Penalynn to notice a marked intelligence in the girl. It seemed as if just beyond those eyes, clockwork spun, every moment thinking, deducing, wondering. Rowena took in every inch of the room. She was no doubt terrified, clutching her Shadow like a child with a doll. But despite her evident fear, her countenance was curiosity embodied.

Daylight streamed through many arched windows, providing Penalynn a clear view of Rowena's odd Shadow. It was clear the thing belonged to her. It, too, had enormous eyes, translucent as mist, which peered quizzically just past Penalynn to the fox atop the desk.

The fox stared back. *It's like a candle blew out, and the smoke decided to stick around.*

Penalynn gestured to the chairs before her desk and said, "Please, have a seat, all of you. And excuse the mess. I've only just arrived a few days ago, and believe it or not, this is not even half of the books I've brought with me."

Only the Myth Keeper moved to sit. Haaris looked to Roderick, and Roderick cleared his throat before saying, "Madame, Haaris has requested that his daughter be excused from our meeting."

Penalynn looked at Rowena again. The girl tucked her chin to her chest so a fringe of curls hid half her face. Her posture drooped in wearied submission. It seemed to Penalynn that the girl was not happy about her father's request. On the other side of Roderick, The Myth Keeper peered around the Lord Overseer, not at the girl but at the Shadow in her hands. His lips quirked in hateful disgust as if she held a demon.

"Yes, perhaps that's best," Penalynn allowed. "You may wait in here." She slid open a heavy oak door in the wall. It led to a private library with floor-to-ceiling bookcases, mostly empty, and a large fireplace. Mounds of boxes were stacked about the room like a maze. The entire west wall was made of glass doors leading to a spacious balcony.

Rowena passed Penalynn through the door, leaning away as if she were afraid to touch the Scholastic. Her father said, "I'll come get you as soon as we're done." Then he slid the door shut.

Penalynn resumed her seat and faced the three men across the empty desk, all of whom looked particularly upset.

CHAPTER FIFTEEN

J UST ON THE OTHER side of the sliding door, Rowena lingered. The voices from the Scholastic's office were muffled through the solid oak. She knew she wouldn't be able to make out what they said, and she wasn't sure she wanted to. What could be said in there that could possibly save her now? She saw how they all looked at her Shadow, that man with the canary in particular. She had nothing to do but await her fate.

After weaving a path through boxes, she sat in a squashy chair before the fire, alone, except for Ghost. She held her bag in her lap, with the discomforting awareness that, behind that door, her father and three strangers talked about her. Perhaps the whole town was talking about her after what had happened. She stared at the rug, following lines in the weave and feeling terribly sorry for herself.

Her mortification was soon interrupted by a *tap-tap-tap* on a glass door. She looked up to see, of all things, two teenage boys standing on the balcony. Their hair and coats were frosted from the cold. Titus waved a mittened hand. Next to him, his brother jiggled the door handle and pointed at it, his eyebrows raised at Rowena expectantly. She jumped up to unlock it, and they burst in at once, icy wind gusting like fanfare.

"Hey, Spook!" Titus greeted brightly, "This is my brother, Bruce. Bruce, this is my friend Rowena. Gah! It's cold out there!" He bounded for the fire, removing his mittens with his teeth.

"Hi," Rowena said, self-consciously waving to the boy with the raccoon slung across his shoulders. He was stocky and broad-chested, reminding Rowena of someone, but she couldn't quite place it.

Bruce jutted his thumb over his shoulder. "There's a bathtub filled with books out on the balcony," he said as a way of greeting, "Is this Scholastic some kind of weirdo?"

"How—" Rowena stammered, "How did you get all the way up here?"

Titus shrugged as if the answer were obvious. "We know this castle better than the Myth Keeper himself."

"We're on the fourth floor! And how'd you know I'd be in here?"

"My dad," said Titus. Rowena only blinked, and so he added as if it were common knowledge, "He's the Overseer."

Rowena realized that's who Bruce looked like, a shorter, unbearded version of Roderick. A dozen questions filled her mind, but before she could ask any more, Bruce grabbed her hand. "Might I just say how brilliant you were last night?" He bowed over her hand in mock deference. "Easily the best festival of my life. And I was there the year that not *one,* but *two* trials tried to fly and crashed in glory. How'd you come up with the idea?"

Rowena wrenched her hand from his and pushed her curls off her forehead, feeling suddenly hot around the ears. "I didn't do it on purpose!"

"Well, you should have," he insisted, "What a finale!"

"You'll have to get used to my brother," Titus explained to Rowena, "He's an idiot."

Rowena struggled to understand her own feelings. She was at the lowest point of her life, possibly on the verge of arrest, banishment, or worse, but suddenly, all she could think about was how close Titus was standing to her. Half of her wanted to lean away and gain some semblance of control over her thoughts, and the other half wanted to reach out and touch him to confirm he was real and not just a very convincing dream.

Bruce draped himself over an armchair, wholly at ease with his foot bouncing in the air. "So, what's your story, mystery girl?" Rowena's eyes darted to the door behind which three members of the Sceadwe and her father sat. Bruce continued, "No one's ever seen you before, and then you appear out of nowhere to blow up the festival."

"Umm, could you keep it down?" Rowena asked, glancing at the door again, "I'm already in a lot of trouble, and I don't think you're supposed to be up here."

Ghost hovered at her shoulder, staring at Titus's Shadow, who perched nearby. The owl watched the wisp in return.

"So, what are you," Bruce asked, "Some kind of ghost or something?"

"Bruce!" Titus reproached, smacking his brother with a throw pillow.

"It's a fair question! There're some weird rumors going around."

Rowena dropped into the squishy chair. "So, people are talking about me."

"Well, you did blow up the festival," Titus admitted with a pained look. He sat on a stack of boxes and leaned forward, his elbows on his knees. "So, Rowena, what *is* your story?"

She met his gaze and found something in his open look that made her shoulders soften. It wasn't courage she felt, but surrender. No matter what happened from here, there was no use in hiding anymore. With a deep breath, she began. She told them how she'd been born with a misshapen Shadow that had no magic, how her father had raised her in secret. She told them about growing up forced to hide and never be seen. The fear her father placed on her if she were ever to be found out, and what it was like living her entire life in a tiny cottage, avoiding even the windows in case the neighbors might see.

All her life, Rowena's father had promised that sure danger awaited if anyone ever knew the truth about her. But somehow, looking into Titus's warm brown eyes, she found only attentive wonder, no trace of fear or condemnation. And so, her voice didn't waver as she told her life's story.

When she finished, Bruce scratched his head. "Well, it's about time you showed up. We needed something interesting to happen around here."

Rowena blinked. "You live in a world with magic and can do magic yourself. How am *I* interesting?"

Titus smirked with something like admiration. "You're spooky."

She didn't know how to respond and looked at the closed door again, where her fate was being decided. "I wish I knew what they were saying in there."

"Well, that's easy to find out." Bruce sprang up and wove around stacks of boxes, then pressed his ear to the door. Rowena could just make out a faint hum of magic from the grinning raccoon at his feet.

CHAPTER SIXTEEN

"I EXPECT CONSEQUENCES!" THE Myth Keeper demanded, kicking off the discussion with heat. Penalynn chaffed at his starting the conversation before her. "A holy ceremony was desecrated, and—"

"We will get to that," Penalynn said, "But first, I want to know, Mr. Faye, why did people seem to think your daughter was dead?"

The Myth Keeper answered for him, his Shadow's feathers puffed like an angry chrysanthemum. "Because we had a blasted funeral for her!"

Despite her mounting dislike for the Myth Keeper, she could understand his outrage on that point. "Mr. Faye, is this true?"

"Yes." The word burst from Haaris like a long-held confession. "My wife died in childbirth, and I told everyone the baby had passed with her. The funeral was for them both. I've kept Rowena hidden ever since."

"Her whole life, hidden?" Penalynn asked. "Then why was she at the festival last night?"

"I had to work, so I brought her with me. I managed to hide her—until the end."

"Hide her how?"

"I used persuasion," Haaris admitted, his confession breaking like porcelain. He tugged at the sling around his shoulder.

Penalynn sat back in her chair. So the mysterious persuasion the night before had been his, she thought. "Why? Why the funeral? Why hide her?"

"Because of her Shadow," he said.

"Because of the way it looks?" she asked.

"That and, well, it has no magic."

"What do you mean?"

"Exactly that. She's—empty—in a way." Haaris seemed to struggle to explain. "Look, I'm not a part of the Sceadwe like you people. But I live in a town full of gossips, in a kingdom with serious superstitions about Shadows. I saw how that Wandrel chief looked at her last night. It's how I always knew he'd look if he ever saw her. Because he thinks she's . . . well, I can't articulate it like I'm sure you could. What I know is that when Rowena was born—the birth—it killed my wife. And, suddenly, I had this baby with this barely-there little Shadow. And my best friend worked for the Sceadwe." Haaris's eyes trailed to Roderick, who covered his mouth with a massive hand, sinking back in his chair. The wolf's ears flattened against its shaggy mane. "I just knew we'd all be in danger if...if..."

Penalynn asked, "You suspected she was The Wandering's Shadowless figure?"

"No! Absolutely not. But I knew some people would. Personally, I've never concerned myself with Sceadwe matters, and I'm not a superstitious fellow."

The Myth Keeper wagged his finger. "The Sceadwe should have been notified. Your secrecy belies your culpability. You knew what she was; why else would you hide her?"

"She *has* a Shadow!" Haaris defended.

The wolf's teeth flashed, and Roderick pointed at the Myth Keeper. "That. That right there is why he did it, Julian. Now, I'm not saying it was right, but this kingdom's superstitions—"

"It's not superstition; it's *creed*!"

Penalynn held up her hands to quiet the men. "Mr. Faye, you said that the Shadow has no magic. That she's 'empty.' What do you mean by that?"

Haaris eyed the Myth Keeper next to him, then reluctantly said, "From what I've gathered, they don't have a mind link. What I mean is Rowena can't hear her Shadow. It's just silent. And it's never managed any sort of magic, though the poor thing's tried often enough."

Penalynn could hardly believe what she was hearing. She ignored her Shadow's warning in her head. "She has no magic whatsoever? You've tested this?"

"Yes. There's nothing there. I've done some basic homeschooling. Rowena will learn anything you put in front of her."

"What have you taught her?"

"More like what she's taught herself. I showed her the basics: reading, writing, sums, what-have-you. But after that, she got hold of some of her mother's old books. She's most fond of physic. Anything manual. Whatever she can do with her hands. In that regard, she takes after me, I suppose."

At the mention of physic, the Myth Keeper snorted derisively, but Penalynn's eyes glittered. "How old?"

"Fifteen."

Penalynn fell silent, lost in thought. Her Shadow paced back and forth across the desk. The lull turned awkward as the men waited for her to speak. At last, the Myth Keeper said, "Madame Scholastic, it is plain to me that thing is an abomination in every way. The death of her mother. Hardly a body. No magic. No mind link. I suspect it lacks even a soul! This is more than enough evidence to report the child to the king."

"I disagree," said Penalynn.

"Madame! I know you are young, but as a Scholastic, surely you must be familiar with the sacred texts. You know this child fulfills the qualifications of the Wandering's Shadowless."

"Except for one key point, Mr. Keeper. She has a Shadow."

The Myth Keeper slammed his fist on the arm of his chair. "That abomination will be reported. As a servant of the Sceadwe, it is my duty to know and keep the ancient texts. I must report anything malignant I see as represented in my teachings."

"You're right," Penalynn allowed, "It is your job to know and keep the ancient texts. But you are a mere *keeper*, not an interpreter. Interpretation is a Scholastic duty. And based on my Scholastic interpretation, her lack of magic seems odd and certainly interesting, but not malignant. And certainly not a threat to the throne." She looked at Haaris, who appeared to be holding his breath. She said to him, "Your daughter is safe and free to live as a citizen of Wyre. No more hiding, I should think."

Haaris blinked as if the air were filled with dust.

"I will vouch for her on behalf of the Sceadwe," Penalynn promised.

Roderick smiled broadly, his teeth a shock of white behind his mustache. But Haaris's anxiety escaped in gusting breaths as his posture buckled like a fallen statue. He held his head in his hand and whispered repeatedly, "Thank you. Thank you."

"Mr. Faye, I would like to speak with Rowena. Would you please let her in?"

On the other side of the door, three ears pressed against the wood. They sprang back at the Scholastic's words. Titus and Bruce dove behind stacks of boxes.

The door slid open to reveal Rowena just standing there as if she'd been waiting there the whole time. With shining, wet eyes, Haaris said to her, "Rowena, Madame Scholastic would like to speak with you."

CHAPTER
SEVENTEEN

ROWENA TOOK THE ONLY open seat between the sour-looking Myth Keeper and the Overseer, avoiding the shaggy wolf as best she could and wondering at the strange look on her father's face.

Behind the desk sat the Scholastic woman. She was short in stature and appeared even shorter, framed in high-backed leather. Even so, she filled the office more than the Overseer and wolf combined. Her superiority suffused the very air they breathed. And somehow, her Shadow was even more intimidating. Rowena cowered under its interrogating glare.

When the Scholastic spoke, her voice was neither loud nor quiet. She spoke clearly as if she'd held authority all her life. She asked, "Why were you onstage last night?"

Rowena looked down at her lap where Ghost hovered atop her folded hands. She bit her lip, unsure how to explain her Shadow's strange behavior or the mysterious dog who had saved her. "My Shadow ran away, and I tried to get her back. I think she saw something that..."

Rowena tucked her chin to her chest so that her hair covered her eyes. It was easier to keep her feelings in check that way.

The Scholastic must have leaned forward because she heard the leather chair squelch. Then the woman said, "Yes?"

"I'm not sure what she saw."

Past the fox and across the table, Penalynn frowned thoughtfully as she beheld the girl with the strange Shadow. By every accountable measure, she was leagues beyond Rowena in status, power, luxury, and advantage. But instead of pity, which she ought to have bestowed in plenty, Penalynn felt jealous of the girl. She asked her, "You don't hear your Shadow's thoughts?" The girl shook her head, and jealousy ran down Penalynn's throat like bile.

The fox, knowing her every thought and feeling, shot her an injured look. Penalynn changed the subject. "Your father says you enjoy the study of physic. What do you like about it?"

"It allows me to do things that magic would."

The Myth Keeper muttered, "Preposterous."

Penalynn ignored him. "Do you have a favorite physic scholar?"

Rowena nodded. She wore a bookbag like a piece of clothing and rummaged in it then pulled out a tattered book. She slid it across the desk to Penalynn.

"*Theory of Physic* by Atticus Wolder?" read Penalynn with a wry smile, "He's a personal friend of mine."

Rowena sat up straighter. It was as if the Scholastic had bragged she dined with the king himself. "You know Atticus Wolder?" she asked. A dozen questions sprang to mind, and she had to bite her lip to keep from pressing her for every detail about her intellectual hero. This woman knew Atticus Wolder: the most extraordinary mind for physic Wyre had ever seen.

She watched the Scholastic thumb through the book's pages. When she lingered over her cramped writing filling the margins, Rowena felt suddenly embarrassed; like when her father walked in on her singing to herself when she thought she was alone.

"It looks like you've attempted to make several of these inventions," Penalynn observed.

"Yes."

"Successfully?"

"Some, yes."

Penalynn closed the book, tapping her nails on the cover. "Is there any other field of study you'd be interested in? Literature? Art, maybe, like your father?"

Rowena wrinkled her nose, uninterested in any of those subjects. Then, an image came to mind of the little brown bottle her father had brought home from the apothecary. Her answer burst without thought. "I want to make potions." As soon as she said it, the desire bloomed deep in her heart, as if it had always been there, like a seed, waiting to bud. "But potions need magic, and I haven't got any."

Penalynn didn't respond. Again, she withdrew into her thoughts, but this time for only a moment. Then she dropped from her chair with an infuriating leather squeak and opened a nearby trunk. She pulled out a black box polished to such a high shine she could see her reflection in the lid. "During the ceremony in which I was made a Scholastic, I was given three items," she said, "My cloak and pendant, which signify my status as a Scholastic, and this box. Do you know what is inside?"

Rowena shook her head, but the Myth Keeper seemed to understand the box's significance. His breath whistled through his hooked nose. Penalynn turned a key in the lock, then opened the lid to reveal a blue cape in the same fabric as her Scholastic cloak. It was shorter, meant to stop at the elbows and fasten down the front in a line of sterling silver buttons.

Rowena leaned forward to get a better look. Ghost hovered by her ear.

"Every Scholastic is charged the duty of appointing and training an apprentice," explained Penalynn. "Someone remarkable to carry on their legacy. Most Scholastics are much older than I am, and so they typically appoint apprentices who are just behind them in age. But, as Mr. Keeper has repeatedly remarked, I am uniquely young for my post. And so, I think it is only logical that I should appoint a uniquely young apprentice."

"Madame!" the Myth Keeper cried.

Penalynn ignored him. "Rowena, I would like to appoint you to the role of Scholastic Apprentice. I will train you in the art of physic, and under my tutelage, you will be made a master of the study."

The Myth Keeper sprang from his chair, his canary flipping in the air. "You cannot be serious! You'd appoint a magic-less abomination to be a member of the Sceadwe?!"

"Mr. Keeper, you are excused," Penalynn said serenely.

Behind him, Bran opened the door. The Myth Keeper didn't argue but left as if on a mission, flourishing his black cape as he went. Penalynn suspected he headed for the silver glass to report her to the Sceadwe. But whatever complaint he made to them, Penalynn didn't care. She had faced worse than an angry Myth Keeper from a backwater town.

The door shut, and the room felt oddly still after the Myth Keeper's blustering exit. Penalynn said to Rowena, "As you can see, this will not be a popular decision. It is not an easy thing I am offering you. I will expect much of you. But this position will offer you some level of protection. You will need to be a part of society for the work I intend, which means there can be no more hiding."

Haaris spoke up then. "Madame, surely you cannot give this honor just to protect—that is to say—I am grateful, but—"

"This is not altruism," Penalynn assured him. "Appointing an apprentice is an incredibly personal decision. My realm of study is...unprecedented. I've known all along I'd need to choose the right person. In my experience, magic can impede excellence when it comes to the study of physic. Rowena will not have this problem. Such a thing has never been done before, and I am very interested in seeing what she is capable of. Also, and more significantly, my Scholastic work will, I believe, be benefited by her...singularity." Her smile was wide, though it faltered a bit when the fox jumped down from the desk, wandered behind a stack of boxes, and curled up out of sight. Still, Penalynn asked, "Rowena, will you be my apprentice?"

Rowena's eyes were perfect circles as she gaped at the opened box and the blue velvet cape. Her mind spun over all that had taken place. The Myth Keeper's outburst had shaken her, and she knew she didn't understand the significance of the blue cape nor the role of apprentice. She didn't trust herself to make a proper decision without comprehending things perfectly, so she looked to her father for guidance.

But Haaris only shrugged. "This is your decision," he said. "You don't have to if you don't want to." The world had truly turned upside down, for when had he ever entrusted her with any decision about her future?

"Would I get to go to school?" she asked, "Here in the castle?"

Penalynn nodded. "Traditional schooling will be necessary."

"Yes," Rowena answered.

"Are you sure?" Haaris asked, "Do you want to take some time and think about it first?"

"No. I want to go to school."

Haaris looked over her head at Roderick, who watched the exchange with an ever-widening grin. The giant man's chuckle sounded like a rockslide. "Leave it to you to be unsure about such a positive turn of events."

At this, Haaris nodded his concession.

"It's settled, then!" said Penalynn, sliding the box to Rowena. "This is yours. As Scholastic Apprentice, you must always wear when you're in public to signify your high status."

Rowena could hardly imagine having *any* status in town, let alone a high one.

The meeting was over. They all stood. Haaris mumbled thanks, as did Rowena, both struggling to grasp the sudden swing of fate.

"Oh wait," Penalynn added, "There's something else for you." She rummaged in another box and pulled out a newer book, its spine crisp and unbroken. "Since you're a fan of Wolder's, I think you'll be interested in his sequel. Perhaps we'll get you making potions after all."

Rowena's fingers traced the embossed title: *Physic Potions* by Atticus Wolder. Her heart seemed to dance in her chest. "Thank you!"

Penalynn took her hand and shook it firmly. "I look forward to working with you, Rowena. We start at the first of the week."

They left, Roderick, Haaris, and Rowena. Behind them, the Scholastic's door closed with a *click*, and they all stood in the corridor, hardly believing what had just happened. A nearby door flung open, and the Ashworth brothers came spilling out, eager to congratulate Rowena on her good fortune.

"Were you eavesdropping?!" Roderick growled.

Bruce elbowed his father in the ribs. "Hey, Dad, now that she's a member of the Sceadwe, does this make Rowena your colleague?" The three Ashworths laughed at the notion while Rowena and her father exchanged a look, both dizzy by the sudden, happy reversal.

Roderick clapped Haaris on the shoulder. "You're having dinner at our house tonight; don't even bother arguing. As soon as I tell Fern what's happened, she'll be knocking down your door."

"Mom's going to be thrilled," Titus told Rowena. "She was really worked up this morning." Rowena marveled that his mother would care about her at all. Titus chattered as they walked, "I think you'll like her. She's about as nice as anybody you'll meet but like a pillow: soft, with the potential to smother you. She's a good cook, though. I'll ask her to make a cake. What kind do you like? She can do anything."

In the span of a moment, nearly every aspect of Rowena's existence had changed. She felt unsteady as they walked down the stairs as if the ground rocked under her feet. "Umm, vanilla?"

"*Vanilla*? Wow, you were right; you don't get out much. Okay, vanilla. Simple. I like it."

He rattled on, but Rowena didn't catch much, too engrossed with the castle's interior. She slid her hand into Haaris's and whispered, "This is my school now."

At this, Haaris did something Rowena had never seen him do before. He threw his head back and laughed, looking fifteen years younger and lighter than ever.

CHAPTER EIGHTEEN

WHEN THE FAYES ARRIVED at the Overseer's house that evening, Fern Ashworth waited for them on the front stoop. Her willowy frame leaned against the railing, reminding Rowena of a daisy, slender and cheerful. From around her skirt peered her bashful Shadow, a fawn with chestnut fur dappled with spots and impossibly long lashes.

"Rowena," Fern murmured as she wrapped her twiggy arms around her shoulders. Rowena stiffened in the embrace, but Fern laid her hand on her cheek, and suddenly, it was as if a gentle breeze and warm blanket encircled her, unknotting her nerves with maternal care. With Rowena now relaxed, Fern leaned back to examine her, her tongue clucking like a hen. She tucked a wayward curl behind her ear, but the curl bounced back, unwilling to be tamed. It seemed to remind Fern of something because she smiled but in a sad sort of way. The corner of her lips pinched.

Rowena didn't know how to respond to this intrusive welcome, but thankfully, Fern backed away to usher Rowena and her father into the house. It smelled of baked bread and sweet vanilla. Rowena noticed that it was much brighter than their small cottage. The drapes were open wide, allowing in plenty of evening light.

Rowena sat at the table next to Titus, her father and Bruce across, and Fern and Roderick at either end. Everyone's Shadows lounged at their feet or perched on the backs of chairs. Even Ghost managed to attract little attention, sitting atop

Rowena's shoulder. The meal was perfect for the cold weather outside: potato leek soup with crusty bread and generous scoops of butter. Their centerpiece was a frosted ivory cake atop a crystal pedestal.

The brothers talked through most of dinner, and Roderick often joined them. Haaris spoke only when asked a direct question, and Fern said even less. Rowena couldn't help but notice Fern's increased glances. When their eyes met, Fern's were filled with tears, though she smiled through them. "Are you okay?" Rowena asked.

"Yes, dear." Fern dabbed her eyes unconvincingly. "It's just, oh, look at you! So grown up. I remember when you were only a few minutes old. You were such a tiny little baby."

The table fell silent. Tension crackled among them like static before a storm. The hairs on Rowena's skin prickled. Although, she didn't quite understand the sudden change in the room. Roderick's wolf stood to look directly at Fern, his shaggy shoulders surpassing the tabletop. But Fern was oblivious, too lost in her feelings. She spoke with the distant look of someone remembering.

"Hazel was my dearest friend in the world. She'd asked me to be her midwife. Did Haaris never tell you?" Rowena shook her head, and Fern looked hurt. She cried in full now. "I was the one to hold you those very first moments. It happened so suddenly, Hazel passing. It was horrible...oh, but you were the daintiest little thing. My boys had been such stout babies. But you were so little. Saying goodbye to you was the most awful thing I ever had to do." She slid her bony hand around Rowena's, grasping her tightly. "But you're here now. And so much like your mother. Hazel's hair was just as—"

"Fern!" Haaris cried, startling Rowena. "*Please.*" A dark cloud seemed to color his face. His shoulders were ridged, the tendons in his neck visible.

Rowena touched her hair as if she might find her mother buried within. So, her mother had had curls, too. The information felt strange. She tried to picture it, her hair on another person. But a faceless image came to mind, clumsy and incomplete. Her mother was the greatest mystery of her life—other than Ghost, that was. Haaris never spoke of her. Never. His daughter's birth coincided with his greatest grief, so he'd never even taught her the tradition of celebrating her birthday. She didn't even know what date it was.

Haaris and Rowena weren't the only ones disquieted by Fern's words. Like a thunderstorm off in the distance, Roderick's voice rumbled. "Boys, Rowena, give us a minute."

Bruce and Titus both argued, but Roderick wouldn't budge. So, reluctantly, they left the table, Rowena trailing behind, the most hesitant to go. How many adults would know her own story better than she did, she wondered. Titus seemed to sense her thoughts because he tugged her arm and jutted his head toward the back door with a conspiratorial look. On the porch, he held his finger to his lips and led her around the corner, then stopped under a window. Fern had cracked it earlier to let out some of the heat from cooking dinner.

They sat on either side of the window, their backs pressed to the outer wall of the house. It was dark out; their only light filtered through the curtains inside. Stars blinked awake in a navy blue sky, and Rowena began to shiver. Luckily, Bruce rounded the corner carrying a couple of blankets. He tossed one to each of them, then settled down beside his brother as if eavesdropping through a cracked window were a common evening occurrence. Rowena remembered how casual they had been about listening through the Scholastic's door; perhaps eavesdropping *was* common for the Ashworth boys.

Inside, they heard a chair scrape across the floor in the way it does when someone is sitting back, getting comfortable. Then Roderick's voice: "You know, Haaris, something about your story has been bothering me ever since you told it this morning." Rowena wrapped the blanket tighter around her shoulders and leaned in close, her head resting against the windowsill. "The funeral."

Haaris's voice sounded hollow. "What about it?"

"You were always terrible at persuasions. How'd you magic the minds of so many people to believe your lie? Besides, I sat right next to you at the funeral. Where was the baby?"

There was a long pause.

"I helped him." It was Fern's voice.

Rowena and Titus locked eyes, mirroring one another's shock.

"I kept her here with me. Titus was still a baby himself, and Bruce was too young to understand."

"That's why you wouldn't go to the funeral," said Roderick. "I've always wondered. She was your best friend, and you wouldn't go."

"The persuasion was mine too." Fern sighed as if relieved of a heavy burden, one she'd obviously shouldered for many years.

"How? I know you're good at it, love. But not *that* good. The whole town believed she was dead."

"I didn't have to persuade the whole town to get them to believe it," she said. "Just you."

The air seemed to sizzle with tension, palpable even through the window where the brothers and Rowena listened. For a moment, Rowena forgot to breathe.

Then Haaris's voice cut in. "It was my idea, not hers. I knew that if Greymere's Lord Overseer believed it to be true, the townspeople would all believe with you. They trust you, Rod."

The wolf growled, and something shifted. Rowena could hear the plea in

Fern's voice. "We needed to protect you. As a member of the Sceadwe, you had to remain innocent. I would have asked your permission first, but consent weakens persuasive magic, you know that."

"We couldn't chance it," Haaris added. "There was too much at stake."

There was another long silence. They all, inside and outside, weighed Fern's and Haaris's words. Roderick broke the silence. "I congratulate you both on your cleverness," he chuckled, though even Rowena could tell it was forced levity. "Although, I wouldn't have minded being criminal with you."

"You're the Lord Overseer!" Fern cried.

"But I'm a husband and friend first."

"The Sceadwe would disagree," said Haaris.

"I could have helped. I *should* have helped."

Rowena sat up on her knees, chancing a look. It was hard to see through the lace curtains, but she could just make out the outlines of figures seated around the table. Fern reached across to take Roderick's hand, but he pulled his arm away.

For some reason, Rowena felt guilty. The tension between husband and wife was her fault. After all, Fern had lied to protect Rowena. She pushed away from the window, and Titus went with her. They sat down on the porch steps, huddled under their blankets. Behind them, they could still hear the adults talking, but their voices were muffled. It sounded like they'd moved on, conversing about something else. The tension was gone, at least.

Rowena pulled her knees to her chest, shivering even under the blanket. There was some comfort in knowing that they could talk about her all they wanted, but they wouldn't be deciding her fate for her. That had already been settled, and for the first time in her life, Rowena had been given a choice in the matter.

"What does a Scholastic Apprentice even do?" she wondered aloud. Her breath looked like her Shadow, though the puff of steam evaporated instantly.

Titus shrugged under his own blanket. "Who cares? You're practically royalty now."

Above them, Ghost spun lazy circles, lost in her own world with vacant expression and even more vacant translucency. Rowena tucked her chin to hide her face. "I'm not sure the rest of the town will agree."

"You'll attend proper magic classes now. Maybe one of the Sages will get some magic out of her after all." His owl hopped up to join Ghost in aerial loops.

"I can't even imagine. But then again, there's a lot about today I never would have imagined." After a moment, she voiced her worry. "I hope your dad's not too mad."

Titus didn't seem as bothered by what they'd overheard. "They've had much worse fights, trust me. They get mad at each other, but they get over it quickly."

Sure enough, a moment later, Fern called for them with surprising cheer. They went back inside to see her cutting the cake, dividing heaping portions onto matching crystal plates.

Dessert was enjoyed with little tension. Through a mouthful of frosting, Titus admitted that vanilla had been an excellent choice, and everyone else all agreed.

After dessert, Fern wouldn't let Rowena and Haaris leave before burdening them with basket upon basket, each filled with homemade bread, muffins, slices of cake, preserves, cheeses, a ham, various knitted things, and even a new dress for Rowena. After saddling them with so many gifts, she still wouldn't let them leave until Rowena promised to return the next day for what she called a "proper haircut."

"I'll not have Hazel's daughter traipsing around town looking like a hermit in the woods! Honestly, Haaris. You couldn't have bought her a *brush* all these years?"

"Fern, let the poor people go," Roderick urged, sweeping her aside. Rowena was glad to see Titus was right. Roderick had already forgiven Fern, his great big arms wrapped around her tiny waist, which allowed the Fayes to make a break for it.

Titus helped load the cart, and then he and Bruce gave it a hefty push. Haaris's magic caught the movement with deft animation. With a final wave, they sped down the street, not only with a full cart but their lives suddenly full as well.

CHAPTER NINETEEN

T HAT SAME EVENING, PENALYNN enjoyed dinner in her own quarters in the castle. As a goodbye present, she had ordered Bran's favorite meal from the kitchen. The aroma of roasted duck in plum sauce filled the space between them. They sat beside the wall of windows in her private library, overlooking the city. Black steeples jutted against a setting sun.

"A meal with a view," Bran admired through a mouthful. "So, how do you like it so far?"

"It's fine," Penalynn answered quickly. Too quickly. Bran stopped chewing. "It's a bit foreign."

"And the people?"

"They're fine too. Different from Riven, but it's not like I made many friends there either." She stabbed her fork as if her dinner had done her an injustice. "That man gets under my skin for some reason."

Bran knew she meant the Myth Keeper. He snorted.

"Was I wrong?" she asked.

Before answering, he wiped his mouth and sat back. "Look, Pen. It's like I've said. You're an idealist, but you won't win much as one. Things that matter to most people are the same things you snub your nose at." He ticked off his fingers: "Seniority. Experience. Politics. And most of all, if you are to have any semblance of friendship out here—any allies—you've got to attempt being likable."

"Ouch, Bran."

"Am I wrong?"

Her fork clanged against her teeth. "You sound like my Shadow."

"Which means a part of you knows I'm right. The wise, not-so-rash part."

"So, I'm rash now, too?"

He chuckled. "You chose an attendant when you'd been here less than a minute. Refused advice from people who already live here and know her. You chose a *kid* as your apprentice despite all the warning signs that you'd get heat for it. You forced us to travel by *horse* with no thought to the expense or appearance of it. Carted across the kingdom a bathtub of all things, because, what? You thought they didn't bathe out here? What else—"

She held up her hands. "Alright. But I can explain every one of those decisions. Except the bathtub. That was just—"

"Pompous."

"Uninformed." He gave her a withering look, and so she admitted, "Fine, you're right. I'm a pretentious brat. Why do you care enough to lecture me?" She regretted the question immediately; it left her feeling bare and vulnerable. She hated that she cared what he thought of her, but she couldn't help it. His esteem seemed to mean more to her than anyone else's.

He answered sincerely. "I care because I won't be here, and you'll be alone."

She swallowed thickly. "Thank you for making the trip."

"It's my job."

"All the same, thank you."

He took another bite. "I didn't tell you before, but you're not the only one with a fancy new job. I've been promoted. Soon as I get back to Riven, it's no more guard duty. You're having dinner with a bona fide Black Guardian to the throne."

Penalynn tried to look happy for him, though she stabbed at her plate.

"You disapprove, don't you?"

"Of course not," she lied. "What does your mother think of you becoming an assassin?"

"They're not assassins. Okay, fine. They're not *just* assassins. And uh, I haven't told her yet."

It was Penalynn's turn to chuckle. "Ha. Good luck."

"What can she do? I'm a Black Guardian now. My mother can't kill a Black Guardian."

Penalynn quirked her eyebrow, but inside, her stomach roiled. The plum sauce suddenly tasted sour. She'd miss this. The friendly arguing that only comes from lives lived in close proximity to one another. All familiarity had been stripped from her. It was like she was trying to hold water in her hands, sitting here with Bran. Their friendship, the joy of knowing and being known, was trickling through her fingers, and there was nothing she could do to stop it.

Bran took his last bite with a satisfied sigh. "Besides, you've got a bigger task than me, training up that apprentice of yours."

"I'm guessing you disapprove," she said.

"Honestly? I should have seen it coming the moment she walked in. I think you were looking for someone to save. You gave her a future, at least. That's something she didn't have before."

Penalynn chewed thoughtfully. He certainly knew her. She wanted to savor the feeling of being known like this. Starting tomorrow, there would be no more.

Bran wiped his mouth, then stood. "I better get some sleep. It's a long road home." He paused, looking at her with something she rarely saw in his eyes: genuine concern. "It's not right, what happened to you. I've hated bringing you here. Like I'm complicit or something."

"Oh, your conscience will be clear soon enough," she said, "You'll be back home and will forget all about me just like the rest."

"Impossible," he said, but Penalynn knew better. In fact, he had already begun to forget, though she didn't know yet how much. Soon, he'd forget everything. She would hate him for it, though that wouldn't be fair.

"I'll write you," he promised.

She nodded, though she knew he wouldn't.

When he left, she locked the doors and drew the curtains. Then she scooped up her Shadow and wove among the stacks of boxes until she stood before a tall, flat shape leaning against the wall, covered by a tapestry. The fox's tail twitched. Penalynn tugged the fabric, and it pooled at the foot of a large rectangle of pure silver. The silverglass glittered like treasure in the firelight.

It had been ages since she'd done magic. She couldn't help but enjoy the smoldering power, like an ember kept from the wind lest the fire reach fearsome potential. Like burning passion clutched in the hand of denial.

The fox's ears perked. Magic rose in her throat, anxious to be poured out, but, as usual, the Shadow tamped it down.

It will only make us feel worse, Penalynn's Shadow said.

I know. Do it anyway.

Regret flared between them. The fox was right. This magic would yield no satisfaction. She longed for something real, a magic she could sink her teeth into. Her magic hummed like a song, her Shadow's skill undiminished with time. The silver swirled in concentric spirals until it dissipated to reveal...nothing, only empty blackness in a gilt frame.

I told you. The accusation was barely a whisper in Penalynn's head.

Hot tears rolled down her cheek, falling into the fox's fur. Despite the clutter of unopened boxes, she felt a gaping emptiness all around. The last familiar connection was gone, and she was truly alone now.

Taiosech sat alone by the elder fire. All around the Wandering camp, tents were full of sleepers. Karah approached from the dark. He settled beside the chief to whisper a report after a day of spying. "Rumors fly about the girl. She is infamous in ways I do not understand."

"Infamous?"

"She is said to have died. They eulogized her when she was just born."

"It was a lie," the chief dismissed. He had heard the same spoken by the crowd the night of the festival.

"It is rumored her Shadow possesses no scead-magic."

Taiosech's Shadow shifted, flexing its papery wings.

Karah continued. "But my chief, it is odd. She was made Scholastic Apprentice this very day. She is of the Sceadwe now."

The chief's face seemed to smolder in the firelight. "Did you see the animal with her?"

Karah nodded.

"I've seen this creature many times before," Taiosech murmured. To him, the dog was unmistakable, visited upon him night after night for months now. "It is the creature from my dreams."

"What do you make of it all, my chief? A Scholastic of the Sceadwe travels by horse and then appoints a magicless child to carry her legacy. Is this Scholastic a fool?"

"No. She is savvy. Perhaps she suspects us and has given the child a position as a guard."

"But why would a servant of their king want to protect the Shadowless? It would be foolish to keep a king-killer in their midst."

"Who says the Scholastic is protecting the girl?" Taiosech countered. The last ember winked out, and his face was cast in darkness. "She keeps the child out of reach, perhaps to deliver her to another."

"Should we capture her then?"

"Not yet," said Taiosech, "Let us watch and wait."

Chapter Twenty

THREE YEARS LATER

Cold air caressed Penalynn's skin. She stood within a ring of light, darkness expanding all around. The floor stretched like glass to unseen reaches. Tentatively, she stepped forward, heels clicking on slick black obsidian. A slab of red-veined marble appeared. An altar. Atop it, a fox curled tightly in on itself.

She climbed onto the altar; her movement strained as if through water. The fox burrowed against her chest. "It's alright, we're alright."

From the darkness, figures approached. Men in black velvet cloaks. Their faces were obscured, but she thought she knew them, though she couldn't recall their names. They circled the altar. A hand emerged from a cloak, putrid and decayed. It reached out to bury its fingertips in the fox's fur.

She wrenched her Shadow back. "No!" Penalynn attempted to scream, but her voice was gone.

The floor quaked. The marble slab split down the middle, with Penalynn on one half and her Shadow on the other. The hooded figures chanted in a language she once knew but now forgot. It sounded like music and a lecture and howling all at once. Strong hands pinned her like a bug, the fox also. She held the fox's gaze and wondered if she was mistaken, and it was not her Shadow after all, but a mere animal. Its thoughts were closed from her. The fox stared, silent as a tomb.

A silver dagger flashed as if in moonlight. The chanting rose in pitch and passion, echoing off unseen walls. Penalynn lay immovable, unable to scream. She was all eyes. Watching. She looked to the outer darkness for someone—any-one—who might save her.

Something stirred. A flash of blue flickered across the ground. There it was again. It swished into view, then disappeared. Its motion reminded her of the tip of a tail, but thick as a tree and covered in blue scales. All efforts to escape ceased. She knew that whatever lay in the dark would not help her. She looked back at the fox as the knife buried into its side. The Shadow exploded in a cloud of ash.

Penalynn sat bolt upright. She'd found her voice and screamed. Her fingers clutched cotton sheets, and she panted in the dimness. Moonlight cast her bed-room in a lilac sheen, falling upon her Shadow, who lay on a pillow. The fox stood, shaking her body like a dog as if she might shake away the dream's lingering horror. *Oh, that was awful.*

"It was just a dream," Penalynn whispered, "We're home."

Home, repeated the fox.

Penalynn stroked the Shadow's tail, the feel of coarse fur tethering her to reality. Her eyes scanned the bedroom, comforted by the solidity of her bedposts, the curve of the stone wall, and the domed ceiling overhead. *Home.* She had come to like Greymere and even her role as Scholastic. In the ensuing years, work had become her life and her life had become her work—a quiet, studious existence. She was content—except when the dreams came, her last, lingering piece of Riven.

"Well, there's no use trying to sleep." She stretched, her joints popping pleas-antly. "Shall we work?"

The question lingered between them like an echo. The fox didn't move, still shaken from the dream. There was a connection, somehow, between the nightmare and Penalynn's study. Now that she thought about it, the nightmare wasn't her only relic from Riven. It had been a question—asked long ago—which hurled her down this path. Soon, she and Rowena would finish their study, and Penalynn would have her answer at last. Another question arose: was she ready?

"Might as well distract ourself, rather than sit here and mope."

Ready or not, answers were coming. She shrugged into her robe and left the bedroom. The fox trailed behind.

In the beginning, there had been much commotion against her laboratory. Nothing like it had ever been seen in Greymere. And like most towns, Greymere was skeptical of anything novel. The room had become famous as it took a small army of servants on rotation to maintain its function. But the laboratory servants were all compensated so richly in gold that most complaints quickly diminished.

Penalynn stopped outside the laboratory door, where heavy clothes hung on hooks in the wall. She selected a thick cloak, buttoning it up to her chin. Then, she donned a fur-lined hat and her favorite pair of gloves (the fingertips cut off for dexterity's sake). She finished the ensemble with fleece-lined boots. When she heaved the laboratory door open, a blast of cold air hit her square in the face. She inhaled appreciatively. The frosty temperature chased away the last fragments of sleep.

At the far end of the room sat two men bundled head to toe, playing a card game. "Madame Scholastic!" They startled to their feet and swiped the cards out of sight.

"Good morning, gentlemen," Penalynn greeted, "I couldn't sleep, so here I am."

A vast expanse of stone stretched between her and the men, covered with a host of mechanical instruments that had just been whirling noisily. But as soon as Penalynn entered, they slowed to a halt as if caught in the act. Among the machinery stood a squirrel. Like the Shadow's human counterpart, the squirrel had startled, breaking its concentration. The only movement was everyone's steamy breath.

Penalynn pointedly said to the man belonging to the squirrel Shadow. "James, you're neglecting your job."

James bent down guiltily, raking the deck of cards into his hands. "I'm sorry, Madame. The night shift is long, so sometimes we pass the hours playing—"

"Not that." She pointed to the squirrel hunched among polished machines.

"Oh! Right!" James smacked his tobogganed forehead. His Shadow pushed a machine with tiny paws. Then, his magic caught the movement and sustained the instrument in a continuous spin. The squirrel scurried down the table, sliding, pumping, and twirling every instrument, magicking them to life. So long as his magic continued, the instruments could operate indefinitely.

The second servant had startled like James, but his Shadow had had the presence of mind to maintain his magic. The laboratory's glacial temperature never wavered.

The frozen laboratory hummed with magic and metal, soothing Penalynn until her nightmare faded from consciousness. The fox leaped onto a high stool before the countertop, shivering, though not from the cold. She hated the laboratory, but she hated more the itchy feeling of waiting in the hallway, so far away from Penalynn. So, she bore the tedious hours with the stoicism of a martyr.

Penalynn slid a tray toward herself. The items were exactly where she had left them the day before. She moved by rote, her exposed fingertips long used to the cold. She said without looking up, "Gentlemen, don't let me stop you from finishing your game."

The men grinned behind thick scarves, and James shuffled the deck, the sound inaudible against the noise of magicked contraptions all around.

CHAPTER
TWENTY-ONE

I T WAS AN AVERAGE morning in Greymere, the sky overcast as usual. Mist drizzled atop steepled homes as a breeze swished playfully through autumn leaves. Rowena stood at the foot of the famous castle doors, oblivious to the mist soaking her curls like a sponge and even more oblivious to the throng of people giving her ghostly Shadow a wide berth.

Upon entering society, with the blue cape of a Scholastic Apprentice shrouding her shoulders, the kindest in Greymere dismissed her Shadow as a mere quirk. But the dogmatic among them still wondered if she was an honest-to-goodness abomination. But no matter their opinions, Rowena's cape mollified most. After all, as a member of the Sceadwe, she was nobility—or at least impending nobility. Still, her Shadow posed a conundrum. Even with three years to ponder, most of the townspeople hadn't managed to sort through their conflicted feelings, and so they vacillated between fits of warm welcome and cold indifference.

Rowena never knew what she would get in any given encounter, so she had developed the habit of ignoring most people.

Standing before the castle that morning, her eyes traced intricate details within the door's surface. She liked to play a game with herself to see if she could find a new picture hidden in the woodgrain, something she hadn't noticed before. She lingered over the image of a dog nestled in looping ivy. It reminded her of her father's Shadow, its droopy ears looking soft to the touch even in wood. Just under its paw, in the lower left corner, she found encircled by a spoke of spiraling leaves, a rose the size of a baby's fist. Within a petal was a minuscule rendering of a bird no bigger than her pinky nail. She smiled, triumphant over her little find.

"*Ahem!*" Someone plucked the sleeve of her cape. "Spook, human beings are talking to you."

"Huh?" She noticed then that Titus had joined her. "Oh, hi."

"Not me." He rolled his eyes. "*Them.*"

Rowena turned to see Gloria Patterfold standing just within the passageway, waving. She was ringed by a circle of girls, beckoning in a way that made Rowena's skin prickle.

"That means she wants you to join them," Titus interpreted for her.

"I know what it means," she muttered, mystified. "But *why?*"

"Go find out."

He pressed the small of her back, steering her to the circle of girls. The circle opened for her to join. She clutched the strap of her bag like a ward against evil. Titus kept walking to meet some friends, leaving her to fend for herself.

"Good morning, Rowena," Gloria greeted. Her Shadow was a cream-colored cat cradled in her arms like a fluffy infant. Rowena knew Gloria primarily as Dr. Patterfold's daughter. Patterfold Potions was the only apothecary in town that Rowena could peruse with limited side-eye. It was her preferred shop. She'd seen Gloria there a few times after school, usually when Dr. Patterfold was gone on house calls.

"We were wondering if you want to join us after school. We're all meeting at Ronan's Pub."

Gloria's smile was so dazzling that it looked like Rowena spoke directly to her teeth. "I can't. I've got apprentice duties." The answer was reflexive. After a beat, she added, "Thanks, though."

"Okay, we'll just ask you now," another girl said. Her name was Anna, or Abigail, maybe. Rowena could never remember. The girl glanced at Ghost, then quickly looked away as if she'd seen something indecent, so Rowena didn't feel so bad for forgetting her name. The nameless girl lowered her voice like a secret. "Tell us, is Titus taken?"

"Has Titus taken what?"

The girls chuckled in a way that made Rowena squirm. "Is he *taken?*"

They all looked over to see Titus sitting on a low wall, chatting with a group of boys. A slight grin belied his awareness of being watched. He dragged his fingers through his sandy brown hair, causing it to swoop back, artfully disheveled. The girls all sighed at the gesture. Rowena considered buying him a comb.

"Ask him to come over here," the girl urged. "Gloria wants to tell him something."

"Shut up, Amber!" said Gloria. The cat in her arms hissed.

Rowena asked, "Tell him what?"

"Leave it," Gloria told the group, flicking her impossibly shiny hair. "She doesn't understand what we're talking about."

Rowena frowned. She didn't like someone insinuating she was ignorant, especially when she felt her ignorance so acutely.

Just then, an arm wrapped around her shoulder. "Alright, I've been gone too long, leaving you poor girls to fawn over a lesser Ashworth. Take heart, ladies. I'm back." Bruce Ashworth grinned devilishly around the circle of girls.

"What are you doing here?' Rowena asked, ducking under his arm and nearly stepping on his Shadow. Ghost greeted the raccoon with a pat on the head. "Aren't you supposed to be at school—in *Riven*?"

"It's a quick visit," he said, "What's this about you not understanding something? I didn't know there was anything our Scholastic Apprentice didn't know."

Gloria answered for her, "We were talking about boys."

"Ah, boys, I see." Bruce nodded sagely. "You know, Rowena, I'd be happy to give you a tutorial on the subject if you're interested."

Gloria huffed. Bruce's grin widened as he looked her up and down. "May I say, Gloria, I love what you've done with yourself."

Her icy blue eyes narrowed. "What's that supposed to mean?"

"That your beauty abounds more and more each day. My compliments to your Shadow."

"You're a pig." She sneered, then marched toward the courtyard, her hair flowing down her back like a blonde waterfall. The gaggle of girls bustled after her, firing hateful looks at Bruce as they went.

Rowena was left utterly baffled. Though she'd had a few year's practice by now, any conversation with more than one person tended to leave her lagging. She asked Bruce, "What did you mean about her Shadow?"

He sniffed, unapologetic. "Gloria Patterfold is what we call 'all magic and no looks.'"

"You think she manipulates her appearance?"

"Look at her. There's no way *that* exists in nature."

Rowena couldn't help but stare. Gloria's perfectly trim features had always reminded her of painted porcelain, embossed and polished to a shine. She frowned, feeling like a lump in comparison. "I think she likes Titus."

Bruce squeezed her shoulder. "Trust me. He doesn't feel the same."

His look was knowing and all too significant, causing Rowena's stomach to flip as if she'd been walking downstairs and missed a step.

"No wonder she gets such bad marks in class," she deflected, "She's using all her manipulation on her face. What a waste."

Just then, bells rang over the city, signaling the first class of the day. Bruce left her to join the students and Sages all rushing past in a hurry. But Rowena remained rooted to the spot. She felt naked, as if Bruce's words had cut her open, exposing her heart for anyone to see. She understood now what the girls had been talking about and cringed.

Titus bounded to her side as if summoned by her thoughts. "Hey, Spook! I heard Animation's in the courtyard today. I'll walk with you."

"Sure." She hugged her arms to her chest, afraid he might see what Bruce had uncovered.

CHAPTER
TWENTY-TWO

A T THE CENTER OF the grassy courtyard stood a green-cloaked teacher beneath an ancient oak tree. Sage Anura called the class to order, her froggy Shadow peeking from a pocket of her cape. Animation magic required plenty of room, and so Anura's classes were often held outside. Across the lawn lay intermittent piles of river rocks, smooth and round, stacked in miniature towers waist-high.

The Sage explained to the class, "Today's assignment is a simple one. Your Shadow will use animation to move the stones without touching them. I will grade your magic based on creativity and order. Lay them out in an organized fashion, and you will receive high marks. Scatter them about like a brute animal, and you will receive low marks. The more creative the magic, the higher the points. Got it?" The class nodded. "Good. Find a pile and get to work."

The students dispersed. Their Shadows stepped, hopped, or winged toward a pile, ready to exert their magic upon the stones. Ghost, however, followed Rowena under the wide-reaching branches of the oak tree. Rowena settled herself at the base of the trunk and then pulled a book from her bag.

In her first year of school, the Sages had required her Shadow to attempt all classwork. But, day after day, Ghost displayed not a single drop of magic. After a year's fruitless trying, the Sages eventually gave up, excusing Rowena from participation. She was still responsible for all reading, papers, and exams just like any other student—everything except actual magic-doing. Since nearly everything in class required magic, she was mostly left to herself. It turned out, however, that the extra time in class was essential for her to keep up with her Apprenticeship. Half of her work involved experimenting with non-magical potions, and the other half was spent assisting Penalynn. Ultimately, Ghost's incompetence afforded Rowena crucial study, which allowed her to outstrip every apothecary in town—something few of them took kindly.

She opened her book, enjoying the way the spine crackled, and settled into a chapter about extracting oil from herbs. Ghost lounged on the grass, picking clovers. An owl swooped in under the leafy canopy and landed on a low-hanging branch.

"What are you doing?" Titus asked.

"Reading," Rowena answered.

"But I need your help with the assignment." He pointed to the nearest stack of rocks.

She spoke from behind her book, "You're the one who can do magic, not me."

"You heard Sage Anura. She wants creativity. I need whatever obscure knowledge you've got rattling around that brain of yours."

"Just throw something and animate it."

"That's what everyone else is doing."

Sure enough, he was right. Their classmates showed little creativity. Most merely threw a pencil or coin and then animated the object midair to nudge the rocks to the ground.

"You know we could do it better." Titus nudged her foot with his, and Rowena's lips twitched behind her book. "Please, Spook. I need you."

She snapped the book shut. "Fine."

He grinned, looking far too much like his brother as he pulled her up to stand. "Okay, what do you have for me?" he said.

Her fingers tapped the book in a thoughtful strum. "Well, Atticus Wolder has a theory about unseen forces I've always wondered about."

"Who's Atticus Wolder?"

"A physic scholar."

"There's such a thing?"

Rowena looked him straight in the eye. "You know *I'm* training to be a physic scholar."

"Yeah, but I thought you were, you know, weird."

"Alright, good luck with your assignment." She turned on her heel and opened her book.

Titus caught her by her wrist before she could sit back down. "I meant unique, not weird. Amazing, really. Terrific. Brilliant! Please, tell me more about whatever you were just talking about."

"Invisible forces," she repeated, finding the subject much more interesting than any hurt feelings she might have. "Wolder says there are these non-magical forces happening all around, unseen."

"Aren't invisible forces just called magic?"

"Yes, but magic is performed by humans—or at least a human's Shadow. But Wolder writes about other forces that happen *non*-magically. There are some we already know about, like the wind. You can't see it, and no Shadow causes it, but it's an invisible force that affects the world around us."

Titus looked up at the thick canopy of orange oak leaves, noticing how they appeared to dance on their own. "Yeah, I get what you're saying."

Rowena added, "So, it's logical that animation could be used upon these forces..."

"Because animation enhances an already-occurring natural energy," he said as if quoting from a textbook. "Like animating the wind like this."

Rowena looked up at his Shadow who already hummed with magic. A few dancing leaves sprang from their branches, ripped by a tiny but sharp gust. The wind died the second the owl's magic stopped.

"Exactly," she said. "Animation enhances unseen energy, so long as you know *where* and *what* the energy is." With the tone of a teacher, she asked, "What would happen if I dropped this book?"

Titus answered like a dutiful student. "It would fall."

"Why?"

"Because things fall when you drop them."

"Yes, but *why?*"

"I...don't know." His brow furrowed, and he cocked his head. Like Rowena, he loved a good puzzle.

"Why wouldn't it fall up?" she asked, "Or to the right or left? Why do things fall straight down to the ground? Is something pulling it down, pulling everything down? Is there a force at work causing the book to fall?"

Titus's face lit up. "If there is an energy pulling the book down, then that energy can be touched with animation magic—"

"Since animation enhances already-occurring natural energy," she recited. Her Shadow may have been ignorant about magic, but Rowena had faithfully read every textbook assigned to her.

Titus turned to the pile of stones he was meant to rearrange. "So, you're saying there is an energy that is pulling these stones down so that they don't float away into the sky?"

"That's the theory. Wolder calls it *grounding*."

Titus's Shadow landed on the grass near the pile of rocks, his round eyes intent.

A few seconds passed. Rowena still mused over the theory, thinking out loud, "Of course, if there is an invisible energy pulling everything down, then it pulls *straight down*."

Titus didn't hear her, his concentration engrossed with the magic.

She continued, "Which, now that I think about it, I'm not sure that's going to—"

The ground rumbled under their feet. The pile of rocks vibrated and then toppled haphazardly to the ground. There was a terrible ripping sound, like a glacier cracking in spring, and an enormous tree limb smashed to the ground, burying the stones in a mound of limbs and leaves. The limb barely missed the owl, who stopped his magic to flee for safety.

Titus and Rowena had both dodged the falling limb and lay tumbled on the ground. They got to their feet, pulling leaves from each other's hair. Rowena had to retrieve Ghost who had been pinned beneath the limb. The Shadow appeared dazed but unhurt and utterly confused by what had just happened.

The entire class stared at the wreckage, struck dumb with shock. A tree branch as thick as a barrel and as long as a classroom had peeled from the trunk like a banana. It appeared as if a giant's hand had flattened half the tree. Even the ground had collapsed under the magic. A large crater was filled with leafy debris and, somewhere amongst the wreckage, Titus's assignment. Students and Shadows gathered in a semicircle, their mouths agape.

Sage Anura pushed students aside to reach Titus and Rowena. "WHAT IN BAZILEUS NAME HAVE YOU DONE?!" she shrieked.

With a guilty grimace, Titus said, "Well, you did say you wanted creativity. Though I understand if you need to deduct points for lack of 'organization.'"

Rowena looked around the courtyard. Most students had managed to complete their assignments. Their stones were laid in neat rows and tidy circles. She looked back at the sinkhole buried in half an oak tree. The other half of the tree was still upright, though shards of wood jutted from the trunk like jagged fangs.

"This tree is over two thousand years old!!" Sage Anura screamed. "This very castle was built around it to preserve its majesty!! And *you've...you've...SQUASHED IT!!!*" Her Shadow's froggy eyes looked near to popping.

"Perhaps it could be fixed?" Rowena suggested. Ghost cowered behind her shoulder, flippers wrapped over her smokey head as if another tree might squish her again at any moment.

"Oh yes," the Sage said sarcastically, "Let she-who-knows-nothing-about-magic tell us how such a disaster can be undone."

Titus took a step forward. "Hey! For someone who can't do magic, she sure knew enough to help—"

Rowena pinched the back of his arm, and he caught himself. He was the son of the Lord Overseer and, therefore, a town darling. His reputation could take a hit. But, despite being a Scholastic Apprentice, Rowena had zero social capital to spend.

The Sage's eyes narrowed, her tone formidable. "Help with *what*?"

"I helped pull Titus out of the way," Rowena said, "When the tree came down."

"Well done, Miss Faye. At least the teenage idiot was spared while an *ancient treasure* was destroyed!!"

They winced at the reality of what they'd done. The bell dismissed class, but Sage Anura leveled them with a finger. "Expect consequences. Both of you." Then she marched off the lawn like a soldier.

Their Shadows flew somberly overhead as they made their way to their next class: Manipulation. Thankfully, the rest of the day was much less exciting. Rowena sat at a desk near the back of the class, quietly reading. Ghost floated by a window, bored as always, and drawing doodles in the frost rimming the glass. When the final bell dismissed school for the day, Rowena and Ghost headed toward the Scholastic wing. The day was far from over. Her real work had not even begun.

CHAPTER
TWENTY-THREE

WHEN ROWENA ENTERED THE laboratory, she was greeted by the mechanical chorus of instruments bobbing and twirling as if alive. In an instant, frost sprung on her cloak like icy dew, but Ghost was impervious to the cold. She plopped atop a machine, enjoying how it bucked her like a horse. A young man sat hunched at the back of the room, dressed more for work outside in the dead of winter than for sitting inside a castle.

"Hi, Tom," said Rowena through chattering teeth. "Just dropping off some samples. Weren't you here yesterday?"

He shrugged under his heavy coat. "I need the extra pay." A grey ferret sat on a pillow beside him.

A wall of glass cabinets spanned the length of the room, housing a few thousand compartments, each containing labeled vials and rolls of parchment covered in Rowena's handwriting. From her bag, Rowena pulled out identical vials. The bottles rattled in her shivering hands.

"Wanna borrow my coat?" Tom asked.

"No, I'll be quick." She opened a cabinet door and winced. A gust of freezing air hit her head-on. Tom winced in sympathy, but his magic persisted. She deposited the vials and parchment into empty compartments, double-checking everything was labeled properly, then closed the door and hurried across the room where it was warmer. Though even there, metal contraptions were frosted like cakes.

"You're here alone?" she asked, "How can you do both magics simultaneously?"

"Years of practice. Madame Scholastic pays well, especially for double duty. Besides, looks like I need to take my chance at a cushy job while I have it. Those cabinets are getting full. Rumor is, you're coming to the end of it."

Rowena grabbed empty vials and fresh parchment from a shelf. "To the end of my part, at least. Who knows when Penalynn will finish? See you later, Tom."

She was eager to leave the laboratory. Across the hall, the fireplace enticed her with the promise of thawing her poor hands. Penalynn had converted her private library into a second office so her apprentice could work close by. Much like at home, Rowena seized ownership of the place, altering the library for her inquisitive purposes. Bookcases were crammed not only with Penalynn's vast collection of books (surprisingly, most of them were novels) but also with all manner of jars, plants, and odd equipment. The balcony blossomed like a cramped garden overflowing with exotic fauna. Rowena had even repurposed the old bathtub, filling it with rich black soil from which a creeping vine spiraled up and over the balcony ledge. At the center of the room sat a large table littered with pens, paper, dried leaves, crushed shells, used matchsticks, and an odd-looking instrument made of bulbous glass.

Rowena dropped her bag with a heavy thud. "Ghost, I need you to learn magic so you can make my bag lighter. One of these days, it's going to snap my back."

As usual, Ghost ignored her. She flitted across the room and tapped on the balcony door. Rowena was used to her Shadow's eccentricities and obliged the unspoken demand. "Here you go," she said, propping open the door. From either ignorance or indifference, Rowena's work bored Ghost. She spent most of her time in the castle gazing out over the city.

The sliding door was ajar, and a voice called from Penalynn's office. "Don't get too comfortable in there! I have work for you."

"Hi, Penalynn!" Rowena called back.

The door slid open all the way, and the fox entered, followed by the Scholastic herself. Quick as she could, Rowena swiped the nearest leatherbound book and threw it hard, aiming for Penalynn's head. Penalynn didn't even blink. She tucked her chin an inch and let the book whizz past her nose. It smacked the wall and fell to the carpet with a resigned *whump*.

"Now you're just getting desperate," Penalynn sighed with a disappointed air, wholly unfazed by the assault.

The fox, however, jumped onto the cluttered table and leveled Rowena with a stern scowl. Rowena met the fox's look and mouthed, "Sorry," though her teasing smile was hardly apologetic.

Penalynn asked, "Is that one hundred yet?"

Rowena dropped her smile. She approached a piece of paper tacked to the wall where a host of pencil marks lined in tidy rows. "Ninety-eight," she said, adding a tally. She pointed her pencil at Penalynn. "One of these days, I'm going to see your magic in action."

"Aren't you bored of this enterprise yet?"

"It's a matter of justice!" Rowena cried, "Magic is completely wasted on your Shadow. If I could do magic, I would never lift a finger again. My Shadow would do everything. I'd even brush my hair with magic."

"How would you manage that?"

Rowena sat at her desk and leaned back in the chair. "I'm smart. I'd figure it out."

"Speaking of..." Penalynn sauntered over with her arms crossed like a scolding nanny. "I caught wind of quite an impressive feat today. I had to go downstairs and see it for myself. The famous oak in the heart of the castle has been destroyed—a pretty unusual feat for animation magic, don't you think?"

Rowena suddenly became very interested in the wood grain of her desk.

"I heard your boyfriend did it."

"He's just a friend," Rowena corrected, feeling her neck and cheeks flush with heat.

Penalynn mused like a cat playing with its snack. "Did you loan him my copy of Wolder's book? *The Theorem of Non-Magical Forces*, I think it's called. Or did he somehow come up with the idea all by himself?"

Rowena wilted. "I only *mentioned* the concept to Titus."

"So, you did help him!" Penalynn confirmed with equal parts triumph and anger. "Rowena, the Sceadwe allows you to wear that cape, but they could just as easily take it away. Your position is tenuous. You must never forget that. I've a mind to fire you myself."

Rowena looked away, feeling embarrassed like a spanked child. She worked tirelessly to win Penalynn's respect, her approval a scarce and fleeting prize. But in a moment, she'd lost it, showing off to Titus.

Mercifully, Penalynn added, "Since you helped make the mess, your expertise can clean it up. Where's that healing sap you made a while back?"

Rowena recognized a life raft when she saw one. She latched on, eager to rescue herself from trouble and win back Penalynn's esteem. "Let me make you a fresh batch. That stuff doesn't keep well." She flipped open a well-worn journal and scanned a complicated recipe in her own handwriting. "I've added a few tweaks to the compound, which I've been meaning to try."

"So, you destroyed the tree to show off your potion skills?"

"Yeah. I was getting too popular with the locals, so I thought I'd color my reputation a bit."

Penalynn snorted. Rowena dashed about the room, gathering ingredients and feeling grateful for Penalynn's laugh. It was a rare sound and meant she wasn't in nearly as much trouble as she should be. However, she couldn't be sure if it was her relationship with Penalynn or Titus's relationship with the Overseer that protected them from harsh punishment. It was probably best not to ask.

She joined Ghost on the balcony, but only to tear a few leaves from the wild vine in the bathtub, making a mental note to prune it soon. It was making a move for Sage Maudvale's office again. It liked his window and tended to worm its way through a chink in the frame if left unattended. The Sage was a rather fussy fellow. He allowed no spots or smudges in his office, manipulating the walls to an unnatural white. There was no tolerance for quizzical vines.

She went back inside, thoughtful as she ground the dry ingredients with a mortar and pestle. "Why was it so easy for Titus to magic the grounding energy? I'd only given him the barest explanation."

"The Sages tell me your friend has a pretty strong Shadow," said Penalynn.

Rowena wasn't convinced. "That's it? Just raw power?" She sprinkled the powdered ingredients into a clear cylinder and then set it onto the instrument of blown glass. Penalynn handed her a box of matches. She lit the wick, and soon, steam gathered in droplets within the looping glass tubing.

"I've always believed *imagination* was more important in the magic process than mere power," said Penalynn. "Obviously, Titus could picture the invisible force in a way that worked. Not just any mind can do that. I'm impressed. He's creative."

Rowena gathered the wet ingredients next, shielding the jar of pickled slugs so Penalynn wouldn't see. She got squeamish when it came to Rowena's "juicy specimens," as she called them.

Penalynn continued, "I imagine the Sceadwe will be eager to have him in Riven next year. The university loves Shadows like his."

Rowena stirred the ingredients into a paste and added the droplets from the glass tubing at the very last. After a good stirring, she poured the concoction into a bottle, corked it, and then handed the potion to Penalynn. "This is a concentrated tree sap. As soon as it's applied, reassemble the pieces of the tree and have someone manipulate the sugar particles so they bond properly. You'll need to find someone who can tell the difference between sugar particles and acid. Otherwise, you'll poison the whole thing. If done right, the tree should heal nicely in time." She shook the bottle in front of the fox, enticing. "Care to do the magical honors?"

"Nice try," Penalynn swiped the jar from her. The fox's tail shook like a rattlesnake's.

It was her ninety-ninth failed attempt. Rowena added another tally to her sheet.

Penalynn asked, "Have you finished your interviews yet?"

Rowena knew the change in subject was meant to be a jab. She frowned, grumpy at the reminder. "No, not yet."

The most significant aspect of her apprentice duties involved interviewing every citizen in Greymere, or at least everyone who volunteered. Since volunteers were compensated in gold, and Greymere's social scene was fueled mostly by gossip, nearly everyone signed up to be interviewed. A memorable encounter with the Scholastic Apprentice and her eerie Shadow was juicy social currency. In only three years, Rowena had interviewed a couple thousand people. She hated the process. Even with constant practice, she still felt inept when it came to people. Thankfully, she had only a handful of interviews left. Her goal was to be done before the Festival of Shadows in a few weeks.

"I need another sample," said Penalynn. "He hasn't volunteered, but no matter. I need this one. He's a hermit, apparently, named Craefog, and he has quite the reputation. I'm surprised I haven't heard of him before now."

"No way." Rowena shook her head. "That guy is supposed to be insane. There's no way I can convince my father to let me wander into the woods to interview some deranged lunatic."

"How about a deal? You do the ones you have scheduled for today and then Craefog, and I'll let you be done. No more interviews after that."

The hope of finishing early proved far too tantalizing for Rowena, so she agreed.

Penalynn said, "I want a full work-up on him. If what I hear is true, he will be pivotal in our findings."

"And what exactly is it we're finding?"

"You still haven't figured it out? I thought you were supposed to be clever."

"You won't tell me what it is we're studying!" It was a well-worn accusation in a years-long argument. "You hole up in that laboratory and won't share your results."

"I need you unbiased," Penalynn said for the hundredth time. "Objectivity is crucial for information gathering. I promise I will show you my findings as soon as I'm finished."

Rowena didn't argue but couldn't help but wonder aloud, "You're a Scholastic who doesn't use magic, but you interview people about it. Does it have anything to do with why you were kicked out here to Greymere?"

Penalynn startled. "Excuse me?"

"Everyone knows you were banished here. You just said so yourself that the

Sceadwe prefers people with powerful Shadows."

"No. My work is not why they sent me here." Penalynn grimaced but would say no more.

Rowena tried another track. "Is it because you're a jilted lover of the king, and he cast you out here to keep from causing drama in court?"

"*WHAT?!*"

The fox snarled, thoroughly offended.

Rowena held up her hands. "You have me interviewing the whole town. I hear things."

"That's what people say about me?" Penalynn marveled.

Rowena was tempted to giggle at Penalynn's agog face, but she knew better. "It's not the most popular theory, but it's definitely my favorite."

"You tell those gossiping fools directly from me that it is *untrue*."

"You've met the king, though, right?"

Penalynn dabbed her forehead with her cloak, seeming oddly breathless. "Yes."

"I hear his Shadow, the Bazileus, is more powerful than the entire High Consul combined. Do you think he uses physic to make his magic so powerful? Like Titus did with the tree?"

"No." Penalynn's tone made it clear the conversation was over. "I want Craefog's samples by the end of the week."

"Done. But how am I supposed to find him?"

"Ask your boyfriend. It appears he owes you a favor," Penalynn said, then turned to leave. "Skip class if you need to; I'll give my permission." In the doorway, she stopped and held up the potion bottle. "Do something like you did to that tree again, and I'll fire you. Got it?"

It was as if the temperature had plummeted like the laboratory across the hall. There was not a trace of jest or banter in her voice. This was a promise. Rowena was shamed, calling to mind the moment they first met, just after she had burned the festival down.

"Yes, madame," she said.

She waited until she heard the door to the laboratory close before hoisting her bag with a groan. "Come on, Ghost! Let's get these interviews over with."

CHAPTER
TWENTY-FOUR

BRAN HEADED WEST, UP and down narrow alley stairs, doubling and redoubling from the road's many switchbacks as it hugged a jagged cliff. The city of Riven was ancient, founded upon the Bazileus's sacred mountain. Buildings stacked upon buildings, the mountain adorned Riven like a skirt, its folds trailing into the valley like jagged lace.

Bran traversed Riven's poorest neighborhood, coined Cheapton, the oldest and most dilapidated part of the mountain. Some dwellings were mere alcoves hewn, no doubt, from primitive generations of bygone eras. The further into Cheapton he went, the narrower the roads became until they were just a maze of alleyways and broken ladders, homes piled upon one another like forgotten trash. The air hung thick with the stench of poverty.

Around his bicep wrapped a snake. Every Black Guardian's Shadow was the same, a serpent varying in color only. His Shadow's bright orange scales shone like a badge, signifying his employment to the king.

He stopped before a tired-looking door. "This is it," he said to his partner, Rankin.

Rankin was a man of gristle and guile, his snake black as shale. "My money says this 'uns a runner," he said with a hungry grin. He loved it when they ran.

"Just keep your mouth shut and let me talk," said Bran. His knuckles rapped

117

on the door, and Rankin's smile turned manic.

The door cracked only an inch to reveal a sliver of a woman, one eye and half her mouth visible. "What?" Her question sounded like an accusation.

"Good morning," Bran greeted. "We're looking for a man named Patrick Breagadhor."

"Who?"

"You might know him by the name Patrick Nobble. We were told he used to live here."

"'Trick don't live here no more."

"Do you know where I can find him?"

She muttered some instructions and then shut the door. In a neighborhood like this, men with snakes around their arms were bad luck. Death always seemed to follow them.

They turned down an alley and then another, winding back and forth along the narrow streets until they came to a dead end. The woman had sent them to the underside of Wrackington Bridge, comprised mostly of hanging tarps and heaps of garbage. A homeless camp. Bran consulted the nearest person he could find awake. The filth-smeared boy pointed to a lump leaning against a tower of empty apple crates.

"Trick!" the kid shouted. The lump of blankets stirred.

Rankin walked over and gave the lump a kick. A man emerged. Bran knelt before him, urging his nostrils to close against the smell. The man called "Trick" rubbed his fist against his eye socket. Bran suspected he was either inebriated or hung over. But, seeing two snake-clad men standing over him, he sobered quickly. He sprang to his feet with surprising litheness, threw his blanket over Bran, and then sprinted. Bran gagged as he emerged from the blanket.

Why do they run? his Shadow thought.

Beside him, Rankin cackled with pleasure. He grabbed the snake around his arm and hurled him with practiced precision. The snake's magic stretched his body like a grasping python. Nobble was halfway up a flight of stairs when the snake caught him by the ankles. He fell face-first, breaking his nose on a moldy stone step.

Bran jogged to catch up. "Mr. Nobble," he said to the man who attempted to staunch the blood flowing down his lips and chin. "Are you the one who's been going around by the name 'Patrick Breagadhor?'"

"Uhh." Despite his bound ankles and bleeding face, the man attempted to crawl away, inching like an enormous caterpillar.

Rankin's boot pinned Nobble's neck to the ground. "We'll take that as a yes."

"Sir, you are under arrest," said Bran.

"What for?" Nobble squeaked, "What've I done?"

Rankin wrenched him to his feet. His snake returned to his previous size and slithered back around his arm. "You've got yourself a ripe reputation for being a king-killing, Wandrel-savior type, Patrick."

"That?! That was nothing. It was a rag, was all! A fake! I lied to them Wandrels!"

Despite having emerged from a pile of trash, Patrick Nobble was well-dressed and clean-shaven, although greasy, like an oil slick come to life. His clothes were woven in the intricate style of The Wandering, though it was clear Nobble himself was not a native member of the tribe. The garments were at best borrowed, most likely stolen, and long since laundered. No amount of artful style could distract from the impoverished ilk about him.

"I swear, it's not me!"

"That's for the king to decide," Bran said, shackling his wrists.

"Don't go callin' yourself the Wandrel's Shadowless," snarled Rankin, "Bad for your health."

"But look, I can't be! I've got a Shadow!"

An acid-green lizard emerged from his coat, eager to show himself and secure Nobble's freedom. It reminded Bran of his own Shadow, back before he had taken the mandatory form of a snake.

"I never meant it," Nobble sputtered, blood flinging with his spit. "I was only fooling those Wandering high-ups, honest! Thought it'd be a lucrative gig. Get some food and a bed, and all I had to do was pretend to be their whatever-you-call-it. Change my name, hide my Shadow. It was easy. But I was never going to go through with anything, I swear! Just a short-term gig. I left soon after—didn't even go with them when they took their long walk north. I never woulda' hurt the king or no one, I swear it!"

Bran pulled him along by the cuffs down the alley the way he'd come. "It's clear you've got a Shadow. Perhaps the king will be merciful."

"Or he'll kill you like the rest of them," Rankin countered. "Teach you not to lie."

They escorted Nobble to the palace, taking a longer route to avoid the wealthier neighborhoods. A perk of a high-status station was being able to pretend that things such as tramps and assassins didn't exist.

By the time they made it to the palace, Nobble's whimpering protests had lagged. When they stopped outside the throne room, he muttered feebly, "But I've got a Shadow." But then the doors opened, and someone emerged to announce, "The king will see you now."

CHAPTER
TWENTY-FIVE

PENALYNN WAS ABOUT TO enter the Hall of Sceadwe for her weekly meeting with the High Consul when a voice called from the end of the corridor. "Ah, good. I was told I would find you here," breathed Sage Anura, marching down the corridor with her Shadow in hand. "I hear you provided a potion to mend the tree in the courtyard."

Penalynn confirmed and added, "As well as a crew to help fix it. It's a big tree."

"Why did you ask *her* to make a potion and not one of the apothecaries in town? Or better yet, one of the many Sages in the castle?"

Penalynn entered the Hall of Sceadwe, and Anura followed. "Because she is a high-ranking member of the Sceadwe and more gifted than any apothecary in town. I knew Rowena's potion was the only solution that could accomplish such a task, and, I might add, it worked! It's impossible to tell where the break was. I involved her because of her *ability*, not her culpability. Everyone knows it was the Ashworth boy who did it. And you should know better than anyone. It happened in your class."

They reached the dais, where an attendant sat beside the Silver Glass, ready to receive a message from Riven should someone magically appear in the frame. He passed the time reading.

Sage Anura pressed, "Several students saw her plotting with the Overseer's son when it happened. I believe she was just as responsible, if not more so!"

"The tree is mended, Anura. What do you want from me?"

"I want consequences!" shouted the Sage, gesturing with the hand still holding her Shadow. The frog's eyes bulged. "She tricked him to wreak havoc. Do not dismiss this, Penalynn. Everyone knows not all is right with that apprentice of yours, and I have sat silent for years as you have inflicted her upon this town with those impertinent interviews!"

Penalynn turned to the Silver Glass attendant, who had abandoned his novel to watch the unfolding drama between them. "Give us a minute alone, please." Reluctantly, he left, sour to miss such a show.

The Sage demanded, "That girl is polluting the dignity of this castle and ought to be reported to the Sceadwe."

"She *has* been reported. Multiple times, actually. And the High Consul, in their wisdom, dismissed every complaint. Say one more thing against my pupil, and I will strip you of your measly position."

Sage Anura, being a head taller, peered down her nose at Penalynn. "Only the Sceadwe has the authority to fire me."

"I AM the Sceadwe here!" Penalynn's voice echoed off stone walls.

But a part of her wavered. What if the Sage—and the rest of Greymere, for that matter—were correct? What if there really was something sinister in Rowena's quirks? She had tasked the girl to question every citizen in Greymere, giving her ominous Shadow the opportunity to touch and tinge the entire town. Many had made complaints against the girl. In fact, the Myth Keeper himself had been the first to do so. But so long as she had a Scholastic's protection, Rowena went unrestricted. Why would she protect someone who so clearly—

"How dare you!" Penalynn gasped. "*How dare you use persuasive magic upon me!!*"

The Sage blanched, caught in the act of illegal magic. Her frog dove for safety inside her green cape. "But you weren't using intuition," she whispered.

Nearby, a purple banner hung against the wall. Penalynn reached for its silk cord and, with a mighty tug, ripped it free. The fox's long-held magic released like a faucet, animating the rope's movement. It wriggled as if it were alive. The cord struck out like a lasso, looping round and round the Sage in seconds, pinning her arms to her sides. The frog belly-flopped onto the floor.

Penalynn's magic surged like angry rapids, urging the cord to crush. The release of power felt euphoric. She growled, stepping toe-to-toe with the Sage. "I don't need magic to know which are my own thoughts and which are not."

The rope constricted painfully. "Madame, I'm sorry, I didn't—"

"You didn't think you would be caught!" Penalynn's magic tightened.

The frog sagged against the floor, her eyes bulging as the woman's breath choked.

Penalynn purred, "I could rip your job from you, and no one in Riven would bat an eye. They neither know who you are nor care about your future. It is by my sheer *mercy* that I don't end your career this very instant."

"I'm sorry—I'm sorry. Please, I beg you..."

There was a flash of yellow in their periphery. Penalynn looked down the center aisle to see she and the Sage were not alone after all. The canary landed on the Myth Keeper's shoulder; his grey eyes locked on hers. Her throat constricted. At once, the fox's magic ceased; her power extinguished like a candle. The silk cord fell to the floor, dead. Sage Anura breathed in gasps, wincing as her bruised ribs expanded.

"Your indiscretion is forgiven," Penalynn said in a raspy voice. Her mouth was suddenly dry.

"Thank you, Madame." The Sage scooped up her Shadow and scurried down the center aisle, past the Myth Keeper, and out of the hall. The doors banged shut behind her.

Penalynn dropped onto the front bench and raised a quivering hand to cover her mouth. Footsteps clicked against stone, steady and measured. The Myth Keeper joined her on the bench with a swish of his black cape.

He spoke in a light tone, almost amused, "Oh, all of it."

"What?"

"You were going to ask me how much of that did I see, and I'm afraid I saw all of it."

Her hand shook as she wiped her face, outrage swapped for shame. "I over-reacted."

"Bah. During my university days, I was on the receiving end of a Scholastic thrashing or two. Oddly enough, it made me respect the Scholastics all the more."

"Respect or fear?"

"Is there a difference?"

Penalynn exhaled through her nose. "Are you going to tell the High Consular?"

"Ha! No. My tattling days are over. I think you could have suffocated that Sage back there, and the Consul wouldn't even blink." He was right. But somehow that only doubled her guilt.

A voice boomed behind them. "Am I late?" Roderick Ashworth entered the hall with his giant wolf loping at his side.

The Myth Keeper rose to meet him, and they both ascended the dais. Penalynn, however, hung behind. Shame clung to her like cobwebs. She'd lost her temper and done the unthinkable without a moment's consideration. Her skin crawled with self-revulsion. Her Shadow, however, basked in the aftermath of magic, finally satiated after so much restraint. She practically purred with satisfaction, as if she'd just enjoyed a feast after years of fasting. With half her soul elated, Penalynn's regret clung all the more. She shrunk in on herself, cringing.

"Madame Scholastic?" said Roderick.

His wolf growled with magic, and the silver glass swirled to reveal the magnified image of High Consular Webley. His silver robe glittered, and because of the severe angle, no matter his mood, he always seemed to scowl.

Penalynn schooled her face as she stepped up to the silver glass. But she was too lost in her thoughts to notice the initial greetings and what followed. Her attention was only caught when the Consular's tone became barbed. "The Wandrel caravan usually spends the first half of autumn outside of Riven," he said, "but they left early this year. We haven't heard word of their migration since they left."

"The Wandering are here, sir," said Roderick. "Arrived outside the bounds of Greymere just a few days ago, in their usual location. They went a different route, which brought them quicker than usual."

"How do you know this?"

Roderick hesitated. "I, uh...have a man on the inside."

"A trustworthy man? Who is it?"

"I trust him." Although Roderick grimaced oddly. "He's Wyrian if that's what you're asking."

"Yes, good. That's good foresight, Overseer. The king has asked us to keep tabs on The Wandering of late, but it's difficult as they never keep still. Did your man mention their reason for traveling faster?"

"No."

"If he can find out, let me know. Also, have him keep his ears open for anything regarding that Shadowless character of theirs."

The Myth Keeper interjected. His canary puffed its feathers the way it always did when the Myth Keeper spoke to someone he deemed important. "Has someone emerged who fits the prophesy?"

The face in the silver glass said casually, "There was a recent candidate, but the king has already seen to his execution." The Consular brushed his hand as if the notion were an unsavory bug. "It's the same every handful of years. Someone shows up who they claim to be their Shadowless, we hear of it, and the king has whoever it was arrested and killed. You'd think they'd get better at hiding their seditious icons."

Penalynn entered the conversation then. "Was the person without a Shadow?"

"Of course not."

"Then why—?"

"It is not our business to question the king, madame. Roderick, have your spy keep on the lookout. I want word of any mention of the Shadowless from those heretics—even if it's just talk."

When they'd finished their meeting the Consular's face dissolved, and the silver glass resumed its flat gleam once more. The Myth Keeper exited the hall through a side door, while Penalynn and Roderick walked back the way they'd come in.

"I thought you liked The Wandering," she asked him as they walked down the center aisle. "Why would you place a spy among them?"

Roderick sighed. "I didn't."

"You said you have a man on the inside."

"I do. But I didn't put him there." He stopped before the wall of statues, and Penalynn turned her back on them to look at Roderick directly. He said, "It's Bruce."

"Your son? I thought he was in Riven at university."

Roderick spread his arms and dropped them to his side, at a loss. "Apparently, he dropped out a while ago, only I've just found out. He's been living with The Wandering for months."

"As a spy?"

The wolf shook his shaggy mane, and Roderick let out a humorless laugh. "No. As a love-sick idiot."

Penalynn's eyebrows raised nearly to her hairline. "He dropped out of university for a *Wandering girl?*"

"Like I said, he's being an idiot," grimaced Roderick. "Fern and I are trying to convince him to go back and finish his education. But now..."

Penalynn finished for him, "Your lover-boy just turned Sceadwe-appointed spy."

"Fern is going to kill me."

"Maybe she'll be happy to welcome a daughter-in-law?"

"I know my son. It's not as serious as that. This is just one more instance of him choosing immediate pleasure over responsibility."

"Maybe this is perfect. He gets whatever this is out of his system, and the Sceadwe gets the information it wants. Although, he ought to be careful. The king could misunderstand his presence in their camp and do something rash."

"Bruce is Wyrian. Besides, no one would mistake my son for a prophetic figure. I'm surprised they haven't kicked him out of their camp already, if not from sheer irritation. Any advice on convincing my wife that our son's idea to forgo his education in order to shack up with a Wandering girl is not only a *good* idea but somehow in service to the Sceadwe?"

She winced with sympathy. "Good luck."

He touched the door but paused before opening it. "By the way, the tree in the courtyard...?"

Penalynn held up both hands. "I've already seen to its reconstruction."

"Thanks for that. But as to *who*—"

"It was my apprentice and your son," she confirmed, and he nodded, having heard the same. "I'd go easy on him, though. I'm pretty sure mine was more to blame than yours."

His expression darkened. "Right."

Penalynn chuckled. "Rough day for the Ashworth boys."

"Bazileus help me."

CHAPTER
TWENTY-SIX

ROWENA STOOD ON THE sidewalk outside the mail menagerie, one hand on the door handle. After a girding breath, she entered, the shop bell tinkling. Behind the counter, Greymere's mailman stood before a wall of cubbies. Each cubby contained an animal, most of them some species of bird. A crow sat on the counter while the mailman read out loud the address on an envelope. A large brown moth fluttered above the bird, his magic inaudible so as not to startle. The bird took the envelope in its beak, then winged out an open window. The mailman whistled, and another crow hopped from a cubby.

Rowena approached the counter, and the man grumbled, "All my dogs are out. Only letters going the rest of the day."

"Oh, no," she said politely, "I'm here for your interview."

It was then he noticed her blue cape. He muttered, "Forgot that was today."

Ghost peeked from behind Rowena's bag, and the man's countenance hardened. Rowena pretended not to notice. "Can I set my things down here?" He nodded, and she unrolled a kit comprised of parchment, a pen, two clean vials, a jar of apothecary's alcohol, a packet of needles, cotton, and most importantly of all, a fat, jingling coin purse.

"What's all this? A doctor's visit or an interview?" he asked.

Rowena ignored the question and jumped straight into the interview. "First,

I must verify your name. Are you Nester Brown?"

Nester Brown grunted his assent.

"How old are you, Mr. Brown?" she asked, then scribbled his answer. They continued through demographic questions, his answers perfunctory but easy enough. She checked off the questions one by one. "Alright, that's all settled. Let's move on to the main portion. Does your daily activity involve performing magic?"

His eyebrows constricted at the absurdity of the question. "I've got a Shadow, haven't I?"

"So, yes." She scribbled. "On an average day, about how many acts of magic does your Shadow perform?"

Behind him, a raven shrieked from inside its cubby. Mr. Brown answered, "I don't see why the Sceadwe needs to know that."

"The Sceadwe is not asking; Scholastic Penalynn Graft is."

"She's a *member* of the Sceadwe, isn't she?" he asked. Then he caught sight of Ghost again and quickly looked away, his frown furrowing into a scowl.

"This is not a mandated study. You volunteered. If you want, you can withdraw your commitment, and I will leave you alone."

"I had no idea you'd be asking such personal questions! It's not right, askin' about people's magic."

"Alright." She gathered her supplies as if she wasn't bothered in the slightest. She made a show of picking up the coin purse, jostling it so the gold tinkled inside. Nester Brown's face fell, and she reminded him, "I'm only allowed to pay those who've completed the exam. Scholastic's orders."

Clearly, he was torn. After an amusing show of indecision involving several sighs and muttered complaints, he released a gritty cough of surrender. The reward of two whopping gold coins consoled his indignation, and he grumbled, "About two hundred."

"What's that?"

"On an average mail day, my Shadow does about two hundred bouts of magic. Give or take."

Rowena jotted his answer. "Wow, that's a lot."

"Well, lots of mail comes through here in a day."

Rowena read from the sheet: "Does your Shadow prefer the exterior or interior magics? Or both?"

"What?" The lines of his forehead crinkled almost comically.

"Persuasion and intuition are interior magics—performed in the mind. Animation and manipulation are exterior magics—done visibly on physical objects," she explained.

"I'm a mailman, aren't I?" he asked as if it were obvious. He gestured to the menagerie behind him, where a choir of squawks, bleats, and grunts rang in discordant chatter. "All day long, I'm persuadin' this lot where to go and what to do."

"Right." She scribbled her notes. Then, more out of curiosity than data collection, she asked, "Are some animals easier to persuade than others? I mean, would a big one, like a horse, be more difficult to magic than something small, like a mouse?"

"Size's got nothing to do with it," said Mr. Brown. "Most of the big ones are the easiest, almost like they were made for taming. Dogs, for instance. Nearly every dog I've worked with practically *wants* me to bend his mind. Especially the big ones. I use them for packages. Very obedient minds, the big dogs. Birds are similar if you catch them young enough. But then there's other species that it depends on the animal. Goats are good for heavy loads. But I had one once that was like tryin' to persuade a cat. Impossible. Kept throwin' packages in the river!"

Her curiosity was piqued, and she wished she could ask more. But she needed to keep to her schedule. And so she swallowed her questions and moved on. The mailman's apprehension eased as they made their way down the line of questions. When she'd finished, she took a deep breath before unstopping the vials. With forced nonchalance, she said, "Now all that's left is a sample of blood and hair, and we'll be through."

Nester Brown pulled himself upright, having expected the request. Word in Greymere got around about this part of the Scholastic interviews. He wagged a gnarled finger. "Now see here. I've given this some thought, and I refuse on principle. It ain't right you asking for somethin' like that."

Rowena expected the response. Even the most accommodating volunteers became provoked at this final portion of the exam. Unfortunately, Penalynn insisted the physical samples were the most necessary portion of the study.

Gaining steam, he continued, "Where do you get off asking a grown man for his *blood*?! And all casual-like, as if you were asking for a cup of tea. What's that Scholastic doing with all the town's blood and hair? Nothing good, I'll tell you. And let me tell you another thing—"

But Rowena never did find out what that other thing was because, just then, she pulled out two shining gold coins and placed them beside each vial. Like a kettle removed from the stove, Mr. Brown's complaint lost steam. Gold reflected in his pale, heavily wrinkled eyes.

She tapped a coin with her fingernail. "Come on, Mr. Brown. You can do it."

He relented, though he muttered curses the entire time. Thankfully, years s of practice had made Rowena quick. It took less than a minute. She corked the vials, one with blood, one with hair, then slid the gold across the counter with a professional "Thank you." Without a word, the coins disappeared into his vest pocket, and he was back to his animals and ignoring her like before.

Rowena had to pull Ghost away from the wall of cubbies. The Shadow had found a floppy-eared rabbit and nuzzled her smokey face against its fur, relishing the softness. After that, the mailman looked at his rabbit as if considering giving it a bath. Rowena had to tuck Ghost under her arm to get her to leave. The bell jingled its goodbye much too cheerfully, she thought, for such a proprietor.

Walking down the street, she did feel some relief to have another one done. The interview had been less than pleasant, but she didn't mind the cranky volunteers. There was something about their unveiled frankness she could respect. After countless interviews, she'd learned that the worst aggression was wrapped in subtler packaging, like a present hiding venom inside.

Her second volunteer twittered like a little girl. Her Shadow bounced like an excitable cotton ball atop twiggy legs. The woman even erupted into giggles of all things when Rowena drew blood. "I'm sorry to laugh," she sputtered hilariously, "Only I told old man Crabbit my interview was coming up, and he went on and on about how your hands are as cold as a corpse. I knew he was teasing me, but what with your funny little Shadow, I wasn't so sure. His interview was a few months ago. Maybe he was telling the truth? What with all those rumors—well, you've heard them, I'm sure. But look at you, sitting there as whole as anybody and with warm hands after all!" She giggled as if it were all a joke.

Rowena's humiliation rang in her ears as if the woman's giggles had been clanging symbols, shame reverberating from the top of her head to the soles of her feet.

The one after that was nearly a waste of time. The volunteer asked, "What do most people say?" after each question. So self-conscious, she changed her answers multiple times over for fear of seeming "abnormal." Rowena drew question marks beside the dubious answers, including the woman's age, which she claimed was thirty-five, but the backs of her hands were mottled like an old woman's.

After that was the dishwasher at Ronan's pub, which was easy enough. But the town duster, who lived in a shed by the river, made such a fuss that Rowena was forced to hide Ghost behind a tree several yards away.

"It's still too close!" he cried, eyeing the tree as if her Shadow might jump out and curse him then and there.

Rowena's chest pricked painfully, her Shadow's distance tugging at the invisible string that bound her soul together. "She can't go any further," she said. Still, the man grumbled insults until Rowena was tempted to throw the questionnaire and the man into the river—and perhaps kick his Shadow for good measure.

And so, that's how she arrived at the final house of the day, weary and trembling. She banged on the door, eager to be admitted. The door swung open, and Ghost shot inside as if from a cannon.

"Hey, Spook!" Titus greeted, dodging under her Shadow. He took one look at Rowena, with her cape on crooked and her hair frizzing, and wrinkled his nose in sympathy. "Interviews got the better of you again?"

CHAPTER
TWENTY-SEVEN

"Madame Apprentice, is it time for my interview at last?" Fern welcomed Rowena by wrapping her willowy arms around her like a blanket smelling of lavender and comfort. Long fingers smoothed the velvet cape across her back in a way that sent pleasant tingles rippling down her spine. Fern's mothering touch was exactly what Rowena needed after such a day.

Titus led the way to the kitchen, where Bruce rummaged in the pantry.

"Rod!" Fern called, "Rowena's here!"

Boots tromped down the stairs, and the kitchen seemed to shrink when Roderick and his Shadow entered. "I hear we've got important Scholastic business to do," he boomed in greeting.

"I saved the best for last," Rowena said. Though her smile quaked in the Overseer's presence.

Titus scoffed. "Hey! What about me?!" His interview had been Rowena's first, followed by her father and Bruce. She had needed the practice before interviewing strangers.

"You whined like a piglet when I took your samples," Rowena teased.

"What can I say? My hair's my best feature." His fingers raked their habitual route along his scalp, his hair springing back in place.

Rowena rolled her eyes, then turned to Fern with her pen at the ready.

"Alright, let's get started. How old are you?"

"Forty-six," answered Fern. Rowena's pen scraped the parchment.

They flew through the preliminary questions with ease, even when the questions turned to matters of magic. Fern made no objections, no unfair assumptions, no back-handed remarks about Ghost, who kept trying to provoke Titus's owl to a game of chase. For the first time, Rowena actually enjoyed her work. It was only when she asked, "Does your Shadow have a preference for interior or exterior magic?" that Fern hesitated.

"Umm...well...interior, I suppose."

Behind her, leaning against the kitchen cabinets, both Titus and Bruce chuckled.

Rowena asked, "How many acts of magic would you say your Shadow does in a day?"

"Hmm. I'd say thirty? Forty, maybe?"

At this, Bruce openly scoffed. "*Mom!*"

Fern's eyes rounded with innocence. "What?"

"Answer honestly." His tone was playful but accusing.

"I did answer honestly!" Her Shadow's ears flattened against her dappled neck. "Bruce, you're the one who has difficulty being honest."

"Fair enough," he allowed, "But in this house, the biggest lawbreaker isn't me."

It was apparent Rowena had stumbled upon a family joke, and she looked back and forth between them. The brothers grinned knowingly at their mother.

"Mom, come on," Titus coaxed, his tone softer than Bruce's. "You've used about ten persuasions since Rowena got here."

"Titus!" Fern cried as if he'd said something distasteful.

She looked at her husband who sat quietly in the chair next to her, but he only chuckled. "Fern, love," Roderick said, laying a consoling hand over hers.

She flushed a rosy shade of pink. "I work hard to make this home as comfortable as I can. It's not illegal to be hospitable in my own home!"

"You do a wonderful job, and we're all grateful," Roderick said. However, he winked at his sons.

Understanding came slow for Rowena until Fern pleaded with her: "I only set people at ease! It's really just for making people happy..."

Rowena wanted to avoid Fern's tears (which threatened to break at that moment), so she said, "It's okay, Mrs. Ashworth. I don't mind." However, she wasn't sure she meant it.

Of course, Rowena knew of Fern's talent with persuasions from her confession to Roderick years ago—how she'd persuaded him in order to help Haaris hide Rowena. But she had no idea that she used persuasions still, perhaps even at that very moment. Rowena ducked her head, allowing her hair to fall across her face while she gathered her thoughts. The smell of bread and melting butter filled her nostrils then, and she felt the tension in her stomach unfurl like steam.

Feeling suddenly—oddly—better, she unstopped a vial. "Let's move on to the samples," she said.

Titus and Bruce exchanged knowing grins, which Rowena chose to ignore. In less than a minute, she had two full vials, one of blood and the other with a lock of silky hair.

"My turn?" Roderick asked. His voice was like fireworks after his wife's gentle murmurs.

Over the course of his interview, Rowena struggled to meet the Overseer's eyes. It felt as if no time had passed, and she was still that cowering girl hiding under a tarp, fearful of being seen by the giant-man. And yet, the fear was different. The barrage of disapproval from strangers always stung, but eventually, she managed to push the indignities out of her mind, or so she told herself. But Roderick Ashworth's estimation mattered to her in a way she could not explain. Different even than Penalynn's. His presence was like a beam of light, illuminating the places she lacked, not in magical ability, but in ways undefined. She felt an overwhelming desire to be more than she was. More brave. More mature. More clever. Simply *more*. Perhaps he was persuading her as well, she wondered.

Despite her timidity, the interview went quite well, and when she secured her finished kit, she sighed. "Only one more, and I'll be done for good."

"It's getting dark," said Fern, "Surely you're not going to work so late."

"No, I'm done for today. The last one might take me a bit. I don't know where he lives."

"Who is it?" asked Roderick.

"That hermit everyone says is crazy. Craefog, I think is his name."

Bruce spoke up, "I know where he lives."

Roderick shook his head in a fatherly fashion. "You're not going to see that man alone."

"I've interviewed some hermits already, each one by myself," she said.

"Not like this one."

"I could take her, Dad," Titus offered.

Fern asked her husband, "He was never violent, was he? Do you think he'd do something to a kid?"

"We're nearly of age!" Titus said, offended at being called a kid. "Dad, you know I wouldn't let anything happen."

"You're right, I trust you. But Bruce will go with you just in case."

"What?!" the brothers cried in unison. Bruce argued, "I said I know where he is, not that I'd take her!"

Roderick asked Rowena, "When do you need to go?"

"Tomorrow if I can. Penalynn needs it as soon as possible."

"Fine. You must be careful, all three of you. Craefog's not one to mess with."

"We'll be in and out of there quick," Titus assured him.

Roderick slapped him on the back. "Got my best man on the job. Now, would you two please excuse us? Fern and I must discuss a matter with our eldest son." He slid out a chair, allowing the legs to scrape the floor ominously. Bruce turned unusually somber, and his raccoon ducked out of sight.

Titus chuckled as he and Rowena left. "I love it when he's in trouble."

"What'd he do?" Rowena asked.

"Something stupid, no doubt."

The following morning, Rowena ate breakfast as she always did: with an open book propped against the teapot. Haaris broke the silence. "You'll be late for school."

"I've got an interview in the woods," she said absentmindedly, still reading. "I'm waiting for Titus and Bruce to take me."

Without realizing it, she'd captured her father's full attention. He cleared his throat. "A father is going to need more information than that."

"I just told you, apprentice business." She took a sip of tea and turned the page.

Haaris's Shadow reared up on his hind legs and knocked the book over with his nose. Rowena looked up, and Haaris said slowly, as if explaining something elementary, "When a boy tells you he wants you to interview him in the woods, that's boy jargon for—"

Rowena sputtered, spewing tea across the table. "What? No! They're helping me find some hermit Penalynn's hung up on! Craefog something-or-other. *Ugh.* Please do not say *boy jargon* ever again." She cringed, wiping spittle from her book.

"Craefog?" Haaris tilted his head, his relief evident in his voice. "Ewan Craefog? I went to school with him."

"One of your classmates became a hermit?"

"He dropped out of school our last year, went into the woods, and never came out. He was always a bit...off. Even now, he's got a reputation. I'm not sure I want you talking to him."

"Titus and Bruce will be with me," she said just as a knock sounded at the door.

When Haaris opened it, Titus greeted him with a hearty handshake. "Hi, Mr. Faye!"

"Good to see you boys," said Haaris. "I hear you're doing Scholastic work this morning."

Bruce leaned against the door frame. "If delivering Rowena to some freak in the woods is Scholastic work, then yeah, sure."

Haaris's smile dropped to stony disapproval. He turned to Rowena and said, "I'm taking you instead." But she only rolled her eyes and kissed him on the cheek.

"See you at dinner, Papa." She donned her bag as she passed the brothers on the porch and strolled down the garden path, Ghost chasing a cardinal as they went.

Haaris leveled the boys with a warning finger; his voice dropped to a growl. "She doesn't leave your sight."

The brothers both nodded, swallowing. "Yes, sir," they promised before scrambling after Rowena, who had already entered the edge of the forest.

Chapter
Twenty-Eight

T HERE WAS NO PATH to follow, so they made slow progress through the woods, the underbrush thick with fallen limbs and last year's decaying leaves. The brothers took turns course-correcting every so often. Rowena didn't mind the pace. She was glad to be free from the stone confines of Greymere for a change. Torborough forest glowed bright despite the dense canopy above. In summer, sunshine trickled through emerald leaves, reflected from white tree trunks. But in autumn, the forest was transformed into a ceiling of golden yellow, light breaking in soft, buttery beams.

After a while, she asked, "How do you know where Craefog lives? Have you met him?"

"Anyone with a Shadow can find him easy enough," said Bruce. Titus smacked his arm, and he winced at his blunder. "Whoops, sorry."

"It's alright. I know what you meant," said Rowena. Ghost floated at her side. "So, your Shadow is using magic to find him? How does that work?"

"Intuition magic," Titus explained. His own Shadow winged from limb to limb overhead. "All magic lets out a kind of—oh, how do I explain this? A kind of *scent.* And intuition picks up that scent."

"Your magic can 'smell' Craefog so far away?"

Titus stopped to look at her as if seeing something for the first time.

"What?" she asked.

"Nothing. It's just...I forget sometimes what it must be like for you." He looked at Ghost, then back at Rowena. "It's such a regular thing in Greymere. People don't talk about it much, but we all feel it. Something we all share, like the Festival of Shadows or the first snow in winter. It happens to everyone...except..." His look bordered on pity, and Rowena frowned.

"What are you talking about?"

"I guess you've never noticed that people in Greymere don't use intuition magic. And there's a reason for that. If we did, we'd feel it all the time, this magical pulsing, never stopping"—he pointed straight ahead—"coming from this direction. I've felt it my whole life—or at least when my Shadow used his intuition. And with every step we take, the pulse grows stronger."

Rowena made her confusion evident.

"It's Craefog," Bruce chimed in, "He doesn't live out here because he likes it."

"I asked my dad about it," Titus said, "When my Shadow first learned to use intuition, and I felt it. He told me the Sceadwe banished him years ago because his magic had become too much. Now and then, someone new will show up in town, using intuition like normal, and they'll ask about it, and the gossip will kick up with stories about Craefog. It's just this annoying thing we all live with. It's easier not to use intuition."

Rowena's skin prickled. She wasn't sure which was more disturbing: walking toward someone whose magic was so disruptive that the Sceadwe had to banish him or the fact that every citizen she lived among experienced something about which she was clueless. She felt exposed and hazardously incompetent. Meanwhile, her Shadow floated blithely along, batting at specks dancing in sunbeams. "What are we headed toward?" she wondered aloud.

Just then, she felt a vibration through the soles of her shoes. "Is he here?!"

"Can't be," said Bruce, looking around.

Titus placed his palm against a tree to feel the vibration through the trunk. "We're not close enough for this to be Craefog."

"Then what—" The ground lurched beneath her feet as if the world had been tipped like a pitcher of water. She gasped, her feet slipping. Dirt and leaves slid along the forest floor, angled like a seesaw.

Titus seized her by the hand. The noise of rumbling earth was so loud he had to shout, "Quick! Grab on!!" With one arm, he pulled Rowena to himself. With the other, he grabbed the tree next to him, which now appeared as if it were above him on a steep incline. His muscles strained to hold on as their weight shifted. The ground had transformed into a massive slide, urging them to tumble.

Rowena hugged the tree. Her feet slipped, and she fell, her legs splayed below.

She screamed. "Titus!"

He hoisted her up and then sandwiched her body between his and the tree, his torso pinning her in place. "Wait, this isn't right," he muttered in her ear, "Look at Bruce."

She peeked under his arm to see Bruce standing upright as if on level ground, though at an unnatural angle. He ought to be falling head-first down the hill, but he stood, unbothered by the world upturning. Titus let go of the tree then, and without his support, she screamed, catching herself just in time. Somehow, impossibly, he joined his brother. Both of them stood as if their feet were planted in the dirt.

Rowena, however, struggled to maintain her hold. Her muscles twitched with effort. The earth didn't stop rumbling until the ground was no longer a hill but a sheer cliff with trees sticking out at right angles. With only her hands, she managed to hang on. Her feet dangled below. "Titus!" she cried. "Help!"

"Spook, it's alright," he said with a smile in his voice. Gently but unhelpfully so, he placed a hand on her back. "Let go. You won't fall."

She loosened her grip just enough for her stomach to lurch and clutched the tree with renewed fervor.

"Sersha?!" She heard Bruce holler. "Sersha, I know you're here!" A feminine laugh rang out, close but hidden. "Very funny." His tone was oddly cloying. "You've had your laugh; now let up."

A young woman's voice spoke in an unfamiliar language.

"She's just a friend," Bruce replied in answer. "And she can't do magic, so give her a break, darling."

Through her labored breath, Rowena heard Titus make a choking sound. "*Darling?*"

"TITUS!!" Rowena screamed, her hands slipping.

Next to her, Ghost seemed wholly unaffected by the changed scenery. She hovered near Rowena's face, bobbing up and down with evident concern at Rowena's distress. Something rustled nearby, and Rowena opened her eyes to see a snow-white otter approach to sniff Ghost tentatively. Ghost, in turn, tapped the otter on the nose in a friendly hello. Rowena suspected this was not a true otter but a Shadow, no doubt belonging to the voice. Just then, Bruce's Shadow sprang atop the newcomer, and the raccoon and otter wrestled one another.

At that moment, the world righted itself with a sickening flip; the ground was no longer topsy-turvy but upright as normal. Rowena fell on her belly with a painful "*oof.*" The shift churned her stomach and brain like a badly shaken jar. She pushed herself to her knees, her arms twitching with exhaustion and terror, struggling to catch her breath. Ghost pulled a twig from her hair and patted her shoulder in sympathy.

From behind a tree stepped a young woman no older than twenty. She wore a flowy dress despite the autumn chill. Her eyes and mouth seemed too big for her face, but somehow, the imperfection intensified her beauty. Green eyes sparkled with wild energy held barely in check. Rowena didn't need intuition to know that no part of this girl's appearance was magicked.

Without a care for Rowena's shaken state, the girl ran for Bruce. Her body crashed into his, and they fell to the ground in a roving embrace, their faces locked in a passionate kiss. Rowena and Titus exchanged bewildered looks, then quickly averted their gaze, blushing deeply and unable to block out the noises from the writhing pair, all smacking and giggles. Titus cleared his throat, and the two paused their kissing to look up.

The girl seemed perfectly comfortable lying on the ground with Bruce on top of her. She spoke once more in the unknown language, but this time, Rowena heard her voice echo in her mind. Her Shadow's magic translated: "Bruce, who are your friends?"

"I'm Rowena," she answered flatly, incensed the stranger dared to use persuasive magic after what she'd just done, even if it was to provide a translation. "Who are you?"

Bruce stood and then pulled the young woman to his side. Leaves clung to his jacket like ridiculous souvenirs from his romp with The Wandering girl. "Rowena, Titus, this is Sersha. Sersha, this is my brother and his friend Rowena."

"You have a girlfriend..." Titus said, struggling to reconcile the image of his brother in the arms of such a woman. "Who's...a Wandrel."

"That's an offensive word," Bruce chided, although his lips quirked smugly. "But yeah."

Rowena snorted. "She attacked us with illegal magic, but calling her Wandrel is offensive?"

"It was easy," Sersha said, flicking her waist-long hair. "Your Shadow is pitiful."

"Hey!" Titus said. "Watch yourself."

Sersha pulled Bruce by the hand. "Come, my love. I am bored with them and want you for myself."

He grimaced, clearly wanting nothing more than to obey the stunning woman pulling his arm, but somehow, he stood his ground. "I have to help her first." It looked as if the words caused him physical pain. He explained his father's demand to deliver Rowena to the hermit Craefog.

"Let her go herself to see the zealot," said Sersha, "He is not hiding."

"She can't."

She looked at Ghost, seeming to understand. "Fine. I go with you."

"No," Rowena said, crossing her arms.

"I did not ask permission, *Scead Demortas,*" Sersha said the last words with marked sarcasm as if they were an insult. Rowena struggled to decipher the word, divided translations echoing in her mind simultaneously.

Titus understood, however, because he said, "She *has* a Shadow."

But Sersha ignored him, walking in the direction they had been going before her persuasive prank had stopped them. Rowena threw up her hands, but Bruce only shrugged, mouthing, "I'm sorry," before jogging to catch up with his girlfriend. Titus walked beside Rowena, who walked slowly to provide plenty of space for the two lovers up ahead. She tried to ignore them, but every few minutes, a lilting laugh drew her attention, and her mood darkened. She wanted justice for the trick played upon her imagination, but more than that, she wanted Titus to stop looking at Sersha's legs like that.

After an hour, her mood had darkened to outright vengeance. Soon, they crested a low hill and found a break in the trees where a house was tucked in the middle of the forest.

Titus whistled low. "Well, there it is."

Rowena jerked her chin at Sersha and asked, "Is she messing with me again?" Surely, what she saw couldn't be real but a fiction painted in jest upon her unguarded mind.

"Nope," said Bruce, his voice and countenance full of wonder.

With some satisfaction, Rowena noticed that even Sersha seemed to shrink in the shade of the hermit's house.

# CHAPTER
TWENTY-NINE

T HE HOUSE LOOMING BEFORE them couldn't really be called a house—more like a manor stretching several stories high. A couple of turrets jutted here and there, and dark glass windows scattered like patchwork in a stone-made quilt. The longer Rowena beheld the house, the dizzier she became, unable to reconcile the countless architectural oddities. Something felt disconcerting about the roof's many gables. Or how the shingles curled at the ends not only impractically but impossibly. Her eyes roved over the edifice, wondering at magic's reach. Could manipulation alone—merely enhancing material substance—perform such architectural feats? Or was the whole scene a persuasion, their minds tricked to see what did not, could not, exist?

Bruce led the way up the steps, Sersha's fingers entwined with his. The raccoon's fur camouflaged against the flagged stone, but Sersha's otter scurried like a swath of snow come to life. Rowena and Titus followed close behind, leaning against one another in united apprehension. When they reached the towering front door, it wrenched open with a groan of iron and wood.

A middle-aged man of measly stature stood before them, merrily clapping and bouncing on bare tiptoes. He wore a periwinkle bathrobe made of silk, his chest bare underneath. White hair swooped charmingly atop his head, his grin so wide it nearly reached both ears. He effervesced with frenetic energy, buzzing like a kid with a sugar rush. Rowena looked just past him to see, barely discernable against the darkness of the manor's interior, a panther with glossy fur so black as to be nearly blue. The Shadow sat perfectly still with unblinking lime eyes. Yet, like his human counterpart, the panther emanated an insatiable energy, although restrained. Like a spring, coiled and ready to pop.

"Hello, Mr. Craefog?" Rowena stepped forward. "I'm Rowena Faye, Apprentice to Scholastic Penalynn Graft. If you don't mind, I would like to—"

The man grasped both her and Bruce's arms at the same time and wrenched them across the threshold with alarming strength, practically singing as he said, "Come in! Come in! Come in!"

Titus and Sersha were jerked along by Rowena and Bruce's hands, and together, they were all jostled into a foyer wallpapered in dark velvet. A glittering chandelier hung from the high ceiling, all crystal and candlelight. To their right swept a staircase of black marble buffed with polish. Ahead, a wide corridor led to a mahogany-paneled room.

"I knew you were coming," the man said, clapping his hands ecstatically. "OOHHH!! Let me look at you, let me look at you. Let! Me! Look! One, two, three, four. Just as I expected." He tapped them each in turn as he counted, tapping Rowena last. "And YOU! You, you, you, you, you! Just look at you!" He took Rowena's hands and spread her arms wide like wings. He asked, "May I?" but before she could grant permission, he placed his ear on her chest. A terrible, rotten smell filled her nostrils, and she nearly gagged.

"Yep, there's a heartbeat," he said. "You're not a corpse after all. My Shadow felt you coming. My intuition's always at it, you know, and I thought to myself, WOO-WOO, what is that? Four bodies, three Shadows? Is there a *dead man* walking my way? But nope, you've a HEARTBEAT!! HA! HA! *Fascinating.* Absolutely fascinating. Were the noble Wandering right after all? Are you the long-awaited Shadowless they've looked for all these centuries?"

At this, Sersha spoke up, although she clung to Bruce's arm. "She's not the *Scead Demortas.*"

Again, Rowena's mind tripped over the numerous translations bouncing around her mind. "What is that word? Shade de-something."

"*Scead Demortas,*" Sersha repeated, her Shadow providing translation. "Your people call it Shadow-less. It's not you, though. Worthless as she is, you do have a Shadow."

It was then the hermit spied Ghost, who hardly dared to peek over Rowena's shoulder. With chilling reverence, he whispered in a way that made Rowena's skin crawl. "What is this?" His grin widened to reveal every tooth in his mouth. "Oh, I've never met such a mind."

Rowena nearly choked, equal parts horror and hope seized hold of her. "You can sense her mind?!"

"Not at all," he breathed. Slowly and with a manic gleam, his attention turned to Rowena. The panther's tail flicked like a snake slithering on the marble. "Amazing. You're completely defenseless. Not an ounce of intuition in you. Why, a Shadow could do *anything* to a mind like yours."

The panther sprang to all fours, licking his lips, a flash of pink against black fur.

Titus slid himself between Rowena and the panther. His owl spread his wings in warning. "Easy there, Mr. Hermit. We might be far from town, but you still have to follow the law. No persuasions."

"Oh, my lovely boy." Craefog chuckled, patting Titus's arm, "But you've brought me such a *treat* today. It's only been animals for so long, and even they won't come close anymore. I don't think they liked my Shadow's games." He winked at Rowena as if they shared a joke. "But then four human minds show up, and one of them so deliciously *exposed*. But no, I promise I'll be good."

Rowena mustered the bravery to ask, "Are you Mr. Craefog?"

"Craefog? Craefog! Yes! That's me, that's me! Excuse me, but it's been years since I...Yes, I am yellow, no yodel, no ewe..." he muttered like a man who'd misplaced something.

"Ewan Craefog?" Rowena offered, remembering the name her father had mentioned.

"That's the one! Ewan Craefog. Hideous really. No wonder I forgot it." He laughed, and Rowena exchanged a look with Titus. The buffoon before them was wholly unexpected.

"EAT!!" Craefog screamed, causing Sersha to startle. "I've prepared a feast for you."

He led them to the wood-paneled room, gesturing grandly at a buffet under a wide window. An impressive spread stretched the length of the table. At the sight of food, Rowena suddenly realized their walk through the forest had worked up quite an appetite. Her stomach growled.

"I made that," said Crafog, pointing at each dish as he spoke, "And that, and that, and that, and that. Not that. I bought those ages ago, but it's still good, probably. Oh! Here, try this. Do you like pears? I never did, but my nanny always told me to eat them when I was young, and so I've magicked some bits and bobbles, and LOOK! STEWED PEARS! Just ignore the, *hmm*, aftertaste." He held what looked like a steaming bowl of cinnamon-honey pears, cooked to tender perfection. "Or ham! I found a pig, so it's real. Well, the pig wasn't real; it was a squirrel, but the meat is real. Tastes just like ham. Dip it in the mustard, although that's sand, but you won't notice."

As hungry as Rowena was, she wasn't sure what to do. She glanced at Bruce, who shook his head firmly, and so she said, "No, thank you. You see, Mr. Craefog, I'm here on business."

"Ooh! Business! How delightful! I do love *business*. Here on business. What sort of business?" He was like a child who'd just discovered a new word, enjoying how it sounded in his mouth.

"Scholastic business. I've come to interview you if you wouldn't mind."

"How splendid!"

He led them to a limestone fireplace ringed by a semi-circle of wing-backed chairs. She took the seat nearest Craefog. Her companions followed, clutching their Shadows as if the furred and feathered companions were anchors to reality. Ghost, however, hovered in the air, her smokey eyes roving about the room unceasingly. She patted a flipper against the arm of Rowena's chair as if testing something, then proceeded to rub the fabric with vigorous curiosity.

"That Shadow answers an ancient question," said Craefog, settling into his chair. His manic energy sagged in languid leisure. The panther sprawled at his feet, his eyes never leaving Ghost; tail thumping rhythmically.

"What question is that?" Rowena asked, dreading the answer.

"Is magic worked upon the Shadow mind or the human mind? Or do we have the same mind, just two bodies? It's impossible to know. A person can't cut the mental connection with their Shadow, *snip-snip*. Only death can do that. *Snip-snip*, your mind is dead. But now we know, don't we? You, the human mind—*knock-knock*—" he rapped his knuckles on his head— "You see everything I want you to see. But your Shadow, *woo-woo*. I'm not so sure she does. It doesn't seem like it, does it? Are you learning all my secrets, little Shadow? What is real? What is not? I think she knows."

Ghost ignored him as she looked about the room. Her usually dim eyes were lit like a flame, wondrously alert.

"So, you *are* using a persuasion?" Titus asked. "My intuition can't decipher…" Rowena looked at the owl who practically trembled with magic, his concentration focused with intuition.

"My boy," Craefog said with pleasure, "I'm using *all* the magics."

"I'd like to ask you some questions about that," Rowena said, pulling a kit from her bag. The hermit nodded his consent. "Mr. Craefog, how old are you?"

"Ooh, now that *is* an interesting question." He leaned forward, his knees bouncing. "I'm forty…I think."

"You think?"

He shrugged. "It's an assumption."

"Okay, how often does your Shadow use magic?"

His eyebrows lifted as if she were stupid. Bruce answered for him, "Always." Craefog nodded. She scribbled the answer.

"Does your Shadow prefer one branch of magic over others?"

"Well, I enjoy persuasions the most. Such fun to play with the mind. *Things* don't object to being manipulated. Where's the fun in that? I like the push-back of a resistant mind, the dance of wills. Although, your wide-open mind is awfully tempting..."

Titus leaned forward. "NO!" he said in a way reminiscent of the Lord Overseer.

The interview continued. Later, Rowena would admit to Penalynn that she had been right; his interview was the most unique among all the others. Never had Rowena met someone who performed magic to the raging, obsessive extent as Craefog. While most people used magic as a tool to accomplish a given task, Craefog performed magic with an insatiable lust for the practice itself. Even as they talked, his Shadow used animation to play with the fire in the hearth, to throw various items about the room, or to touch the breeze outside. The décor shifted ceaselessly as he manipulated the colors and textures across every surface. Even the chair Rowena sat upon morphed from blue to green, tweed to brocade. The visitors had to keep their eyes trained downward to not grow faint from the room's constant change.

Finally, Rowena uncorked two vials, took a deep breath, and said, "I will need a blood and hair sample if you don't mind."

At this, Craefog burst into laughter, the sound erupting like a cannon. Sersha was so startled that her Shadow tumbled off her lap to land clumsily on the rug. The otter hissed at the hermit, and he winced as if in pain.

"Ouchy! What is this?! The Wandering princess has *fire* in her! No persuasion taboos with your kind." He tilted his head as if noticing Sersha for the first time, then turned back to Rowena. "Now, where were we before this lovely lady proved her worth? Ah, yes. Blood—and—hair." His eyes bore into hers with undiluted sanity, so intense Rowena felt nearly hypnotized. "So, after all these years a Scholastic has finally asked the right question. Magic and blood, blood and magic. Ooh, Bravo!! Congratulate Madame Scholastic for me, won't you? Of course, you can have my blood and hair. Take it! As much as you need!"

Never had this request produced such a response. Rowena gulped as she took his hand into her own. His skin felt papery in hers, so delicate she feared she might hurt him. Using a sterile needle, she pricked his finger, and squeezed several black-red droplets into the vial. Craefog leaned close, his breath hot and smelling like mold.

"You can't tell I'm touching her, can you?" he whispered.

"What?" She looked up, startled to see their noses were only an inch apart.

"Your Shadow."

As always, Ghost hovered nearby, Rowena's constant, silent companion. But, without her realizing, the panther had wrapped his glossy tail around Ghost's torso. "She's remarkably solid," Craefog observed.

Titus clapped his hands. "That's it, we're done. Let her go!"

"I'm not done looking," said Craefog like a boy who hadn't finished with his toy. The panther raised Ghost to the man's eye level so he could get a closer look.

On a nearby table sat a crystal bowl filled with walnuts. It shifted in hue like a roving rainbow under the panther's magic. Titus grabbed a walnut and threw it at Craefog's head. The owl animated its speed for painful effect. The panther, however, proved too quick. His magic touched the walnut as well, making it arch in a loop, then aiming it at Bruce. With a jolt, the raccoon's magic flared. The walnut disintegrated in a shower of brown dust, but the speed had not been altered. Bruce coughed and sputtered, wiping specks of walnut shell from his eyes.

Sersha leaped to her feet. Untamed malice crackled across her features like lightning. The otter reared onto its hind legs, magic grumbling. But Craefog merely sighed.

"My dear, Wandering enchantress. Your attempts at persuasion embarrass you and your people. No subtlety. No art. You work too hard when my own imagination can do just fine."

The otter dropped to all fours, and Sersha's eyes darkened.

"Don't throttle the mind with magic," Craefog instructed. The panther purred. "Let the persuasion sneak in as if through the back door of the imagination. Silent. Unnoticed. Look around in there; what do you see? I assure you, the mind has enough already with which to torment itself."

Sersha's face crumpled, making her appear much younger, her chin pursed and quivering. "Please," she groaned. "No...please..." Soon, tears streamed down her face and neck.

"STOP!!" Bruce hollered. He lunged for Craefog but toppled to the ground, the muscles in his legs seizing in the grip of magic.

Sersha's cries came in gulps, her imagination in the throes of whatever scene the panther painted. Rowena's stomach knotted. Not an hour ago, she would have been happy to see The Wandering girl receive a persuasion like the one she'd inflicted upon her. But now, as Sersha's tears and snot wet the rug, Rowena felt no satisfaction. But she was helpless against magic.

"Sersha!" Bruce cried desperately, his legs wriggled useless in magic's grip. "It's not real! Whatever he's doing to you, it's not real! *Sersha!!*"

Both of their Shadows were frozen in place; whether through physical manipulation or mental persuasion, Rowena couldn't tell. She felt as if she ought to do something, anything, to stop the cruelty.

Meanwhile, the panther still held Ghost close to Craefog's face, although their attention had turned toward their prey. Ghost reached her flippers to grasp two tufts of Craefog's white hair. With a flick, she ripped out the hair, leaving a patch of scalp exposed in an angry shade of pink. Craefog hollered, but Ghost didn't stop there. She slipped from the panther's tail and soared to the back of Craefog's head, where she ripped one tiny fistful after another. White tufts littered the chair like cotton.

The panther batted his massive paws, but Ghost soared out of reach. Craefog scurried like a frightened rabbit. Ghost tore after him. Not much hair was left atop his raw and bleeding head, so she settled for smacking him with her flippers, the sound like a spatula hitting flesh. He cowered and dodged, but Ghost persisted, slapping every bit of skin she could find.

With the panther distracted, Bruce and Sersha were free. But none of them moved, all four of them watched the tiny Shadow clobber the hermit. Never had Rowena seen her Shadow exhibit such violence, but she was loath to stop her. Clearly, magic was ineffective on Ghost which reduced the panther to pounce like a real cat, his gait awkward and clumsy. Craefog batted as if at a wasp, but Ghost was too quick. At last, she stopped darting and hovered coaxingly above Craefog's head. The panther took a mighty leap, but Ghost zoomed out of reach just in time, bowling into Rowena's chest. The panther crashed into Craefog, and together, they landed in a defeated heap on the rug.

"Spook, get your last sample, and let's get out of here," Titus said.

Thanks to Ghost, Craefog's hair lay everywhere in clumps. Rowena swiped the nearest tuft and shoved it into her last vial. She threw the kit into her bag, and all four rushed into the foyer. Bruce propped a deeply shaken Sersha, whose head sagged against his chest. They were all desperate to leave. The door was already ajar, and they fled at once. Rowena was the last, but a voice stopped her on the threshold.

"Shadowless!" Craefog called, emerging from under the panther. He leaned heavily against the wall, panting. "You'll want another sample."

She hesitated, one foot outside. "Why?" she called back

"Do you not know?" He asked, genuinely surprised. The effort to stand seemed too much, and he slid down the wall, his chin falling to his chest. "My Shadow says we have...how long is it? Months. Maybe a year. At the end, I'll leave another sample for you. The door will be open." He chuckled, his eyes rolling back. "I figured it out early on. At the capacity I used magic, there was no mistaking the truth. He doesn't sleep, my Shadow. Every morning, I wake up and see all he's done during the night, some horrible, terrible things. Yes, yes, it won't be long now. Soon, I hope, and then you'll come back. I've made a path for you, you'll need it if you are to return. It was hard doing, but my Shadow managed. You'll have more questions then, but I won't. Use the path when you come, *Scead*

Demortas." He lay on the floor, but he continued to speak. "If I were Shadowless, I could close my eyes and finally sleep. That's a nice thought, isn't it? I'm so tired. Soon, Shadowless, I'll leave it for you."

Titus pulled Rowena's elbow, and she left the hermit's house. At the foot of the steps, they met up with the others. Sersha drooped against Bruce as if she might faint.

"Was that here before?" Titus asked. He stepped onto a dirt path stretching into the forest precisely the way they had come.

"I don't think so," said Rowena.

Sersha whimpered as new tears rolled down her cheeks.

"I have to take her back to her camp," said Bruce. "Titus, do you know how to get back?"

Rowena answered, "We'll take the path."

"I wouldn't trust that guy if I were you," Bruce warned.

But Rowena shook her head. "Craefog's a lunatic, but I don't think he was lying. This will take us home, I'm sure of it." She looked at Sersha, feeling guilty. "I'm so sorry. I shouldn't have brought you here. This is my fault."

"You didn't do this. She's strong. Her people will know what to do."

They parted at a crest in the woods, Bruce and Sersha angling for The Wandering camp, Rowena and Titus following the path north. They were both still jittery.

Titus spoke with a slight tremor in his voice. "So, we're walking on a path magically created by a madman who violently attacked us and mentally tortured my brother's girlfriend." With a grin, he added, "Good thing we have your Shadow to protect us."

Rowena snorted, but eyed Ghost nervously. "I've never seen her act like that."

Rowena wasn't sure if she felt impressed or disturbed by Ghost's violence—or merely grateful. If it weren't for her Shadow, there was no knowing how far Craefog's torture would have gone. Neither of them could help but glance over their shoulders as they followed the path that led them straight home, just as Craefog had promised.

CHAPTER THIRTY

PENALYNN SAT IN HER private quarters, chin in hands, brooding. Since her conversation with Rowena, Penalynn couldn't help but wonder about the numerous rumors apparently circulating around about her. The table was littered with her half-eaten lunch. Her attendant cleared the dishes, and Penalynn took the opportunity to ask, "Freya, you're in the castle's servant quarters. A chatty atmosphere, no doubt. Have you ever heard any...stories...about me?"

"You're a very important lady." Freya measured her words as carefully as she stacked the dishes. "There is talk here and there, but I never give it any mind."

Penalynn feigned disinterest by inspecting her cuticles. "I hear there is a rumor that I'm a scorned lover of the king. That people think I was sent here to avoid scandal in court."

The mouse on Freya's shoulder slipped from her perch and landed in a teacup with a minuscule splash. Freya's voice quaked. "Yes, madame, I might have heard that one once."

"It's nonsense, of course."

"Of course, madame." Freya rescued the mouse and tucked it in her apron pocket to dry off.

"You will inform anyone who tells that story that it is nonsense," said Penalynn.

"Yes, madame. Is that all?"

Penalynn bit her lip. She wanted to ask what other rumors there were, but that would leave her feeling vulnerable and infantile, so she merely said, "Yes, that is all."

Freya curtsied, then hoisted her tray and left.

The fox sat in Penalynn's lap and scoffed: *You're a fool.*

"Thank you, I was unaware." Not for the first time, Penalynn wished she could hide her sticky embarrassment from her Shadow.

She searched for a distraction and slid open the library door. Rowena was out on the balcony. But a door was propped open, so she called, "Congratulations, madame apprentice. Your years-long task is complete!"

Each day, the temperature dropped a little more, sending the balcony garden into hibernation. Rowena stood among her leafy creations, selecting the pots to bring inside before winter fell. She dragged a young lemon tree inside as she said, "You saw the hermit's sample, then? Almost lost my life for it, but it feels good to be rid of those infernal interviews." It took both her and Penalynn to carry the heavy pot over the carpet, to set it in a spot that got plenty of light but was far enough away from the windows to avoid frost. Rowena brushed off her hands and looked at Penalynn with a proud smile, "Now that I'm finished, can I help you in the laboratory?"

Penalynn sniffed the last lemon holding on, and carefully avoided eye contact. "No, thank you," she said.

Rowena faltered as if she'd tripped. "But I finished. Aren't you at least going to tell me what it is we're studying?"

"I've got at least another year before I'm through. The easy part has been done, collecting the data." Rowena blanched at the notion that her interviews had been easy, but Penalynn continued. "It takes an enormous amount of time to process each sample, I might not even finish by the time you graduate next year."

"But I'm your apprentice. what do you expect me to do if not help you?"

"You've still got school, haven't you?"

"Hardly. I have no magic, Penalynn."

The lemon snapped off in Penalynn's hand, and she frowned. "Right. Well, get a head start on your graduation trial. Knowing the Myth Keeper's prejudice against you, you should probably start early."

Rowena snatched the lemon from her, anger rising. "My trial isn't for another year."

"Exactly. Time's running out."

She bit the inside of her cheeks to keep from arguing. Penalynn was not going to budge, and Rowena knew from experience that when she got like this, there was no amount of pressure that would get her to change her mind. All this time, she had regarded her interviews as a sort of finish line, expecting to win the answers she desired as soon as she was finished. But now, instead of entering a new phase of her apprenticeship, she found herself right back where she had always been—clueless to Penalynn's work but with three years of resentment built up.

"Oh, by the way," Penalynn said, interrupting Rowena's disappointed sulking. "I need one last sample."

"What?! You said I was—"

"Calm down. It's yours. I need a sample from you."

Rowena sat on the arm of a chair. "I already gave you my sample years ago. It was the first one I ever collected."

"I need another one. Why are you looking at me like that?" Penalynn's eyebrows pinched together. "You can have two gold coins for it if you like."

Rowena crossed her arms. "Are you going to want a second sample from everyone else, too?"

"No."

"Then why do you need one from me?"

"To note any changes."

At this, Rowena leaned forward to place her elbows on her knees. "Changes in what?" she asked. But Penalynn's jaw set, and her lips pressed in a tight line. Rowena sighed. "How about a trade? You give me an idea of what you're doing with all that blood and hair I collected for you, and I'll give you my second sample."

"That is not how our arrangement works."

Rowena shrugged. "Then I won't give you my samples."

Penalynn shrugged as well. "Then you're fired. Enjoy life without the benefits of that cape. I'll leave you to think about it. You know where the vials are." And with that, Penalynn left her apprentice to stew.

Across the hall, through the laboratory door, at the far end of the glass cabinets, on the bottom row, sat Ewan Craefog's samples, deposited only that morning and waiting for Penalynn.

Penalynn decided to skip the other samples that waited, snatched the hermit's vials, then shut the glass door. With practiced precision, Penalynn conducted the routines of analysis: separating and dissecting each hair with delicate tools and chemicals, distilling, elixerating, and filtrating in sequential stages until the samples were winnowed and percolating in contraptions all across the counter.

She'd been at it for a few hours when a strong odor smelling of burning peat caught her attention. A loud *bang!* erupted from a whirring machine followed by an ominous *hiss.* Immediately, she called for the servant to stop his magic so she could open the machine. An acidic vapor invaded the laboratory. Penalynn struggled against the urge to retch, and pulled out the sample of blood, now resembling black tar, and placed it under a magnified lens.

Behind her, Rowena burst into the room. "Penalynn, are you alright? I thought I heard an explosion." She stopped short, gagging— "Gah! What is that *smell?!*"

A chorus of coughs rounded the room as Rowena and the two servants battled the stench.

The room was frigid as always but eerily quiet. All the machines had stopped. A haze of smoke gathered overhead, still wafting from the offending sample. Penalynn appeared composed, but her eyes were oddly distant. The fox sat atop her stool and shivered, despite her thick fur. Rowena stepped forward to place a hand on her mentor's shoulder. "Penalynn, are you alright?"

At this, the fox slipped from the stool, landed clumsily on her back, rolled, and then dashed out the door. Rowena was jostled aside as Penalynn followed her.

"What's happened?" Rowena asked. But Penalynn was already across the hall. She followed, demanding to know, "What's the matter?!"

They found the fox hiding in a far corner of Penalynn's office, burrowed among folds of heavy drapery. Penalynn said with forced calm, "Rowena, would you please go to the laboratory and ask the men to resume their magic." Her Shadow spasmed as if Penalynn had screamed, clawing the drapes like an animal.

Disturbed by the Shadow's behavior, Rowena hesitated. She'd never seen the fox drop her prim demeanor.

"Go, now!"

The laboratory was already warming. The two servants gagged from the stench too distracted to do any magic. They had thrown open a window, and each leaned out in turns to gulp fresh air.

"Madame Scholastic needs you to keep up your magic," instructed Rowena. She shut the window, though she regretted it instantly. The stench burned her throat.

"What about this one?" The man pointed to the still-smoking device.

Rowena peered at the black sludge inside. "Umm, I guess leave it alone."

Within a few seconds, the temperature magically plummeted, and the machines resumed their tinkering movement. The hairs on Rowena's arm stood up, and not only from the cold. Something had happened in here. Penalynn had discovered something; she knew it. Two vials sat on the countertop; their contents nearly used up. Rowena's minuscule writing labeled the samples: *Ewan Craefog*. His blood had turned to black tar in the machine, smelling like poison and sending Penalynn's Shadow to flee as if for her life.

Questions swirled like a windstorm as Rowena returned to the library. She sat at her desk, then swiveled in her chair to stare at Penalynn's closed door. Her mind roiled with wonder. She wondered if the fox was still hiding. Wondered what it was that had frightened her. Wondered what Penalynn had learned. It had always been like this with Penalynn: Rowena was left alone to merely wonder. Nearly everything about the Scholastic was a mystery. She looked at the paper tacked to the wall with its hundred tally marks. A hundred lines marking Penalynn's secrets.

Rowena continued to wonder, and a creeping foreboding tip-toed up her spine. She had always assumed that what she did as a Scholastic Apprentice was good, morally speaking. That whatever was discovered in that frozen laboratory would benefit each person she had interviewed. But Penalynn shared so little with her that she couldn't be sure. She wondered whether a pile of secrets could ever prove harmless.

And as she wondered, something bitter settled behind her breastbone. Penalynn had harbored one secret too many, breaking her trust at last. Rowena's resentment soured near to hatred for the Scholastic and her countless secrets. She considered the closed door as she sat there, convinced that anything concealed could be nothing good.

CHAPTER
THIRTY-ONE

ONCE A MONTH, THE entire school assembled in the Hall of Sceadwe to hear a lecture from the Myth Keeper. Students filled nearly every row with Sages posted along the walls, watching for mischief. At the front of the hall stood the Myth Keeper behind a podium. His Shadow amplified his voice to reach the back. Most listened respectfully, including Titus. But beside him, Rowena slumped with arms folded, her gaze resolutely downcast. It was only when Titus elbowed her sharply that she realized she had been sighing the whole time.

"Something wrong?" he whispered out of the corner of his mouth.

"Nothing," she lied.

From the dais, The Myth Keeper's monotone persisted in a lulling cadence. "I shall ask an easy question. From where does your magic come?" He stepped around the podium. A few students looked around, unsure if the question was rhetorical. The Myth Keeper said again, "Let's try this again, shall we? From where does your magic come?"

Everyone except Rowena answered in a drone: "The Bazileus."

"Correct. The Bazileus. That great Shadow of our king is the one who gives every—single—one of you—magical power." He pointed emphatically at each word for emphasis.

Meanwhile, Ghost draped across Rowena's lap, magicless as always. Rowena grumbled, following the Myth Keeper's thought to its logical conclusion and finding herself wholly left out. "*Hello.* I'm sitting right here."

Luckily, Titus was the only one who seemed to have heard her.

The students watched the Myth Keeper with, if not rapt, at least quiet attention. Many of them Rowena had interviewed. And if not them, then certainly their parents. She had collected hair and blood and answers to personal questions, then stored it all upstairs in Penalynn's laboratory. None of them seemed bothered by this fact. None of them were left to wonder until the wondering turned to brooding, and the brooding turned to bitterness. She moaned like an angry cat.

"Now for another question," the Myth Keeper continued. "Is your magic as strong as you wish?"

"Nope!" Rowena said more loudly.

A few students chuckled, and the Sage closest to her leveled her a warning look. Titus elbowed her again. The Myth Keeper, however, had not heard. He continued. "It's one's devotion to the Bazileus and their understanding of the Great Myth which will grow one's magical ability."

Rowena chafed at the speech and all it insinuated. Penalynn didn't trust her with the truth, and apparently, the Bazileus didn't trust her with magic. A headache bloomed from the base of her jaw to her temples as she chewed on the implications of the Myth Keeper's words. More questions added to her growing bank of doubt, and her mood darkened even further.

Eventually, the students were dismissed for the day. Free to talk at a normal volume, Titus turned on her. "Care to share what that was all about?" Rowena attempted a look of innocence, but he wasn't convinced. "Spook, you heckled the Myth Keeper."

"It wasn't heckling," she mumbled.

Titus wrapped an arm around her shoulders and steered her toward the exit. "Come on, let's go do some homework. That'll cheer you up, you weirdo."

When they neared the door, Rowena lingered before the wall of statues where row upon row of past kings and queens stood memorialized in stone. She scanned their faces. "They all look so grumpy."

"Well, you would know," said Titus.

Behind them a voice snapped, "Students are not permitted to linger in the Hall of Sceadwe." The Myth Keeper's heels clicked loudly in the already nearly empty hall. He stopped several feet away from Rowena with an imperious smile. "Interested in the royal genealogy, are you? Wondering why they forgot your Shadow?"

Rowena stammered, hearing her fears confirmed in the Myth Keeper's mouth. "I was... just..."

"Sorry, Mr. Keeper," Titus interjected smoothly. "We'll leave." Together, they ran, and the doors slammed behind them.

They had to trek all the way across the library, but eventually, they reached the Scholastic library. Titus sniffed the air. "Mm, what's that smell? You making perfume or something?"

"It's a potion," said Rowena, indicating the iron pot she'd left simmering since that morning. Atticus Wolder's potion book lay open on the desk, and vapor filled the room with a heady aroma.

Like usual, Ghost zoomed to the balcony windows, tapping her flippers impatiently on the glass. Rowena released the Shadow who stared wistfully at the street below. Inside, she cleared room on her desk so Titus could join her while he did his homework. "What are you working on today?" she asked him.

"That essay for Internal Magical Theory." He pulled books from his bag and pointed at the simmering pot. "What is it?"

"I'm trying a new potion for my father."

"He break another limb again?" It was a fair question. Haaris always seemed to be either healing from a recent injury or on the brink of incurring another one.

"Thankfully, no," she said. "This is meant to be preventative."

Titus snapped, remembering something. "Speaking of, do you have any more of that stuff you gave my mom? She said she's out."

Rowena frowned with concern. "She's still having headaches?" Titus nodded, and she retrieved a bottle and then tossed it to him.

"Thanks," he said, "You ever thought of making potions for your trial next year?"

Potions were by far Rowena's greatest skill, surpassing even her penchant for tinkering. She'd solicited a few of her concoctions at Patterfold Potions, but despite the apothecary's goodwill toward her, he'd had little success selling her work to the public. No one in Greymere was brave enough to drink something the ghost girl made—no one except her father and Titus's family. And occasionally Penalynn when she needed a remedy.

Rowena asked, "Speaking of trials, when will you tell me what you're doing for yours?"

"I've already told you. It's a secret."

"It's so soon, though; you might as well tell me."

He crossed his arms. "Fine. But you've got to give me something in return."

"What?"

"Wear a costume to the festival this year."

She huffed. "No."

"Then I'm not telling you my trial."

"I don't wear costumes," she said flatly.

He shook his head as if she were crazy. Soon, they entered the routine of study, stopping every so often for Titus to ask about homework, trusting Rowena to have read their textbooks word for word. Twice, Rowena requested his Shadow's help since various steps of her potion required magic. The owl hummed over the simmering pot as she instructed and soon the potion turned a pale shade of lilac.

"Thanks," she said. Titus resumed writing and Rowena turned to a high shelf for her last ingredient. But her fingers slipped, and the bottle bounced off the desk and rolled across the room. It stopped under an ugly old tapestry hung between bookcases. She knelt to pick it up, worried the fall had made the effervescent liquid pressurize. As carefully as she could, she twisted the top. Sure enough, the cork popped like champagne, ricocheted off the wall, then smacked Titus in the back of the head.

"Ouch! What was that for?!"

Rowena gasped. "No!!" A splash of neon green splattered the tapestry. Rowena groaned and dashed for a rag and cleaner. "Penalynn's going to kill me. She's really precious about this thing. She won't even let me touch it."

She muttered under her breath as she dabbed a damp cloth to the stain. Titus helped, and together, they scrubbed. Eventually, the stain began to lift one layer at a time.

Titus stopped scrubbing to look behind the tapestry. "*Woah*, you seen this?"

Rowena lifted her corner. "It's a...a..."

"That's a silver glass," said Titus, tracing the curious symbols etched along the edge with his fingers.

"I thought silver glass was only for the Sceadwe," said Rowena.

"Only because silver's scarce and seriously expensive. It's not like it's illegal or anything."

"What is Penalynn doing with one?"

"Isn't she loaded?"

"It's got to connect to the Sceadwe in Riven, right?" Rowena assumed.

"Sure. Or maybe family or something?"

Rowena clenched her shoulders, her previous irritation flaring with sudden heat. "Then why would she hide it?!"

How many times had she sat in this room with this same old tapestry, ignorant of the treasure it hid? A silver glass! They were rare—beyond rare. Surely, only the king of Wyre was wealthy enough to own a private silver glass. But all this time, one had been hidden not two yards from Rowena's desk. Her entire body was filled with a sense of rebellion. Rowena was angry. And she was done being left to wonder and question.

"Titus," she said, suddenly smug. "How would you like to learn to use a silver glass?"

"You think we can?" he asked, meeting her eyes.

"We ripped down a tree using a force no one's ever heard of."

He seemed intrigued by the challenge. "How're we supposed to figure it out?"

"There's got to be books about it in the school library."

Titus cocked his head. "Silver glass is famous for being difficult to magic. Rumor is, not even the Myth Keeper's Shadow can do it."

"You scared?"

"A little. I don't think whoever is on the other side will be happy when a couple of teenagers suddenly show up in their glass."

Rowena dismissed his concern with a wave of her hand. "We'll stand out of sight so no one can see us. They'll see an empty room. And if they're of the Sceadwe, I'll explain that I'm a Scholastic Apprentice. Easy."

Titus shook his head, although with a grin. "I think you've been hanging out with Bruce too much."

Rowena wasn't deterred. "I'll go to the library tonight, and we can start as early as tomorrow."

Without another moment's hesitation, Titus clapped his hands and stood to finish his assignment. "Right! Today, we're dutiful students. Tomorrow, deviant lawbreakers."

Rowena stood as well. "Using silver glass isn't against the law," she argued.

"You think Madame Scholastic will be happy with us poking around that thing?"

Rowena grinned. "Nope," she said, utterly thrilled. For once, it was Penalynn's turn to be the outsider to a secret.

CHAPTER
THIRTY-TWO

F OR WEEKS, THEY CLOSETED themselves in Rowena's study, hunched behind armchairs in case anyone appeared in the glass. They kept the doors
locked, but there was no need. Penalynn rarely left her laboratory these days.
With classes winding down and her apprenticeship dwindled down to nothing,
Rowena had plenty of time to devote to their covert project. Yet, all of their
practice, experimentation, and last-ditch guesswork were fruitless. With every
failed attempt, Titus's determination outstripped Rowena's. The glittering glass
taunted him, the first challenge he couldn't overcome. But no matter what they
tried, the glass remained unchanged. Rowena was nearly out of ideas.

One morning in the final week of classes, they relocated to the castle library
under the pretense of studying for final exams—a ruse since Rowena was exempt
since her Shadow couldn't pass a magic test to save her life, and Titus had an
annoying habit of barely studying and passing with high marks anyway. Rowena
scanned the shelves upstairs while Titus sat at a table on the ground floor pretending to read. Eventually, Rowena plopped into a chair across from him.

"Nothing?" he asked.

"No," she grumbled, disappointed in the library for the first time in her life.
"I've scoured this place so many times; Ms. Spruce is starting to ask questions."

"There's got to be more than two books on silver glass," he pressed. "Go ask the librarian."

However, the librarian, Ms. Spruce, was unusually busy that morning. Nearly the entire school was crammed inside the library to study. Though not much learning was happening as Shadows soared and scurried about in a circus of distraction. Students coped with the mounting stress of finals with bursts of magic. Books were thrown from balcony to balcony, magicked to fly loops overhead. Bits of wadded paper were aimed at the heads of studious kids who struggled in vain to ignore the chaos around them. One Shadow had gone so far as to magic the famous statue at the library's center, the carved effigy of the Bazileus. Its marble scales had been manipulated a blinding shade of pink. When Ms. Spruce noticed, shrieks filled the echoing library with cries of *"Heresy!"* and *"Blasphemy!"* Students leaned from the balconies above, craning to witness the librarian's meltdown.

Rowena was wary. "I'm not sure it's wise to let her know our interest in silver glass."

"So, what do we do?" Titus thumbed through a book that described at agonizing length the history and construction of the first silver glass, but not once did it mention how actually to use the thing.

"I've got a few more ideas," said Rowena. "But if they don't work, I guess we give up."

A sniffling sound drew their attention. The librarian wagged her finger in the face of a young boy on the brink of tears. "I don't know how!" he pleaded, denying manipulating the statue, which had now turned a sickly green. "It's only my second year!"

Ms. Spruce abandoned him to interrogate someone else.

Just then, Gloria Patterfold approached their table. "Hi, Titus," she greeted with a smile. "A bunch of us are practicing our trials in the courtyard, and we were wondering if you wanted to join. Rowena, you can come too, only, your trial is next year, so I guess not." She pouted her perfect lips in what Rowena knew to be mock regret, then she smiled back at Titus, brimming with hope.

"Thanks. But I can't," said Titus.

For the briefest second, Gloria's cheeks flushed, but in an instant, her skin returned to its illustrious porcelain once more. "Okay, well, bye then," she said quickly, then met with a waiting gaggle of girls by the library door.

Despite herself, Rowena felt a little sorry for Gloria, who had done a brave thing by inviting a boy she obviously liked, only to be rejected at once. She nudged Titus. "Why didn't you go with her? Hang around some normal people for a change."

He grimaced. "Normal's boring."

Rowena rolled her eyes, whole-heartedly disagreeing. *Normal* was all she ever wanted. Not for the first time, she considered how much normalcy was wasted on the ungrateful.

"Look, you don't have to do this for me," she pressed, stacking their two measly books. "Let's give it up. You should enjoy your last weeks in Greymere."

Titus grabbed the books from her and slid them back to himself. "I'm not ready to quit just yet," he insisted. "It feels, I don't know, like something I got to see through."

He flipped a few pages, and Rowena looked back at the library door where Gloria and her posse had left. "In all that's been going on, I'd forgotten about the trials. Soon you'll leave for university. Are you excited?"

"Sure," he said, noncommittal.

Of the two of them, Titus was usually the chatty one. But every so often, a topic came up that rendered him uncharacteristically introspective. When this happened, Rowena wouldn't press him. After all, she was used to her father's reserved ways and was comfortable with silence. But time was running out; soon, Titus would be gone. "Have you figured out what you'll study?" she asked.

He waited almost an entire minute before answering: "I want to be an Overseer one day, so I'll just do whatever my dad did when he was at university." He said it as if his fate was a path he simply had to walk. "Then I'll return to Greymere and work with him until he retires. Then take over as Overseer after that."

Rowena marveled at his confidence. It was the confidence of a young man whose life would go exactly as it was supposed to, the confidence of one satisfied with his fate, though a bit uninspired, it seemed.

"Have you ever thought of something else?" she asked.

"Like what?"

"I don't know. You're talented enough to be a Sage."

"I don't want to teach."

"What about Scholasticism?"

"Not enough action."

"Myth Keeping?"

Titus laughed, looking more like himself. "You hate the Myth Keeper."

"*He's* the one who hates *me*. Maybe you could be a good one. Less..." Her gaze trailed back to the librarian, who had been joined by Greymere's Myth Keeper. They stood before the dragon statue, which was now purple with orange stripes.

"AH-HA!!" The Myth Keeper crowed at a pair of students, his cry nasal and pinched. "It was *you!!* My Shadow's intuition caught you in the act!"

Titus pointed with his thumb. "You want me to become that guy?"

"Well, no, obviously not. But you could be the first-ever likeable Myth Keeper."

He frowned at her, shaking his head. "What gives?"

"I don't know," she relented. "It's just that…don't you want more than just living in Greymere your whole life? Didn't you just say that 'normal is boring?'"

"I like it here. Don't you?"

She didn't know how to answer, but she didn't have to. Another shriek echoed among the bookshelves. Nearly everyone in the vicinity jumped as Ms. Spruce pointed dramatically at the Bazileus statue, her hand pressed against her mouth.

Titus sprang to his feet, suddenly energized and pulling Rowena to stand. "We should probably leave."

"Why?" she asked.

Laughter drowned out her question, and she craned her neck to see. From the dragon's face sprouted a pointy goatee, mustache, and bushy eyebrows; its scales were bright yellow, and its talons were shrunk to the size of bird feet. The statue looked like a cross between a dragon, a canary, and the Myth Keeper himself. The real Myth Keeper stared aghast, his goatee quivering with rage, and his canary puffed like a yellow cotton ball.

"That last one was me," Titus admitted with a devious grin. He seized her by the hand, and together, they ran for the door, their Shadows racing overhead. The library door shut behind them, muffling the Myth Keeper's offended bellows.

Rowena chortled. "You're right. You would be the worst Myth Keeper ever."

The owl landed atop Titus's shoulder and winked at her as if it were a compliment.

CHAPTER
THIRTY-THREE

BELLS CHIMED TO DISMISS final exams. Students poured from classrooms, cheering and chattering within the castle corridors. Titus pressed against the rush of students to catch up with Rowena, then pulled her into an alcove. "I did it!" he said, ruffling his hair excitedly.

"Did what?" she asked.

"The silver glass, I made it work! But I think it's broken or something. Do you think Madame Scholastic is out of her office? I want to show you."

"What do you mean you made it work? When?!"

"I've been sneaking in at night to practice." He said this as if it was nothing. "And last night, I finally did it! Let's go." He pulled her along, pressing against the stream of students.

"Are you *insane?*" Rowena hollered, startling a younger student who walked by. She dropped her voice, "You've been sneaking in at night?"

"It's not the first time I've broken into that room, you know."

She did know. He'd done the same thing with his brother the morning after her infamous fireworks catastrophe—the same morning she had won her apprenticeship. "Titus, Penalynn sleeps only two rooms away! What if she caught you trespassing, or even worse, using a silver glass *you're not supposed to know exists?!*"

He shrugged off her worry. "My Shadow keeps his intuition up. Madame Scholastic never even came close."

When they reached the Scholastic corridor, it was empty. The owl glided the length of the hall, his intuition sniffing out nearby Shadows. "She's not on this floor," Titus confirmed, then held the door open for Rowena.

As usual, Ghost zoomed to the window and tapped impatiently on the glass. Rowena obliged her Shadow and propped the balcony door ajar. Titus dragged two wingback chairs across the room, angling them before the silver glass, and they each took one to hide behind. The owl perched atop a bookcase just out of view.

"Here's hoping this works again," Titus said, peering around the chair. He didn't blink; his mind perfectly synced with his Shadow, who silently willed magic upon the silver.

After only a moment of bated breath, Rowena gasped. The surface swirled like water in a drain until it dissipated, revealing a dark, black expanse. "How," she whispered, "How did you...you're amazing!"

Titus was clearly pleased with himself, but the black surface seemed to bother him. "I think it's broken. Or maybe I didn't do it right?"

Fearing someone would manifest within the glass, they remained hidden, squinting as best they could. Eventually, Rowena huffed, "Oh, this is ridiculous; I can't see a thing." Her curiosity won out, and she abandoned her hiding spot. Up close, she could make out infinitesimally small specks pricking the black like stars. She brushed her fingertips along the dots but only felt smooth glass.

"What does this look like to you?" she asked, her voice low.

"Nothing." His volume matched hers. "It was the same last night." Their noses touched the glass as they looked closer. "Wait, is that...light?"

"I think there's another tapestry covering the other glass," she said. "And the white specks are light shining through the fabric. It's not broken. It's covered."

"Do you hear that?" Titus whispered.

They pressed their ears to the glass and heard a muffled noise. It sounded familiar, human even.

"Is someone crying?" she mouthed, not daring to speak aloud in case someone was on the other side of the glass after all.

Titus mouthed back, but she couldn't make it out, so he repeated more slowly. "It. Sounds. Like. They. Are. Hurt."

Rowena wondered where in Wyre that voice might be, but her thoughts were suddenly cut off. A terrible, stabbing pain sliced her chest, so sharp she thought her heart was being carved from her ribs with a knife. Bone-chilling howls pierced the silence, and it took her a moment to realize she was screaming.

Beside her, Titus had frozen. Beyond the black came a voice. "*Penny?*" Fingers appeared within the frame's edge, and a hand pulled fabric away to reveal a face. It was only a second, but it was all the time Titus needed. In that brief flash, he saw something in those bloodshot eyes that chilled him. Madness. The person who lived on the other side of the silver glass was not of sound mind. He stopped his magic at once, and the face disappeared in a wink. The silver glass resumed its original gleam.

On the carpet, Rowena had fallen to the floor, her forehead pressed into the carpet, her arms wrapped around her chest. Her screams came from a deep, forbidden place of pain and horror. It was as if someone dug a knife into her very soul.

Beside her, Titus dropped to his knees. "What's happening? Are you hurt?!" He pushed back her hair so he could see her face.

"G...g...Ghost," she stammered in jagged gasps. "Where's...Ghost?"

She dragged herself across the carpet. Titus hoisted her to standing, and she careened toward the balcony, knocking into furniture and nearly tripping with every step. Her hands pressed her chest as if her heart might spill out onto the floor. Her Shadow was gone from her usual spot near the balustrade.

"Ghost!!" Rowena screeched, her voice brittle and tortured. She nearly fell head-first over the rail, but Titus caught her around the waist just in time. Still, she wailed, "Come back!! GHOST!!"

She reached over the stone ledge as far as she could. Titus restrained her by the hips. He followed her gaze, raking his eyes across the street below until he finally noticed a tiny wisp of smoke, nearly invisible against the cobblestones. Ghost floated at the far end of the street, a dangerous distance for any Shadow. She seemed to strain against something as if an invisible leash kept her in check. Still, she inched further from Rowena with her flippered arms outstretched, grasping for distance. Every centimeter gained was like an icepick in Rowena's chest, unleashing fresh cries until suddenly her screams choked off entirely.

Ghost had stopped. She'd reached her prize—a hulking figure covered in short, mottled black and white fur. Her flippers wrapped around the thick neck of a massive dog. Rowena strained to see across the distance, pain strung like a clothesline between her and her Shadow. At the sight of the dog nuzzling her Shadow, she fell back into Titus's arms.

"What? What is it?" he asked, shaking her.

Rowena's skin tinged a ghastly green; sweat beaded down her neck. Pain laced with horrified comprehension, and she nearly retched. This was not just any dog Ghost had found. It was *the* dog. The dog from the Festival of Shadows—the night Ghost had fled to terrible, calamitous ends. Now, three years later, in broad daylight for anyone to see, her Shadow had leaped from the castle's top floor, withstanding painful, almost deadly separation from Rowena just so she could reach this creature.

"She's going to kill you if she doesn't come back," said Titus. He was right. Two halves of a soul could only survive so long this far apart. Her eyelashes fluttered. Her eyes rolled back into her skull. Titus shouted, "Rowena, stay with me! Stay awake!"

"I...can't..." she moaned. Waves of exhaustion crashed over her. Sleep promised to ease the agony, and she closed her eyes, welcoming oblivion.

"Rowena! Listen to me!" Titus shook her shoulders, and her head flopped back. Seeing the whites of her eyes sent him into a panic. His voice cracked. "Rowena, wake up!"

"Bad dog," she mumbled, "Ghost..."

"Yes, let's get you to Ghost." He hooked his arm under the backs of her legs and scooped her up like an oversized baby. Adrenaline hardened his muscles like granite, and he barely felt her weight as she cradled against his chest, whimpering.

He took one step forward, just one step from the balustrade, but Rowena's body convulsed violently. "NO!!!" she screamed. Her pain resurged with a slicing flourish.

Titus's face crumpled at what he had to do. Tears filled his eyes, and he pressed his lips to her ear like a kiss, whispering fiercely, "Spook, I'm so sorry, but this is about to get a lot worse before it gets better. Just stay with me!"

He placed one foot after the other, forcing himself to ignore her cries. Somehow, his Shadow had the presence of mind to drop the tapestry over the silver glass before they left. With every step, Rowena shook violently, but by the time they reached the courtyard on the ground floor, she fell silent, her body frightfully still in his arms. Titus looked down at her closed eyes, her ashen skin, hoping with all his might that she was merely unconscious.

He swallowed. "Nearly there."

The castle was empty, students and teachers alike having sprung from containment to celebrate their freedom and the upcoming festival. He sprinted through the massive doors undeterred. Rowena's head lolled side to side. When he'd rounded the final corner of the castle, he heard the booming tones of a dog's bark. A massive hound galloped at full speed directly for them, coming to a screeching stop just in time. Ghost sped at the creature's side. When she reached them, Ghost crashed into Rowena so hard it was as if she wanted to lodge herself inside her ribcage.

As soon as Rowena's Shadow touched her skin, she spasmed, gulping air as if emerging from deep water.

Titus nearly dropped her in relief, but he caught himself. His knees buckled and crashed against the pavement so he was kneeling when he lowered her to the ground. His adrenaline dried up in an instant, and his arms shook with fatigue.

Panting, he bent in half so low his hair grazed the ground.

Rowena squeezed her Shadow against her chest, reveling in the closeness. Ghost hugged her back, though she angled her head so she could see the dog who sat nearby. It had creamy white and black fur splattered like ink. Intelligent brown eyes seemed to appraise Rowena before it bobbed its head in greeting.

Rowena scowled. Twice now, this beast had nearly upended her life, sending her Shadow into fits and nearly killing Rowena in the process.

They all sat in the middle of the street: Rowena and the dog surveying one another, with Titus fully laid out on the cobblestones.

"You all right?" he croaked, his voice jagged with emotion and fatigue.

Rowena nodded. "You?"

Slowly, he sat up, wincing but also nodding. "But if your Shadow ever does that again, I'm going to kill her."

"Agreed," Rowena muttered, pressing Ghost tighter against her chest as if to imprison her under her own skin.

For the first time ever, Titus eyed the wispy Shadow with a look of suspicion. "What got into her?"

"This dog."

"Why?"

"No idea." Rowena felt baffled and even more betrayed—and by her own Shadow of all things. Although, she wondered if she could really count her Shadow as a person. The pain of their separation proved that Ghost harbored some portion of Rowena's soul, but still, she'd nearly killed her. Ghost had proved once again that she was not to be trusted. Rowena reminded Titus: "It's happened like this before."

It took him a moment to remember. For weeks after that unfortunate Festival of Shadows, they had pondered over the source and whereabouts of the mystery dog. Now, years later, here it sat. The memory returned, and Titus gasped. "That's *the* dog?"

Rowena confirmed, "The one when the fireworks burned everything down."

"Didn't you say it saved you?"

"After causing Ghost to misbehave in the first place." She glared with venomous accusation but then relented with a sigh. "But yes. It saved me from a rocket that would certainly have killed me. It pulled me to safety, then blocked the explosions from me with its own body."

"Where'd it come from?"

"Maybe it's one of the animals from the mail menagerie?" she wondered.

Titus shook his head. "This is definitely not a work-dog." At this, the dog raised its head, its posture ridged as if it sat upon a throne.

Rowena asked the question which had lain in the back of her mind for years.

"Could it be someone's Shadow?"

"No," Titus answered firmly.

"How do you know?"

"Intuition." Rowena didn't understand, so he explained, "Intuition doesn't just sniff out magic. It can also sense the presence of other Shadows nearby." He cocked his head as if realizing something. "Actually…that's not entirely true now that I think about it. My intuition has never been able to sense your Shadow. It's like she's invisible to it."

This information wasn't exactly new. Even Rowena's own father described Ghost as "empty." Craefog had said she was "like a dead person" when he described Ghost's invisibility to magic. But hearing it confirmed by her best friend felt disturbing.

"Intuition doesn't see your Shadow because she doesn't have magic, don't you think?" asked Titus.

"How would I know? Maybe this dog is a Shadow like that?"

"Where is its other half?" Titus looked around the empty street, the castle wall on one side and the backside of shops on the other. "Are they hiding?"

Rowena's energy suddenly flagged in the wake of the crisis. "I'm too tired to solve this mystery right now. I'm going home." Slowly, she rose to her feet.

"Can you walk okay?" Titus held out his arms as if she might topple again.

Reunited with her Shadow, though, she felt stable and whole once more. Still, Titus insisted on walking her home. Rowena insisted she was fine, but Titus would only leave her once they reached her front porch. The dog followed them the entire way. They kept looking back expecting it, or rather *hoping* it would eventually wander elsewhere, but it never did. And when Titus reluctantly left Rowena at home, the dog remained with her.

Before entering the house, Rowena held Ghost up to eye level as if talking to a small child. "Papa won't let you keep it," she told her Shadow.

Ghost blinked blandly at first but then seemed to understand. She jerked out of Rowena's hands and dropped like a leaf to sit atop the dog's back, making it clear that wherever she went, so would the dog. Rowena considered kicking her Shadow; she was so irritated. But there was no point in arguing with a voiceless, mindless mist. So, she opened the door. Ghost entered the house astride the dog as if on a horse. Apparently, and completely against her will, Rowena had a new pet.

CHAPTER
THIRTY-FOUR

I T WASN'T UNTIL BEDTIME that Ghost finally parted with the animal, and then only because the dog couldn't climb the ladder to Rowena's lofted bedroom. Rowena supposed she should be grateful her Shadow chose to sleep with her instead of the animal.

The following day came the Festival of Shadows. As soon as night fell, Rowena and her father walked the lantern-lit path with the dog resolutely following. They stopped at the entrance before the bulbous arch of pumpkins. A lively group paraded past them, decked in elaborate costumes, each one an opulent version of their Shadow. Haaris wore a simple ensemble comprised of a headband with furry ears and painted nose and eyes, but compared to the rest of Greymere's pageantry, he looked a bit dour.

Rowena wore no costume. Her apprentice cape buttoned down the front, and her bookbag slung across her chest, looking as if she were headed for class, not a kingdom-wide festival.

"I still think you should sit this one out," Haaris said, eyeing their guest. The dog sat at Rowena's side, much like the spaniel did by him. "It's wrong to have an animal pose as your Shadow."

"I'm not pretending it's my Shadow!" she said.

"People don't walk around with wild animals. It would be a fair assumption."

She threw up her hands. They'd been over this nearly a dozen times. "I don't have a choice, Papa. Ghost won't give it up."

Someone interrupted their argument by calling for Haaris.

"Go," Rowena urged him, ready to be rid of his disapproving glower. "You know the festival can't function without you."

He grumbled, "You'd think people didn't have magic of their own." Yet, despite his resentment at being roped into festival duties, he preferred the work, leaving everyone else to do the actual effort of merry making. He wagged his finger in a warning fashion. "Keep your Shadow out in the open at all times." He scowled at Ghost for good measure, then left.

Rowena grumbled under her breath, focusing on her irritation rather than the complicated hurt that simmered down deep. Her father was just as scared and ashamed of her Shadow as he had been when she was a child, smuggling her from view. But after recent events, she couldn't blame him. Even her own doubts had renewed. She usually ignored Ghost's quirks. But the dive from the castle balcony and the sudden friendship with a wild dog, of all things, reminded her that Ghost was still a stranger—a mystery she might never solve.

She scooped Ghost from the air and held her to her face, forcing the Shadow to look into her eyes. "Ghost, pay attention. The festival is for *people* and *Shadows*. No dogs. She can sit here and watch, but—" At the word "sit," the dog plopped its bottom onto the grass. Rowena stopped short. "Right...good. Stay there."

The dog bobbed its snout in an unmistakable nod. Rowena stepped back. The dog understood her. She was lucky if Ghost understood her own name. "Alright, Ghost, the dog will sit here, and you will come with me."

Ghost floated between Rowena and the dog, considering, as if they were clues to a riddle. After a beat, she patted the animal's neck and then flew to Rowena, who felt rather pleased at having successfully communicated with her two mute companions. She swung her bag off her shoulder, then hid it under a squashy fern beside the dog. "Watch that for me, will you?"

The dog nodded again, and Rowena patted its head. She walked through the archway of pumpkins, looking over her shoulder to confirm the dog hadn't moved, then entered the Festival of Shadows and joined the throng of people to meander—past rows of market stalls with their colorful tents, past performers and their come-and-go audiences, past children playing and couples flirting. Rowena wandered without a target until a flash of glitter caught her eye. On the dancefloor, Titus stomped to a fast-paced melody, hand in hand with Gloria Patterfold. Her joy radiated like a halo, her smile dazzling. The song ended, and at once, another tune drummed up. A new partner claimed Gloria.

Rowena searched for Titus, but he was lost by the crowd churning in a kaleidoscope of costumes and Shadows. Suddenly, a voice spoke in her ear, "Spook, what are you wearing?" She jumped.

"This is the Festival of *Shadows!*" he practically hollered in her ear to be heard over the music. Rowena chaffed at his condescending tone. "Every person here is dressed like their Shadow. In every town of Wyre, people are dressed like their Shadows. Tonight, in Riven, the King himself and the entire Sceadwe—which you are a member of, by the way—are dressed like their Shadows. You say you don't want to draw attention to yourself, but by not participating, you *really* draw attention."

It was Rowena's third festival living out and among society. Every year, Titus made the same argument. At this point, it was tradition. A tradition Rowena hated.

She shouted over the din of drums and violins. "Let's not spend your last days in Greymere fighting!"

"You're making it worse!" he yelled.

"What?!" she yelled back.

"The superstitions about you. You're MAKING IT WORSE!!"

The music stopped cruelly. Titus's last words screamed in the abrupt silence. Everyone in their vicinity stopped to look at them. The first eyes Rowena noticed were Gloria's, who seemed annoyingly pleased. Rowena stomped away, and Titus followed her.

"I'm sorry. I didn't mean—"

Rowena jerked away from him and changed directions toward the dance-floor. The music kicked up again, and she wove through the tight crowd of spinning couples. Someone grabbed her hand, and suddenly, she found herself standing in the arms of Bruce Ashworth. His eyes glittered behind a black mask; his raccoon counterpart slung roguishly across his shoulders. The music slowed as couples swayed like reeds under the glow of the bonfire. Rowena, however, stiffened like a plank.

"You afraid you'll fall in love with me or something?" Bruce teased.

She sputtered. "What? No!"

"Then loosen up. It's like dancing with a tree." He jostled her waist, and she exhaled, softening her posture and allowing his touch to lead her through the steps.

"Where's your lady friend," she asked, swaying in time with his movement.

"She's back at camp getting ready for something. I think they've got a ceremony tonight or something."

"The Wandering don't celebrate the Festival of Shadows. What's the ceremony for?"

"No idea." He spun her, then caught her waist to draw her along. "Sersha and

I don't do a lot of *talking* when we're together."

"Gross."

"You jealous?" She felt his thumb tickle her rib playfully.

She made a face. "No."

He chuckled. "She told me to bring you and Titus along with me if you wanted. But sounds like you two had a spat. You know, The Wandering don't wear costumes. Just tell Titus you've joined the tribe."

"As a future Overseer, I'm sure he'd love that."

Bruce grinned. The song ended, and they spun to a stop, clapping politely. Then he patted his stomach. "Time for a turkey leg," he said and left the dance-floor, saying over his shoulder, "I'll find you later."

Rowena found a nearby stall serving cider and grabbed a cup, then retreated to an empty patch of grass out of the way of the crowd and quieter by comparison. She sat cross-legged and sipped the foamy drink. The front half of her body grew deliciously warm from the bonfire nearby while her back prickled pleasantly, the cool of the forest pressing in close. The next song was slow. It unraveled her nerves into a mellow reverie. Notes of cinnamon and clove clung to her tongue, and she swayed, her mind contentedly blank for once.

"That's a nice dog you've got there."

Her moment of peace was over. She looked up to see a man standing over her. Firelight exaggerated the lines of his face. It took her a moment to remember him. The mailman, Nester Brown, looked with uncanny admiration. Rowena followed his gaze to see a prodigious figure planted on her right. The dog had left its hiding place to join her, or rather Ghost, on the grass. It sat, poised as if for a portrait.

"What I wouldn't give for a beast like that on my crew," said the mailman. "Just look at the size of her! The strength of a horse but the mind of a dog. That's the dream combination there." He walked around them, admiring the dog from every angle. Rowena was unsure what to say. He asked her, "Do you mind if I...?"

"Mind what?"

"Just a peek at her mind is all. See what sort of beast she is—on the inside."

"It's not my dog," she said, unconvincing as her Shadow sat atop its back. Rowena's curiosity lit like tinder. Maybe the mailman's magic could discover the reason the dog followed her. Perhaps he could unearth the appeal that Ghost managed to understand. "Go ahead," she allowed.

The man's moth-Shadow fluttered above the dog's head, magic flaring. After a moment, Nester Brown's rapture shifted to confusion; then, he yelped and hopped back as if he'd been stung. "That—that's an odd creature," he said, covering his mouth with a trembling hand. Without another word, he hastened away, throwing suspicious glances over his shoulder before disappearing among the crowd. The moth twitched fitfully to catch up.

"That was less than unhelpful," Rowena muttered, scowling at the dog as if it had insulted her. Ghost hung on its neck like a child with a favorite grandparent.

Rowena considered depositing the dog back in the forest. But the last thing she needed was for the creature to come looking for her in the middle of the ceremony where the entire town would undoubtedly notice. So, when the lights flashed overhead, she retrieved her bag from its hiding place near the entrance, then allowed the dog to follow her into the arena. Thankfully, so many people jockeyed about to find good seats, no one seemed to care.

CHAPTER
THIRTY-FIVE

As soon as Penalynn arrived at the Festival of Shadows, she wanted to leave. It was always more a chore than a celebration, but this year more than others.

As soon as she entered the meadow, her Shadow soured. It was a celebration of magic at every turn, everyone paying homage to their Shadows. The fox itched to use her own magic, burned with unused power. Soon, her mood was too bothersome, so Penalynn abandoned the crowd and entered the arena early. She and her Shadow passed the sign reserving the section for members of the Sceadwe and sat on a grassy bench cut into the steep hill.

The fox burrowed into Penalynn's skirt, making a nest of taffeta and toile, nearly invisible against the orange fabric. Her thoughts rushed in a reproaching torrent.

The muscle in Penalynn's jaw twitched as she held back her retorts. But no thought could ever be hidden. The fox knew what she meant to say, even if she didn't say it. Penalynn had been born with a voice imprisoned in her mind that constantly told her what to do and how to do it, judging her mercilessly if she ever failed. Her life flowed with twin undercurrents of disdain and resentment. Undoubtedly, one day, the conflict would rip her apart beyond repair.

The fox chuckled darkly. *I am not the one who will rip the world in two. All you have to do is stop. Stop this shameful work and be done.*

"No," Penalynn whispered, her lips barely moving. "It's too important."

Claim moral superiority all you want, but I'm right. You'll ruin lives, and for what? Your career? For the ability to say, 'I told you so'? If I'm wrong, tell your apprentice. Tell Rowena what she wants to know, what she deserves to know.

"She's not ready."

Claws punctured layers of fabric to prick Penalynn's thigh. The fox's voice was distant, barely even a thought. *Why do you hate me?*

Penalynn's heart wrung like a sponge, careening a tear down her cheek. She flicked it away. "I don't. I didn't want to be right. Not about this."

You'll come to regret it.

Penalynn laughed, the sound knocked from her chest as if she'd been hit. "I already do."

People began trickling into the arena, oblivious to the Scholastic's invisible fight. The fox watched them—every pair of human and Shadow—every costume borne from self-love towards their soul's magical half. Every Shadow was free to use his or her magic to the fullest extent. The fox brimmed with envy, and Penalynn ached to give her Shadow's magic release. Impossible as it felt, she hated the Shadow and loved her at the same time—simultaneously adored the fox and longed to be rid of her. It wasn't sympathy she felt for her Shadow, for sympathy required separation, a sense of otherness. But there could be no separation between them. Penalynn *was* her Shadow. Every thought, feeling, itch, and pain. Her mind, heart, and will—all of it hers—all of it theirs. Perhaps this was what it meant to have a soul. To be trapped within one's own being. Bound to something which strained against nothing because she strained against herself. What relief it would be to strain against something that was not herself. Freedom could be attained then. Penalynn had strained against Riven and had ultimately found freedom in Greymere, even if forced. She strained to be free from her own mind but would never win such a fight. Surely, the struggle would eventually cannibalize her.

In Penalynn's periphery, she saw Rowena walking down the row. Guilt clenched her stomach. She knew she had been unfair. Her decision to shield Rowena from the truth robbed her of a proper apprenticeship and kept her cruelly in the dark. With a sweep of her arm, she tucked her billowing skirt to make room on the bench.

"What's that?" she asked when Rowena sat down.

"A dog," Rowena answered. Her tone was icy in a way that seemed to agree with Penalynn's guilt. She hadn't forgiven Penalynn for withholding their re-search findings.

Penalynn didn't know how to respond. "She's pretty."

There was plenty of room in the reserved section, as the Overseer, Myth Keeper, and every Sage helped with the ceremony onstage. So the dog had plenty of space to lay down, taking the length of three seats at least. Rowena's strange little Shadow sat among its folded legs as if on a couch.

The tense silence between mentor and apprentice was only relieved when the ceremony began. Compared to previous years, the show was rather average. All the customary participants played out a tired routine, and while the audience and Penalynn showed polite attention, Rowena fell into a sort of stupor until the Shadow trials began. The trials were always her favorite part, but this year's displays seemed woefully unoriginal. Her focus waned again, disappointed, and she found herself stroking the dog's head, which had found its way into her lap. Suddenly, a familiar figure caught her attention.

Titus stood center stage, illuminated in the ring of manipulated moonlight. His Shadow perched on his outstretched arm. The moment stretched into another, and soon, people shifted in their seats. A few coughs broke the silence, and Rowena fidgeted uncomfortably, nervous for her friend. Impossibly, Titus was freezing up, though he didn't seem the type for stage fright.

"What was that?" someone said nearby.

Several voices echoed similarly back and forth until Rowena felt it too, first through her feet, then through her seat. Rumbling tremors rose from the ground. As one, the crowd gasped to witness Titus's magic. She flinched, grabbing Penalynn's arm, but Penalynn didn't notice, trying herself to make sense of what they saw.

The stone stage, the width and breadth of a house, slowly rose from the ground as if a giant's hand lifted it like a platter. The slab of mountain floated several feet in the air with Titus perched atop, looking as if he rode a massive stone eagle. Across the arena, Shadows flared intuition only to discover it was no persuasion upon their mind. What they saw was real. Somehow, Titus's Shadow magicked a chunk of granite to lift upward, neither animated on the wind nor persuaded by trickery. But animation wasn't possible without existing energy.

Everyone knew that. The stage had no energy, yet his magic had moved it—from static to mobile in a single act. Such magic was impossible. Together, they all witnessed something new. Surely, something never seen before in Wyre.

Slowly, as if tucking a sleeping baby into its crib, the owl's magic lowered the stage, setting it deftly in place where it had been. Then Titus bowed. That was it. No pageantry. No music. No fanfare or flourish. His trial was over. The crowd sat speechless. He stood self-consciously, about to flee the stage in embarrassment, when the crowd finally found its voice. Like dynamite, they exploded. Every person jumped to their feet to clap and cheer at the top of their lungs. Some even wiped away tears, awed at their good fortune at seeing such a raw display of power.

None of them knew what Penalynn and Rowena did, that his magic was the average animation magic everyone used. He'd simply animated the invisible force called grounding, which Atticus Wolder had theorized. Instead of touching the energy to pull down like he had done to the tree in class, Titus tweaked the technique to push upward instead.

"Impressive," Penalynn said close so only Rowena could hear. "Riven will be glad to have him."

The Wandering fireworks came next, lighting the sky, far and safe as they were designed, but Rowena hardly noticed. Though Penalynn had meant her words as a compliment, they stung Rowena. Despite her argument with Titus, the thought of him leaving ached like a bruise. With his trial complete, nothing stood between him and University. Tears threatened to spill from her eyelashes as she found herself wholly unprepared to say goodbye.

When the ceremony ended, Penalynn left, but Rowena remained seated. She watched people swarm the stage, eager to congratulate the Overseer and his talented son. Eventually, Titus spied her sitting alone in the near-empty arena. With some difficulty, he extricated himself from his newfound fans to join her.

Rowena congratulated him. "It looks like you invented a new magic."

"Nah, it was a trick I learned from a friend," he said, heady from success and attention.

"She sounds smart."

"Smarter than me, that's for sure." His face and tone turned somber, and he took her hand in his. "Spook, I'm so sorry about earlier. I hate how people treat you as if there was something wrong with you. I figured a costume would help you fit in better."

Rowena squeezed his hand. "A costume won't change things, Titus. Look at your Shadow. He's powerful, beautiful, *whole.* I don't expect you to know what it's like for me with Ghost. But it's not something..."

"What?"

Ghost hovered close—oblivious, silent, and always there. Rowena's voice was no louder than a breath, "She's not something I want to celebrate."

Titus hung his head. "I'm an idiot. We have officially established that. I'm sorry. Genuinely. I promise I won't ever bring up costumes again."

She shrugged. "You won't be here next year, anyway."

Her words were like a slammed door. Unspoken promises strung between them were abruptly cut off. They stared at one another, speechless.

Suddenly, Titus's face quirked, and he said, "So you think my Shadow is *beautiful?*"

Her face fell. "What? No!"

"Yes, you do. You just said it."

She blustered, "No! I meant, as far as owls go, your Shadow does a pretty good imitation."

"Uh-huh, I get it. You think I'm beautiful."

She struggled to pull her hand away, but he held on tight, pulling her arm across his chest. She dropped her forehead to his shoulder, her hair obscuring her blushes.

Behind them, someone said, "Oh good, you made up." Bruce took the stairs two at a time, holding a turkey leg in each hand. "You two ready for a party, Wandering style?"

Rowena gaped at him. "You live with them, are in love with one of their own, and yet you still manage to be so offensive? How?"

"Raw talent." He wiped turkey grease from his chin, then pointed at the dog beside her. "What's that?"

"A dog."

"Fair enough. If you're coming, then come."

Rowena looked at Titus. "He's invited us to the camp. Want to go?"

"Well, I'm not about to let you go with my idiot brother alone," he said, pulling her to stand. And so, they followed Bruce into the forest, hand-in-hand all the way to The Wandering.

CHAPTER THIRTY-SIX

IT WAS WELL PAST midnight when they entered Torborough Forest. Bruce led them by lanternlight. Black knots etched in white bark seemed to make faces at them as they passed. After a night of dancing, a lengthy ceremony, and the long walk, Rowena leaned heavily against Titus when they arrived at The Wandering. A sleepy Ghost cradled in the crook of her arm.

Two men stood at the entrance, their Shadows white as the moon trickled through the canopy. It wasn't clear if the men were guards posted to keep visitors out or doormen to welcome visitors in. Bruce spoke with them. After a quick exchange, they looked at Rowena and Titus, who heard voices in their mind: "The chief told us you might come. He invites you to the elder circle."

They passed the guards, and Titus asked, "What's the elder circle?"

"The chief's fireside," said Bruce, awed but confused. "Only the elders and their families are allowed there."

They walked a circuitous path, passing tent after tent. Around every bend, Bruce craned his neck as if searching for someone.

Rowena clung to Titus's arm. "*This* is their camp?" she whispered.

All these years, she had assumed The Wandering lived in primitive conditions. They were a nomadic tribe, after all. Certainly, the lifestyle would favor the practical over the comfortable. However, Rowena could think of only one word to describe their camp: *elegant.* They traversed among cunning domed dwellings of various sizes, each with a round thatched roof perched atop thick, polished tree trunks. Rich canvas stretched taut to make up the tent walls. Closer observation revealed every inch of fabric to be painted in intricate white, barely discernable against the creamy canvas. Entire scenes wrapped the dwellings—some beautiful and placid . . . others violent and graphic. But each was rendered in a sophisticated style Rowena had never seen.

The tents were arranged in circles, facing inward toward an earthen courtyard with a fire at the center. Some circles were large, nearly twenty or thirty tents in wide open loops. While others were small—only a handful of tents squeezed in a tight ring. Around the fires, people congregated, standing, sitting, or lounging on cushions. And from every side, music swelled.

When they reached the centermost ring of tents, more lavish than the others, Bruce hesitated on the path. "I'm not allowed in the elder circle. Do we just walk in?"

"How should I know?" said Titus. "Where's your girlfriend? Ask her."

Bruce cautiously stepped into the ring. A fire greeted them, blazing high and bright. Most people sat on cushions, while a handful sat on carved chairs. These were the elders. They recognized the chief at once, seated at the center of elders, with his iconic white bat hanging from the arm of his chair. Several children were also present, though most lay asleep in their mother's arms or cuddled their Shadows atop pillows.

Sersha stood before the fire, singing to those who had gathered. Rowena was glad to see that Sersha had evidently recovered from their trip to Craefog's. The fire illuminated her from below, dramatizing her jaw and cheekbones. Rowena thought the effect looked rather skeletal. Sersha's voice lilted in a complicated melody alongside a reeded instrument played by a slightly older woman seated on a cushion by her feet. Though Rowena didn't understand the words, she listened carefully. With every note, her emotions ebbed. She felt as if she knew the story being sung, a tale of bravery and loss. Greymere's music somehow seemed blunt compared to this lilting voice and trilling reed—light yet haunting, like a playful breeze over a misty grave.

Seeing Sersha seemed to relax Bruce. He led them to empty cushions and plopped himself down. Someone passed them a platter heaped with bread and cheese. Around the courtyard, hands exchanged similar platters, primarily laden with spiced vegetables, bread, and various aromatic sauces to dip. Rowena snatched a seeded loaf, then passed the platter to Titus. They were glad to sit after their long walk, their Shadows sagging with exhaustion. With each passing minute, Ghost's smoke-made eyes drooped lower. Only the dog seated behind her seemed unphased by the hour. It sat upright and regal as ever.

"Ugh," Titus muttered through a yawn, "I'm not sure I'm going to make it just sitting here like this."

Bruce snatched a bottle from a nearby mat. He took a deep swig and then handed the bottle to his brother.

"What is it?"

"It'll wake you up."

Titus took a tentative sip, debated briefly, and then pulled two long gulps. He shook his head like a dog out of water before passing the bottle to Rowena. The drink was sour with a bite at the end, but after only one swallow, she felt the pressure behind her eyes lessen and so took another. The effect was immediate; the drink roused her with intractable clarity.

"Careful," Bruce warned as she raised the bottle for another taste. "That stuff will make you crazy after a few swallows."

"How so?"

"The first time I tried it, I drank a whole bottle and didn't sleep for three days. By the end, I was so out of my mind I tried to climb a tree stark naked, and, uh, it didn't end well."

Rowena's eyes popped, fearing the sips she'd already taken might cause her to spontaneously strip down as well. But she felt awake, not manic. She corked the bottle then turned in her seat so no one would see her stash the potion in her bag. As soon as she returned to the castle, she intended to decipher the drink's makeup. Maybe replicate it.

The music stretched on. Sersha's voice swelled in increasingly complicated measures. Rowena was certain her otter Shadow used magic to accomplish the harmonies, sure no human was capable of such high-pitched, double-toned feats. When the song ended, Sersha swept deeply into a bow, but no one clapped or cheered. Instead, another woman took her place, and the girl with the instrument began a new song.

Bruce smiled at Sersha as if he expected her to approach him. Instead, she walked around the fire, her bare feet pale against the black forest floor. She stopped at the chief's chair, and he whispered something. Rowena's stomach nearly flipped when suddenly they both looked directly at her. She felt as if they spoke about her. It seemed confirmed when Sersha left the chief and walked directly toward Rowena. But she stopped before Bruce. She bent, her auburn hair trailing down his arm as she kissed him on the lips.

Sersha then greeted Titus and Rowena in the common tongue, not relying on her usual mind-talk. It sounded odd to Rowena, but more because of the politeness of the gesture than her command of the language, which was surprisingly good. "My uncle welcomes you to his fire," she said, then indicated the dog by Rowena. "And who is this?"

"Oh, um…it's just a dog," Rowena said awkwardly. "Is that allowed?"

"Beasts are welcome here."

The chief watched them from across the fire. Sersha shared Bruce's cushion, so close to Rowena that their hips touched. A new singer approached the fire for another song. Rowena listened politely, understanding none of the words, until suddenly, a voice filled her mind.

Who is that?

She startled, her head swiveling.

The voice answered her unspoken question. *Over here.*

At the end of the row of elders, aged eyes caught her attention. The firelight played with the copious lines on the old woman's face to seem almost grotesque. At her side, a table with spindly legs held a bowl of water where a milky white fish swam weary circles. Rowena had never seen such a Shadow. Before she could consider the impracticality of a nomad with a fish for a Shadow, the woman spoke again. Her voice sounded just as cracked as the top and bottom of her lips.

The creature with you. Who is it?

Rowena looked at her friends, but both Titus and Bruce seemed oblivious to the inaudible conversation. The woman's questions were just for her. Rowena sat dumb, unsure how to answer. If she spoke aloud, she'd have to shout to be heard across the way. She could walk over and answer but didn't dare approach the elders and chief. Instead, she tried answering the same way she heard—in her mind.

It's just a dog, she thought.

That is no dog.

It felt as if the ground dropped, plummeting her into the earth like a grave. Rowena knew Fern persuaded her every now and then, nudged her thoughts and feelings in ways that never felt entirely right. But that was just a touch, fleeting. This woman ravaged. To listen in on the most private of things, her own thoughts—she was a thief looting a temple, a marauder infiltrating the most sacred of places. Her mind. By spying on her thoughts, the woman exposed Rowena more thoroughly than if she stood naked in the crowd.

The woman was unconcerned with Rowena's discomfort. She said, *The beast is no Shadow either.*

Rowena seethed. She imagined herself sprinting across the distance, reaching into that fishbowl, and throwing the woman's Shadow into the fire.

The woman's cheeks folded like an accordion into a mocking sort of smile. But if she saw Rowena's murderous thoughts, she didn't say. Instead, her focus remained on the dog.

She calls herself...Isla.

Wonder shoved Rowena's hate aside, and even in her mind, she could hear the hope in her words: *She spoke to you?*

Yes.

Did she say anything else?

She will usher the Scead Demortas.

Rowena remembered that word. Both Craefog and Sersha had called her that, though Sersha sarcastically. And like the other times she'd heard it, several translations overlapped simultaneously, the most discernable being *Shadowless.* Or was it Shadow-*death?*

What is that? The Shadowless?

Perhaps you are.

Did the dog say that?

No. But Isla will bring the Shadowless.

Is that why she is following me?

The old woman did not answer. The courtyard had fallen silent. The song ended. The chief reached out to take the old woman's hand to help her to stand. Rowena's mind felt oddly quiet in the aftermath of their conversation. All eyes watched as the elder shuffled to where the singers had stood. A young boy carried the fishbowl behind her, his face strained as he carefully planted each step, terrified of spilling even a drop of water. There was a change in the air as a thick silence settled over the entire camp. Only the wind in the treetops dared make a sound, the tribe holding its collective breath.

Sersha whispered to her Wyrian guests, "Now for the Shadowless legend. Shall I translate for you?"

They each nodded, though Rowena's mind still chafed at the old lady's persuasion. Leaning on her cane, the elder sang in the same brittle voice Rowena had heard in her mind, only now in the indecipherable language of The Wandering. Her voice reached up and out over the entire encampment.

Sersha's Shadow translated:

I am a herald, awakening an ancient truth erased.

The Shadowless is coming to rescue back his people from the waste.

I entered the king's court; upon his throne he sat and watched me come.

The Bazileus was hidden, in his cave, a phantom he had become.

I am not animal, nor Shadow, a beast's body I wore like a veil.

I opened my mouth, and the people were amazed to hear me tell:

The Shadowless is coming, searching for the lost child.

His people now exiled,

Broken and lost in the waste and wild.

The people did not tremble, no omen in my words did they discern.

But the Bazileus saw truth,

And so struck me down, never to return.

I watch and wait,

For the Shadowless to give me my command.

When he appears before you, I will herald the very end.
The Shadowless is coming, searching for the lost child.
His people now exiled,
Broken and lost in the waste and wild.
Then on the last day, Bazileus you will meet your enemy at last,
Shadow death once done,
This ancient curse will be the outcast.
The Shadowless is coming, searching for the lost child.
His people now exiled,
Broken and lost in the waste and wild.
I am a herald, reminding of an ancient truth erased.
The Shadowless is coming to rescue back his people from the waste.

The song ended, and after a hallowed silence, the camp resumed its easy chatter. Music swelled once again. More platters were passed around, and everyone ate and drank. Bruce and Sersha talked in low murmurs, their voices seeming oddly strained. But Rowena didn't notice. She sat rigid, her limbs filled with what felt like mutinous bees. She might have wondered if she'd had too much of the wakening drink, except all she could think about was how every single elder glanced her way, their gaze darting to the corner of their eyes, taking turns so no one would notice. But she noticed.

"I want to go home," she told Titus.

He agreed, and so they stood to leave. Bruce ignored them, thoroughly engrossed in whatever he and Sersha seemed to be bickering about, and so, they took his lamp and left. By the time they left the camp, night waned in cerulean light. Morning dawned in full when they reached Rowena's porch, having been led by the dog named Isla, who people kept telling her was, in fact, not a real dog.

Chapter
Thirty-Seven

Two days after their visit to the Wandering camp, Rowena had yet to catch up on sleep. When she woke the sun was high, but the light seemed thin somehow. The first thing she noticed was her father's face outside her window, standing on a ladder. He battled the rosebush whose reaching tendrils threatened to devour the house every summer. It would take him a few days to prune it into submission. She thought about helping him as she went downstairs, but then Ghost flopped onto Isla. Rowena didn't have the energy to argue, so she dropped to the couch beside them. A while later, voices roused her from a nap, followed by a knock at the door. She opened it with a stifled yawn, hugging her sweater close against the cold.

"Hey, Spook," said Titus. The bags under his eyes proved he also had yet to catch up on sleep from their all-night jaunt. Behind him stood Bruce with his hands in his pockets, looking uncharacteristically grumpy. "I came to say goodbye. We're leaving for Riven...today."

His words were like icy water, rousing her awake. "But...but I thought that was next week."

Titus spoke through his teeth, clearly unhappy, "We're leaving early. Bruce is in a bad way, and Mom and Dad are taking the opportunity to get him back to university as quickly as they can. They hope it'll cheer him up."

"What happened?"

He dropped his voice. "He and Sersha split."

From behind him, Bruce interjected loudly, "She thought I was a spy! Can you believe that? A spy! All I did was tell my dad a few things, and suddenly I'm—" he threw up his arms sarcastically— "*spying for the Sceadwe!*"

"Your dad works for the Sceadwe," said Rowena all too reasonably.

Bruce huffed. "You sound just like her! Did you know The Wandering are all vegetarians? I gave up *meat* for her!"

"Bruce, can you give us a minute?" Titus said with exaggerated patience.

"Careful, brother," Bruce warned. "They're nice and all in the beginning, but eventually, they break your heart and ruin your life. No offense, Rowena."

Titus shoved him, and Bruce acquiesced, stomping to the gate where he blatantly sulked.

"Thirty days to Riven," Titus muttered with dread.

He looked at her, and Rowena felt her heartbeat in her ears. Titus's departure had always been an impending reality, one they avoided, conveniently deluding themselves with distraction. Now, suddenly and wholly unwelcome, goodbye was here. But it was too soon. They were supposed to have had another week.

"I'll see you next year when you come to university," said Titus.

"I don't have magic. There's a good chance—"

"You're already a member of the Sceadwe. They have to invite you." He grabbed her hand, abandoning her nickname with a somber look. "Rowena, you've a magic all your own. You'll graduate and join me in a year." He tucked her fringe of curls back so he could see her eyes. They were wet and glistening, mirroring his own. "I hate that I'll miss your trial. It's going to be truly special."

The pressure behind her eyes threatened to break. She didn't want him to see her cry, so she gave him a swift hug. "Bye," she choked.

"See you, Spook."

His owl reached a wing to cup Ghost's chin. Then Titus joined his brother, both of their Shadows atop their shoulders, all heads downcast. And that was it. Titus left.

Haaris watched the pitiful scene from his perch on the ladder. Rowena met his eyes before she closed the door. The latch sounded too loud, like something final. She fell against the door and let the tears loose, and with them, a complicated knot of unspoken words. She wasn't sure, if given the chance, what she would have said differently, but she wished Titus had said more. Although she doubted anything could have made parting with him easier. Other than goodbye, what more needed to be said?

For once, Ghost seemed to understand what had happened. She clung to Isla, her face buried in her fur.

Rowena threw herself back on the couch, her heart a miserable eddy of confusion. At some point, she fell asleep again. When her father jostled her awake, the light from the window had moved across the room.

"Come help me paint," he said gently, "Some work will do you good."

After the annual tending to the rosebushes, Haaris gave the cottage shutters, doors, and eaves a fresh coat of paint. Haaris's spaniel licked Rowena's face. She batted at him, but he wouldn't relent. So, she emerged from the couch to slather cherry red paint on the front door while Haaris painted the shutters the same shade of green they'd always been. It was foolish to paint so close to winter she told him. But his Shadow took care to dry and cure the paint, so the cold didn't matter, except to Rowena's bare hands.

Her fingers were numb by the time their buckets were empty, but they still had more to go. Haaris fetched a can of paint from his workshop and was about to round the corner when it happened. Rowena could hear it all the way from the front porch, like a twig snapping in winter, followed by a guttural groan. He didn't cry out. Of course, he didn't; it wasn't Haaris's way. But from the look on his face and how his hand flopped back, Rowena knew it was the worst injury yet. This was no sprain, but a full break.

By evening, Dr. Patterfold sat at their kitchen table, spectacles balanced on the tip of his nose. His Shadow, a sleek grey crane, used magic to send gentle vibrations through Haaris's arm, giving the apothecary enough information to diagnose him with "brittle bones."

"What does that mean?" Haaris asked.

"It means you have the bone density of a much older man." He splinted the injury, then slid a bottle of potion, not to Haaris but to Rowena. "I'm sure you'll want to make one of your classic adjustments before you give him this."

She tried to look sheepish, but he was right. She had every intention of examining the potion as soon as he left.

Dr. Patterfold chuckled. "I'm not offended. Just so long as you share with me whatever improvements you make."

"Certainly."

He left them with strict instructions for Haaris to rest. Rowena's father obeyed, retiring to bed early, which left Rowena alone with only her thoughts—and Ghost and the giant dog, who both lay on the rug in front of the fire. She sat on the couch, thinking about The Wandering elder. The old woman had called the creature—who at the moment nuzzled Ghost like a mother hen—Isla.

She will bring the Shadowless, the woman's voice echoed in her mind. Rowena shivered.

The fire died out, and she was cast into darkness but didn't move from her chair. She pondered the long stretch of time before her, like pool of moonlight trickling through the window. A year. Titus was gone. Her father injured, for how long she didn't know. All she had was the sham of classes and barely an apprenticeship to mention. A mountain of tension still divided her and Penalynn. Thinking of Penalynn, Rowena remembered that she still expected another sample of Rowena's. But she wasn't ready to give it up, though she couldn't articulate why, not even to herself. The woman's words, The Wandering song, the dog Isla, Penalynn's study…it was the same problem she'd had all her life. Sure, she was no longer hidden from society, but still, too many people had intentions for her fate, robbing her a choice of her own.

Even so, she was not without agency.

She dropped another log onto the fire, stoking it until she had enough light. Then she grabbed Atticus Wolder's book, a notebook, and a pencil from her bag. She angled herself on the couch so the light could illuminate the page. Then she sketched. And as she drew, her mind settled into something resembling peace. An hour later, she had the first drawing of many. It wasn't an original idea but a sizeable improvement upon Wolder's. Her pencil scratched, tweaking the design into something truly special. She smiled. That was the word Titus had used. Her trial would be special. The log spent its last embers, and eventually, she slept, no longer caring what the Wandering sang about nor what Penalynn did with her samples. Let them all do what they wanted. Her future was hers to decide, and she had a year to make it happen.

CHAPTER
THIRTY-EIGHT

Everyone in Greymere liked to stretch out the festival holiday for a few days after the main events, but not Penalynn. She didn't take holidays. But she did give Freya a few days off, and so she was surprised to find breakfast waiting for her the next morning. She eyed the three-tiered tray piled with scones, cream, jam, stewed apples, biscuits, gravy, bacon, and even an iced cinnamon cake. Freya intended for her mistress to celebrate the holiday properly, even if only with breakfast.

Penalynn barely made a dent in the feast, so she brought the tray across the hall, stopping to don her usual accouterments. As she did, a heavy loneliness settled upon her. Or was it regret? She looked down at her Shadow. The fox looked back, and the aching weight doubled.

The servants magicking the laboratory were already happy amassing double pay for holiday hours, and so the mini feast Penalynn brought them only added to their cheer. They had to eat quickly, however, before it all froze.

Penalynn sat at the counter and cocked her head at two corked vials that sat as if waiting for her. The label read: "*Rowena Faye—2nd Sample.*"

The lonely feeling ebbed, replaced with affection for her young apprentice. Penalynn knew she had been too harsh with Rowena, barring her from their study. But letting her in seemed harsher still.

The cork popped and Penalynn set to work. It took an entire day of meticulous testing, but by dinner, Rowena's samples were nearly used up. Both bottles rendered dozens of tests; each result the same. She logged the data points into her massive book, then stared at the page. The book was enormous, as thick as it was wide, crammed with every scrap of data her tests produced. Each page represented a citizen of Greymere, with Rowena's the topmost page. The book felt magnetic, the knowledge pulling, relentlessly tugging Penalynn's spirits. She beheld Rowena's results like welcome good news. Relief filled her like a hot drink, warming her despite the frigid temperature. She allowed the feeling full bloom, knowing it would not last but grateful at least for the moment.

"Thank you," she whispered, tracing her fingers over the page. She didn't know who to thank for such news, but the gratitude needed voice all the same. Staring at Rowena's results was the only holiday Penalynn would allow herself. But it was enough.

CHAPTER
THIRTY-NINE

T HE SCHOLASTIC AND HER apprentice passed the entire winter on cordial terms, entering springtime in amicable friendship. So, it was strange for Penalynn to enter Rowena's study one morning, screaming. In her defense, she had to scream to be heard over the searing torch in Rowena's hand. The girl turned awkwardly where she knelt in the mouth of the fireplace. She cut off the blazing torch, then raised bug-like goggles to her forehead.

Penalynn's nose wrinkled at the molten smell of metal. "Are you black-smithing? *In the castle?!*"

Rowena's voice was muffled by a thick mask, "Technically, it's called brazing, which is a form of weld—"

"WHY?!" Penalynn demanded, then gagged. "*Ugh,* I can't breathe!" She wrenched open the glass doors to release the noxious fumes onto the potted balcony garden. Isla (who after all these months still followed Rowena like an adopted Shadow) sprang for the balcony as well. Ghost joined her, as did the fox, each gasping like divers surfacing for breath.

"It's for my trial!" Rowena defended.

"Doesn't your father have a workshop?" Penalynn choked, "Blacksmith there."

"But all my stuff is here."

"If you insist on stinky purposes, I insist you relocate."

Rowena knew better than to argue. She lifted a lump of cooling metal with tongs and dropped it in a pot on her desk.

Penalynn peered at the molten mass. "You're melting rank metal for your trial?"

"All metals smell when you melt them." Rowena sniffed, offended. "And no. I'm making two devices that will allow me to administer potions non-magically. This will be a canister that vaporizes liquid to gas, allowing the potion to be inhaled. I'm also working on a few new potions. Something amusing for the audience, but also useful."

"Very impressive," said Penalynn, picking a yellow flower from a basket brimming with them. "Are the weeds for a potion?"

"Dandelions," Rowena corrected. "I'm making rubber out of them. I need an air-tight seal for a hollow needle, which I'll use to inject potions directly into the bloodstream."

Penalynn cringed at the notion of a needle piercing someone's skin but continued scanning the bottles on Rowena's desk. She picked one up, unstopped the cork, and sniffed the contents inside. "What's this one? Mmm, it smells good."

"Oh no, Penalynn, don't do that!" Rowena snatched the bottle from her before she could sniff it again.

"Why? What-igga-fuuu?" Penalynn's eyes popped as the potion took immediate effect. Her face sagged, numb, and lifeless. She felt her slack jaw, gargling in horror. "WHA!! *WHA-AAGH!!*"

Rowena whipped open a drawer crammed with all manner of odd assortments. She rummaged until she found a sewing pin, lit a match, and then set the flame to the pin's tip. Penalynn gargled something indecipherable, banging her fist on the table. Assuming she asked why she was heating a pin, Rowena said nonchalantly, "It's not important. Now, would you mind looking up for me?"

"*Wha?*" Spit traced a ribbon down her Scholastic cloak, splashing her pendant.

"Just look at the ceiling," instructed Rowena. She dipped the newly sterilized pin into a second bottle of potion.

"*O!*" Penalynn refused, belligerent despite herself.

"Trust me, you'll want to look up."

Penalynn refused again, and so, with a roll of her eyes, Rowena stabbed the Scholastic's cheek with the pin.

"*AAGHH!!*" Penalynn recoiled. But just as quickly as it had gone numb, her face regained life, her outraged objections articulating into words. "*Ow dare you stab me in the face!*"

"Did it hurt?"

"Actually..." Penalynn rubbed her cheek in reluctant wonder. "Not at all. Wow, that's incredible." The Scholastic side of her couldn't help but be impressed. Still, she said, "I can't believe you stabbed me in the face!"

"Don't go sniffing potions you don't recognize," Rowena said mildly. "I'm glad to see the antidote works well. I've been meaning to test it. Isla was going to be my subject."

Hearing her name, the giant dog looked over. "That's right," Rowena said, "If you're going to stick around, at least make yourself useful." The dog growled as if daring Rowena to stab her with a potion.

Still massaging her jaw, Penalynn asked, "With all this potion-making, are you keeping up with your mathematics?"

"It's hard to do physic without it."

"Do you have any classes today?"

"Yes."

"Are you getting anything out of them?"

"They're magic classes," Rowena said flatly. "So, no."

"Good. I'm excusing you from class for a few weeks. I need your help." Seeing the look on Rowena's face, Penalynn held up her hand, "Not to analyze nor read any results, mind you. In fact, you needn't even enter the laboratory. I need you to check my equations."

"Equations for what?"

"There's a number I use that I distill from the interviews you conducted. The entire project hinges on this number, and it'd be bad form to present inaccurate findings to the Sceadwe."

She spread two pieces of paper on the table. Rowena scanned them. The first was a complicated line involving multiple measurements, resulting in a number on the far side of the equal sign represented as *Pt*.

"What does *Pt* stand for?"

"Potent."

"And a potent is...?"

"A measurement."

Rowena looked at her. "You know I can just look it up in the library, right?"

Penalynn's lips puckered. "A potent is a measurement of magic. Like a cup of sugar or a yard of fabric."

"A potent of magic. I didn't know such a number existed. What do these numbers here represent?"

"Duration and type of magic. Each type of magic has its own equation, which I've put here."

Rowena examined the key where four short equations resulted in numbers for manipulation, animation, intuition, and persuasion. Each equation could be plugged into the larger equation, resulting in a complicated mass of numbers and letters lining the page. Rowena was used to Wolder's complicated physic equations, so she could read these almost like a book. "Yuck, no wonder you need a second pair of eyes. This is tricky numbers work."

She moved on to the second equation, tracing her finger slowly down the line, which spanned two page-widths, ending in *AGG-Pt*. "You're trying to find the *aggregate potent?*"

"Very good," said Penalynn. "I've already completed the math; all you need to do is check the accuracy. Of all of them."

"All of them? You mean for every person interviewed? But the aggregate potent would be a sum of all the magic a person ever used. That's a lot of math per person. And there's a couple thousand of them!"

"Why do you think it's taken me so long?"

Rowena grew engrossed with the numbers. "Grading a Scholastic's homework," she murmured, "I feel so powerful."

Penalynn returned to her office and came back with a crate of loose papers which she dropped to the table with a *bang*. Rowena took the top page. Penalynn's handwriting crammed both front and back.

"I'm assuming one of these pages is mine?" Rowena asked.

"It might be a complicated equation, but anyone could deduce that a zero plugged in at every point would result in a zero aggregate potent of magic."

Rowena frowned. "Ah. Yes."

"The order is randomized and coded, so there is no point guessing identities. Whatever you get done each day, just leave it on my desk." Penalynn paused before opening the door. "I'll have Freya send up some tea for you. An hour or two into that, and you'll be cross-eyed."

"Cheers."

It wasn't long before Rowena lost all track of time, absorbed in endless calculations. She barely noticed Freya enter with the tea, nor when she refilled the pot not once but three times over the course of the day. And only when the bells dismissed school did she finally put down her pencil, her hands grown jittery from the tea. She stacked the finished pages, tapping them into order, and dropped them on Penalynn's desk.

But her work for the day wasn't done yet. She still had a trial coming up, and with months' worth of equations to check, she was suddenly behind schedule. Sending Freya for a hand cart, she carefully packed her welding supplies, hoping her father didn't mind sharing his workshop.

CHAPTER FORTY

I N THAT ODD TIME between summer and autumn, when the nights were cold, but the days still sweltered, Taiosech stood outside Riven's gates. The Wandering filed past, laden with their belongings. For those of his people who met his eye, Taiosech nodded encouragement, urging them on. He was asking too much of them, he knew, forcing them to leave like this, earlier than planned and with barely time to pack. Thankfully, the trade among the Wyrians had already afforded them plenty, so the tribe didn't lose much by leaving early, at least not financially. In other ways, they lost more than they had in years.

In the east, the horizon budded pink in a lavender sky. It was early. But it was not fatigue that weighed their heads to bow as they did. Even the children walked somberly, not skipping as they usually did. If there was talk, they whispered.

Only Karah's face turned upward. "Black Guardians," he muttered out of the corner of his mouth, "On the left and right, my chief."

Taiosech did not look up immediately, letting his gaze drift casually. His eyes grazed past the guards atop the outer wall. It was not half a second, but all the time needed. Only one kind of man had a snake for a Shadow.

"Has the king lost his mind?" Karah wondered.

"He wouldn't be the first," said Taiosech.

"Do you think he will grow suspicious from our early flight north?"

"Can he grow more suspicious than he already has? Let him wonder what he will."

Karah raised his eyebrows at the chief's uncharacteristic flippancy.

The sun broke the horizon, gold reflected in the chief's eyes like fire. Karah followed his line of sight, and together, they watched the final family pass in complete and utter silence, the couple's Shadows black to signify their mourning.

When the king's guards infiltrated The Wandering camp the night before, it was the birthing tent they ransacked. Taiosech knew why they'd done it. Everyone knew. There hadn't even been an investigation. Thankfully, the execution was not public—the only decency a Wyrian king had ever shown as if he felt shame at the atrocity he committed in the name of self-preservation.

"He could have waited," Karah seethed under his breath. "What harm could two infants—" Taiosech touched his arm to quiet him.

They watched in honorable silence as the last two Wandering passed under the gate. The husband and wife walked nearly bent in half, and not just from grief. The man wrapped his arm around his wife's shoulder while she leaned heavily on his arm. With extreme patience, he matched her gait, which was bowlegged and slow. Having given birth only the day prior, the woman ought to be resting in bed, nursing her twins, languishing in the care of her fellow women. Instead, she migrated north, bleeding and childless. And her Shadow black as death.

When they finally passed, Taiosech and his elder fell into step at the rear of the caravan, allowing plenty of space so the couple would not hear them talk. His voice was like stone, hard and cold. "Who told?"

"As soon as the sons entered the world, the men of the family went out to celebrate. Drink was involved, and one of them—I don't know who—made mention of the boys' Shadows, how they were...different. A Wyrian must have heard, and word got back to the king."

Taiosech sighed. "Fools. How am I to protect my people if they will not protect themselves? I see now my task is an impossible one. I am not sure who is more impatient to find the Shadowless: myself or this Wyrian king."

"Pardon me, my chief, but if the king will kill our people without reason, then perhaps our discretion is in vain?"

"I hear you, my friend, and at last, I agree. I am done with patience."

CHAPTER
FORTY-ONE

T HE NEXT SPRING AND summer passed in a haze of endless work. When autumn returned, it painted Torborough Forest in a hundred shades of gold, scarlet and umber. When Rowena entered the kitchen that morning she was met by a cheerful father.

"Surprise!" Haaris declared in a rare display of parental enthusiasm. He gestured to the table, which was spread with a mini feast of cinnamon buns from Corrie Cunningham's Confections and the last remaining berries from summer, magicked a bit for freshness.

"What's this for?" she asked, taken aback.

"Your trial audition." He slid out a chair for her. "I thought we could celebrate."

Rowena pressed her lips together, gratitude and pity vying for purchase. "Papa. This is amazing, really...but...my audition isn't until Tuesday."

"What's today?"

"Sunday."

"What?" His face fell. "How did I...I thought..." His Shadow hung his head so low his floppy ears pooled on the floor.

"It's okay," she said, her heart wrenched by the look on his face. "We'll just celebrate early." She threw herself into the waiting chair and grabbed a bun.

Haaris joined her, his embarrassment evident. "I'm sorry, I don't know what's wrong with my head lately. I fear I'm becoming a moron."

She squeezed his hand. Though it had taken half a year, Haaris's wrist had finally healed, but even with his hand restored, ever since the injury, something had changed. He wasn't himself anymore, and they both noticed.

"If you're going to be a moron, at least you're a generous one," she gently teased.

They ate silently, Haaris watching his daughter from the corner of his eye. A familiar cloud seemed to descend upon her countenance. She was worried, he could tell. But Rowena had done all she could do. Her trial accouterments were ready for show. Soon, the Myth Keeper and Sceadwe would either approve her work and admit her to university or deny her and keep her from fulfilling her life's goal of leaving Greymere and joining society on her own standing. Her future was in the hands of others—again.

She rolled a blueberry between her thumb and forefinger. "They're making me audition in front of the silver glass."

"That's new. Back in my day, it was just the Myth Keeper who oversaw auditions."

"It's just mine. Turns out they want a Consular to weigh in since, you know, my trial is a bit different."

Haaris cleared his throat before saying, "Let me tell you something. If you do your audition exactly as you showed me the other day, you'll do fine. More than fine. Amazing. There's no way that Myth Keeper, or some Consular, or even the king himself, I'd say, can do anything but approve you. You'll be the hit of the night come festival time. You'll see."

She smiled under her father's praise and finished her breakfast. "Thank you for this. It was delicious." She kissed him on the cheek.

"The work of a moron," he muttered grumpily.

"Hey, you can't be the best magician in Greymere *and* a genius. It's not fair to the rest of us. So, you'll be talented and dumb." She shrugged. "Could be worse."

He chuckled. "You headed to the castle?"

"It's *Sunday!*"

"Gah! Right! Sunday. *Sunday.*"

"I'm going to practice my trial some more," she said, then left through the front door.

She felt self-conscious practicing her trial within hearing, even of her father, so she decided to take advantage of the cooler weather by practicing in the woods. Ghost and Isla trailed so close that they banged into the back of her legs when she came to a halt halfway down the path. A pile of brown leaves impeded her way. But on second glance, she noticed the pile had eyes and breathed heavily. After a moment's confusion, she realized it was a dog with absurdly shaggy fur. It sat as if waiting.

Rowena's stomach dropped. "Oh no. Not another one." She eyed Ghost. But her Shadow didn't dart after the ugly dog like she had with Isla a year ago. Ghost's expression remained vacant and bored, as always.

The morning was chilly, but the dog panted heavily, its thick fur matted into dreadlocks. It stepped forward, and Rowena noticed the red collar, signifying the dog as a member of Greymere's fleet of mail delivery animals—a small brown package was strapped onto its back like a little saddle.

"For me?" she asked. The dog stared dumbly; clearly, it was no Isla. Rowena untied the package, and as soon as the dog was free, it took off down the street. Ghost watched the dog go with a bland look, and Rowena felt grateful not to have unwillingly adopted another pet.

She inspected the paper-wrapped parcel addressed to *Rowena Faye of Greymere*. She knew the handwriting and ripped open the package. A small, heavy object tumbled into her hand. It was oval-shaped, made of thick, flat metal small enough to fit snuggly in her palm. It reminded her of a pocket mirror, the kind she saw Gloria Patterfold and her posse of giggling girls use. Except the surface was too dull to see her reflection. In the discarded wrapping, she found a note that read:

Spook, keep this with you after sunset.

—T.

Rowena and Titus had only managed to exchange a few letters in the past year since he'd left. With a month's distance between Riven and Greymere, the post was a frustratingly slow form of communication. In fact, she had been waiting for some time for a letter, and so was disappointed by the brevity of his message. Just one sentence. And a cryptic one at that. But it didn't matter. Titus had written to her—had sent a present even. Turning the burnished metal over in her hand, she wondered what it could be. Then she tucked it into her bag.

She pushed open the gate and crossed the gravel street where a line of trees stretched like an entryway into Torborough Forest. She spent nearly the entire day in the woods. At first, she practiced her trial, rehearsing her speech over and over. But there were only so many times she could say the words until they became so familiar as to sound foreign, words and letters losing all meaning in her agitated state. She needed a break but wasn't ready to return home to be watched by her father with his constant sympathetic smiles. And so, she found a pleasant meadow and alternated between reading and dozing until, at last, dusk drew her home. She emerged from the woods just as the first stars winked overhead.

Thump-thump, thump-thump.

Just over the hedge, her neighbor, Archibald Cutter, stood in his famous pumpkin patch. He rapped his knuckles against a thick orange rind while his Shadow scurried atop looping vines, manipulating the pumpkins with magic. As soon as he saw Rowena, Archibald stopped his magic long enough to glower at her. He had never quite forgiven the Fayes for their secret.

When it had been discovered that Haaris's child was alive, Archibald had been nearly inconsolable at the apparent disrespect they'd done him. How many years had he lived in fright of a possible haunting next door when there had been a perfectly reasonable explanation for all those voices and sightings? And the persuasions! It was clear to him that Haaris must have magicked his mind. And how many times had he done it, Archibald wanted to know! Countless, he reckoned. Haaris Faye ought to be locked up for what he'd done. It wasn't legal. But worse than that, it wasn't neighborly. None of this did Archibald ever tell his neighbors, the Fayes. No, all he ever did was glower at them. It was only when he frequented Ronan's pub, and only then when he'd had enough pints in him, that he would muster up a gripe. And his fellow drinkers would tell him the same thing: report Haaris Faye. What he'd done—allegedly or not—was punishable by law. You can't go around persuading your neighbors, they reminded Archibald, their inebriated words drawn out like cursive. But then others would chime in how they themselves had reported the girl, usually after one of those confounded Scholastic interviews, but nothing ever came of it. Likely, her standing with the Sceadwe protected her father too. And so, Archibald's complaints dwindled until it was just mutterings only his Shadow could hear.

After he'd sufficiently glowered at Rowena, he went back to knocking on pumpkins.

Rowena went inside.

When night grew black, figures emerged from the forest, their cloaks so dark as to be invisible. But their Shadows were unmistakable, moonlight reflecting off their white bodies like ghosts in the night. At first, Archibald thought they were the girl's misfit Shadow. But when he saw more than one, he threw himself at the window to press his nose against the glass. The mysterious strangers knocked on the Fayes' front door and waited.

Haaris opened the door, looking startled to see two members of The Wandering standing on his front porch: a young woman and a man. It was the young woman who spoke first, her accent thick. "Good evening. We have come to speak to one called Rowena."

Hearing her name, Rowena approached from inside. "Hi, Sersha," she greeted. "Would you like to come in?"

"No," Haaris said, curt. Rowena winced at his rudeness, but the two visitors didn't seem to mind. No doubt they were used to it.

Sersha spoke directly to Rowena, "I have come to introduce you to my uncle, chief Taiosech of The Wandering."

"Hello," Rowena said to the chief's shoulder, too self-conscious to meet his eyes. And not daring to look at the red-eyed bat hanging from his arm.

"Out of courtesy, he will not use your forbidden magic, so I will translate for him."

Taiosech spoke in The Wandering language, his voice husky and deep. Sersha translated, "I invite you to The Wandering camp, Rowena Faye of Greymere. You will have a place of honor at my own fire."

Rowena asked, "Why?" simultaneously as Haaris said, "No."

The chief answered her. Rowena preferred to look at Sersha, who translated, "I wish to speak with you."

"Why would he want to speak with me?"

Sersha translated to her uncle. The chief did not answer at first. He beheld Rowena with a piercing look, his pulse visible in his temple. Finally, he said, and Sersha translated: "I had a dream. In it, a creature spoke to me. It appeared like the creature you keep. When you came to our camp, you brought with you this very creature from my dreams."

Rowena looked at Isla. She felt betrayed somehow, even if it had only been a dream version of the dog. She turned back to The Wandering visitors, disturbed by Taiosech's open stare, too much like admiration.

Sersha asked, "Will you join our camp? Perhaps after your festival celebrations?"

"No, she will not," said Haaris.

Rowena was puzzled by their word choice. "'Join your camp?' Do you mean for the evening or..."

Sersha grinned. "Let's start with the one evening. For now."

"Leave." Haaris pointed towards the forest. "Get off my property, and never speak to my daughter again."

"Papa!"

In deference to Haaris, Sersha and the chief retreated, though Taiosech nodded at Rowena significantly before stepping down from the porch. Their dark cloaks seemed to melt into the night, and soon, their shock-white Shadows winked out of sight within the forest.

Haaris locked the door, but only after forbidding Rowena from talking to a member of The Wandering race ever again, then checked the windows and back door as well. Still not satisfied, he decided to sleep on the couch, just in case they came back.

That night, Haaris wasn't the only one who stayed up late to watch for them. Next door, Archibald Cutter fell asleep in his armchair where, long after the Wandering left, he'd watched the tree line, waiting for them to return or, possibly, for the Faye girl to follow after them.

CHAPTER
FORTY-TWO

ROWENA LAY AWAKE IN bed. She could hear her father's snores through the floorboards. A patch of moonlight cast pale light across her quilt. Her mind was too busy for sleep, turning the encounter with The Wandering over and over until she buried her face in her pillow with a groan.

"Spook." A voice cut the silence. *"Pssttt! Spook!!"*

She sat up, clutching her quilt to her chin. "Hello?" she whispered to the air.

"Is it working?" another voice said, oddly muffled.

"Yeah."

"No, it's not, it's all black."

Completely bewildered, Rowena left the safety of her bed to tiptoe across the room. She lifted the trapdoor in the floor, half expecting The Wandering to have returned and be standing in her living room. But she saw only Isla curled on a pallet at the foot of the ladder and her father asleep on the couch, ready to ward off any other visitors.

Again, the voice called out, muffled and distant. *"Spook! Are you there?"*

Only Titus called her by that name, and now that she thought about it, the voice sounded a lot like him. But he was in Riven. How could his voice be in her bedroom?

"I don't think you're doing it right."

"Yes, I am. She's probably just left it in her bag or something.'"

Ghost hovered by Rowena's desk and poked her bookbag. Sure enough, the voice came from inside, muffled under leather and books.

"Great. I get you a highly powerful magical object, and your girlfriend forgets it under a bunch of books."

She rifled through the bag, shoving aside the odd assortment of items until she found the small gift from Titus. As soon as it was free, she heard clear as day, "There you are! Turn me around."

She turned the metal over, saw a tiny hand waving up at her, yelped, and dropped the thing. The gift rolled under the bed and Ghost zoomed after it like a cat with a toy.

"Careful, Spook! Silver's expensive!"

"Like you had to pay for it," the other voice said.

Rowena retrieved the thing full of voices. "Silver," she muttered, turning it over. There, in the palm of her hand, was Titus's face, smiling up at her. *"You gave me a silver glass?!"* Her father snorted loudly, and she clutched the silver glass to her chest, straining to hear if he'd awakened.

"Hello? Spook, where'd you go?"

But Rowena pressed the thing to her chest. Only when she was sure her father still slept did she look down at the silver glass in her hand. "How...how...?"

Bruce's tiny face appeared over his brother's shoulder. "I'm an excellent card player, that's how." He waved. "Hiya, Rowe."

"Bruce won a pair of broken silver glasses in a card game," Titus explained, "But *I* was the one who figured out how to fix them and—I'm sorry, I can't talk to you like this. Spook. You look like you're in a cave made of hair."

She held the glass in her lap, her shoulders hunched so her hair cascaded down around her face.

"This thing isn't a book you're reading. Hold it up at eye level."

She did as he instructed, holding the silver in front of her like a mirror. Her hair fell to her shoulders.

"Much better."

"Titus, how are we talking through silver glass right now?"

Bruce answered for his brother. "Because I'm an excellent gambler."

"No, because your friends are all drunks and chronically stupid," Titus corrected.

"Rowena, send all your thanks my way," said Bruce, "Because, without me and my seedy friends, you two wouldn't be having this little tryst of yours."

"Thank you, Bruce," Rowena giggled, practically giddy to hear them bickering. It sounded comforting and friendly, making the lonely ache she'd borne the past year disappear like fog on a sunny day.

Titus rubbed his forehead. "Cut it out, Bruce. You're messing with my concentration."

"Speaking of seedy friends," Bruce said, "See ya, Rowe!" He waved again, then disappeared out of sight.

"He seems to be doing better," Rowena observed.

"Yeah, after a month-long sulk from being dumped by a Wandrel, he's back to the same old Bruce." Titus rubbed his forehead again.

"Are you okay?" she asked. "It looks like you're in pain."

"Yeah, it's just hard to talk and magic this thing at the same time. It takes a ton of concentration. I think I know now why more people don't use silver glass. It feels like my brain's trying to squish out of my ears."

"Should you be doing it then?"

"I'll get used to it."

Rowena felt guilty their conversation was causing him discomfort, but her curiosity won out, and she asked, "How did you learn to fix silver glass?"

"Your way: with books. The guy who gave them up had no idea these things were repairable. The university library has much more about silver glass than the one in Greymere. Oh, Spook, the library here! I can't wait to show you when you get here."

"I have to pass my trial first. My audition is the day after tomorrow. I've been working forever on it. Look what I made!" She pointed the silver towards her desk, where she'd neatly lined her trial items.

"Woah! Easy where you point that, I'm getting dizzy."

"Oh, sorry." She turned the silver back.

"I know you'll be brilliant," he said. "You better not be nervous."

"I'm terrified."

"Ridiculous. You'll be amazing." Her face warmed at his familiar smile. "Hey, I gotta' go, but keep this thing with you. I'll try and use it around the same time tomorrow. I want to hear all about your trial." Titus paused. After a breath, he said, "Wow."

"What?"

"It's just really good to see you, is all."

Her smile broke like the morning sun. "You, too."

CHAPTER
FORTY-THREE

PEOPLE AVOIDED THE GIRL in the blue cape lingering before the castle's massive front doors. Rowena stood engrossed in the intricate tapestry etched in wood grain, desperate to find a new picture obscured in the door's labyrinthian complexity as if the artwork might lift her spirits somehow. But this was the morning she finally came to their end. Every picture had been found. Every animal, face, flower, and filigree. Each image recognizable, like the face of a friend. She pressed her hand against the carving of a rose tucked within the wing of a bird as if making a wish upon the door.

Roderick Ashworth was headed for his office when he stopped mid-stride, then sidled up beside her. "I've always thought these doors were beautiful." He aimed for a soft tone, but still, his voice rumbled, and she jumped.

"Oh!" She felt alarmed to find herself in the sudden company of the Overseer. "Good morning, sir," she said, eying the wolf at his side.

By now, she was used to large animals, Isla's head just as high as the wolf's. But Isla was sleek and refined, whereas the Overseer's Shadow was clothed in thick fur around a powerful frame, the consummate picture of authority.

"Of course, you of all people would appreciate them," Roderick said about the doors, "But they're special for me too. I was there when he made them, you know. To this day, it was the most impressive trial I have ever seen. He was just

as shy then as he is now, and so he hacked a way to avoid performing on stage."
Roderick chuckled at the memory. "He set up a stall in the festival market like
a merchant. While people came and went, he stood on a ladder with a penknife,
that Shadow of his manipulating the grain. He didn't make a single cut. Just some
magic and a bit of nudging with his knife, and he twisted the woodgrain to make
the picture you see now as if it had grown in the tree like rings. It was incredible.
Took him only four hours to do it."

"Who was he?" she asked.

Roderick looked at her strangely. "Why, your father, of course. Did he never
tell you?" She shook her head, and his face tightened, pained. "Oh, Haaris. Always
so private."

Suddenly, it was as if she saw the doors for the first time. She had always
felt a connection with the pictures in the woodgrain, but discovering it was her
father who had drawn them, the knowledge ached like a bruise. On every side, she
was surrounded by massive figures. The great oak doors. The Overseer. His wolf.
Isla. And now her father's magical talent looming from above. She felt impossibly
small, but even more so when she said, "It's my audition today."

Roderick nodded, seeming to understand how she felt. "Rowena, you might
not know this, having never met her, but you mostly take after your mother.
You're smart. Bookish. And those eyes and hair! You're Hazel Faye made over.
But your creativity? That's Haaris in you. He took something as ordinary as a
door and made art. People pass them every day, not bothering to notice the sheer
genius they pass." Rowena looked up at him, realizing then that Titus had his
father's smile. "That same genius is in you, little one. Even if not everyone sees
it."

She nodded, not in agreement, but in hope that he was right.

CHAPTER
FORTY-FOUR

WHEN ROWENA ENTERED THE Hall of Sceadwe, Penalynn and the Myth Keeper already stood before the silver glass, waiting. She made her way down the center aisle, trying her best to ignore what felt like a wasp's nest lodged in her stomach. A table had been provided, covered in black silk. She unloaded her bag, lining bottles of potion in a row. Then, she unwrapped her two inventions. Their metallic surfaces gleamed like treasure upon the black silk.

Penalynn stepped close to mutter, "Is that animal necessary for your trial?" She indicated Isla, who stood close as usual.

"Ghost won't be without her," Rowena said, glad to hear her voice sounded steady despite her nerves.

"Fine. But keep her out of sight. Best to not instigate more questions than necessary."

Rowena ushered Isla to the side, out of sight of the silver glass. Thankfully, Ghost seemed to understand the importance of the occasion and chose to stay by Rowena and not Isla.

"Good morning, esteemed members of the Sceadwe," a voice called.

They all looked up into the towering visage of High Consular Mac Feargus. His face loomed, his saggy jowls heavy, so no matter his mood, he always seemed to disapprove. Despite Rowena's four years as a member of the Sceadwe, this was her first time meeting a High Consular. She did her best not to shrink back.

Penalynn stepped towards the silver glass. "Consular, before we get started, on behalf of my apprentice, I would like to state how highly irregular this audition is. No other student in all of Wyre is required to perform for an official of your status. I request we end this meeting and allow Rowena to audition for the Myth Keeper alone, like any other student."

Rowena felt a rush of gratitude towards her mentor. But Feargus simply answered, "It was the Myth Keeper who requested it."

Nearby stood The Myth Keeper, his posture rigid, his Shadow unusually still. In fact, Rowena thought he looked angry for some reason. He chewed the inside of his cheeks.

Feargus continued, "The requirement is irregular because the circumstances are irregular. She is not even at university and is already a Scholastic Apprentice. Not to mention her rather peculiar Shadow. Just *one* of those counts would warrant special treatment, but *two?* Well! The Myth Keeper was right to include me."

From the angle of the silver glass, Rowena couldn't tell where the Consular looked, but she was sure his frown was meant for her Shadow. Ghost sank below the edge of the table.

"Mr. Keeper, the floor is yours," said Feargus.

The Myth Keeper stepped forward and turned his back to the silver glass so both he and Feargus faced Rowena. "When you are ready." His goatee twitched.

For a moment, Rowena gaped, the hateful look on his face uncharacteristic, even for him.

She inhaled deeply, then picked up her first instrument. Sunlight reflected off its embellished filigree. This particular piece she had remade nearly a dozen times until it was just right. The minuscule loops fashioned in metal were inspired by the castle doors. She marveled at the irony of the moment, having unknowingly designed her trial after her father's.

The Myth Keeper cleared his throat. His pencil tapped an impatient staccato against his clipboard. With another deep breath, Rowena began her well-rehearsed presentation.

"I have created for my trial two devices: a hollow needle and a vaporizer. These devices allow me to administer potions faster and more effectively than the common method of ingestion. For my demonstration, I have prepared five potions of my own design: a paralytic and its antidote, a powerful pain reliever, a sleeping potion, and an interesting one that, when administered in small doses, can make the mind and body sharp, despite fatigue. If given in larger doses, it can provide a temporary experience of inhuman strength and cognitive function."

"How do the devices work?" asked the Myth Keeper.

She demonstrated by picking up a glass tube and sliding it into the device. "You insert a potion capsule into the base like this." She twisted until she heard a *click,* then handed the device to the Myth Keeper. "The button here will render the potion into gas, which can then be inhaled. Although, I wouldn't recommend it just yet. That stuff is strong. One moment while I prepare a second capsule—"

He interrupted her. "And what aspects of all of this have you accomplished with magic?"

"None. This was all done purely by—"

"But this is a trial of *magic.*"

"If you'll let me demonstrate, you'll see that—"

Again, he cut her off with a curt tone. "The Sceadwe is looking for magical accomplishment, not trinkets. What trial does your *Shadow* have to show us today?"

Ghost peered over the edge of the table, trembling. The Myth Keeper waited for the answer they both already knew. Consular Feargus leaned toward the silver glass; his nose magnified several feet high.

Rowena's voice was low. "My Shadow cannot do magic, sir." Ghost sank heavily to the floor to land upon Rowena's shoe.

The Myth Keeper held up the vaporizer. "I cannot accept this for your trial." He turned to the Consular. "Sir, this is why I requested your presence here today. As witness."

Rowena pleaded, "But what I've accomplished, not even magic could do!"

"If it was not done by magic, then you have accomplished nothing."

At this, Penalynn interjected, "It's more than nothing, Julian."

"I grant you," he acquiesced, "But in regard to magical aptitude, which is the sole priority of the Shadow Trials, I see nothing here that's pertinent."

"Magic enhances the natural world," Rowena quoted from her numerous textbooks. "I *have* enhanced the natural world. I've created four potions, one antidote, and two devices that—"

"But you did not do it *magically.*"

Penalynn said, "Without passing her trial, she cannot graduate. You would bar a Scholastic Apprentice from graduating? Have you lost your mind?"

"Madame, it's in the rules! I would like to note that this was why I was against her becoming a Scholastic Apprentice in the first place."

"No, that was prejudice, and you know it! You've had it in for this girl from the moment—"

The Myth Keeper raised his voice over hers. "—I knew the moment you appointed her that it would come to this one day! And I would be made the villain when I am only enforcing Sceadwe standards!"

"This is absurd," Penalynn said to the face in the silver glass, "What my apprentice has accomplished is ingenious. She has developed potions beyond any apothecary's ability as well as ways to administer them that magic itself cannot do."

"Julian is right, Penalynn," the Consular said. "Trials display magic. Her Shadow cannot do magic, so she cannot do a trial. It's as simple as that."

"How can she attain Scholasticism if she doesn't graduate and attend university?!"

"A university education is hardly the thing standing between her and Scholasticism," said Feargus. His jowls quivered like saddle bags straddling his lips. "You were the one who chose her, not us. Madame, you may disdain magic with your predilections for physic and refusal to do magic yourself. But I will remind you, the Sceadwe is a body overseeing *magic*. Now, the High Consul cannot affect your status as a Scholastic. No, that was always out of our hands. But we will not make special concessions for your pupil. If she finds magic in that Shadow of hers, then fine. But until then, I hereby state she is barred from participating in the Shadow Trials. Now, good day to you all."

And with that final decree, High Consular Feargus disappeared in a swirl of silver, leaving behind his echoing words reverberating like a gong. They all stood there, the decision so swift it took a moment for Rowena to comprehend.

The Myth Keeper said to Penalynn, "None of this would have happened if you'd only listened to me and chosen someone else for your apprentice."

Penalynn turned on her heel. Her Shadow stood at an odd distance, still close but with several feet between them, looking as if they each stood alone. "This will not stand," Penalynn seethed. She took Rowena's hand into her own. "Listen to me, Rowena, I will have this decision overthrown. Trust me."

The Myth Keeper snorted. "Who in Wyre could overrule a High Consular?"

Penalynn didn't answer. She marched down the center aisle, thrusting the doors open, then raced through the castle, the invisible string between her soul's two halves tugging painfully as her Shadow reluctantly followed. When she entered her private library, she locked the doors behind her and then closed the drapes. Despite the fox's welling disapproval, the Shadow couldn't help the spark of joy that flashed between them. She was about to use magic, and so she joined Penalynn, who stood before the old tapestry. The silver glass's counterpart would be covered; Penalynn knew that. But it didn't matter. She would remain here as long as it took, yelling into the glass until he answered. She wouldn't stop until she had her way.

With a tug, the tapestry pulled loose and pooled on the ground, revealing sparkling silver underneath.

CHAPTER
FORTY-FIVE

THE DOORS BANGED CLOSED, leaving Rowena alone with the Myth Keeper. Hope evacuated her heart like water from a burst dam. Her entire future was gone in the span of a moment. Her mind twisted in on itself, unable, unwilling to understand. With fumbling fingers, Rowena slowly wrapped each bottle in fabric and then tucked them inside her bag. She managed to hold back the tears, but only because the Myth Keeper hadn't left yet. He watched with unflinching intensity as she packed her things.

"You really believed you would become a Scholastic, didn't you?" The question sounded genuine as if he could hardly believe it. "It was wrong of Madame Scholastic, giving you hope like that. I am only setting it right. It is my job, to do justice on behalf of the king and Bazileus."

Her hands balled into fists, but she forced herself to speak calmly. "Banning me from graduating is justice? What would my graduation have done to you or anybody?"

"*You* are the injustice," he said softly, as if it were a mere fact. "I have some sympathy for you, you know. After all, one cannot help the circumstances of one's birth. But never-the-less, you are a mistake. Your father knew it. Why else would he hide you? And ever since you entered society, the evidence has been clear. It follows you. Haunts you, more like. And so long as you walk among us, it haunts us all."

Rowena stared at the table, urging the tears not to fall. She would not cry in front of him. Her lips pressed against her teeth, reigning in her argument. But she had no defense. He was right. Somehow, she had eluded the truth for a few precious, wonderful years. But now the truth broke like a prisoner set free. There was no denying her abiding incompetency, more like an incompletion, an entire piece of humanity missing from her. Ghost burrowed under her cape like a worm inching for cover.

The Myth Keeper continued. "I am not out to get you. Truly. I have no ill will against you. In fact, just this morning I received word of your dealings with The Wandering clan and before I reported you to the king, I was going to let you make your defense."

He waited.

She tilted her head, urging the tears to retreat as she said to the arched ceiling, "I have no dealings with The Wandering." Then she held out her hand, pointing to the device still in his hands. "May I have that back?"

His knuckles whitened around the contraption. "You did not spend several hours in the woods alone, followed by a visit from the chief of The Wandering to your home?"

In the span of only a few minutes, Rowena had progressed the spectrum of emotions, from anxiety to shock to heartache, embarrassment, and then landing on shame. But all of those she pushed aside, calling upon something greater, something which simmered just below it all. It bubbled with heat the moment High Consular Mac Feargus had looked at her Shadow with that familiar disdain. She was angry. The impending tears dried up in the molten heat. Now that she touched the anger, and acknowledged its existence within her very soul, she realized it had always been there, simmering, waiting. Her fate was never her own and once again, her future had been decided by others.

She snapped her fingers. "My vaporizer, please."

"You will answer me," he demanded, and she noticed how his sweaty hand smudged the metal's polish.

"I will not." The words felt good. The anger felt even better. She wrapped it around herself like a shield. "Give that to me now."

The Myth Keeper's lips fell apart, offended at her tone. "You leave me no choice then but to make a report. You will find that the king is far more expedient than the High Consul. I tried to give you a chance. Remember that."

Still, she kept her eyes on his hands. "That is mine. Give it to me."

He tossed the vaporizer onto the table, accidentally triggering the button on impact, the sound quiet but prominent. *Click. SSSSHHHH.* Mist gushed from the cylinder's end, enveloping the Myth Keeper in a thick cloud smelling strongly of sickly-sweet valerian. He sputtered. Rowena leaned away from the onslaught, holding her breath as best she could.

"*WHAT HAVE YOU DONE?!*" he bellowed.

The answer rose in her throat like bile, laced with hate, as she quoted his own words back to him. "According to you, *nothing that matters.*"

She snatched her second device from the table, a long cylinder with a capped needle. With expert quickness, she inserted a tube of potion, twisting until it clicked in place. Then she uncapped the needle and plunged the needle into her arm, inhaling deeply as the potion entered her body.

The Myth Keeper's eyes nearly popped from their sockets. "What was that? What did you do?!"

Wincing, Rowena pulled the needle from her arm. "It's a variation of a potion I stole from The Wandering. Though I've tweaked it a good bit. It acts as a counterbalance to the sleeping potion you're inhaling. I really wish you hadn't used it up like that. That big of a dose will knock you out for at least half a day."

As if in evidence, the potion revealed itself in the Myth Keeper's slurred words: "What...*sleep...po-sshh?*" He swooned. The canary atop his shoulder fell to the table with a muffled *thwack*.

"I'd give you the antidote, Mr. Keeper, but surely you don't need it. your Shadow can do *magic*." Anger had reduced her to sarcasm, but it felt satisfying.

The Myth keeper struggled to keep his head from lolling back, outrage and sleep warring for purchase upon his faculties. "*How...dare...you...*" Then, with an indignant eyeroll, he slumped to the ground, his face banging the table as he went. His Shadow lay atop the table fast asleep.

Rowena gathered the rest of her belongings and fled the hall. She didn't have much time. After all, she'd just drugged a member of the Sceadwe—a man who had every intention of reporting her to the king, for Bazileus-knew-what—leaving him snoring in a puddle of his own spit. As soon as he awoke, she would need a solution. Otherwise, she would lose far more than she'd already lost. Graduation was gone. University—where Titus waited for her—was also gone. But there was still Penalynn. Still hope. Before she'd left the hall, Penalynn had said to trust her, that she could contest the Consular's decision.

Rowena ran, desperate to have her future in her own hands once more.

CHAPTER FORTY-SIX

ROWENA BURST INTO THE Scholastic's office, but Penalynn wasn't there. To her right, the door to the library was slid open, and Rowena saw Penalynn sitting in there.

"Penalynn!" she panted, "I really hope your idea works because I just—" she stopped. Something was wrong.

Penalynn stared at the wall, her face as inscrutable as a sphynx. Rowena followed her gaze to see the silver glass blatantly revealed. It was splintered in a spiderweb of shattered glass. It was then Rowena felt the waves of heat wafting from Penalynn like an invisible tide. Ghost burrowed into Rowena's hair, and Isla sat on her rump, tense and watchful.

Penalynn asked, unnervingly conversational, "Rowena, do you know what this is?"

"It's a silver glass."

"No. It's a *broken* silver glass. Do you know how it was broken?"

"No," Rowena answered truthfully.

"Have you seen this silver glass before?"

Her mind cast about for an answer somewhere between the disgrace of truth and the shame of deceit.

Penalynn held up her hand. "I see you are trying to come up with a lie, so I'll stop you. You *have* seen this before. What did you do when you saw it?"

Rowena went pale, still as a mouse cornered by a cat. "I can't use silver glass.

I don't have—"

"You don't have magic. Yes. That has already been thoroughly established today. Does this mean you must, therefore, be innocent?"

"I didn't break your glass, Penalynn."

"No. You didn't. It's broken from the other side, which is far from here."

Despite the tension of the moment, Rowena's curiosity couldn't help but pique. She didn't know that a break in silver glass would reveal itself miles away in the corresponding match.

Penalynn asked outright, "Have you used this?"

"No-o." It was technically true. After all, Titus had been the one to magic the glass.

Penalynn stood, clearly about to leave.

Rowena wavered. This was not the atmosphere she had expected when she'd sprinted upstairs. Penalynn opened the door, and Rowena cried, "Wait, no! You said you had an idea to help me."

Penalynn swung out her hand toward the shattered glass. "*This* was my idea."

"But..." she floundered, her heart racing. "But could you use the one in the Hall of Sceadwe instead?"

"That one doesn't connect to the silver glass this connects to."

"Well...could you...could you write a letter, maybe, to whoever..." It was a useless request, and she knew it. The clock was against her now. Soon, the Myth Keeper would awaken with no one to defend her case. "Please! Please, there must be something. I *have* to graduate!"

Penalynn's face puckered with chagrin. "I'm confused. Your lack of magic won my sympathy earlier, which is why I came up here to help you. But now you use your Shadow's inability as an alibi to lie to me?"

Rowena buried her fingers in her hair. "Okay, yes! Yes, I've seen this silver glass before. I found it a year ago."

"Did you use it?"

"A friend helped me. But it was my idea. I asked them to do it."

"What did you see?"

Rowena shook her head quickly. "Nothing. It was black. I think the other side was covered."

"It was. Did you hear anything?"

"Umm..." She closed her eyes, struggling to remember. "Breathing...and...and a voice."

"What did they say?"

She shrugged, at a loss. "Nothing. It was just...I don't know...it sounded like someone was crying, maybe."

Penalynn stepped toward her, pressing for information, her look more severe than Rowena had ever seen. "And did you do anything?"

"No."

"Nothing? You didn't make any noise at all? Because if you could hear them, then they could hear you."

Rowena did her best to remember that day when she and Titus had successfully used the silver glass. It was difficult, the details overshadowed by…her eyes squeezed tight against the memory of what happened next. She dropped her face into her hands, her heart sinking.

"I, uh…I screamed."

"You screamed," murmured Penalynn. The hair on her arms stood up, her Shadow's tail bristling. "Did something appear in the glass that scared you?"

"No. Ghost jumped from the balcony because of…because of Isla. The silver glass was still working when it happened."

"After you screamed, did anyone appear in the glass?"

"I was in too much pain. We forgot about it after that."

"Did Titus see anyone?"

"No, I don't think so. We never really talked about—wait…I didn't say it was Titus who helped me."

"No. But you've confirmed my hunch," said Penalynn with a grimace. "So, you found my silver glass, showed it to Titus, and convinced him to use it for you."

Rowena stood unmoving, feeling exposed and thoroughly guilty. "I'm sorry."

Penalynn stared out the window, lost in thought. Outwardly, Rowena stood still, but inwardly, her body raged. She regretted dosing herself with the potion, wishing she were passed out alongside the Myth Keeper, unconscious to her suddenly crumbling world. Her limbs hummed, her heart a frenetic ricochet churning her anguish until she felt crazed.

Just then, Freya entered. "Madame," she said with a curtsy.

"Yes?"

Before the servant could speak, Rowena blurted in a rush, "If I can't do my trial, I can't graduate! Penalynn, if I don't graduate, they'll never invite me to university, and I can't become a Scholastic if—"

Penalynn cut her off. "You can't become a Scholastic without your mentor's trust! Something which you no longer have."

Tears welled in Rowena's eyes, and her knees threatened to buckle. "Please. I'm so sorry. Please."

"You're fired," said Penalynn. It was barely a murmur.

All breath rushed from Rowena's chest as if she'd been leveled a deadly blow. Her vision tightened, spots blinking in her periphery. Everything she knew was crumbling away, and surely even the ground would fall away at any moment to swallow her whole. She ached for that to happen. For oblivion from the pain.

Penalynn turned to Freya. "Yes, what is it?"

"Madame, it's happening," Freya said meaningfully. "You asked me to tell you when the hermit's magic changed."

"Has Craefog's magic stopped completely?"

"No. But it's slowing."

Penalynn nodded. "Get the carriage and meet me at the castle doors. I want to be there before he dies."

Freya dashed out the door and down the hall. Penalynn walked across the room swiftly and grabbed two empty vials from a shelf. She spoke over her shoulder at Rowena, "You may leave your cape on my desk."

A whirlwind of feeling raged inside Rowena, tears streaming like a broken levee. She bellowed, "*Why did you choose me?!* I was just a little girl. I had no education. No magic. I had a literal *ghost* for a Shadow. It was the worst possible choice you could have made for your apprentice. The Myth Keeper saw it. The whole town saw it. It's clear from whatever Consular Feargus was talking about, even the Sceadwe never approved your choice. You've faced ridicule and threats because of me. *Why?!* It must have been important, or you wouldn't have gone against every single person you know to have *me* as your apprentice!"

Penalynn kept her face blank. But her jaw quivered. She turned the doorknob to leave, but Rowena's cries stopped her.

"Penalynn, I'm sorry! I'm sorry I lied to you. I'm sorry I used your silver glass." While Rowena talked, her hands were behind her back, her fingers blindly working. "I'm sorry I tried to trick you into using your magic over and over again these past years. I'm sorry I complained about the interviews so much. I'm sorry you were made so unpopular because of me. And most of all I'm sorry I never showed proper appreciation for it all. You saved me. You took a little girl, trapped and lonely, and you gave me...everything."

Click.

"And...I'm very sorry for *this*."

She pulled forth the vaporizer with a new capsule inside and aimed the device at Penalynn's face; her thumb smashed against the button. A bitter, licorice-scented cloud spewed from its end. Penalynn's face contorted from shock to outrage. Rowena held her breath for a count of five, then shut off the gas. Only when the cloud dissipated did she dare to breathe. But just to be safe, she uncapped another capsule and took a sip of antidote.

There wasn't even time to speak before the potion took effect. Rowena caught Penalynn's swaying body and pivoted her toward the wingback chair nearby. Her neck and shoulders were rigid, her limbs inflexible as planks. Guiltily,

Rowena adjusted her as best she could while all Penalynn could do was blink at her in fury.

"It's safe, what I've given you," Rowena assured her. "Just a paralytic potion. You can breathe and see just fine, but the rest of your body is going to have a little sleep. I didn't give you much. Just enough to get me a head start. There's a bottle here on the desk. See it? You're going to have some nausea when the potion wears off. I haven't managed to work out that side effect yet. Take a sip of that—just a teaspoon, really—and it should help. Yes, I know you're mad and you have every right to be. But what are you going to do? Fire me—again? Ban me from school?" Rowena shoved her hair from her eyes to properly look Penalynn in the eye. "There's nothing left I have to lose."

She scooped up the fox, its body also inert and stiff, and set it in Penalynn's lap.

"I hope you'll take the time sitting here to see things from my perspective. I know there was a reason you chose me, and I think I'm about to find out why. Craefog knows. I have to know too, Penalynn. Can you honestly blame me for wanting to know the truth? Haven't you risked everything to find the truth yourself?"

Rowena kissed her on the cheek then unbuttoned her cape and draped it over the back of the chair. She left Penalynn with nothing to do but wait for the potion to wear off. She wasn't sure how much time she had. The dosing measurements weren't fully worked out yet. In her uncertainty, she'd erred on the side of caution.

She broke into a run in the corridor, her body buzzing partly from hurry, but mostly from the two potions swirling through her blood, whipping her adrenaline into action. Outside, she passed a horse-drawn carriage—the one Penalynn had called for. Freya waited beside it; her face drawn with worry. Soon she would go upstairs to find a paralyzed Scholastic. Rowena wondered if she should have left a note. Still, she ran from the castle where two members of the Sceadwe lay, both incapacitated by her handiwork.

She didn't stop until she reached the edge of the woods by her house; the part where Craefog's path ended, now overgrown. Beneath a blanket of leaves and growth Rowena could just make out the trail. She followed it, her muscles eventually tiring as the potions burned off. When all adrenaline and potion were drained from her veins, she was left with nothing but fatigue and the untended emotions of the day. The reality of her circumstances threatened to split her heart down the middle, so she forced those thoughts into a recessed corner of her mind, focusing on the present moment.

She arrived at the towering edifice of the hermit's mansion, sweating despite the autumn chill. Behind that door, she would find a madman, but he was dying,

Penalynn said. Rowena needed to ask her questions before he did. Now, standing on the brink of discovering the truth at last, she hesitated. After all, secrets were secret for a reason.

CHAPTER
FORTY-SEVEN

T HE PARALYTIC DIDN'T LAST long, and having a carriage, Penalynn soon
gained on Rowena until the path narrowed so much that she was forced
to abandon her ride and continue on foot. Penalynn stomped through the underbrush, absolutely furious. In those first seconds of paralysis, she happily considered having Rowena arrested for drugging a Scholastic of the Sceadwe. But
frozen suspension had given her time to think. Rowena's actions had been risky,
recklessly so. But Penalynn had deprived her of the truth—a grave deprivation
she herself knew all too well. While throwing her in prison would be satisfying
(especially after the humiliation of being disarmed even of the capacity to stand),
Penalynn couldn't blame the girl. After all, if the roles were reversed, she would
have done the same thing.

When she caught up to Rowena, the girl stood outside the hermit's abode.
"Put this on," Penalynn demanded, pressing the apprentice cape into Rowena's
hand.

Rowena knew she would come, and so wasn't surprised. "I thought I was
fired."

"I've changed my mind."

"So, how angry are you?" she asked, doing as she was told and buttoning the
cape down her front.

"Livid. And considering your actions, it seems that feeling is mutual. Before we go any further, let me make myself clear. If you ever use a potion on me again, I will drag you down to the castle's dungeon and leave you there to rot."

"Does Greymere's castle have a dungeon?"

"I will have one carved out just for you. This is neither a joke nor an empty threat. Do you understand?"

"Yes."

"Good." Then Penalynn softened. "Look at me, Rowena. You must prepare yourself for what lies ahead. We are about to enter the home of a dead man."

"How do you know he's dead already?"

Penalynn inclined her forehead, and Rowena turned to see the hermit's mansion. Only the mansion was gone, replaced by a sagging, decrepit shack built at the foot of an earthen cliff. It was a haphazard mishmash of crude construction, natural stone, and fallen trees.

"I...I don't understand," stammered Rowena. "His house—it was just here!"

"I read your report. You knew magic was at work," said Penalynn gently. "Most likely a combination of manipulation and persuasion."

With eyes no longer magicked by the hermit, Rowena struggled to assimilate this stark reality compared to the magical fantasy from before. The shack was old. Very old. But there were vague familiarities. A wood door stood where the previous one had stood, though smaller and without hinges. It leaned against a wall of stone and mud, moss caking nearly every surface. The "windows" were just gaps in the wall, hastily covered with planks to stave off the coming winter. To enter, Penalynn pulled the door's edge, allowing it to fall back. She stepped over it, and Rowena followed. Where Rowena had once walked upon glistening tile, their boots crunched leaves. Puddles of rainwater pooled in shallow rivulets. She placed her hand against the lichen-encrusted stone cliff. "There had been a staircase. And marble. And carpet."

"He built his house around this cliff wall," Penalynn observed. "Clever. It's a natural protection from the elements."

There was no roof. What shelter he required, Craefog had found in the natural rock. The makeshift walls of stacked rock and muck served more for privacy than any real protection.

Rowena stared at the bare limbs above. "There was a chandelier."

"It was a persuasion," said Penalynn.

They rounded the cliff where the mahogany-paneled room had been—or had seemed to. Where the fireplace had been, there was a shallow cavity filled with ash. Perhaps the warmth she had felt from the fire had been real. With Craefog's magic extinguished, the table, which once held a massive feast, was now revealed to be stained by rain and what looked like dried blood. There was a bowl, a cup, a pile of decaying mushrooms, and all manner of bones and furs.

Rowena cupped her hand over her mouth to keep from gasping at each new revelation. The reality felt obscene, especially compared to her extravagant memories from before. Everything was dirt and damp and wild. Memories flooded back. It wasn't just what she had *seen*. She remembered the smell of the food, how the feast had made her mouth water. How the wind sounded muffled through glass windows, which now she knew had never existed. How the carpet had felt plush under her feet, not a twig or leaf in sight.

Craefog had tricked every one of her senses into believing his lie.

She turned to where the interview had taken place. In this very spot, she had sat on decadent furniture, but now she saw the truth. Two moldy chairs for her and Craefog, a spindly stool for Bruce, and mere stumps where Sersha and Titus had sat. Thinking back, she remembered how the three of them had sat on the edge of their seat. Had their bodies known what their minds had not, that there was no chair to lean back in?

She pressed the heels of her palms to her eye sockets, cutting off her vision to allow her mind to catch up. She could hear Penalynn's measured footsteps, the fox's prim tread. A brush against her shoulder told her Ghost hovered close. Isla's breath was audible, rapid, and she sniffed as if she'd found something. Rowena opened her eyes.

She rounded a chair to see whatever Isla saw, and as soon as she did, she screamed. Her legs caught the edge of a stump as she stumbled back, and she fell, her feet flying overhead.

"Did you find him?" Penalynn asked, coming over.

Rowena scrambled to sit. Her finger quaked as she pointed where, in the same chair as his interview, sat Craefog, still dressed in that ridiculous periwinkle robe. Or at least what was left of Craefog.

Penalynn's nose wrinkled. "He's worse than I expected."

"But...I thought..." Rowena gaped. "*When* did he die?"

"Just a minute ago."

"No. No. That can't be. Penalynn, *look at him!*"

"I used my intuition the whole time to get here," said Penalynn. "His magic stopped just after I arrived. I assure you. Craefog was alive minutes ago."

"That's not possible," Rowena insisted because there, seated as if waiting for his afternoon tea, sat the hermit's remains, drained of life to the bone. His skeleton protruded under tightly wrapped skin, his body empty of fluid as if it had begun decaying months ago. Patches of skin were missing, but his exposed muscle was still red. She was very glad his robe hid whatever state his belly was in, uninterested in seeing his organs should any be visible beneath his paper-thin skin. "Penalynn, what is it I'm seeing?"

Penalynn spoke with sympathy in her voice, "Rowena, come sit with me."

"I'm not sitting with a dead man."

"You want to know what it is I've been studying. It will take a minute to explain, so we might as well be comfortable."

"There's a man's *skeleton—*"

"Sit."

With a mighty effort not to gag, she obeyed, taking the seat farthest from the corpse.

"Rowena, how do we know a person's age?"

"What?" The question seemed random and dissonant from the macabre scene.

"Think, Rowena. How do we know a person's age?"

She shrugged. "Ask them how old they are."

"Correct. One way of knowing someone's age is by time, measured on a calendar. Starting from their date of birth and marked by years. But there are also markers of time in the body."

"What do you mean? Like rings in a tree trunk?"

"Precisely. And these age markers within the human body are more accurate than a calendar."

"What are the markers?"

Penalynn leaned forward. "Age, in essence, is a measurement of *deterioration.* Every living thing eventually dies, which makes life a spectrum. It can be a spectrum of *time*, measured from their birthday to (for lack of a better word) their deathday. Or I can be measured by the spectrum of deterioration in the body. Birth is the point when the body is least deteriorated, and death is when it is most deteriorated."

Rowena frowned. "But there's no way to know when a person will die."

"True. A person can die from illness or injury. But the body—if given the chance—will eventually die simply of old age. Within every body, there is a timeline. We know what the timeline markers are at birth and death. By looking at physical samples such as blood and hair, I can pinpoint where a person is on their timeline by measuring the amount of decay I find because I can plot where they are between their birthday and...well...their deathday."

Rowena held up both hands. "Are you telling me you can find out when a person will die just by looking at their blood?"

"No. But I can tell you where they are on their timeline," said Penalynn.

"Just ask them how old they are."

"You did that. In your interviews, you asked every person in Greymere how old they are. But, when I tested their samples, the markers in their body did not match the age they provided. Think about it. Some people live to be ninety, while some die peacefully in their sleep at seventy. Why? Take out accidents and illness. What causes a person to die? *Decay.* A nicer term for it could be age. And, as my study shows, a person's age is not accurately measured by time on a calendar. It's in their body."

Rowena held her head in her hands. "I don't understand. You just said so yourself that some people die at ninety and some at seventy. And some younger than that. How can you measure their age if every person's physical timeline is different?"

"Because there's another variable involved." Rowena's eyes narrowed and Penalynn pressed, "Surely you can guess what it is."

Prickles, like tiptoeing spiders, crept across Rowena's skin. "Magic," she breathed.

She looked at Craefog. The skeleton's jaw hung ajar as if screaming from beyond the dead. Rowena's voice dropped to a whisper. "The math you had me check—the number—of all magic a person has ever done..."

Penalynn nodded. "I took what I found in the samples—the markers of decay—and found each person's genuine age. I then compared the sum total of magic they'd ever done. What I found is that the more magic they did, the more decayed their body became. And more than that, the *progression* of decay coincides perfectly with magic. So perfectly, that if you were to take the sum total of magic they've ever done, you could accurately predict their genuine age without ever having to look at their samples."

Rowena's chest tightened. She breathed through her nose, urging her heart to slow. "Penalynn, what are you telling me?"

Penalynn waited, allowing the knowledge to sink in.

After a moment, Rowena said, "The day you studied Craefog's samples you freaked out."

Penalynn nodded, remembering. "Ewan Craefog's age (at least when you took his samples last year) measured over two hundred years old."

At this, Rowena's stomach churned as if she'd been shaken like a jar. Her head swiveled toward the skeleton. Its cheeks were sunken, eyelids so thin pupils were visible beneath, purple like a bruise. "No. He's middle-aged. He went to school with my father. They're the same age! Craefog didn't die today; he died...I don't know...*months ago!* We're just seeing his body after it—"

"I know it's shocking," said Penalynn.

"*Shocking?*" she gasped. "A hermit living in a freakish mansion in the woods is *shocking.* Titus pulling an entire tree down by magic is *shocking.* You've just told me that the more magic a Shadow does the older a person gets! The closer to their—what did you call it? Their *deathday?!* It's more than shocking its..."

She cast about the decrepit shell of a room, hollow and decayed like Craefog's remains. The weight of knowledge pressed upon her. She sagged under the truth, the implications heavy as lead. Desperate, she longed to return to her previous ignorance when she had been free from these waves of horror crashing into her as implication after implication made itself evident.

Her voice was small, like a little girl's. "Penalynn...does magic kill people?"

Penalynn answered grimly. "Well, it's certainly not good for one's health."

Rowena gaped. How could she be pithy at a moment like this? But Penalynn had had years to acclimate to the revelation. Would that happen to her, Rowena wondered. Would she eventually grow accustomed to this truth? *Magic kills people. Oh well!* She struggled to swallow.

Penalynn contemplated the skeleton. "It's obvious Craefog's Shadow used magic to keep his body alive; maybe a manipulation of his organs or something. Or he could have animated his own heart to keep blood pumping. I had hoped to ask him, but I'm too late."

Rowena barely heard her. A translucent flipper touched her cheek, and she recoiled until she realized it was just her Shadow. Ghost wiped her cheek, and Rowena realized her face was wet. She was crying. Ghost looked back to Craefog's body and then back at Rowena with something akin to wisdom in those misty eyes. Thinking back, Rowena remembered Ghost's odd behavior the last time they'd been here. Craefog had insinuated that Ghost was not persuadable like the rest of them. Even then, her Shadow had seen the truth of what Craefog had become. Ghost had watched Rowena converse with a living corpse. No wonder she had attacked him.

The room tilted, and Rowena slipped from the chair to her knees. Her body convulsed, eager to expel all her mind had swallowed, vomiting up what felt like her very guts. When her stomach emptied, her emotions remained, tears streaming in wracking sobs. Isla placed her head under Rowena's hand while Ghost burrowed at the nape of her neck.

Penalynn patted her back. "*Shhh.* Rowena, breathe. Just breathe."

"He...he knew!!" Rowena choked between sobs. Craefog's corpse seemed to watch her unravel like a pulled thread. "He knew what magic was doing to him—and—and—*he did it anyway!*"

Penalynn looked at the fox Shadow's pupils, which were wide and black as the grave. "It's difficult to give up magic."

Faces flashed across Rowena's mind as she remembered her countless interviews. Her neighbors. Classmates. Teachers. It had always been there, this truth, evident in the aged and youthful of Greymere alike. Their bodies held the truth. The Shadows with puny magic always accompanied the smooth-skinned and youthful, while the truly talented in magic had mottled hands or lines around their mouth. She recalled the aged and stooped mailman and his two hundred bouts of magic a day. Or Haaris and his brittle bones.

Haaris! Even now, her father would be in his workshop with his Shadow humming over a piece of material, transforming it into art. How much decay would that one act win for her father's body? At what point would his "brittle bones" be rendered to dust? Rowena's neck grew clammy, and she wondered if she might vomit again, but only bile remained. Her throat blazed with it, sour and raw.

Then there was Titus, with that Shadow of his securing the highest marks in every class. How much had Rowena's "help" cost him the day his Shadow pulled down the ancient oak tree? When she requested his help with Penalynn's silver glass, had she unknowingly requested him to surrender hours of his life? Silver glass required the most powerful of magic, so it could have cost him days. Weeks, even. How much further had Rowena plunged him towards his deathday?

Her lungs quivered, either forgetting how to work or making room for the much more pressing matter of weeping. Tears raged in earnest now, and she wondered if she would ever manage to stop. "They're dying!" she cried, her face crumpled like soggy paper. "Papa and Titus are dying!"

Penalynn knelt beside Rowena, hugging her to her chest. "Not at this moment, they aren't."

"But they will! And what about me? I have no magic. What will I do when everyone I love dies without me?"

Penalynn smoothed Rowena's hair like a mother with a wailing child. "Listen to me. You were right; I did choose you for a reason. When I found you, it was like I had found a prize. Your sample has been the most amazing of all my findings. You were my control. My constant. My standard by which I measured everyone else. Your rate of decay matches perfectly with your calendar age. It's astounding. You are exactly nineteen years old. You will live longer than anyone ever has, but even so, you won't live forever. You will not be left behind all alone."

Rowena croaked, wiping snot on her cape. "But *they* will leave me. And so will you."

Penalynn sighed. Rowena was right.

After a while, when her sobbing ebbed to the hiccupping calm that happens after a good cry, Rowena asked, "How long have you known?"

"It started with just a hunch. Long before I ever came to Greymere. After all, you don't study something without a hypothesis to test. Every sample I've examined has been another piece of evidence added to the growing pile."

Rowena hiccupped. "How can you stand it? Knowing what you know?"

"Well, maybe there's a reason I don't have any friends. You've been a bright spot for me, you know. At least I have one person I don't have to worry about."

Surely, Rowena thought, her body would soon be just a dry husk, drained of fluid like Craefog. Yet somehow, more tears welled. "But for me, every person I love is amazing at magic and will live half my lifespan because of it. Penalynn, I have to tell them. Maybe if they stopped, they could..."

Penalynn shook her head. "It's not that easy. Look at Craefog. He knew what his magic was doing, and he never stopped. If anything, his magic grew."

"But he was crazy," argued Rowena. "Besides, *you've* done it. You've stopped."

"No, I haven't. Really, I haven't. Just this morning, I meant to use my silver glass, and the only reason I didn't was because it was broken. And on the way here I used intuition to find Craefog's house. Trust me, every person, when pressed with the need, will do magic, even if they know the cost. Though I wish never to use magic again, I know it is not a matter of *if* but *when* my Shadow does it next."

"But it's possible to live without it. I do it every day! I'm *proof!*"

"Are you?" Penalynn asked, unconvinced. "How often have you asked someone to do magic for you?"

"But I didn't know the cost. I didn't know that asking Titus to help me took time off his life!"

"Your life has depended upon magic more than you know. Even my work—which found this all out—is impossible without the constant magic of servants in my laboratory." Rowena's stomach flipped as she remembered that even at that very moment, miles away, two Shadows magicked the frozen laboratory. Penalynn's lip quivered. "And yes, I have felt ashamed every second they have been in there, but without them, my work isn't possible. Why do you think I pay them so well?"

"But people deserve to know. We have to tell them."

"And we will. Eventually, I will present my findings to the Sceadwe, and they can decide how or if to tell people."

"*If?*" Rowena cried. "Penalynn, can you imagine how this information will change the world?"

"Can *you?* We're not guaranteed people will even believe us."

"What does belief have to do with it? You have evidence. How could anyone debate against evidence?"

Penalynn sighed like a much older woman. "Rowena. *Everything* is debatable. Trust me, this knowledge will not be received like you think it will. You do not understand the nature of Shadows. How the soul-link works. To have a part of you that wants to do something that goes against your deepest impulses. The war of will within your own heart—you know nothing of this. Knowing the cost will not make the thirst for magic any less. If anything, the thirst becomes more terrible because suddenly your heart has dual purposes. Right now, everyone does as they wish, with no thought to what their magic does to their body. But when you tell them, it will split them in half. Magic and self-preservation will war inside them, pitting their souls against themselves. Human against Shadow. The craving for magic will not bend to the knowledge of self-destruction. No, the desire burns hotter. People want what they want, and they want to do magic. They will forsake anything—truth included—for what they want."

Rowena considered this, then asked, "Is this why your Shadow always looks angry?"

Penalynn grinned, although in a pained sort of way. "Yes. That is exactly why."

They both fell silent, lost in thought. Eventually, with a look of complete and utter hopelessness, Rowena asked, "Penalynn, what do I do now?"

"Let's both go home and get some sleep. Tomorrow, we work. You are right; people need to be told. It's our job now to find the best way to do that. Together."

Rowena allowed Penalynn to pull her to stand. She hugged Ghost to her chest, and Isla leaned against her hip like a bolster. Before they left, Penalynn stooped over Craefog's remains. Her cloak shielded whatever she did from view, but when she stood, Rowena saw a vial disappear in the fold of her cloak. A chunk of flesh had been carved from the corpse's chest. Apparently, *any* physical material could be tested for Penalynn's purposes. Blood and hair were simply the most merciful.

Chapter
Forty-Eight

B RAN'S BOOTS BEAT A steady measure as he exited the throne room, the king already moving on to other matters. Specks of light shone across his vision as he walked, and he tried to blink them away. Time in the throne room often had this effect on him. The court must be prone to dust, he assumed.

Beside him, Rankin complained, "I can't believe he's givin' you time off but not me." He tucked a scroll into his jacket. "Why's he sending Tollers and not you? Think he's cracking up?"

Bran shrugged. "I'm just glad I don't have to go so far north. Too cold."

"It's beastly far," Rankin groaned. "What's it called again? Greymere?"

Another splatter of specks shot across Bran's vision. He batted the air as if they were gnats. "Never heard of it. A teenager this time, right?" He shook his head. "As if a kid could conspire against a kingdom."

"What a waste," Rankin agreed, though he might have meant his time trekking across the kingdom. "So, you going to enjoy your time off like a real man, or are you playing nursemaid?"

"Shut up."

"HA!" Rankin barked, considering that answer enough.

On the gravel drive, they parted ways, each leaving on horseback. Once free from the palace grounds, Bran trotted down bricked city streets where pedestrians gave his steed a wide berth. The first year he became a Black Guardian, he resented the superstition towards his position—made visible by his Shadow's serpentine form. Now he barely noticed the averted glances and babies being whisked out of sight as if he were a sickness they might catch.

He eventually came to a ramshackle row of townhomes, the houses pressed together like slices of stale bread. Leaving his mount on the street, he pushed a gate which creaked in rusty protest. The blinking persisted, so he decided he'd use his time off to visit an apothecary. Maybe some drops would help. But the specks cleared enough to see a woman lying across the narrow porch; her face squashed against the welcome mat and her legs spilling down the steps. He jolted toward her with panic. With a mighty heave, he rolled her over, freeing her crumpled Shadow beneath: a badger, snoring loudly with her tongue lolling out. The woman was asleep.

Bran exhaled with more irritation than relief, then scooped her up like a giant infant. With practiced care, his Shadow twisted his tail around the badger's middle to hoist her along.

The front door was ajar, and he banged it open further with his foot. "Anna! Get in here!"

A frail, meager-looking young woman with girlhood lingering in her round cheeks rushed into the room wearing an apron. Her Shadow (an absurdly skinny chicken) wouldn't leave the safety of the kitchen, so she gandered around the corner.

"Why was my mother asleep on the porch?" Bran demanded.

"She went out," the girl said, her knees knocking in fright before the king's man.

Summoning patience, Bran said through clenched teeth, "She's not supposed to be going out. That's one of your jobs—why I pay you, in fact— so she doesn't overexert her Shadow."

Anna eyes threatened to pop from her face.

Bran heard his Shadow's voice, *Mother would eat her for supper if she tried to hold her back.* Bran sighed. It was true. The girl was no match for the old lady in his arms...when she was conscious and not gargling on her own spit, that was.

"Go fetch the Myth Keeper."

"He's not due 'till tomorr—"

"NOW!"

With a squeak, the girl rushed into the kitchen. Bran heard retreating footsteps and the *tap-tap* of chicken feet, then the back door slam.

So much for time off, his Shadow thought.

Bran lay his mother on her bed upstairs, noticing with some gratitude that his vision had at least cleared for now. Eventually footsteps sounded on the stairs, and an old man entered alone. Anna was probably holed up in the kitchen doing nothing of use. The man appeared in his fifties, though Bran knew he was at least a decade older than he looked. He wore the black cape of a Myth Keeper and held a bag of clanking glass and metal. His Shadow was a raven.

"Atticus, you're late," Bran accused, shuffling to the far side of the bed.

The old man's voice wheezed in the back of his throat, the only evidence of his marked age. "I wasn't expected until tomorrow." He rummaged in his bag.

"Two days a week isn't enough. I need you here every other day."

The man named Atticus pulled out a corked bottle and gently shook its contents. "I have another job, you know. I can't be personal apothecary to whoever asks."

Bran crossed his arms, his biceps bulging. "Does the Sceadwe know the Royal Myth Keeper is an accomplished physic and black-market apothecary?"

Atticus's laugh sounded like a cough. "That's cheap."

"Every. Other. Day."

Striking a match, Atticus held the flame to a long needle. "You need to tell her she's pushing her Shadow too much."

"Yeah, I'm sure she'll listen this time," Bran said sarcastically, pushing the matted hair from his mother's forehead. "She's pleasant like this, isn't she?"

"Almost tempts one to leave her be," Atticus said. He parted the badger's fur then pierced the Shadow's skin with the needle."

Outside on the street below, they could hear hooves clomping at a thunderous pace, followed by a piercing whistle. "Bran! Oy! Ninny-nob!" Someone banged on the door downstairs.

"Lovely company you keep, sir Bran."

"I'll be right back," he groaned, then stomped downstairs to find Rankin on his front porch. "Aren't you supposed to be halfway out of the city by now?"

"I can't go without my partner."

"Where's Tollers?"

Rankin's face cracked into a wicked smile. "Gone bonkers. Spent the night in a dream shop and a right dodgy one from the looks of it."

Bran cursed. "Stupid, useless piece of—*how* a persuasion junkie ever got in our ranks is beyond me!"

"Well, he's gonna' be out of his mind a while. Look, it's a track-and-grab job. Easy." Bran shook his head, and Rankin pressed, "I can go all the way back to the palace and get the king to make the order, or you can just accept it like a man." He thrust a scroll embossed with the king's seal into Bran's hand. "Here, get a feel for it before we head out."

"Remind me to kill Tollers," Bran spat, scanning the page. "Give me a minute to pack."

First, he went to the kitchen to explain to Anna the change in schedule, leaving her with explicit instructions and more money than she'd need. Next, he dashed upstairs, where Atticus monitored his mother's pulse.

"Is she stable yet?" he asked.

"Getting there," said the old man. "Where-to this time, Mr. Guardian?"

"North. Some city in the forest called Greymere. I've never been."

"I thought you had," said Atticus curiously. "Doesn't our Scholastic friend live there?"

The specks resurged, and Bran blinked. "Who?"

With an odd mix of pity and sadness, the old man shook his head. "Never mind. I'm sure you'll meet her when you're there."

When Bran had packed, he dropped a hefty gold purse on the table beside his mother's bed. "For your trouble. Don't forget, she needs this potion every other day."

"You don't want to say goodbye?" asked Atticus. "Before you're gone two months?"

Bran grimaced. "I'm on my way to arrest a teenage girl. I'm not about to be throttled by my mother for it."

"The king's afraid of little girls now, is he? Well, it wouldn't be the first time."

"You're a terrible Myth Keeper. You know that?"

"Meh. I'm the *Royal* Myth Keeper. I'm superfluous. What use has a king with me when he's got a Bazileus to guide him?" His lips twitched with irony. "You're one to point fingers. A Black Guardian afraid of his own mother! Ha!"

There was a grumbling gargle. The sleeping woman mumbled something, but her eyes remained closed.

"Best be off then," Atticus whispered ominously, "*It stirs.*"

"Every forty-eight hours," Bran reminded him, hoisting his bag onto his shoulder.

"Yes, yes, off with you now. And say hello to my old friend when you get there."

"Who?"

"Oh, you'll remember when you see her."

Leaving his mother in the care of the old man, Bran climbed into the saddle.

Rankin said with a crooked smile, "Let's go catch us a monster!"

"She's just a kid."

"If the boss sends us to get it, then it's a monster. *Hyah!*" Rankin spurred his horse, taking off in a blur.

Bran gave one last look at home, the recently painted townhome whiter than its neighbors, like a false tooth in chipped and yellowed smile. He urged his horse northbound. The snake squeezed his bicep for purchase. After all these years his

Shadow still missed his old lizard form. But the orange scales were the same bright orange as always, like a badge, signaling him as a Black Guardian to the King of Wyre. Like an arrow shot from the king's bow, he never missed his target.

CHAPTER
FORTY-NINE

IT WAS EVENING WHEN Rowena returned home from Craefog's shack, now a tomb. When Haaris asked her about her audition, she answered with a blunt, "I failed," and he mercifully knew from her tone and the look on her face not to ask more. But despite the enormous losses of the day, they felt like mere scabs, pain so slight as to be insignificant. What did things like Riven and university matter when the world was turned upside down and inside out?

She went to bed early, watching the evening darken from purple to navy to black. Soon there was a whisper.

"Spook. Pssttt, Spook! Are you there?"

She considered ignoring him, but instead, she shouldered her heavy grief and scooped up the silver glass.

"Hi," she said.

It took only one glance at her face for Titus to demand, "What happened?"

Her voice was mechanical. "They've banned me from participating in the trials."

"What?! *How?*"

"It doesn't matter," she said and meant it. "Titus, I need to tell you something."

"But what does that mean about university?"

"I'm not going to university. There's something—"

"I don't understand. You're a Scholastic Apprentice!"

"Well, actually I had lost that too. Penalynn fired me. Then we went to Craefog's house—Craefog died today, by the way—and while we were there, she hired me back on. But that doesn't matter—"

"Wait. Rowena, slow down."

He rubbed his forehead, and her eyes narrowed upon his fingertips. "Do you have a headache?"

"It's fine," he said, "As soon as we're done with the silver glass it'll go away."

At this, she nearly cried. "Titus, I can't talk to you on the silver glass anymore."

"Really, it's not that bad. And I'm not going anywhere until you explain what happened."

"What happened is I learned what Penalynn had been studying."

"But, what does that have to do with—"

"Titus. Magic kills people."

He blinked. "I'm sorry, what?"

In a rush, Rowena filled him in on all she had learned. As she talked, her eyes never left the crease between his brows, the difficulty of his magic evident in that single line, as if the wrinkle were a ticking clock, counting each second he lost from his lifespan so long as his magic operated the silver glass. Her lungs ached with the speed of her speech until she finished in a rush, "Which means I can't talk to you on the silver glass anymore because you're not going to use magic anymore. Ever. You can't. It's killing you."

"What?" was all he managed to say in response.

"Titus! Didn't you hear me? Magic—"

"Yes, I heard you, but I don't understand. There must be a mistake. Magic can't...I mean...it's magic! I'm sorry, Spook, but what you're telling me, it's crazy. You see that right?"

"It's true. Believe me, it's true. You must promise me you won't let your Shadow do any more magic. I mean it, Titus!"

He sighed. "Okay, let's be realistic here."

"I *am* being realistic."

"It's magic, Rowena. I can't just stop doing magic!"

"*I* don't do magic. I'm not asking you to do anything I haven't done."

"Yeah, except for about the hundred times you've asked me to do it for you," he snapped. "Everything is done by magic. You can't just ask people to stop. The whole kingdom would collapse!"

Penalynn had predicted this sort of response, but still, Rowena chewed the inside of her cheek, incensed. She wanted to reach through the silver glass and shake him.

Titus added, "Even if what you say is true, maybe this is just...natural."

He was wrong; she knew it. She had proof. In fact, Rowena perhaps *was* the proof. Just then something opened inside her heart, like a bud in springtime, pushing up from the soil. Her whole life she had thought that people like the Myth Keeper were right, that she was a mistake. But was it possible, could it be, that she was the answer? If Penalynn's study had birthed a new question: *can a person live without magic?* Then Rowena's very existence was a resounding *yes!*

"Titus, I'm begging you. Please do not use any more magic."

"If I stop, we can't talk through silver glass anymore. And if you're not coming to Riven then...we won't..."

Her eyes watered. Of all his push-back, this was his strongest argument. Her heart ached, enjoying nothing more than these clandestine conversations. "I just got you back," she whispered.

"See. For that reason alone, I won't stop. Being able to talk to you each day is too important to me."

They smiled at one another. It was the closest they'd ever come to declaring their feelings.

"Titus, you have to believe me. Please."

"I do," he assured her, and she knew he meant it.

A tear trailed down her cheek and she whispered close, her lips nearly brushing the silver, "I'm going to miss you so much."

He had barely enough time to understand what she meant before she smashed the silver on the frame of her bed. The glass splintered in jagged rings, and Titus's face was gone. She sprang from her bed, heaved open the trap door, and then slid down the ladder on the insides of her shoes. Ghost followed as they crossed the garden and entered her father's workshop.

It took half an hour to get the furnace hot enough. She squeezed the bellows, fanning the coals until they glowed white. When she finished, the glass was reduced to liquid. She left it to cool, a small fortune of pure silver forgotten in the crucible. After all, without Titus's face shining from its surface, what use was silver to her?

CHAPTER FIFTY

IT WAS DARK, BUT somehow, Penalynn could still see. She lay on her back, her arms in the grip of something. Her head swiveled. It was claws pinning her to stone. Talons sank into the rock like a knife in bread. Something slithered. A snake. No. It wore the same sapphire armor as the claws. A dragon, then. Yes. Its tail wound around her legs. Loop. Loop. Strapping her to the pyre.

A fox tiptoed over the tail around her legs like a fallen tree. It sat on her stomach, its forepaws perched atop her chest. It smiled. Penalynn smiled back. The fox's smile widened into a grimace, teeth bared. Then its jaw hinged open like a yawn. It struck like a snake. Teeth sank into Penalynn's neck, warm wetness spilled everywhere, and she knew it was blood.

With a scream, Penalynn jerked awake, sitting bolt upright in bed, her pulse pounding in her ears. She stretched her legs and arms, testing her freedom. The only thing binding them was the tangled sheets she'd wound around herself. It had been a dream. Only a dream. Beside her lay her Shadow. The fox was awake, of course, but she wouldn't look at Penalynn. Her back was turned with her legs curled underneath herself, her bushy tail covering her face.

Penalynn's heart calmed, and her breath returned to normal, so she smoothed the covers and lay back down, back-to-back with her Shadow. There were no thoughts between them, just the memory of the dream filling their conjoined mind, like a wall dividing her soul in two.

Tap-tap-tap.

Rowena awoke with one thought. It was an unwelcome thought, but even so, she was glad for it, if only for something new to think about. That was all she had left to do now—think. No trial, no graduation, no classes even. Just time and thoughts.

In those first few days after returning from Craefog's, she ransacked the Scholastic wing. Penalynn lifted all restrictions which allowed Rowena full access to the laboratory at last. First, she went for Penalynn's logbook, where she found graphs plotting calendar age and genuine age on a spectrum, just as Penalynn had described at Craefog's. Every page in the logbook featured this graph, and there were thousands of pages, bound in thick leather straps. When closed, the logbook was a cube, as thick as it was tall. It was all numbers and data, but Rowena knew what they represented. Names. Lives. Every page represented a real, breathing person. Her neighbors. Her friends. Her father. She wondered which page belonged to whom. Really, she could have figured it out if she wanted to. After all, she was the one who had painstakingly gathered the information and placed it in the freezing glass cabinets. But she didn't want to know, not really. Truth had lost its luster now that she had it.

At her best, Rowena paced Penalynn's office, engaged in a one-sided argument Penalynn refused to participate in. She was too busy distilling years of work into a single report, which she would eventually present to the Sceadwe. Rowena's anxious rantings raged in the background like an angry bumblebee tapping against a window. Those were the best days for Rowena. Her anxiety provided the illusion of activity, a phantom purpose, however harried and torturous.

But eventually, the illusion broke, and she stopped going to the castle. Those were the worst days when she withered into a stupefied mess. This was when Haaris found out. It took only a look from him, and her resolve to keep the Scholastic secret broke, and her heart along with it. The words tumbled out like a confession. She told him everything—about Craefog and the logbook, the graphs and data, and the stark conclusion to years of interviews.

With folded hands, she begged Haaris to cease all magic at once. His magic was killing him! she cried, his bones disintegrating because of his Shadow.

It was the look on his face that hurt her most. It wasn't dismay or horror like it should have been. Just pity. The kind of pity one gives a child who cries over childish matters. "Rowena, what you and your boss have discovered is only nature. It's the way of things. You might as well ask the river to cease its flowing, for all the good it'll do you. It's a Shadow's nature to do magic."

And that was it. Haaris's Shadow would continue to use magic, no matter if it cost him his life. That was when she took to her room, hardly touching the meals Haaris left by the trapdoor at the top of her ladder. Mornings were the hardest. In that space between sleep and wakefulness, reality splashed like cold water, mercilessly jerking her awake. She would lay in bed pondering the beams in the thatched ceiling until the panic subsided.

After a week of this, she awoke to the sound, *tap-tap-tap,* and a new thought.

"Today is the Festival of Shadows," she whispered.

Tap-tap-tap.

Perhaps she should go, she mused. She could use a diversion. But no. Everyone would be celebrating Shadows and magic. She'd only wind up looking for a megaphone to scream over the music, "*Magic is death!*" Which would only land her with the label of lunatic on top of all the other superstitions against her.

Her eyes glazed over.

Tap-tap-tap.

Her future was gone. Titus was gone. She could barely look at her father.

Tap. Tap.

What more was there to do but stare at nothing? Think about nothing?

Tap.

Slowly, as if the effort were a chore, she turned her head to see Ghost hovering at the trapdoor. *Tap-tap-tap,* her flipper rapped against the door.

How long had they been awake? An hour, maybe? Two? Rowena closed her eyes. Maybe she could fall back asleep.

There was a noise like wind; then something smacked her face with a searing *thwack!* She opened her eyes to find herself nose-to-nose with Ghost. Rowena batted her away, but Ghost smacked her across the forehead, this time harder.

"*Ouch,* Ghost! That hurts!" Rowena's voice was raspy, her tongue like sandpaper. She'd fallen asleep crying. Again.

The Shadow didn't seem to care. She *whooshed* to the trapdoor. *Tap-tap-tap.* Then flew back to smack her again. Rowena might have been fine to hole up in her room for days on end, but her Shadow evidently was not.

Just then, a muffled knocking sounded below. Someone was at the front door. Rowena and Ghost both froze to hear Haaris open the front door. She couldn't make out what was said, but she knew at once who the visitor was. And so, at last, she emerged from her bed, her head spinning with the movement after being immobile for so long, then lifted the trapdoor. Ghost plunged downstairs like a diver and landed on Isla's back. The dog's ears perked when Rowena finally descended the ladder. Her joints were stiff and crackled from inactivity.

Through the open front door, Bruce Ashworth waved past Haaris. "Hiya, Rowe."

"You're supposed to be in Riven," she croaked.

"I've graduated," he said, taking in her unwashed hair and the lumpy sweater she'd worn for days. "I've got something for you."

She noticed his hand was tucked behind his back, holding something large. With a gentle squeeze of her shoulders, Haaris left to give them some privacy.

"Nice to see you after all this time. *In person* that is." Bruce wagged his eyebrows, before frowning. "Just so you know, I'm a bit peeved with you. I skip my own graduation and forego a lovely drunken festival in Riven, all so I can high-tail it here with my baby brother. Then, halfway through our trip, you go and smash that silver glass I worked so hard to get."

"Titus is here?" Something lit inside her chest, thawing whatever lay frozen inside.

"That's not an apology. But yeah. He wanted to surprise you by showing up for your trial. But then…I guess things changed for you. After that, he couldn't get here fast enough. He asked me to give you this." His arm swung around to reveal the large rectangular box he'd been hiding. When Rowena took the package, he plunged his hands into his pockets, his lips and eyebrows dropping in a rare show of sincerity. "Do me a favor, will you? Don't say no."

When he left, Rowena tucked the box under her arm and then made her way awkwardly up the ladder with just one hand. She set the box atop her bed and removed the notecard.

Spook,

Though I don't fully understand all you shared with me, I believe you.

I know I promised I would never again ask you to wear a costume. But if what you say is true, it confirms what I've known all along. You are more extraordinary than us all. Let's show them.

— Titus

P.S. Save a dance for me.

With quivering fingertips, Rowena lifted the lid. Taffeta sprung loose like a cheerful surprise. She scooped the fabric into her arms and turned to the mirror. Holding the bodice to her chest, the dress billowed to the floor like fog as shimmering fabric in hues of smokey grey and alabaster white rippled like mist. Trails of glimmering thread spun in arched loops like smoke. She stared at the costume in wonder, the silhouette an artful match to the ghostly Shadow floating at her side.

CHAPTER FIFTY-ONE

ROWENA LIFTED THE HEM of her skirt off the forest floor as she walked alongside Ghost, a union of figures. Isla trailed behind at a respectful distance from the Shadow and her costumed counterpart. Like a twin tuft of smoke, the gown paid homage to Ghost. She glided with her head held high, her misty eyes clear as glass for once. Rowena's chest rose and fell behind the dress's delicate neckline, anticipation mounting as they reached the festival's entrance.

Titus stood below the arch of pumpkins, waiting. Her skin prickled at the sight of him. He also wore a costume, though more subdued than in years past. From his shoulder, the owl beheld her, golden eyes unblinking. Firelight reflected in the folds of her bodice, warming the gray hues. Titus met her gaze, and his lips quirked in a way that made her stomach lurch into her throat. The time and distance away from each other, followed by whispered conversations through silver glass, had done something. He should not be here, but here he stood, unexpected but welcome. And looking at her like that.

He held out his hand. In that open palm stretched an unseen path, and Rowena knew that if she took it, there would be no turning back.

"Spook?" His fingers reached further.

Swallowing, she placed her pale, calloused hand in his. His was warm and solid, and *here*. Attempting a levity she didn't feel, she asked, "Aren't you supposed to be in Riven?"

"No," he answered with unflinching fidelity. "I needed to be here. With you."

Her throat constricted. The bitter losses of the past month flared like an agonizing sting, but his hand squeezed hers and they soothed. "Thank you," she whispered.

Wordlessly, they wove through the crowd, past the lanes of colorful stalls, past performers, and vendors, and only stopped when they reached the dance floor. There, they held one another, swaying and twirling to the music. Overhead, their Shadows spun circles in an aerial dance of owl and mist. Vaguely they sensed eyes watching them, but that was easy to ignore. Sure, there was gossip behind discreet hands—whispers about Titus's sudden return, how Rowena's costume made her look like a haunted princess, how they held each other, no longer schoolmates but something much more—but they heard none of it, only the music and the thrumming beat of their hearts.

They didn't say much. It had been nearly a year since they stood face to face (truly face to face, breathing the same air), and so Rowena hadn't realized until now the intimacy introduced by late-night whispers across silver glass. Hand in hand, they entered the newness in silence. Like a bell made of smoke, Rowena's dress carved a path among dancing couples, Titus guiding her to slow or quicken in time to the music. She thought about how this night was supposed to have held nothing but pain and loss and exclusion. But Titus had come to dance with her. Instead of staring at her ceiling, numb with grief, she spun under the light of his smile.

Eventually, the music stopped. Rowena arched her head regretfully, wishing the music could have lasted forever. Stringed firebulbs flashed overhead, signaling the start of the ceremony and the trials—what was supposed to be her trial.

The crowd surged toward the arena. But Titus stood like a boulder, unmoved by the current; he held her in place. She felt his lips against her ear when he asked, "Want to get out of here?" She nodded.

Once, this arena held a world in which she longed to belong, but now there was nothing for her but an empty myth and a future robbed. And so, she left hand in hand with Titus, dressed like her Shadow and happy about it after all.

CHAPTER FIFTY-TWO

WHEN TWO BLACK GUARDIANS arrived in Greymere, their horses twitching and slick with sweat, they didn't know what day it was. Riding, then sleep, then more riding was all that had broken up their days. Even so, the trip took longer than necessary. They could have gone faster, but something Bran didn't understand urged him to slow despite Rankin's protests. The closer north they went, the worse Bran's vision became, rendering him nearly blind at points. Still, after weeks of riding, they eventually arrived with horses spent and minds bleary.

Night had fallen quickly, the sky already black despite the early hour, but the town seemed asleep already. No, that wasn't right. Bran's Shadow flared his intuition. It was deserted. They walked the hollow streets until they spied a feather-bedecked straggler locking his front door, and they realized the date.

Rankin approached the man, his voice too low for Bran to hear. In answer, the man pointed one quaking finger towards the woods where a pink haze illuminated the sky; then, he pretended to have forgotten something inside where he would no doubt wait until the two snake-adorned guards left.

When they reached the meadow, the night morphed into a raucous masquerade. Rankin broke from Bran in search of food and drink while Bran hovered at the periphery, his skin vibrating where his snake was wrapped. No one noticed him, their minds persuaded to look anywhere else. Either from laziness or arrogance (Bran wasn't sure), Rankin cut through the crowd with no such precautions, completely visible. Heads turned, and whispers spread. Bran ceased his magic, the effort pointless now. Greymere knew Black Guardians had arrived.

When Rankin rejoined him, he had a bottle of ale in one hand and a skewer of meat in the other. Together they wound through the crowd like vipers in search of prey. There were too many people to count, and most of them used magic of some sort, especially manipulation of their costumes or merchandise, so it was impossible to distinguish anything unusual. Everything was unusual. Voices, color, furs, feathers, and above all the deafening noise all crowded their senses rendering their intuition useless.

"Let's wait for the ceremony," said Bran, giving up.

Rankin spit a chunk of cartilage from the bone he gnawed, nodding in agreement.

The ceremony had commenced, and Roderick left the stage to enthusiastic applause, where he saw the Myth Keeper waiting for his cue under a dim torch. Roderick's shoulders and head blocked the light when he stepped toward him, casting the Myth Keeper into darkness.

"Why did I just see Black Guardians patrolling the steps out there?" Roderick demanded.

The Myth Keeper's Shadow jumped, but the man only said, "I'm due on-stage."

"Did you call them?"

He adjusted his cape with a fidget. "No one calls for the Black Guardians. The king sends them."

"Why did the king send them *here?*"

"Someone brought something to my attention which interests the king. I merely relayed the information."

Roderick's hands balled to fists, and his voice rumbled. "You should have told me. I'm the Lord Overseer, for *Bazileus' sake!* Whoever they're after will not just be arrested; they'll be killed. What you've done—you've sent an innocent person to their death!"

The Myth Keeper attempted a scoff. He would never forget waking in the Hall of Sceadwe after being drugged by that accursed Scholastic Apprentice. *Innocent* was not the word for one such as her.

Roderick shook him by the shoulder, "Who? Who did you report?"

The Myth Keeper yanked away and dared to meet the Overseer's blazing eyes. "Who did you *think?*" he cried like an unloved child defending himself on the playground. Then he turned and walked onstage to mild applause.

Roderick, however, burst through the backstage curtain where he found his wife sitting on the front row with their eldest son. He didn't bother to bend low, stomping down the aisle at full height.

"Where is your brother and Rowena?" he muttered to Bruce.

"*Uh*...I don't know. They left before the ceremony."

Fern's face was a picture of concern. "Roderick what is it—"

"Come with me," Roderick said to Bruce, "Fern, my love, stay here." She might have argued, but he gave her a look, and so, trusting him, she stayed, pretending to attend to the Myth Keeper's speech.

Meanwhile, Roderick and his son ascended the arena steps, the forest on their left, the audience on their right. Bruce hurried to keep up while his father took the steps three at a time, and his Shadow's claws dug into his shoulders to keep from slipping. They pushed past a man dressed all in black, and the raccoon turned to gape at the electric-orange snake coiled around the man's arm.

Penalynn sat alone in the box reserved for members of the Sceadwe. The Overseer and Myth Keeper were involved in the ceremony, and all of the Sages either helped students backstage or sat with their families. So, while the rest of the arena sat shoulder-to-shoulder like tinned sardines, her bench felt conspicuously empty. She didn't fault Rowena for skipping the ceremony.

The Myth Keeper droned on, and like the rest of the audience, her attention soon sagged until the Lord Overseer burst from the curtain like a man on a hunt. He pushed past someone standing in the aisle and she squinted. A vague recognition caught her attention. The person on the stairs was camouflaged against the dark, so it was hard to make out, except for the brazen band of orange around his bare bicep.

Bran.

There he stood, just half an arena away. She noticed then his piercing eyes and square chin, with the always-present line of orange encircling an absurdly swollen muscle.

Bran. Here. In Greymere!

His chin jerked, signaling to someone across the audience. Penalynn turned to see another black-clad figure on the opposite staircase, his Shadow indiscernible save a thin blue line where moonlight reflected off dark scales.

Black Guardians.

Instinct dropped her gaze to the empty seat beside her. There was only one person in Greymere they could be looking for, and so she shimmied down the row and up the stairs to the top of the arena.

Roderick hoisted himself onto the perch where Haaris sat manipulating moonlight into a single spotlight. "Black Guardians are here," he whispered.

Haaris's eyes didn't leave the stage. "Why?"

"I think for Rowena."

"*What?!*" The stage suddenly flooded with light.

"She left with Titus; I'm not sure where they went."

"Dad," Bruce interrupted. He pointed down the ladder where Penalynn struggled to climb up. They descended to meet her.

"Black Guardians—" she said.

"We know. Where is Rowena?"

"I don't know."

Haaris's spaniel audibly whined, and the man said, "I have to find her."

"I'll go with you," said Roderick. "Bruce, stay here and fill in for Haaris."

"Um, I'm not qualified to—"

"*Bruce!*"

"Oh no!" said Penalynn, "They're gone!"

All four pairs of eyes and their Shadows scanned the arena, but the men with snakes were nowhere to be seen. Without a word Haaris took off, sprinting down a row of vacant booths.

"I'll come too," said Bruce, but Roderick held him in place.

"No. Stay here and do the lights." Then he jogged off, his massive strides shaking the ground as he went, and the wolf loping at his side. Penalynn trotted behind, though much slower, with her Shadow impatiently matching her pace.

"Right," Bruce muttered to himself. "Just magically alter moonlight, Bruce. It's easy."

They tiptoed past the castle doors, traversing moonlit corridors. Two Shadows soared overhead, an owl and ghost, while Isla trailed behind, her heavy paws inaudible.

"Wow," said Titus, "Do you hear that?"

Rowena held her breath to listen. "What?"

"Silence."

The entire town was at the festival, leaving the castle temporarily deserted.

Her smile shone like gemstones in starlight. "I've never seen the castle like this. So empty. So quiet."

Their laughter danced across the courtyard where it bounced off columns. Titus tilted his head. "So, you have the whole castle to yourself. Where do you go?"

She squeezed his hand and pulled him along, sprinting down corridors, past alcoves and pillars, turrets and doorways, her gown *swishing* like a whisper. As they ran, her thoughts lifted upward, and she imagined herself peering from on high, witnessing herself race among swaths of darkness and pools of moonlight—like a ghost haunting the castle. Her Shadow zoomed at her side, and for the first time, she felt a profound kinship. For that one moment, they were two ghosts, one soul, united at last. Laugher escaped her chest, and she threw her head back, enjoying the rare sound of abandon—the sound of freedom.

They took the final turn at full speed, crashing into a column and bubbling with giggles before Rowena sprang forward again. Isla followed in a more sophisticated fashion. They stopped before a heavy set of doors made of iron and glass.

"Of course." Titus shook his head. "How did I not know."

Laughing again, Rowena heaved open the library doors. The click of her heels echoed among the arched balconies branching overhead like latticework. Moonlight shone through stained glass transforming her dress into a rainbow of color. She spun, arms outstretched, while crimson, cobalt, amber, and emerald painted her skin like a living kaleidoscope. Titus watched her spin, her dress hugging her hips. She came to a swaying stop, dizzy but radiant.

He took her hand and led her up a flight of stairs across the first balcony to a wide window seat. When they sat, their heads bowed together like swans, silent save cautious breaths, as if too much noise might break this perfect moment.

Titus marveled at her hand enveloped in his own, their fingers entwined like honey and cream. His forehead touched hers and he whispered, "Come with me to Riven." It wasn't a command, but it wasn't a question either.

Rowena winced. "There's nothing for me there."

"Come anyway. *With me*. I've thought about this more than anything. I know we could do it. Riven is so much more than Greymere. While I finish school, I can get you access to books. Whatever you want to learn you can learn. It won't be an official education, but you never needed that anyway. Like when I first met you, and you already seemed to know so much. You'd never even stepped inside the castle and remember the catapult you made? Okay, and yes, I know what you said about magic, and yes, I believe you. As soon as I finish school, I'll do what Penalynn's done. I'll stop all magic. By then, you'll have learned enough physic that we won't need magic anymore. Think about it! With your knowledge and my status, we could really build something. We could build a life."

"Titus..."

"It's you! It's always been you. Us. *Together*."

She bit her lip, wanting nothing more than this future he envisioned. Confidence filled him like cement, solid and immovable, as if his words had the power to conjure such a future. The two of them together, in Riven. Like she'd always hoped.

But before she could accept, she had to be clear. "I know it's a lot to ask, but...I can't watch you do magic. Not now. Not ever. It's up to you what you and your Shadow do, but...I can't watch you do it. Knowing what I know, I can't—" Her eyes rimmed with guilt, and she begged him, "I know it's too much to ask, but would you—could you even—give up your magic?"

He buried his fingers deep into her curls, stopping at the base of her neck. "This past year I learned what it is I can't live without," he whispered. With his other fingers, he touched her jaw, and she swallowed. "I'd give up more than magic before I lost you again."

Then he kissed her, gentle but sure. She sank into his lips, feeling as if she were falling, but with the full assurance that she'd be caught in his arms, never to be let go. And so, she fell with him, locked in his arms, and for the first time in perhaps her entire life, Rowena's mind went blissfully blank.

CHAPTER
FIFTY-THREE

T HE STREETS WERE EMPTY, but still, the Black Guardians preferred to traverse the alleyways shrouded in darkness. Their Shadows hummed with intuition until they found their target in the distance.

"You got that?" Rankin asked.

Bran could hardly believe what his magic sensed. Two humans but only one Shadow. And something else—neither human nor Shadow. "What is that?" he muttered.

Rankin smacked his lips. "This trip might not have been a waste after all. I spy me a proper monster."

Their magic led them straight to the castle where they stalked empty hallways, doubling back when they met dead ends until they reached the library doors and paused to consult their Shadows. Yes, there it was on the other side of the door—two bodies, one Shadow—and whatever *thing* was with them.

The doors swung without a sound, and they entered. They scanned the balconied stories above where bookcases lined concave walls, interspersed with arched windows, each displaying scenes of the Great Myth in cut glass. Everywhere they looked, the image of a dragon peered from blue glass with eyes that followed.

There, on the lowest balcony, sat their target silhouetted against a window.

Rankin snickered at the teenage figures locked in a kiss. He puckered his lips in mockery. Bran's instructions were silent, just a series of hand motions. But his partner understood. They split up, Rankin practically skipping up a back staircase, while Bran positioned himself directly under the balcony rail.

He slipped from his belt a short rope; on each end, a heavy stone clicked against one another. First, he looped the middle of the rope around his palm, then flicked his wrist so the rope spun by his hip, the rocks whistling past his ear. After a few good turns, Bran tucked his elbow and flexed his bicep. The stones broke from their circular trajectory to shoot straight into the air. His Shadow animated the rocks that pulled Bran's arm over his head, and with it, his entire body lifted with a mighty tug. He soared up and over the balcony then dropped like a cat in front of the two teenagers. They ripped apart, gaping at the Black Guardian who had landed suddenly in their midst.

"Rowena Faye?" Bran asked.

"Ye-es...?" she answered.

"You are under arrest by order of the King of Wyre." His voice was far too soft for such cruel words.

"*WHAT?!*"

Titus sprang to his feet to sandwich himself between the guard and Rowena while Isla growled at the second guard who ascended the stairs. Bran reached around the boy and grabbed Rowena's arm. Titus's Shadow swooped upon the guard with wings spread wide.

Several feet away, Rankin threw something, and both Titus and Rowena watched, transfixed, as a black ribbon unfurled himself midair. The Guardian's snake caught the owl in twisting coils. With a heroic jolt, the owl fought the snake, and the two Shadows fell in a wrangling knot of feathers and scales, tipping over the balcony rail to crash atop the marble tile below.

A guttural grunt escaped from deep within Titus's chest. The distance between him and his Shadow was not so far as to be dangerous but not nearly close enough. He winced, feeling the snake wind itself around his Shadow, black bands constricting. It was as if his own lungs were squeezed in oil-slick ropes. He dropped to his hands and knees, his breath ragged.

Bran clasped Rowena's wrists behind her back when something slapped him across the face. He looked around for his assailant, but it stayed within his periphery. It struck again like a spatula stinging his skin. He struggled to see it properly until it moved out of the light, and he could just make out a shape. He gasped. "What in Bazileus' name *is* that thing?"

"My Shadow," said Rowena, smug despite being arrested. "You've made her angry."

Ghost reared back, but Bran dodged just in time, so she smacked the back of his neck instead. *Thwack!!* She zoomed in a circle, slapping every patch of skin she could find. When her tiny flipper ripped arm hair from the root, Bran let out a high-pitched yelp, which might have embarrassed him, except he was too distracted by the darting specter. It was like battling a vengeful wasp. Ghost swatted his ear, and he recoiled, the sound reverberating inside his skull. He shook his head, all too fed up, and pulled a sack from his belt. Before the Shadow could render another humiliating blow, he caught it like a child catching a butterfly with a net. The sack jolted, but Bran held it closed, doubling and redoubling the knot. He dropped it to the ground, rather pleased at the *thump* it made. His tongue traced his swollen lip, tasting blood, and he swallowed the urge to give the sack a good kick.

From behind, he heard Rankin sniggering. "That little rat gave you quite the beating."

"Rank, let up," Bran said, pointing at Titus, who gargled at his feet. The boy's Shadow was still bound one story below.

"He's fine. He can still breathe."

Titus wheezed.

Before Bran could insist further, the library doors crashed open, and two men entered at full speed. "Let go of my daughter!!" Haaris shrieked while Roderick barked a two-syllable boom, "TI-TUS!!"

"Up here!!" Rowena screamed with her arms bound behind her.

Titus pressed his face to the floor, moaning.

The dog and wolf Shadows raced up the stairs ahead of the men. When they arrived on the balcony, Rankin gave the two fathers a welcoming smile as if he were enjoying himself. Roderick dropped to his knees to inspect his son, cradling his head in one massive hand.

With measured professionalism, Bran explained, "This girl is arrested by order of the King of Wyre. He has reason to believe she is The Wandering assassin known as 'The Shadowless.' We will bring her to Riven, where the king will inspect her and determine her penalty."

"She *has* a Shadow!" Haaris cried, spit flying, but then he noticed that Ghost was missing. "*Where is her Shadow?!*"

Bran picked up the writhing sack and looped the drawstring over Rowena's head like a misshapen necklace. As soon as it touched her chest, the bag grew still.

"I'm assuming you're her father. You can follow us to Riven and await her judgment."

"Answer me honestly," Haaris demanded, "Will the trial be fair?"

Bran looked away, unable to answer honestly without committing treason. He pulled on the rope, and Rowena had no choice but to follow. Haaris threw himself at the guard, but Bran shoved him off with alarming strength, hurling

Haaris against a bookcase. Volumes thudded to the floor in a waterfall of leather and paper.

"Let go of my son!" Roderick growled at Rankin.

The guard jumped over the railing, magically slowing his descent with animation until he landed on the balls of his feet. The snake relinquished his hold on the owl and returned to his spot around Rankin's arm like a living tattoo. Free at last, the owl flew to the balcony, attempting to bury himself in Titus's ribcage. Titus breathed freely with his Shadow returned, and Roderick bowed his head in relief.

"Get! *Shoo!*" Bran muttered.

Isla had planted her paws like tree roots to block the staircase. Bran's magic reached for the animal, but the snake recoiled. This was the thing he had sensed earlier, the thing Rankin had called a monster. He hesitated long enough for Haaris to recover and lunge for him again, this time from behind.

But Rankin had rejoined them. He pulled from his belt two blades shaped like crescent moons. *One, two,* he threw them, his Shadow catching the movement with sinister alacrity. The blade clipped Haaris's shoulder, and he jolted back, encircled by a ring of singing metal. The blades flew in a circle around his torso so fast they were just a blur only inches from his skin. He pinned his arms to his sides, unable to move, or he'd be sliced.

"Rod!" Haaris screamed, imprisoned in the eye of the shredding vortex. "Stop him!"

Roderick followed Haaris's gaze where the guard had Rowena. He surged to his feet like a battering ram sprung to life. The wolf's teeth bared, and Bran's snake struck like lightning. He landed on the wolf's back, where he magically lengthened to wrap around the Shadow's thick frame, orange coils buried in fur.

Despite the snake's hold upon his Shadow, Roderick didn't stop. He collided with Bran, and they toppled down the stairs, head over foot, until Roderick managed to stop himself. Bran, however, allowed himself to fall a few more steps and then caught himself on a rail. In one fluid movement, he pulled himself up and slipped behind Roderick, pinning his arm behind his back. He nudged his elbow up and out, threatening to pop the arm from its socket. Roderick growled, flinging his free arm behind. But a flash of silver stopped him; a cold blade pressed against his neck, firm enough to warn but not draw blood.

Despite having disarmed the giant man and his Shadow, Bran cried out in pain. The monster-dog had sunk her teeth into his calf.

"Tell your dog to get off, or I kill your friend!"

"Isla!" cried Rowena. The bag containing Ghost writhed furiously. "Isla, stop!"

Reluctantly, Isla unclenched her jaw, then padded to Rowena's side.

The wolf groaned, a deep hum in his throat, and then Roderick winced. The snake's persuasion blocked the wolf's magic with a sharp jab.

"Sir, do not use magic against a king's Guardian." Bran's knife pressed further, and a drop of blood trailed down Roderick's neck. The wolf slumped to the floor, bound by the snake.

Rankin sauntered towards Rowena, and Haaris's Shadow sprang into action. With a surge of magic, he aimed for Rankin's mind. But the guard swung his boot, kicking the Shadow against the iron rail. Haaris nearly bent from the blow, but a sharp slice from a whizzing blade kept him upright. His Shadow crumpled to the floor under Rankin, who dared him to rise.

"Dad!" Titus shouted. "Dad, what do I do?!"

"Titus!" The words caused the knife to sink further into Roderick's skin. "Get Rowena and get out of here!"

Titus jumped up and grabbed Rowena's bindings. "Papa!!" she cried.

"Go!" Haaris yelled, but another blade clipped him.

"PAPA!!" Rowena struggled against Titus and Isla, who herded her toward the stairs. But before they could flee, Rankin grabbed her around the waist.

"Didn't we tell you you're under arrest?" he chuckled, his voice hot against her ear. She jerked away, but Rankin held on even when Titus clawed and scraped to free Rowena from him.

Rankin rolled his eyes as the boy struggled. He couldn't use magic against the kid; his Shadow too consumed with keeping the ringing blades in motion. "Bran," he called to his partner, who still bound the big man. The orange snake reached out with a persuasion. Titus collapsed, screaming from something unseen. His owl fell to the floor with him.

Isla bit Rankin's forearm, and he hollered. He let go of the girl to pull a knife from his boot, and the dog had to release him to dodge the blade.

Just then, there was a loud *BANG*. The library doors swung wide to admit Penalynn, with cloak billowing in blue ripples like a breathing sapphire. "UN-HAND THEM!!" Her voice filled the space as if it were made for shouting commands and having them obeyed. The fox sprinted for the staircase.

At the sound of the woman's voice, invisible dust blinded Bran's vision. His grip loosened enough for Roderick to rip away. Instinctively, Bran's Shadow, which had reached the size of a python to wrap several spans around the wolf, squeezed harder. The wolf howled in agony until something snapped, and he fell still in the snake's embrace. Roderick swooned, his face smacking the floor when he fell.

Meanwhile, Bran blinked furiously. He could barely make out a woman's figure ascend the steps, though it wasn't until she stepped into the beam of moonlight spilling through the window that he could see her properly. They locked eyes then, Penalynn and Bran, and the specks of dust disappeared as if by a gust of wind.

Penalynn. Those same eyes he grew up with, accompanied by that same furious scowl he'd been on the receiving end too many times to count. *Penalynn.*

He staggered back, bracing himself against a bookcase. His eyes were clear. The invisible dust was gone for good. Still, he shielded them, the truth far more blinding. Like looking at the sun, he couldn't take her in. She had been erased, scrubbed clean from his memory. But now, all memories, all recollections, every moment and thought of her came flooding back with ferocious clarity. A gale of truth washed away the dishonest specks. He had forgotten her, the girl who was practically his sister, if not by blood or station, then from sheer proximity growing up. His best friend. His confidant. Penalynn. But...the next memory returned with bone-cracking severity. His knees remembered before his mind. They buckled, and he fell, bowed in deference. He might have offered his allegiance, except she already had it. He had simply forgotten.

At her feet stood her fox, with petulant eyes blazing at him. He dropped his hand from his eyes and braced himself against Penalynn's boiling glance. The heat filled him as if he had traversed the kingdom cold to the bone. He drank in the full veracity of her existence, the persuasion dead in that angry face of truth.

She looked beyond him, and her anger shifted to horror. He turned to see his snake—his Shadow—his very self—fall to the floor. In his shock, his Shadow had gone too far. With a final, deadly contraction, the snake crushed the wolf. The mighty Shadow evaporated in a puff of smoke. Specks of dust trickled to the ground where the wolf had been, snuffed out like a candle. Roderick lay prone as the dead.

CHAPTER
FIFTY-FOUR

THE LIBRARY FELL SILENT. It took a moment to register what had happened. Roderick's Shadow was dead, reduced to ash as all Shadows are when they pass. They were never bodies, not really, not like a human. Shadows were magical vessels harboring half a human soul. If the vessel died, the soul died, leaving behind only ash. A pitiful pile was all that was left of the magnificent wolf.

It was Titus who broke the silence with a cry wrenched from his guts.

Haaris was still bound in the path of the blades, and so, his Shadow inched toward Roderick's body, nosing his lifeless hand.

Rankin dragged Rowena away, but Isla was still there, her haunches spread, teeth bared. Her bark roused Penalynn, who, seeing Rowena in the hands of the Black Guardian, plunged her arms into the folds of her cloak and pulled out a pen. She broke off the feather shaft and threw the metal nib like a dart. Her Shadow's magic shot the pen like an arrow where the gold tip carved a bloody line from Rankin's nose to his ear. Then, it fell to the marble floor with a metallic *tink*.

Rankin snarled, "You missed."

"I didn't," Penalynn countered. "That will be your only warning."

"The king wants the girl," he spat.

"Then he can come get her himself."

"You think that cloak gives you the right? You're defying your king, Scholastic."

"He cannot have her," was all she said. At her feet, the fox's fur stood on end, teeth visible like a smile. She wanted to fight.

Rankin chewed his tongue as he sized Penalynn up, then nodded, glad for a proper altercation. He shoved Rowena to the side, and his magic shifted. The blades broke their trajectory around Haaris's chest and soared over to drop into Rankin's hand. When Haaris was free, he dashed to Rowena and wrapped her in a bone-cracking embrace.

Penalynn acted first. She grabbed a book off a shelf and threw it at the guard. Her Shadow's magic caught it and sent it hurling toward her opponent. Without looking she threw another and another.

The books were easy for Rankin to dodge, the fox barely using enough force to cause a bruise. The Guardian *tutted* his disappointment. In answer, he threw his blades, one after the other. Penalynn dodged these less easily than she had the books. The second one clipped her ear. Behind her, both blades ricocheted off the wall to change course, Rankin's animation not letting up. He pulled another knife from his boot and sent that at her as well. She had to crouch under a desk to avoid the zinging knife. It bounced off a column to join the crescent blades' melee until all three bounced like rubber balls from surface to surface, singing deadly lines in every direction.

"You guardians and your animation," Penalynn scoffed from under the table, "so predictable."

It was then Rankin realized the books she'd thrown were still airborne, spinning slow circles overhead. One by one, they dropped into the path of a blade; the sharp whizzing stopped with a heady *thump*. Metal lodged in leather and several inches of thick paper. Her magic didn't stop until she sent the books, embedded with a blade each, soaring up to the highest balcony, far from Rankin's reach. They fell with a *thud* and the knives were still. No amount of animation could revive them now.

Penalynn brushed herself off as she emerged from her spot under the table, and she and the Black Guardian paced in a circle, appraising one another.

"You think you're clever." The rasp in Rankin's voice betrayed his frustration. All of his weapons were three stories away now.

"Considering *books* have robbed you of your knives..."

"How *Scholastic* of you."

His snake's magic reached across the circle, aiming for Penalynn's mind, but the fox was ready. Her intuition formed a shield, wrapping her mind like a helmet. The persuasion banged against the barrier, searching for a chink, a break, any way to enter and inflict upon her imagination. Rankin gnashed his teeth, his fists balled.

Penalynn smirked. She felt the persuasion knock her intuition like a vague idea at the back door of her consciousness. Dim. Unimportant. Out of curiosity, her mind's eye peered at the besieging magic. "You think *that* would scare me, Guardian? I've seen things that would shrink your snake to a worm. I expected more from a king's man." Her head tilted with detached sobriety. "But I forget. This king prefers his men weak-minded. All muscle and no guile."

Furious, the snake pressed harder, desperate to enact violence. The fox's intuition knocked the persuasion back with a powerful surge, and the snake recoiled under the backlash of his own magic. Rankin staggered, then tripped over Isla behind him. He cursed. Then, he buried his fingertips in a vest pocket and pulled out a single match. He struck it on the rough iron railing, then raised the flame to his parted lips. The flame flickered under his breath. That was all the snake needed. His magic caught the flame's movement and, using a tricky combination of animation and manipulation, he sent a tunnel of fire searing upon Penalynn.

She hardly had time to drop to the ground, knocking the wind out of herself. Her hair sizzled, but otherwise, the flame missed her.

The snake let go of the fire to magic, of all things, the floor polish that had been used upon the tile floor. He manipulated the substance into something slick like oil, and Penalynn's hands and knees slipped from under her. Her face smacked the shiny floor, and she groaned. Blood trickled from her nostril.

Rankin spit. "How's that for clever, you fat—"

"Penalynn, look down!" she heard someone cry. A stupid request as she was laid prostrate, unable to get up without slipping again. But reflected in the floor's polish she saw a flash of colorful light. Haaris's spaniel manipulated the moonlight pouring through the window. Rankin was blinded. He hollered, shielding his eyes. It was distraction enough to stop his Shadow's magic, and the tile returned to its normal polish. Penalynn pushed herself up, using Isla for help to stand. Her limbs ached in painful protest.

With his hand still over his eyes, Rankin stomped his foot, looking like a toddler having a tantrum, one foot banging the ground over and over. *Stomp! Stomp! Stomp!*

Slowly, the balcony began to rumble and Penalynn realized what was happening. "Grab onto something!" she screamed at the others kneeling around Roderick.

The snake's magic touched the vibrations, animating each tremor with rhythmic precision. Penalynn wrapped both arms around the railing. Her Shadow leaped onto her shoulder.

Stomp! Stomp! The vibrations animated in a steady cadence until tiles rippled like waves. Penalynn's feet jerked under the rolling marble tide; tables and chairs rocked like boats. The plaster walls cracked and splintered at the weight-bearing joints. The fool would bring down the entire balcony with himself still on it.

Penalynn's eyes darted above his head where, two stories up, a lantern the size of a lectern hung from the ceiling. The fox focused her animation, not upon the lantern, but upon the ground below. Her magic found it quickly, that unseen energy Atticus Wolder called grounding. She animated the force, increasing its tug in that one spot, but the chain holding the lantern remained secure. However, it did sway, if just a bit. And that was all she needed. Her magic swung upward to animate that sway. Plaster broke into chunks until the chain broke free. The fox pressed upon the lantern as if with an invisible hand. It bore down upon Rankin who leaped away just in time as the lantern tore a massive hole through the balcony floor, the chain trailing behind like a banner.

Isla was there, however. She dropped her head like a sledgehammer slamming into Rankin's spine. He careened toward the jagged hole of broken stone and marble like a toothy maw. He caught the iron rail, stopping himself from falling through the hole.

The fox animated the falling chain to catch Rankin's ankle like a lasso. The speed sliced his flesh like a hot knife, sending Rankin's severed foot atop the rubble below, still entombed in his boot. He slumped to the floor then, the bleeding stump of his leg dripping into the gaping hole. Shock seized his body in wracking tremors.

Without a scrap of remorse, Penalynn said, "You will not take my apprentice from me." She turned to the others. Though the floor had stilled, they still held onto one another.

But Rankin wasn't done. He grabbed a shard of broken marble and hurled it at her back. Before the serpent could hum his magic, Bran plunged his knife into Rankin's arm, slicing the snake's head from its body. The shard of marble slid to a stop against Penalynn's shoe. She turned to see Bran's blade lodged in Rankin's arm. The black snake erupted in a puff of dust, leaving a muddy ring of blood and dust oozing down his arm. His Shadow dead and empty of life, Rankin's body slipped backward, down through the hole. His corpse landed atop his own boot.

Penalynn looked at Bran whose chest heaved with emotion. He had just killed another Shadow, this time on purpose. The library fell silent in the aftermath, but a noise caught her attention, and she turned to see Titus weeping over Roderick's body. Like a missing limb, the great wolf was gone. Rowena and Haaris knelt at his side. Penalynn joined them.

"Where's his Shadow?" someone asked.

"Gone."

Titus's voice, thick with tears, asked, "How...how do we get him back?"

"We don't."

Rowena warbled, "But, how can he live without—"

"He can't."

"But…"

"No! DAD!"

"There's nothing to be done."

"Wait!" Rowena's fingertips were buried in the tangle of his beard. "There's a pulse."

"What?"

"*Dad!*"

"It's not possible…his Shadow…"

"Wake up! Dad! *Please.* You have to wake up!"

Roderick stirred. The hunched figures held their breath as if anything—any movement, any sound—might knock him back into oblivion. His eyebrows constricted. Even unconscious he could sense something was wrong. Something was missing. His eyes snapped open, and, like water pulled from a deep well, came a terrible scream. The sound of an injured bear roaring in the wilderness. It seemed to come not from his chest, but from somewhere darker. A lonely, fearsome place within his soul ripped asunder.

Rowena's hands cupped her ears—Ghost buried within the folds of her dress.

Haaris and Titus pinned Roderick's shoulder, their combined bodyweight not fully capable. Roderick's bulk overtook them, and he staggered upright. His hands pressed to his chest as if his heart might spill from an unseen wound. The long, drawn-out scream was punctuated only by gulping breaths.

Penalynn and Haaris held up their hands to calm, but he shoved past, unseeing. In two long bounds, he reached the window where he crashed into the rainbow-colored picture, glass and iron shattered like candy. Icy wind whipped inside the library, and he fell. The descent cut off his cries. Several stories below, the river abutted the backside of the castle, and black water swallowed him like a ravenous mouth.

Titus leaped onto the windowsill and, without a moment's thought, dove headfirst into the frigid river below. Immediately the current swept him downstream. The owl flew low over the water, following his wake.

Rowena screamed after him, but Haaris pushed her aside. She grabbed his wrist and cried, "NO! PAPA, *NO!*"

He kissed her forehead and said, "Meet us on the bank." Then he threw himself, feet first, out of the window with his Shadow clutched in his arms.

Before Rowena could see him resurface, Penalynn steered her towards the stairs. Bran watched. His Shadow had returned to his arm, no longer the size of a python strangling the wolf. Penalynn stifled the blame rising to her lips as she passed him. He walked in the opposite direction, jumped onto the windowsill, and dove into the river.

Rowena did a quick tally. Four men had jumped through the window. She half expected the second guard to ascend the stairs and take a dive as well. But he remained below a heap of limbs among shattered masonry. His Shadow's demise had proved deadly for him in a way it hadn't for Roderick. Though the river very well might finish the job.

Rowena sprinted down the staircase with Penalynn at her side. The castle was silent, but her ears were full of her own heartbeat, thrumming with panic. Isla pressed against her hip as if the creature knew she was falling. And surely, Rowena was. Though her feet moved—*step-step, step-step*—propelling her through the castle—she was *falling, falling, falling*. At any moment the ground would swallow her just like the river had swallowed all the men she loved.

No. No. No. The words echoed with every footfall.

Ahead of her, Ghost strained against the invisible string between their soul. Somewhere, deep in her chest, Rowena could feel the thread pull taught. Ghost led them through the castle doors and around the west tower downriver from the library. Up ahead, they could make out the river, its rushing water calling to them. Isla and the fox bounded forward, stopping only when they reached the wet river rocks lapping with water. They arrived just as two figures emerged from the black depths.

Rowena nearly fell to her knees to see Titus dragging Haaris's body. Her father gritted his teeth, his hair slicking his face. His breath was like smoke in the near-frozen night. He moved awkwardly, clutching his leg. Rowena crashed into his side, impervious to the rocks banging against her shins. The train of her dress spilled into the river like melting snow.

As soon as she had hold of Haaris, Titus let go of him and turned back. His Shadow raked back and forth across the water, the tips of his wings skimming lines like white ribbons against the black.

With a hand on his arm, Penalynn stopped him. "Wait."

Titus shivered, his clothes clinging to his sopping-wet body. His teeth chattered. "My dad! I have to—"

"Wait." She pointed at something hidden in the river's rush, where moonlight reflected like shattered glass. His Shadow saw it first. A head bobbed from the water's surface. It was the guard.

"I've got him!" Bran gargled before the white-capped current swallowed him. He struggled against it, aiming for the bank. Something besides the current slowed him down.

Titus dove. Rowena groaned to see him disappear into the river once more. Penalynn darted for the tree line and returned dragging a fallen limb. Rowena jumped up to help her, her legs encumbered by the soaking weight of her dress. She would have shivered—that was if she still cared for things such as cold. But nothing existed now, save those men in that water. If only Ghost could do what the owl did, fly over the water so Rowena could see through her eyes. But the Shadow merely hovered at the water's edge, solemn, incapable of help.

A hand broke the surface and grasped the branch the women held for them, nearly ripping the limb from their hands. They fell to the ground, feet braced against stones as they leaned back like rowers in a boat race. Bran pulled himself up, his other arm wrapped around Roderick's chest. Titus followed, holding his father's legs. They used the branch for balance as they pushed Roderick's body forward, face-up. When their feet found purchase on the riverbed, Penalynn and Rowena dropped the branch and entered the icy water, grabbing wherever they could manage: soaking shirt, leather belt, a boot. With four sets of hands, they managed to lift Roderick up and out of the water, then lay him on the rocky bank.

The women inspected his neck and wrists, searching, hoping, and begging for that tiny bump of a pulse. As they worked, Titus's tears blended with the water streaming from his hair. Haaris scooted toward them, clutching his leg. His Shadow pressed his snout to Roderick's' side, urging, pleading, praying. Here lay Haaris's only friend; the man who had protected his daughter in the name of fatherly kinship.

"Please." The words echoed among them. "*Please.*"

Bran dropped to one knee as they begged the night sky.

At last Rowena and Penalynn hazarded to look at one another. They had both found the same thing: nothing. Rowena's face crumpled, hot tears breaking against frozen cheeks.

It was Penalynn's voice that released the truth like a dove into the air, full of regret and sorrow. "Titus, I'm sorry. Your father is gone."

CHAPTER FIFTY-FIVE

A WEEK LATER, ROWENA and Haaris walked to the Ashworth house. Haaris had wanted to take the cart, but Rowena refused to witness any more of his magic. So, they walked. She felt guilty, seeing her father swinging on crutches, but she remained steadfast. Better for him to get a couple of blisters from crutches than lose time off his life from magic.

When he jumped into the river after Roderick, the current had bashed his leg against a boulder. For most, it would have left no more than a nasty bruise. But for Haaris, and his brittle bones, his leg snapped like a twig. Even a week later, it couldn't endure even an ounce of weight. So, their progress was slow, his foot tucked with care.

The street was crowded; everyone headed toward the same place clothed in black, a cruel contrast to the festival pageantry the week prior. Even the clouds were greyer than usual. The trees held fast to their last autumn leaves as if suspending winter in honor of the late Lord Overseer.

It hadn't taken long for the whispers to make the rounds among pubs and firesides, so when the Fayes approached, pedestrians dashed across the street, unwilling to share the sidewalk with an outlaw.

"A Black Guardian killed him, you know."

"I thought he drowned."

"Yeah, that's how I heard it."

"No, I'm telling you. It was a guard."

"I heard it from my cousin. He's on the crew cleaning up the mess in the library. Half the place was blasted to pieces, and, get this, a guard's body was found in the rubble, and missing a foot, no less!"

"Do you think *she* did it?"

"'Course she did. That's who they came for!"

"But how? She hasn't got magic!"

"She's cursed."

"I knew it! Didn't I say to you—at Hazel Faye's funeral years ago—didn't I? I said this was the work of a *curse!*"

"We all know how she got her hooks in the Overseer's son. She must have gotten to the big man too."

"Shame," they all said, shaking their heads. "And he was killed for it. For *her*. Shame."

Rowena didn't need to hear the gossip to know what was said because they were the same suspicions she pondered herself. Powers beyond her understanding were clearly at work, but even so, she understood enough. Those guards had come for her and her alone. Sent by the king and his godlike Bazileus. And stupidly, they had all fought, as if the will of a god could be deterred. The terrible event was like a tattoo, inking Rowena's skin in memory. Marked forever.

When they arrived, it was Bruce who let them inside, where bouquets of flowers littered the Ashworth house like a well-stocked market stall. Roderick, it was evident, had been quite beloved. His absence was tangible. Fern seemed to wilt in the chair where she sat. Without her husband by her side, she seemed conspicuously small.

Rowena dropped her gaze, unworthy to behold the woman's grief. Haaris muttered, "Rowena, why don't you go fetch Titus."

She hadn't seen Titus since the horrible events at the castle. Her knees quaked as she ascended the stairs. She found him seated at his desk, facing the window. He didn't hear her enter—or perhaps didn't care—because he remained stooped over the table, reading something.

There was a shuffling sound. Rowena looked down to see Titus's Shadow on the rug. His wings flapped as if the owl might fly, but he only managed a half-hearted hop. The owl tried again, this time making it a foot off the ground, then flopped in a heap under Titus's chair. Rowena blanched. She'd never seen the Shadow fail at anything, and certainly not something as commonplace as flying.

The owl wobbled on his back like an upturned turtle. His feathers mashed against the rug. Titus, however, seemed wholly unaware of his Shadow's struggle.

"Umm...Titus?" she asked.

"Hey, Spook." He didn't look up, but the use of her nickname was some reassurance.

The owl made an odd hiccupping sound, almost like a sneeze, which propelled him backward so aggressively he rolled under the bed.

"Is your Shadow alright?"

The owl crawled out from under the bed, smeared with dust. His talons scraped the floor.

"Don't know." His voice was distant as if he were in a different room. "I can't hear him anymore."

Her breath hitched in her chest. "What do you mean you can't hear him?"

He turned then, but his eyes were glazed as if he saw something Rowena couldn't. "Ever since the river, he's been silent. I think his magic's gone too." By his tone, it sounded as if he didn't care all that much. He turned back to the paper and folded it carefully.

"What's that?" she asked.

"My speech. I'm giving the eulogy." There was something in the way he said it that made her think someone had challenged him on this. His jaw set, his lips a line.

"Are you sure you—" she shifted, keenly aware of the owl's continued struggle on the floor and how Titus refused to help him. "I mean, isn't that the Myth Keeper's job? So, the people in mourning can, well, mourn?"

"I'm doing it!" The words ripped from him like a snarl, and she swallowed her protest. No, she wasn't the first to voice this concern.

He stood, and for a moment, she thought he walked toward her. Her face flushed; her stomach wrenched. But he brushed past into the hall, sending her heart to plummet. He waited at the top of the stairs with something like disgust etching across his face. He couldn't go downstairs without his Shadow. The owl managed a stuttering *hop-hop*, finally making it onto the bed. From there he made the short glide to Titus's shoulder.

He walked downstairs, the growing distance between him and Rowena gaping. The dance they'd shared. The kiss. All of it was gone now. Shattered, along with Rowena's heart. Titus walked away. She didn't blame him. After all, it was because of her that his father was dead.

CHAPTER FIFTY-SIX

Downstairs, Penalynn stood with Haaris in the foyer.

They stood solemnly while the Ashworths donned coats nearby. Fern walked out the front door with a son flanking her on either side, propping her like bookends. When they reached the street, people gave them a wide berth of deference.

Rowena eyed Penalynn suspiciously and asked, "Why are you here?" But before Penalynn could answer, she realized the answer and snapped, "No. No magic."

"Fine," Penalynn retorted. "Then you'll stay here."

Rowena opened her mouth to argue but Penalynn cut her off. "I'm not sure if you remember, but there's another guard out there with a warrant from the king to arrest you."

"Besides," Haaris added, "your presence at the funeral will cause a stir and that's not fair to Fern and the boys. I'm sorry. You can go, but you can't be seen."

Rowena pressed her lips together. She should stay. She knew she should. But Titus would be there, saying his last farewells to his father. He'd come all the way home from Riven to support her on her darkest day. She wanted to do the same for him. Besides, she wasn't about to revert to the days of her childhood, hiding at home, alone.

With the slightest of nods, she assented to their terms.

On the street, no one shrank away or muttered low. No one even noticed her. The spaniel's magic was inaudible, but Rowena was sure it was her father's magic at work. Penalynn didn't strike her as the persuading type. Rowena pictured an hourglass, each grain of sand representing a minute of a person's life. So long as his Shadow did magic, her father's hourglass would drain. Rowena's heart crushed under a swell of guilt. She should have stayed behind.

At the arena, a single line formed as people trickled into their seats. The meadow was empty. The only festival remnants were matted grass and a few lonely streamers forgotten in the trees. There was no music. No cheer. Only tearful sniffles.

They sat in the topmost row at the very back. Far below, the stage was empty save for a podium and a wide, stone altar. Roderick's body lay like a snow-covered mountain range atop the altar, shrouded in white fabric that pooled on the ground.

"See him?" Haaris asked Penalynn.

At first, Rowena thought he meant Roderick's body. But their eyes scanned the perimeter where the forest rimmed the arena. It was a different *him*, he meant. The Black Guardian—the one who had survived. The one who had killed Roderick's Shadow. But he had also killed his partner's Shadow to save Penalynn's life. Rowena had surmised enough to realize he knew Penalynn from her previous life in Riven. But beyond that, the man was a mystery. Though, in all honesty, Rowena hadn't the energy to care. The past week had been like a waking nightmare from which she couldn't awaken. The missing guard was the least of her worries.

"No," said Penalynn, scanning the crowd row by row.

Yet even in this living purgatory, Rowena's curiosity had not been fully extinguished. A question remained. Two Shadows had died that night in the library. Roderick's and the Black Guardian's. A wolf and a snake.

"Penalynn," she murmured so no one else could hear. "The guard with the black snake, he died when his Shadow was killed. But...for Roderick..." she gulped, the horrors of that night flashed in her memory, and she cringed.

"I've been wondering the same thing," Penalynn admitted. "I've never heard of someone living even a second beyond their Shadow, nor vice versa. I don't know. Perhaps Roderick had an extraordinary soul. One that was so great that, even with half his soul gone, he could carry on in a...I don't know...a sort of half-life."

Rowena's gaze locked on Roderick's shrouded body onstage. "If he hadn't jumped," she whispered, "would he still be alive?"

Penalynn shook her head. "Half of his soul was gone. It sent him mad. Was he even still himself when he jumped?"

"But could he have lived?"

"I don't know. Can you imagine what kind of life that would be?"

A thick silence fell over the crowd, and their conversation ended. The Myth Keeper ascended the stage and tapped papers on the podium, arranging his speech just so. His Shadow perched atop his shoulder, like usual, but there was something off. If Rowena had sat closer, perhaps she would have noticed the droop in the canary's feathers, how sallow, sickly even, the Myth Keeper appeared. Rowena was not alone in her guilt. It was the Myth Keeper, after all, who had sent for the king's men.

Despite the waver in his voice, the Myth Keeper did his duty for his fallen colleague. He spoke of the Bazileus—that great dragon who bequeathed magic to Shadows. He spoke of souls, divided but united. Two bodies but one mind. How they represented something immense, something beyond themselves. And the more he talked, the less he trembled. The message was like a balm, soothing himself far more than the gathered crowd.

Rowena leaned forward as the Myth Keeper droned on, monotonous yet effusive for the Bazileus, despite it being a king's man who'd murdered Roderick. She'd heard the Great Myth before, but never like this. Because now, Rowena knew magic's cost. Their investigation had made plain what had always been secret.

The question she had asked so many times since she'd learned the truth resurged once more. *Can a person live without magic?*

Titus, Haaris, and even Penalynn had all answered her with a resolute, *no.*

But something had happened: Roderick lived. If only for a moment, he had survived without his Shadow.

Onstage, the Myth Keeper hammered the necessity of Shadows and magic. This creed was the reason he hated Rowena. But someone—not just anyone, but Lord Overseer Roderick Ashworth—had lived without a Shadow. He had moved and breathed, his body utterly alive.

The question now was, *could he have lived that way for long?*

Titus ascended the stage, and her thoughts were cut short, her attention sharpening with sudden intensity. She noticed how his shoulders stooped with his arms slack at his side. His hands crinkled the paper he carried. Even from the back row, Rowena thought she saw his lips quiver and she couldn't help but remember their kiss.

A tear fell to her cheek, but it wasn't for Roderick. She didn't cry for Fern, the closest thing she had to a mother. Nor for Bruce nor even Titus. Rowena cried for herself, for all she had lost. She would never get back to that night in the library, that perfect moment in Titus's arms before the world had broken into chaos and death. She chided herself. The Ashworths were the closest thing she'd found to belonging. Roderick had given his life in defense of her, and at his funeral, Rowena's tears were for her own broken heart. Self-pity and guilt revolved in a round, churning tears into tiny rivers that pooled at the hollow of her neck.

"My father—" Titus said loudly, then stopped short. He stared at the paper in his hands. Wind whispered over the trees, and the audience shifted in nervous sympathy. Atop Titus's shoulder, the owl swayed, nearly toppling forward. With a jerk of his wings, he righted.

Titus cleared his throat. "My father was big enough to be two men in one. In many ways, he *was* two men. One man was strong, the other gentle. One was powerful, the other soft. He was an authority in command but could laugh at himself. He was admired, respected..." his voice cracked, "loved by all."

The owl tipped, catching himself just in time on Titus's shirt collar. Titus squeezed his eyes shut, forcibly ignoring the owl's odd behavior. With a shake of his head, he continued. "The day he...*umm*...the day he died...I had gone to his office to talk to him about some ideas I had. About my future. He told me he was proud of me."

Rowena's gut tightened. *She* was what he'd talked to Roderick about; she knew it. About his plans to take her with him to Riven to build that wonderful life he had imagined for the two of them. A life together. Rowena hung her head, hiding her sobs behind her hair.

"I'm sorry." Titus shook his head like a dog shaking water off its fur. He shoved the paper from the podium. It glided back and forth until it stopped on the stage. "I'm sorry, but I can't do this. I can't eulogize my father like I intended because...because he shouldn't be dead. It's wrong. This is all *wrong!*" He pointed at his father's shrouded body. "This cannot be allowed! IT IS WRONG!"

A wracking wail erupted from his chest and his Shadow slipped from his perch. Before he fell to the ground, however, the owl morphed in a grotesque flurry of feathers and fur until he exploded to ten times his size. He landed in a bulky heap of thick fur and long limbs. Slowly, and trembling violently, the Shadow managed to stand atop four quivering legs. Massive paws gripped the ground with inch-long claws instead of talons. His knees buckled, unused to the weight they now carried. The Shadow shook his head. A mane of grey fur bristled around broad shoulders. Ears the size of envelopes flattened against his skull. He was a perfect replica of Roderick's famous wolf, but instead of an authoritative stance, Titus's Shadow curled his tail under his newfound body, head hunched, paws tucked inward.

The crowd gasped as one, shocked to see what looked to be the Overseer's Shadow, sprung to life before them. Titus merely stood there, gaping at his Shadow. No one was as shocked by the transformation as he was. In fact, from the look on his face, it appeared to everyone watching as if Titus had come face-to-face with his father's ghost.

Mercifully, Bruce rushed on stage, his stocky shoulders blocking his brother from view. He steered Titus down the steps and onto the front row where Fern waited to wrap her son with her outstretched arms. The wolf followed clumsily, unused to four legs and no wings.

"He'll be fine," Rowena heard her father say close. It was then she realized she had jumped up, about to race down the steps toward Titus. But Haaris tugged her arm, and she sat. "It's only grief, is all. It does strange things, even to a Shadow. Time will sort it all out. He'll be fine. Eventually."

The Myth Keeper ascended the stage to perform the final rites. He dipped a torch onto the white cloth, and flame engulfed the pyre. The crowd watched in hallowed silence. When the flames diminished, only a pile of ash remained atop the altar. Roderick was gone.

Everyone stood then, filing silently out of the arena; however, the three in the back row remained seated.

Rowena said to her father, "Titus is right. Roderick shouldn't have been the one to die. This is all wrong."

Haaris regarded her pensively before saying, "Titus has learned the secret every person who loses someone must learn. We know it to be true in the deepest places." He touched his stomach as if that's where the secret was held. Rowena met his eyes, and she saw something she hadn't noticed before: wisdom, won through sorrow.

"All death is wrong, Rowena. Not just this one. It doesn't matter how or when it happens. Every death is wrong. We who grieve know this in our bones. It's not just the missing, it's the injustice of grief. They *should not have gone.*" Haaris stared at the empty altar, where the ashes of his best friend blew away in the wind. His voice caught in his throat. "Death is wrong."

There in his eyes, amidst flecks of brown, lay something she had never seen before, and Rowena wondered how she had never noticed. Grief blazed like an ember. She recognized it now, and in doing so, she crossed the threshold from childhood into adulthood. This ember had always been there, burning in her father's eyes. Before, she had mistaken it for thoughtfulness or loneliness, or some low-hanging emotion her young heart could understand. But now, mounting loss aged her, and she was able to accurately name the fire in her father's eyes. Sorrow-filled anger. Grief tinged with outrage. As if, even years later, in the wake of his loss, some punishment was still due. For surely such a tragedy could never be pardoned. His dear wife had been taken by death, leaving Haaris to raise their daughter alone.

For the first time, Rowena beheld Haaris's life as his own. Not as her father, but as a man. Haaris. There had been another funeral, long ago, where Haaris had watched his wife's body smolder to ash like Roderick's. Guilt resurged in Rowena's chest. She had been selfish. In her own self-pity of being robbed of freedom, not once did she consider her father's losses. Losing a mother she had never met had always been a mere fact, banal and unemotional. But for Haaris, his eyes would burn forever after. She wondered if Titus's eyes would do the same now.

Suddenly, the back of her neck prickled, sucking her attention to the present moment. People continued to flow out of the arena, but someone was watching her. She could feel their eyes. Rowena turned in her seat and found, standing off from the crowd, The Wandering chief with a small entourage behind him. From Taiosech's arm hung his Shadow, the bat's filmy wings wrapped tightly around its body. He approached them, and as he did, Rowena realized his gaze was on Penalynn. He offered his hand, and Penalynn took it, accepting his condolences for Greymere's loss.

Rowena lost track of what they said to one another because a voice bloomed in her mind.

My offer still stands, Rowena Faye.

She recognized the chief's voice. Aloud, he continued to converse with Penalynn, pretending to submit to the persuasion's magic. But invisibly, he spoke in Rowena's mind.

There is a seat at my fire should you want it, Shadowless. All you must do is come and take it.

He nodded farewell, his eyes carefully avoiding Rowena. Then he turned and walked away.

CHAPTER
FIFTY-SEVEN

Penalynn waited by the fire, too hot for comfort, but instead of pulling her chair back, she opened the balcony door. Frosty air entered in timid gusts. On a table sat a cup of cherries, the last in Greymere. It wouldn't be until summer when she tasted them again, so she savored them. Balanced on the arm of her chair was a plate where she discarded the pits piled like drops of blood against white porcelain.

She pulled the last cherry pit from her stained lips when he landed atop the balcony like a cat. "Hello, Bran," she said without looking up.

"Pen." His expression was pained. Since the persuasion had broken, his mind churned with found memories. The king's magic hadn't managed to erase Penalynn from his mind. She had merely been locked away as if behind a door. But now the door hung wide, memories released like a flock of birds.

Penalynn leaned luxuriously in the wingback chair, her legs crossed. She brushed the pits to one side of the plate, then, with her fingertip, singled out one. "We have some catching up to do, you and I."

"How long has it been?"

"Four years."

The memories continued their relentless flood. There was an image of her as a child. Another of them as teenagers laughing in the palace kitchens, his mother chiding them. Another of him training on the lawn while she watched from a high window—the look on her face. He had taken that look as a challenge. It was why he pushed himself so hard in practice. For her. To win her approval. After all, his future as a royal guard had rested in her hands back then...before...

More memories flashed across his mind. He pressed the butt of his hand to his forehead.

With a perfectly manicured fingernail, Penalynn tapped a cherry pit. He watched, the back of his neck prickling. He moved to sit in the chair opposite her, but something whizzed past, missing him by hardly an inch. Stuffing and feathers shot from the back of the chair where the cherry pit exited like a shot. She had flicked the pit, her Shadow catching the movement with deadly speed. The magic sounded like a growl in the fox's throat.

"Stand," she commanded.

He obeyed, facing her head-on. Everything about Penalynn seemed relaxed, except her jaw, the tendons of her temple flexing. She singled out another pit and Bran braced himself.

"You killed a friend of mine." Her voice was deceptively soft.

"It was an accident."

"An accident." She looked at Bran's Shadow wrapped around his arm. Firelight reflected in her eyes. "So, when your...snake...wrapped himself around Roderick's Shadow and squeezed the life out of him, that was an accident?"

"Pen—"

She flicked the pit. Magic sent it whistling like a bug past his ear to lodge in the spine of a leather-bound book just behind him.

"Why are you here?"

"The king, he—"

Another pit shattered a glass jar near his shoulder. Broken shards sliced the back of his arms. "*Do not mention him to me!!*" All calm was gone.

"Please, Pen. I'm sorry—"

"What exactly are you sorry for?" She slid another pit to the center of the plate, heat rising in her voice. "For arresting my apprentice on baseless grounds?" The pit shattered the potted plant near his head. Chunks of terracotta and dirt pelted his skull. His boots remained planted at attention.

"For killing my friend and only ally here?" Another pit shot so close it sizzled the hairs on his arm, before knocking a dozen books to the ground. Sweat beaded on Bran's forehead. Still, he didn't move. Whatever she had for him, he would take.

"Or are you sorry for forgetting me for half a decade?" She met his eyes then, and his stance wavered. A jar exploded behind him, cutting a line down his neck. He gritted his teeth.

"For all of it. I swear it was a persuasion. I *never* would have…" Her eyes dropped to the plate where the largest pit lay. Bran hardly dared to say, and so he whispered, "You know your brother's persuasions better than anyone. And now with that dragon of his—"

With a grunt his words were cut off, his chest constricting. The seed, which a second before had sat innocently upon porcelain, ripped a path through his chest. It landed on the carpet behind him, soaked in blood.

"*I said, do not mention my brother to me!*" she hissed. The fox sneered, a single white tooth visible under a curled lip of brazen fur.

Blood trickled from the twin holes in Bran's chest and back. He gasped, staggering.

She spoke carefully. "I obeyed your king. I allowed him to scratch me from my kingdom's memory. I didn't fight him. Somehow, I managed to carve out a life within these walls, cut off, isolated, and forgotten. To slave away as a *Scholastic* when royal blood courses through my veins. Still, I was silent. I let the kingdom go on without me. But now his lackeys have come to my castle, laid hands on my apprentice, and killed my friend. Bran," she purred with something akin to murder in her meaning, "I am done obeying."

Stars shone across his vision. He clung to a bookcase. He would stand. He had to stand.

She spoke with care. "If you or one of your associates touches her again, I will slaughter your king." This was no pretense; it was a promise.

With every breath, he lost more blood, but still, he spoke. "I will protect the girl with my life. If more come, I will be there to stop them. I was your guard before I was his. I am yours to command…princess."

Penalynn cocked her head. He held his breath, hoping. But all she said was, "Leave the way you came in."

Chapter
Fifty-Eight

IT WAS DARK WHEN Rowena reached the Ashworth house. She'd turned
back half a dozen times, Isla and Ghost becoming increasingly confused at
the turnabouts. But when she finally reached her destination, she stood on the
walkway, her feet unwilling to make the last steps to the door. However, it wasn't
long before the door jerked open. She recoiled in surprise.

Bruce was preoccupied with buttoning his coat, so he didn't see her at first.
When he did, he stopped. "About time you came. He's in a bad way, but he won't
talk to us. He needs *you*."

Rowena clutched the strap of her bag.

Bruce brushed past her. "He's on the back porch."

She turned. "Where are you going?"

"Out," he called over his shoulder.

Bruce had never been one for sitting still, and with the ease of a life well
provided for, amusement had always been easy to find. But tragedy is inevitable,
even for a seemingly charmed life. It had finally arrived, but perhaps too late for
the Ashworth boys who had little experience with the darker sides of life. Whereas
for Rowena, her entrance into the world had been a tragedy itself. Her father's
eyes still bore the scars from the wreckage.

She watched him go, chewing her lip with worry. Bruce was hurting, and he had just left home in the dark of night, unarmed with the necessary wisdom to grapple with his pain. She debated going after him but knew she also lacked whatever it was he needed. Besides, he said Titus needed her. Isla and Ghost followed as she rounded the house.

Titus sat on the porch steps wrapped in a blanket, gazing at the low-lying clouds. When he saw her, he didn't say anything; he merely held out his arm, the blanket like a wing beckoning her to nestle. The knot lodged in the pit of her chest melted; her sigh rose like steam. She settled beside him, and he dropped the blanket around them both, tucking her close against his hip. She laid her head on his shoulder, and his chin rested on her temple. It was warm under the blanket, and she relished his closeness.

It might have been a peaceful moment if it weren't for Titus's Shadow. Because there, at the foot of the steps, sat the owl, shuddering. The tremors grew worse until he couldn't control himself any longer. With a violent noise somewhere between a hiccup and a snarl, the owl exploded into the shape of a wolf, still trembling. The wolf vacillated between pitiful whimpers and a horrible snarling and snapping, spit flinging from his fangs. Eventually, he gained enough control to transform back into the owl, but he could hold the form for only a few moments before the tremors returned and the whole process repeated.

It's only grief. Rowena remembered her father's words at the funeral. *It does strange things, even to a Shadow.* She kissed Titus's cheek.

The Shadow morphed into the wolf once more, and Titus stiffened. His torment came in buffeting waves, it seemed, ebbing then rising, exposing Titus's sorrow.

"It's like he's mocking me," he muttered.

His fists opened and clenched reflexively. Rowena drew his palm open so she could lace her fingers between his. "He's not. He's just sad like you."

"Do you think the king knows?" The question burst from him, loud. "It was his man who killed my dad. Do you think he cares?"

"The king was after me," she said softly, "Not your dad."

He nodded, the movement sharp with bridled energy. "Because of your Shadow, right?"

She nodded.

"If you're right about magic, it means you're the only person I can trust."

"What do you—?"

"You said magic kills, right?"

"Not directly, but—"

"But essentially, though, it kills, just like a king's guard. And the king was after you, because why? Because of your Shadow. Who *has no magic.*"

The wolf growled before imploding into an owl. He toppled onto the grass, feathers drooping, dazed by the transformation. Titus flung himself off the steps, the frigid air infiltrating Rowena's warm cocoon. Back and forth, he paced in the yard.

"You're the only one I can trust, don't you see? Before my dad was killed, his Shadow was already doing the deed! No one can be trusted so long as their Shadows...not the king of Wyre, not even my *own Shadow!* From far away in Riven to the closest thing of all." He tapped his chest where the string bound him to his Shadow. "I can't trust anyone...but you." His eyes blazed toward Rowena.

She'd never seen him like this. For Rowena, sorrow projected inward, rendering her a morose mess as it had done the past several weeks. But for Titus, his grief was a storm. He bellowed with it, his sorrow thunderous and spitting as if the pain offended him; grief an invasion he would not abide.

"Titus, please..."

"And I'm supposed to just *live* like this?" he hollered, his chest rising and falling. He had found what many people discover: anger is easier to bear than sadness. "I can't hear my Shadow's voice!"

"I've never heard *my* Shadow's voice." She didn't argue; she pleaded.

He waved his arm at his Shadow, once again a replica of his father's Shadow. It growled at him, mimicking his pacing. "What is this?! It's sick, that's what it is! It's demented. WHAT'S THE MATTER WITH YOU?" Titus screamed. The wolf panted, his fangs dripping. "SPEAK!"

The Shadow sneezed, imploding back into the owl. He sneezed again, and the wolf nearly flipped from the velocity. Muzzle wrinkled, he snarled as he paced between Titus and Rowena, the energy building inside him, ready to recoil any moment. Grey fur bristled like a frightened cat.

Rowena could see the whites of Titus's eyes. He didn't look like himself, ravaged by grief, changed by it. "It's normal to feel upset," she said, reaching for him, beckoning. The wolf snapped at her outstretched hand. She recoiled with a yelp.

Immediately, she regretted the sound because it seemed to break something in Titus. He looked at the wolf as if it were no longer half of his soul. It was a wild animal, and it tried to bite Rowena. He reared back his foot and kicked the wolf in the side. It fell to the ground.

Titus's hands flew to his head, grabbing his hair in fists. "I didn't feel that," he whispered with a mixture of awe and terror, his breath visible in heady puffs. The wolf rounded on him, jaws smacking indeterminately as if trying to catch flies. His fangs drew close to Titus's legs. Titus batted the wolf's muzzle with his boot. "I can't feel it!" he cried, oblivious to the tears coursing down his cheeks.

Rowena stood, the blanket falling to the ground. "Titus, you're scaring me. Please, stop—both of you."

He swung to kick his Shadow again, but the wolf rolled out of reach. They stared at one another, Titus and the Shadow, both trembling. Somewhere from deep in his belly, a noise rose up and out of Titus, a growling wail, all pain and sorrow and hatred. It reminded Rowena of the noise Roderick had made when he'd awaken to feel his Shadow severed. An animal sound. Except such sorrow could only ever be human, borne from a soul torn asunder. The tendons in Titus's neck stood out like shards of bone as he screamed. The wolf lunged for him, and Titus jumped back, scared into silence. They considered one another for a moment, their feet planted like a standoff. Then the wolf flinched, and Titus responded by turning and sprinting across the lawn to the alley between houses. The wolf tore after him.

Isla and Ghost flanked Rowena on either side, waiting for her to respond. She jumped from the porch and ran down the alley. Ghost zoomed beside her and Isla up ahead. The alley was empty. They reached the end where it opened up to a street, and Rowena stopped, looking both ways.

"Isla," she panted. "Where is he?"

The dog sniffed the air, then lurched left, barreling past sleepy houses. Rowena chased after her and soon saw Titus up ahead. He ran at full speed, the wolf on his heels, then turned right. Rowena turned as well, nearly careening into a lamppost, and then saw the wolf disappear into the woods up ahead.

When she entered the trees, it was too dark to see beyond a few feet ahead. Isla's ears pricked forward. Rowena held her breath, hearing her heartbeat in her ears and the river off in the distance. They traversed among white pillared trees, the dark knots like eyes watching.

Finally, she found him—Titus and the wolf locked in an embrace on the ground. She didn't understand what she saw until she was right before him. He wasn't hugging his Shadow; he was choking him. Titus's arm scissored the wolf's throat tight, the fold of his elbow buried in the wolf's shaggy mane. He gargled as if his own neck were held in someone else's grasp.

Rowena threw herself at him, attempting to pry his arm away. "Titus, stop! Please, stop!"

"He's trying to kill me!" Titus's words gargled in the back of his throat.

"No!" Rowena cried. "No, he's just confused. You both are. It's grief! It's only grief!" She echoed her father's words. Coming from her own lips, it sounded more like a plea.

Titus gasped for breath, but still, he squeezed tighter. The wolf jerked and bit him on the jaw. Titus cried out. Rowena let go, fearing she'd only make matters worse. With his other arm, Titus felt along the ground until he found a sizeable rock. He raised it high and brought it down upon the wolf's head. It was at that moment the Shadow transformed. When the rock landed, it was against the owl's skull.

"NO!" His voice cracked. The owl dropped to his lap, its golden eyes mere slits. Titus scooped the owl to his chest and cradled it like a child with a doll, tears streaming, begging. "Please, no! Please!"

Rowena cupped her mouth with her hands, her eyes round as she watched the owl fade like morning fog. A high cry rose from Titus's lips, fading like the final note of a piano until all that remained was a shower of dust plastering his shirt. His arms were empty, and in an instant, he fell to the ground, lifeless as a corpse.

"NO!!" Rowena shrieked. "No. No. No. NO! NO!!"

The clouds broke then, sending snowflakes through the treetops to catch in Titus's eyelashes as if he merely slept. Winter had arrived at last.

CHAPTER
FIFTY-NINE

Rowena cupped Titus's jaw, searching for a pulse. She gasped, then kissed his face. He lived. Like his father, whatever remained of his soul was powerful enough, or tenacious enough, or whatever was required to stay alive. In the span of only a few breaths, his heart rate doubled, and she remembered, then, how Roderick had coped when he awoke in this same state.

Instantly, her hand plunged into the bag across her shoulder, her always-present source of power. She hadn't opened the bag in weeks, not since her trial audition. Wearing it had been more for comfort than necessity. She extricated a cloth-wrapped cylinder and then rifled some more. Glass vials clinked like marbles. She needed to calm down. Panic would cost her time in this race against Titus's mounting pulse. Already his eyelids began to flutter. Finally, she found what she was looking for. Glass scraped against metal as she inserted the capsule into the base. With a twist and *click,* the potion was ready.

"Please work," she whispered as she pierced his skin and pressed the piston. She allowed only a few drops to enter his bloodstream. He must remain unconscious, but not so deeply that his heart stopped.

Recapping the needle, she slipped the device into her pocket. No doubt, she would need it again soon. His heartbeat slowed to the steady rhythm of deep sleep. The potion had worked. With a heavy exhale, she dropped her forehead to his chest. He lived—at least for the moment.

The snow fell thick now. They needed shelter, and fast.

Rowena attempted to pull Titus's limp form with little success. "Isla, help me."

The dog didn't move. Something like doubt welled in those near-human eyes, as if she had assessed the situation and found Rowena's efforts lacking.

Rowena hoisted Titus under his armpits. "Please, I need help!"

Just then a man stepped from around a nearby tree as if he'd been waiting for Rowena's request. She froze, taking in the black-clad guard with the orange snake. He hadn't left Greymere after all, no doubt biding his time until she was at her most vulnerable. With Titus dying at her feet, her heart sunk lower than it ever had before.

"Is he alive?" Bran asked.

She blinked. Those were not the words she expected him to say. "Yes."

"Where do you need him?"

"The castle."

He stepped forward, and Rowena flinched, but he didn't come for her. He went for Titus.

Her hands plunged back into her bag, and she pulled out her second device, the one with the paralytic potion still inside from when she'd used it on Penalynn. With quivering arms, she aimed it at the guard. "Do not touch him!"

Bran eyed the device. "What is that?"

Her voice was steadier than her hand. "Enough potion to stop your heart."

At that, he stopped and then pulled from his belt a long knife. Before Rowena could press the vaporizer's button, he flipped the knife and caught the blade between his fingertips, then offered the handle to Rowena. She stared, incredulous. "Take it," he said.

It was a trick. She knew it had to be a trick. He grabbed her hand, and she whimpered, but he pressed the handle into her palm. Instinctively, she smashed the button of the vaporizer, but he grabbed the device before any gas could emit. So, she grasped the knife with both hands and pressed the tip to his chest, cutting a gash in his leather vest.

"I promise I'm not going to hurt you," he murmured, then slipped the vaporizer into her bag for her. He stood just a foot from her, his bulk looming over her slight frame. Their eyes met, and she noticed how blue his irises were, clear and earnest. Rowena clutched the knife like a lifeline, but it merely rested against his vest.

He said quietly, "Take this." He held out his hand as if making an offering, his Shadow draped in surrender. "I know you don't trust me, so take him." Slowly, so as not to startle her, he draped the snake across her palm. "Hold him behind the head like this," he instructed, wrapping his gloved hand around hers to make a fist around the snake's neck. "Squeeze hard."

With buttery smooth scales, the snake hung lifeless like a rope, submissive. Bran grabbed her other wrist, and she resisted until she realized what he was doing. Her eyes widened to saucers.

He made her hold his knife to his own Shadow. "Hold the blade to the neck like this. If I do anything suspicious—anything you don't like—you slice off the head."

"W-won't that kill you?" she stammered.

The corner of his lips pinched. "Gives me reason not to double-cross you."

"But you have magic."

"Holding my Shadow like that, you'll feel the vibration. Trust me, I'm not interested in dying tonight."

With his life in her hands, he turned his back on her, then scooped Titus up like a doll. He grimaced under the weight, groaning as if in pain. "The castle, you said?"

Her palms slicked with sweat. It would take just a flick of her wrist, that's all, to kill the guard. That was if his soul was like his partner's and not like Roderick's or Titus's. She wondered what sort of soul this black guardian had, who willingly placed himself in the hands of a girl who had every incentive to kill him just so he could win her trust.

Snow frosted Titus's hair. His lips were already blue.

Rowena squeezed the snake. "This way."

When they reached the castle, she turned towards the entrance, but Bran went opposite.

"This way," he said.

"But the entrance is—"

"Shortcut," he insisted.

When he stopped, it was right under the balcony outside Penalynn's offices. He hoisted Titus over his shoulder, freeing one arm to pull a rope from his belt. Polished rocks the size of a man's fist hung at either end.

"I'm going to use magic," he warned, "But it's just to get him up there, so please don't kill me, alright?"

"*Umm...*" was all Rowena could think to say.

He spun the rope, the rocks *whizzing* like a wheel at his side. The snake in her hand vibrated with magic and the rocks hoisted Bran straight into the air. Rowena craned her head back to watch the guard disappear onto the balcony with Titus in tow.

The street was empty, the entire town tucked in their homes while Rowena stood alone in wakeful terror. She had put her trust in a man who'd been sent to arrest her. But she still held his Shadow, she assured herself. He couldn't get far without him.

The snake vibrated again, and she startled, nearly slicing off his head. The guard dropped to the ground as if from a few steps and not several floors up.

"Your turn." He held out his arms as if for a hug.

She didn't have time to protest before he grabbed her wrist and bent her over his shoulder. The roped rocks buzzed like an insect. The snake vibrated and the guard's arm shot into the air, pulling him with inexorable force. Her stomach cut painfully into his shoulder until her weight shifted in an arch and they dropped.

Bran set her down on the balcony. She steadied herself against the rampart, then peered down. The whole ascent had taken mere seconds. Below, Isla stood alone on the sidewalk. With a bark, she took off at a sprint towards the front of the castle.

Ghost watched her go. "Isla's just coming the long way," Rowena reassured her, then turned and entered the Scholastic library.

There, across her desk lay Titus, looking more dead than asleep.

CHAPTER SIXTY

R OWENA REACHED FOR TITUS only to realize her hands were still full.

"I'll take those back," offered Bran, "Unless…"

For a moment, she considered keeping them. But he had helped her; he had done exactly what she needed by bringing Titus to the castle. She wasn't sure this warranted trust, but still, she allowed him to extricate his Shadow. The knife, however, she kept.

"That's fair," Bran consented, "I'll get Pen for you." Then he disappeared through the sliding door.

There wasn't time to wonder about the guard who'd arrested Rowena one minute, killed Roderick's Shadow the next, and then come to her rescue. She shoved her mounting curiosity aside to give Titus her full attention. First, she dashed to her stores of potions lining the shelves, then proceeded to clean the puncture wound in his arm where she'd administered the sleeping potion.

Penalynn soon joined her, followed closely by the guard. Seeing Titus's lifeless body sprawled atop the table, with his Shadow nowhere to be seen, she hollered into her private quarters, "Freya!"

The servant entered immediately. "You're all packed, madame. The carriage will be waiting first thing in the morning."

"You're leaving?" Rowena asked, stopping her ministrations to look up.

"Freya, go to the Overseer's house and fetch Fern Ashworth," Penalynn instructed, "Tell her that her son is injured and bring her here."

When Freya opened the door to leave, Isla entered. The dog resumed her post near Ghost who hovered above Titus. The smokey Shadow's head swiveled back and forth, searching for the missing owl.

In her periphery, Rowena noticed the guard rummaging among her shelves. She turned to point the knife at him and asked, "What are you doing?" But looking directly now, she found herself at eye level with a grown man's bare back, his shirt discarded on the ground. Rowena's jaw dropped.

Penalynn huffed. "*Honestly*, Bran."

"I'm looking for gauze," he muttered while still rummaging, unconcerned with his half-nakedness. A wound the size of a thumbnail nestled in the crease of his shoulder blade. A thin line of blood trickled down his back. Penalynn found cotton rolls for him and pressed them to his mirrored wounds—one on his back and the other on his chest. The top of her head barely passed his shoulder.

"Thank you," he said.

"Don't think this means I'm sorry I did this. Because I'm not."

"I know." Although he did smirk.

"This needs stitching." She grabbed a basket for such purposes, opened a bottle of astringent and said, "This is going to sting," looking rather pleased at the prospect.

Meanwhile, Rowena's hands traced along Titus's body, checking for signs of injury or distress. She lingered at his hands, lacing her fingers through his, lifeless as they were. They were still warm. That was good. Warm meant life. Life meant hope.

Quite a bit of time had passed since she'd given him the sleeping potion. His eyelids fluttered again. Rowena retrieved the needle from her pocket, sanitizing the tip properly this time. Then, she pressed a few more drops into his bloodstream. His eyelids fell still once more.

When Penalynn finished stitching Bran up, she pulled the thread with a jerk. He winced. "Please tell me this wasn't your doing," she said.

Rowena was the one to answer. "Titus did it himself."

"He needs help," said Bran.

"Stupid. Of course, he needs help," Rowena retorted, "His Shadow is *dead*."

Bran said to Penalynn, "If he can be helped, Wolder is the only one who can do it. He needs to go to Riven."

Penalynn's jaw clenched, but she didn't disagree.

Rowena frowned. She knew that name. "Did you just say *Wolder*? As in *Atticus* Wolder?"

"That's just his alias when he writes," said Bran, "His real name is Bernard Wolder. He's treated my mother's Shadow for as long as I can remember. Although hers is only sick, not dead. But if that boy's Shadow is gone, and he's managed to survive it, then Wolder's the only person in Wyre who'd know what to do about it."

Rowena rounded on Penalynn. "Freya said you're all packed and something about a carriage. Are you going to Riven?"

After a beat, Penalynn said, "Yes."

"Take me with you. If Wolder is in Riven, and he can help Titus, then take us with you."

Sympathy softened Penalynn's usually stern features. "Rowena, his Shadow is gone, and Riven is further away than you think. He'd likely die on the journey there."

"I can manage his state with potions. I know I can! Take us with you. While you're giving your report to the High Consul, I can go to Wolder—"

"My report is not why I am going."

This stopped Rowena up short. "Why not?"

Penalynn didn't answer. Instead, she said, "It's not safe for you in Riven, and I won't take you there."

"Titus needs help!"

But Penalynn merely shook her head. So, Rowena changed course. She turned to the guard. "Your mother has a Shadow sickness?"

"Yes."

"And Wolder treats her—successfully?"

"Yes."

As he had done in the woods, she flipped the knife, catching the blade between her fingers. "You can have this back. What's your name?"

He sheathed the knife. "Bran."

"Hello, Bran. I would like you to take me and my friend here to Riven."

"Absolutely not!" Penalynn interjected. "Rowena, I know you're upset—"

"I can save him," she insisted.

"He doesn't have a Shadow anymore! No one can live without their—."

"Yes, they can! I will prove—"

"It is not possible! You're only setting yourself up for more hurt—"

"Oh, get over yourself, Penalynn!"

Penalynn's mouth snapped shut. The fox's fur stood on end, but Rowena continued. "You study Shadows! You know what they do—what magic does. And for years, you've been dallying with the information, not telling a single person. Why? I know why. You don't have a solution. Sure, you've managed to diagnose the world, but you haven't a cure to offer them. Penalynn, open your eyes! The solution is right here! I'm proof that a person can live without magic and Titus...Titus will prove a person can live even without a Shadow. Look at him! He's alive! You found the problem. Now, help me find the solution. Help me save Titus!"

There wasn't time for Penalynn to answer because, just then, the door burst open. Fern Ashworth rushed in, followed by Bruce. Someone had sent for Haaris as well because he brought up the rear, swinging on crutches.

Crying, Fern cupped Titus's face in her hands. His eyes remained closed, his lips parted and already chapped. Bruce stood at his feet, hugging his raccoon to his chest, his face inscrutable. In hushed tones, Rowena filled them in on what had happened.

"But I don't...I don't understand!" howled Fern. "Why would he do this to himself?"

Rowena couldn't answer, so Haaris did it for her. "Grief does terrible things to a man."

"He wasn't right anymore," said Bruce. His voice sounded odd, hollow, and aching. "His Shadow...he had gone all...funny."

Fern seized Rowena's hand with alarming force. Her nails dug into her skin as if grasping for purchase in a roiling sea. "Your potion, it'll help, yes?"

"It's just to keep him asleep. When—excuse me for saying it—but when Roderick woke up in this state, he was...wild." She swallowed against the terrible memory of Roderick crashing through the window, bellowing like a fearsome creature. "I don't know what Titus will be like if he wakens. So, for now, I'm keeping him asleep."

Fern's Shadow pressed against Rowena's leg, the woman unable to give proper thanks through wracking sobs.

"What do we do now?" Bruce asked thickly.

There was silence. Everyone beheld Titus's sleeping form with horrified awe, his missing Shadow as gruesome as if his heart had been carved from his chest and lay on the table. They all instinctively reached for their Shadows, petting and even cradling them with automatic tenderness. All except Rowena. Like usual, she had hardly a thought for her Shadow, who still looked about, utterly confused. No one had explained to Ghost what had happened to her friend, the owl. It was as if she watched through a window, cut off, removed, but all the more heartbroken in her isolation.

At last, it was Penalynn who answered Bruce. "There's a man in Riven. An old friend of mine, actually. If anyone can help Titus, this man is the one. Rowena has offered to bring Titus with me to Riven, and I'm confident that with her potions and expertise in physic, she can keep him stable until we get there."

Gratitude filled Rowena like rising water. Penalynn returned her thankful look with a curt nod, though she still had her doubts.

Haaris spoke up then. "What is this murderer doing here?" Fern gasped, and

Haaris explained, "He's the one who killed Roderick. The one who tried to arrest my daughter." What color was left in Fern's cheeks drained from them then.

"Papa, he helped me get Titus here to the castle," Rowena said, "if it hadn't been for Bran—"

But Haaris snapped, "Don't be a fool."

"When he found me in the woods, he could have arrested me again, but he didn't. He helped me. He's the one who recommended we go to Riven to—"

Haaris threw up his hands. "Of course, he wants you in Riven, Rowena! At first chance, he will take you to the king!"

Bran spoke up then. "I won't. I promised Penalynn my allegiance—"

"How nice," Haaris spat, "The promise of a murderer."

Bruce interjected, "The person who should take Titus to Riven should be me, his brother."

"No," said Haaris, "Your mother needs you. Roderick's wife will not lose all three of her men in one week."

Fern's head rested upon Titus's chest, her tears soaking his shirt. "Is it true?" she asked Rowena directly. "Is it true he can be saved?"

Rowena swallowed. The last thing she wanted to do was offer the only mother she'd ever known false hope. "I believe I can help him," she whispered.

Fern looked at Penalynn, who nodded. "If it can be done, we will do everything in our power to save him."

At that, Fern stood up, wiping her face with both hands. "I give you my blessing. Rowena, Penalynn, please take my son to Riven. Bruce, stay here with—" she hiccupped pitiably "—with me."

Haaris, however, shook his head. "No. Penalynn, you'll have to manage without Rowena."

"Papa, I'm going," said Rowena. "I'm not asking your permission."

The room fell silent, everyone looking back and forth between the father and daughter as if she had slapped him. She spoke as respectfully as possible, "The plan had always been for me to go to Riven. Before, when I had thought my trial—"

"The king wants you dead!"

Bran crossed his arms. The muscles in his arms and chest bulged like rocks, still bare and shirtless. "Not if I have anything to do with it, sir."

"Haaris, I promise I won't let any harm come to her," said Penalynn, "I have more sway with the king than you'd think."

"I'm not going back into hiding," said Rowena.

It was apparent there would be no deterring her, so Haaris relented. "Then I'm going with you."

"Look at your leg! You can't trek across the kingdom like that."

"Titus is unconscious, and you're taking him!"

Rowena wrapped her arms around her father's shoulders, kissed his cheek, and then tucked her head into the crook of his neck. "I'm going, and you're staying here. Fern will need your help. All of Greymere will."

He sighed, his only sign of concession, but it was enough.

"So, when do we leave?" Bran asked the group.

"Now," said Rowena.

"No," said Penalynn. "We need a good night's sleep, and we need to pack."

Rowena disagreed. "The sooner we can get Titus to Wolder, the better."

"Is Titus stable?" Penalynn challenged her, "That's an important question. Because if you can't keep him stable, this trip will be for naught. It's a long way to Riven. A very long way."

"He's stable," said Rowena, then admitted, "But I'll need to re-brew more potion along the way. You're right; I need to pack supplies."

They remained in the castle only a few minutes longer, finalizing plans. Those going to Riven would meet at the Faye's cottage at first light. Bruce and Fern hugged Rowena before they left, Fern smoothing her cape the way she always did. "Thank you, my dear." She attempted a smile. Not for the first time in Rowena's life, she wished she could perform a persuasion if only to ease Fern's pain even a little. "Bring my son back to me. Whole."

There was a fierceness in the request, and Rowena noticed the smoldering ember in Fern's eyes, like the one that burned within her father's—which burned in her own now, too.

"I will. I promise."

CHAPTER SIXTY-ONE

TITUS SLEPT ON THE couch, Rowena dozing on the rug not a yard away so she could monitor his pulse every hour. Already, she found a rhythm to the doses. At some point in the night, she fell asleep properly, curled against Isla. Haaris nudged her awake just before dawn. She shot up with a jolt, scrambling towards Titus.

"He's fine," Haaris said.

Sure enough, Titus slept peacefully still.

Haaris joined her on the rug, offering a plate of food and a cup of strong tea. She needed strength for the long journey ahead. He jutted his chin at Titus. "How're you going to feed him like this?"

This was one of the dozens of questions that had run loops around her mind all night. She took a few bites before answering. "I haven't figured that out yet."

"You will."

She yawned. "I'll have to."

"I have a present for you," he said, then pulled from his shirt pocket a silver necklace comprised of a long chain and a bulbous, heart-shaped pendant. "I noticed you left some silver in my shop. I'll not ask how you came by it, but I assumed you didn't need it anymore."

The pendant was the size of an egg nestled in her palm. Her fingers traced the meticulous design, silver curlicues rendered in her father's distinct style. "When...?" she murmured.

"It took me all night."

Rowena's face fell. "Did your Shadow help?"

"Now, don't look at me like that. So, it's a couple minutes off my life. I've got plenty to spare."

"That kind of thinking adds up! You must promise me you'll stop using magic."

He sighed. "I promise." But they both knew it was a lie.

Rowena considered the threads of silver molded into the image of a bird and a rose with looping vines all around. Light shone between the lines, and she realized the pendant was hollow. Her fingernails found a hinge at the side, and with a click, she swung it open. Ghost hovered close to eye the charm curiously.

Haaris cleared his throat gruffly. "That Shadow of yours has a bad habit of running off, so I wanted you to have an option. It's large enough for her to squeeze inside. Riven's a busy place. Now, that dog of yours will work fine as a dupe. So long as you're someplace busy, no one will think twice about her being anything other than a Shadow. It might help you blend in."

A lump rose in Rowena's throat. This wasn't a necklace. It was a cage for Ghost. That old shame of her father's hadn't changed at all. His compulsion was still to hide her, thinking it was protection. "Okay," was all she could say, unable, or perhaps unwilling, to offer thanks for such a present.

A carriage rolled on the gravel drive, interrupting the awkward silence. Haaris managed to shoulder her bag, even with his crutches, which allowed Rowena to get Titus. She rolled him from the couch onto Isla's back. The dog managed his weight easily enough so long as Rowena held his feet, and together they carried his sleeping body outside, his cheek squashed on the back of Isla's neck, his fingertips trailing along the ground. It was rather an undignified way to carry him, but it was all she had.

They stopped at the gate, and Haaris turned to her. She was leaving. The impending goodbye crashed into them with cruel finality. For years, all Rowena had ever wanted was to leave Greymere. But suddenly, with her bags packed and the road stretched out before her, she felt an overwhelming urge to stay. Rowena threw her arms around her father, all resentment towards his gift gone in an instant. She had never spent a single day away from her father, and now she didn't know when she would return—or what might happen before she did. With a mighty effort of composure, Haaris kissed her cheek. Ghost hovered near the spaniel, but the Shadow merely nodded his head and then turned away, leaving Ghost to dart for cover under Rowena's hair, who said, "I love you, papa."

"You too," he muttered gruffly, then extricated himself to retreat inside.

She turned to the carriage but shrank back from the team of horses, having never been so close to such large, *real* animals. There was a dullness in their eyes and a wild way they moved, tame as they were. On the driver's bench sat Freya, holding the reins. The door swung open, and Penalynn emerged, although the fox chose to remain inside, the gravel drive too dusty for her liking.

"No," a man's voice barked, and Bran rounded the carriage with a modest-sized sack slung across his back. He kicked a wooden wheel. "There's no way we're taking this monstrosity. There aren't any roads the way we're going."

Penalynn scowled up at him. "You can't mean for us to *walk* to Riven."

"Yes," he said without an ounce of jest. "A Black Guardian is dead. I will have gone missing. You will have gone missing. Your apprentice—the king's target—will have gone missing. Guardians will be patrolling every major route in and out of Greymere from here on out. Your brother won't give up, but let's at least not make it easy for him."

"Brother?" said Rowena. "Who's your brother?"

Penalynn's lips pressed into a line, and she fantasized about slapping Bran.

The wheels of Rowena's mind turned, deducing. Understanding dawned in her eyes, and Penalynn admitted through grit teeth, "King Callum is my brother."

From the front of the carriage, Freya's head swung around so fast she nearly toppled from the upper bench.

Rowena cried, "Penalynn! You're a *princess?*"

"Yes," Penalynn growled like a wet cat, "demoted to Scholastic."

"But...how...what..." Rowena's mouth opened and closed like a fish out of water, the reality of this long-held secret crashing into her with significant consequence. Her ears turned red. "Your brother tried to arrest me!"

"I didn't say we were *close*," Penalynn demurred.

"I have so many questions! First, how—"

Penalynn cut her off, rounding on Bran. "The most important question right now is how are we going to get to Riven without a carriage."

"You can take *one* horse," he allowed. "It can carry either luggage or the boy." He jutted his thumb at Titus, who had begun to drool onto Isla's speckled fur. For her part, Isla held her head high, regal, despite being used as a gurney.

"If Titus slid off a horse, I'm afraid he'd break his neck," said Rowena. "Isla is at least closer to the ground. But we'll all need to take turns holding his legs."

"Fair enough," Bran allowed. "Luggage it is."

Freya selected a horse, and they loaded their bags, two for each and an extra for the potion supplies Rowena would need for Titus. After a five-minute argument wherein Bran and Penalynn negotiated her baggage count, Rowen's front lawn became strewn with opened luggage as Penalynn and Freya rearranged the Scholastic's belongings.

Beholding the mountain of finery pouring from half a dozen crates and countless bags, Rowena wondered how she'd never noticed before Penalynn's luxuries and little comforts, her proud countenance, and the way she spoke in commands as if expecting unflinching obedience.

"Princess Penalynn," she mumbled to herself. It fit.

Having heard her, Penalynn held up a warning finger. "Say that again, and my Shadow will rob you of the ability to speak."

"Good grief," Rowena shot back, "Or you could just say *please*."

When they'd finished loading up the horse, they were still left with a pack for each of them to carry. Bran shouldered Penalynn's, saying, "Can't let you break your royal back."

She scowled. "So where are we sleeping each night if we're avoiding the highways? I'm not sleeping on the ground. I'd rather be arrested than sleep outside."

"Actually," Rowena said, remembering, "I think I know some people..."

They both rounded on her, eyes narrowed, arms folded.

"Who?"

She licked her lips timidly. "They're used to sleeping outside and traveling across the kingdom. In fact, they're scheduled to leave for Riven any day now."

"The Wandering." Bran snorted. "Do you *want* the king to kill you?"

"Wasn't he planning on doing that already?" Rowena sniffed. "I have a standing invitation with their chief. Do you have a better plan?"

None of them did, and so, after much scoffing and groaning, it was settled. They left the remaining horses grazing in Haaris's garden, with the carriage parked in front of his workshop. Rowena felt some consolation that at least he'd have something to care for, as well as magic-free transportation. She just hoped he would use it.

Bran led the way into the forest, with Freya bringing up the rear and leading the horse. Rowena held Titus's feet as Isla sauntered under his weight. Penalynn walked beside her, cradling her Shadow.

"Thank you," Rowena eventually said, "For helping me save Titus."

"You're welcome," said Penalynn, "But I was already planning on traveling to Riven."

"Why?"

Penalynn's countenance smoldered with something like hatred. "It's time I had a talk with my brother." After a minute, she added, "You've met him, actually. Well, heard him, at least. His was the voice you heard in my silver glass."

"That silver glass was connected to *the king*?"

Penalynn's knees rose high as she stepped over underbrush, jerking irritably when branches caught her cloak. "In hindsight, it was probably a bad idea to put that thing in the same room as your workspace."

Rowena nearly lost her grip on Titus's shins. She had, in essence, worked in close proximity to the King of Wyre for years and had never known it.

They walked in silence for a while; everyone lost in their own thoughts. Eventually, Bran switched places with Rowena so her arms could have a break. She walked beside Titus, her hand resting atop his back. His breath came in steady measures. Soon, she would have to figure out how to wake him, but in a way that hindered him from harming himself further. But for the moment, all that mattered was that he was alive. And they were together.

To her right walked a Scholastic and forgotten princess. Her mentor. In some ways, her dearest friend.

Behind her, a king's guard-turned-ally, who'd sworn to protect her.

And at the end of this long journey was Atticus Wolder, her lifelong idol of knowledge and their only hope of saving Titus.

Until then, she had her own savvy with potions to keep Titus alive.

Examining her prospects, Rowena's confidence grew. They would succeed; she felt it in her bones. Shadow or not, Titus would live.

The sun was high in the sky by the time they entered The Wandering camp. Rowena introduced herself at the entrance, and they were quickly rushed to the chief's fireside. When she explained their situation, requesting sanctuary and safe passage among their tribe, Taiosech said nothing. His eyes were unreadable as he scanned the small troupe. There was a Scholastic, a Black Guardian, a mousy castle servant, and the deceased Overseer's son. These were not mere Wyrians standing in his camp but people deeply entrenched in the Sceadwe.

But his gaze settled on the dog—the creature from his dreams, visited upon him too many times to count. And slung across its back, the Overseer's son. It was then Taiosech noticed the boy had no Shadow.

"Is he alive?" he whispered, hardly daring to believe.

"Yes," Rowena answered. "And I need to get him to Riven, but without the king knowing."

It was then the chief's face cracked into a most uncharacteristic smile, sending gasps among his elders. "Welcome to The Wandering."

ACKNOWLEDGEMENTS

I am in awe of the people surrounding me. When I said the absurd words "I'm writing a novel" out loud, I expected polite, mild support. Like when someone says they've started a postcard collection. A quick, "That's nice," followed by a change in subject. But every one of my friends and family responded with genuine enthusiasm. I will never forget my brother's response, "Of course you can do it. It's perfect for you." I am so grateful. To everyone who offered a kind word of encouragement, thank you. To those of you who pounced on me with hugs and squeals of delight, you are my favorites, you know who you are. I am amazed to have so many people who believed, without hesitation, that I could do this. Thank you for lending me your faith when I struggled to have any.

To my top-tier supporters, my Beta and ARC Readers, you all gave me a precious gift: your time. To my brilliant sister-in-law, Margaret Kelly, and my generous, bookish friends, Lisa Hawkins, Hayes Parnell, Kristi Booth, Cindy Barksdale, and Courtney Szollosy, thank you for being my first-ever readers, for your feedback and encouragement, and for being my early champions.

Special thanks to Anna Hartzog at Village Editorial for your expertise, polish, and invaluable insights. I'm so thankful to have someone to accompany me on this difficult road to publication. To J. Caleb Designs for the <u>cover art of my dreams!</u> And Racheal Smithson for capturing just the right whimsy in each of your illustrations.

To Tal Prince, you reached out when all around me seemed dark, you listened when it seemed no one would. In the wake of trauma I wondered if my ability to write had been lost forever. Thank you for helping me recover it. And to Becky Whitson, I am convinced your mere presence is healing. You introduced me to my inner child, sparking my imagination in a way no one ever has. Ghost would not have been found if it were not for my time with you.

To Mom and Dad, words like "thankful" or "grateful" just don't seem big enough. Your integrity, hard work, and faith are the solid foundation upon which I have built my life. The older I get, the more your work proves to be bedrock. I do not take for granted everything you have done for me. If I could go back in time and select my parents myself, I'd still choose you. I love you.

Rose, my Rose Petals. There is no one brighter or more beautiful than you. Of all the daughters in the world, I can't believe I got the best one. You have been with me from the very beginning of this book. When I first saw Ghost in my mind's eye, you were busy wiggling and hiccupping inside my belly, just months from being born. I love sharing your delight, hope, fear, and laughter from a story told well. Thank you for always being willing to read with Mom.

Becoming an author has been a terribly long, messy endeavor, and there is one man who has been tied to me, body and soul, in every step. Adam, my love, saying "thank you" would be ridiculous at this point. It's not enough. You have read every word, every chapter, over and again. All feedback you've balanced with your classic blend of honesty and kindness. You've celebrated the wins and embraced every twist in this process. You've talked me down when I wanted to give up, and your wisdom and insight have helped shape this story into what it is today. My champion, my rock, my love—thank you. Sorry, I cried so much.

ABOUT THE AUTHOR

Alison is a Christian writer of YA fantasy, exploring human nature with a dash of magic and adventure.
She lives in Birmingham, Alabama, among stacks of books with her husband, daughter, and a cat named Watson.

alisonrobinsonwrites.com